Praise for
Dark to Mortal Eyes

"In *Dark to Mortal Eyes*, Eric Wilson coils suspense as tight as a snake prepared to strike."
—ROBERT WHITLOW, best-selling author of *Life Support*

"Eric Wilson peels back this story with razor sharp suspense, revealing a robust, multilayered plot; rich, descriptive color; and intelligently drawn characters. God willing, writers like Eric Wilson will be the future of Christian fiction."
—JAMES BEAUSEIGNEUR, author of The Christ Clone Trilogy

"*Dark to Mortal Eyes* is one of those excitingly fresh, thrilling tales that linger in the mind. The titanic clash between good and evil is memorable, and the characters unforgettable. The rush-to-the-next-page adventure will make you hunger to read it all again. Eric Wilson is a terrific writer."
—GAYLE LYNDS, *New York Times* best-selling author of *The Coil, Masquerade,* and others

"Eric Wilson's *Dark to Mortal Eyes* is a wonderful discovery. Frightening in places, provocative in others, this deeply spiritual, powerful story moves with the intricacy of a chess game played at the master's level combined with the speed of a runaway locomotive. Eric Wilson is a great new voice."
—STEVEN WOMACK, *New York Times* Notable Author of *Dirty Money*

"*Dark to Mortal Eyes* is intelligent and ambitious. Eric Wilson takes the reader through a fast-paced thriller that is as thought provoking as it is riveting."
—ALAFAIR BURKE, author of *Missing Justice*

"Packed with intrigue and suspense, *Dark to Mortal Eyes* weaves a tale that awakens the mind toward eternal things. Don't expect much sleep!"
—CINDY MARTINUSEN, author of *The Salt Garden*

"With bravado and compelling prose, Eric Wilson delivers a debut that will surely expand the minds and speed the hearts of readers. *Dark to Mortal Eyes* is a compelling tale that is surprisingly told. Wilson is set to leave his mark on the world of fiction."

—TED DEKKER, best-selling author of *Thr3e* and *Black*

"From the first page, Eric Wilson takes us on a relentless and intriguing ride in his debut novel, *Dark to Mortal Eyes*. With unique characters and a thought-provoking plot, he transports us beyond the physical realm, illuminating the spiritual forces at work in our world. Put it on your must-read list—Eric Wilson's novel is an eye-opening read."

—RANDY SINGER, Christy Award–winning author of *Directed Verdict* and
　Dying Declaration

"From the opening scene, Wilson's characters in *Dark to Mortal Eyes* hook us by the nose and pull us headlong into a suspense-filled, action-packed mystery that consistently rides the razor's edge between life and death and blurs the lines between the natural and the spiritual realms. This book is a delight for the imagination and a challenge for the soul."

—MICHAEL D. WARDEN, author of *Gideon's Dawn* and *Waymaker*

DARK TO MORTAL EYES

DARK TO MORTAL EYES

A NOVEL

ERIC WILSON

WATERBROOK
PRESS

DARK TO MORTAL EYES
PUBLISHED BY WATERBROOK PRESS
2375 Telstar Drive, Suite 160
Colorado Springs, Colorado 80920
A division of Random House, Inc.

ISBN 1-57856-744-0

Library of Congress Cataloging-in-Publication Data
Wilson, Eric (Eric P.)
  Dark to mortal eyes / Eric Wilson.— 1st ed.
     p. cm.
  ISBN 1-57856-744-0
  1. Young women—Fiction. 2. Birthparents—Fiction. 3. Missing persons—Fiction.
  4. Antiquities—Fiction. 5. Oregon—Fiction. I. Title.
  PS3623.I583D37 2004
  813'.6—dc22
                                   2003027964

Printed in the United States of America
2005

10 9 8 7 6 5 4

In fondest memory of
Robert Ludlum *(The Bourne Identity)*
and J. R. R. Tolkien *(The Lord of the Rings)*

To my grandparents, with love:
Dorene and Alan Wilson—
through many difficulties you've made our family stronger;
Barbara and Vincent Guise Jr.—
your years of cheers from the sidelines have meant more than you know.

Author's Note

Through the ages, story and metaphor have been used to examine life's mercurial nature. Jesus himself told parables to highlight spiritual truths. In *Dark to Mortal Eyes,* I try to put these same tools to work. To establish doctrine? No. To explore earth's tension between heaven and hell? Absolutely. I see fiction as an adventure—enlightening, frightening, and inspiring. I'm thrilled to share this novel with you. Together, let's uncover hidden things.

> I will open my mouth in parables,
> I will utter hidden things.
>
> PSALM 78:2 (NIV)

Devil's Elbow

Oregon Coast, November 1945

"Eerie, isn't she?" said Captain Bartlow. "But beautiful."

"She's all that and more, sir. Feisty as they come."

Bartlow jabbed a thumb over his shoulder. "The lady in back? She's a looker, all right. Should've known that's where your mind was. No, I'm talking about the lighthouse." With gloved hands, he drew himself to the windshield. "Now there's a sight for sore eyes."

His driver downshifted, and the truck groaned. Headlights poked at the mist, no match for Heceta Head Lighthouse as she rose from the shoulder of a cliff ahead.

"You think there's any truth to the rumors, Captain?"

"That she's got a ghost?" Bartlow's scoffing breath fogged the glass. "It's a lighthouse, goes with the territory. Now keep your eyes on the road."

"Yes, sir."

Bartlow fell silent. Ghosts? Things of this world were much more worrisome.

As Captain of the Port in the small town of Florence, he had been responsible for security throughout the war. He issued ID cards, controlled anchorage and inspection at the ocean's mouth, and—as delegated by President Truman through the secretary of the navy—oversaw the stowage of military munitions. Two hours ago, with coastguardsmen pacing the pier, Bartlow had supervised a shipment's transfer to the back of this vehicle—crates, canisters, shrouded machinery.

There beneath the dock lights, he had spied the twisted cross.

Though weathered by sea and brine, the swastika had refused to fade from the exterior of a wooden bin, and he'd hurried the item onto the truck.

Now, with the engine battling a steep grade, he threw a glance at the cargo in the darkness. He was following orders, yes, but this was the first shipment he'd ever received without the president's endorsement. As for the woman? Her beauty made her no less a part of this violation. Discerning her profile in the shadows, he winked before letting the canvas back down.

"Almost there," the driver informed him. "Be glad to get this over with."

"Don't you let up now, guardsman. Or are you forgetting what's on board? One good bump and our eyeballs'll be turned to jelly. Is that what you want? You want them finding the lady in that condition?"

"Don't like that kind of talk, sir."

"Good. You just get us there in one piece."

The driver turned left off Highway 101 and wrestled the vehicle over mud tracks toward the lightkeeper's house. With the war over and decommissioning under way, the Coast Guard would soon vacate the house so that life could return to normal.

Normal? Bartlow cupped his gloves over cold lips. Not quite yet.

"Sir? Where to?"

"Round back. Yeah, there at the cellar doors. That's good."

The engine cleared its throat, fell silent. As Bartlow stepped down, the Pacific boomed against rocky ramparts more than a hundred feet below, and an icy gust whipped foam across his brow. Turning, he found a Doberman pinscher sniffing at his leg. Cutter was the lone remaining watchdog from the wartime kennel on the premises.

"Attaboy, Cutter." He patted the dog. "Now stay back. We've got work to do."

From the back stairs of the house, sleepy-eyed guardsmen tramped into position and saluted. Bartlow's driver yanked back the cellar doors, pointed to the truck's cargo. "Well, get moving. Captain hasn't got all night to wait on your lazy backsides."

The men shuffled to the tailgate, then halted as one unit. A woman had materialized between rows of crated munitions, facing them with unblinking eyes. She was young and enchanting, her shape—to their disappointment—hidden by the captain's wool greatcoat.

"I can let myself down," she said. And none seemed to doubt her.

Captain Bartlow chuckled. "Kelso, show the lady to the drawing room.

Those'll be her quarters for the night." Once she was gone, he added, "And hers alone. I know what you're thinking, you filthy sea dogs. Now hop to it."

During the unloading, Bartlow fretted over the lightkeeper's return. With his son in tow, the hardy old keeper had puttered to the lighthouse on the neighboring cape for routine maintenance of the Fresnel lens. Nearly midnight now. Father and son would be back in five minutes, ten tops. Though the keeper had endured the Coast Guard's intrusions, his presence jeopardized the secrecy they desired tonight.

From the truck, a cry of pain cut the air. Two men set down a crate while a third eased a formidable sliver from his palm.

Bartlow, detecting movement from the doghouse, turned to see Cutter strutting forward. "Stay back, boy. Back."

Cutter's ears cocked toward the command, but his low-slung hindquarters caught a fourth man behind the knees. With hands full, the guardsman was unable to halt his backward motion, and he sprawled on the ground.

Ka-chika-chink...

A silver canister spilled from his grasp onto the lawn. The dog prodded it.

"Careful!" Bartlow barked at his subordinate. "That's nothing to toy with. On your feet, man. Pick it up."

Before the man could comply, Cutter went on alert: eyes fixed, hairs bristling, a growl escaping through bared teeth. He tried biting the canister, then clawed at it, nails clicking against the metal. He ignored Bartlow's whistle and gave chase as the canister began rolling along the slope. The object hissed through the grass, trailing tendrils of vapor that stained the night air green.

"Cutter, get back here!" The captain joined the pursuit. If they lost this thing, it'd be his hide.

With a mind of its own, the canister headed for a gap in the white picket fence. The thing was alive. It clattered against wood slats, spun through the gap, then hop-skipped into brush that shielded the last yards to the cliff. Vapor coiled around leaves and twigs. On the Doberman's heels, Bartlow hurdled the fence and briars, grabbed at low branches to brake his headlong dash.

Only to watch the object plummet over the precipice. Spinning. Gone.

Far below, the waves of Devil's Elbow clutched at it and tucked it from view.

The captain swore into the night, then coughed to dislodge phlegm from his chest. He ignored a knot of heat around his ribs. He knew he must report this screwup, but who would believe him? His competence would be questioned, his years of service compromised by one surreal moment.

Hot needles poked at his throat. His vision blurred.

"Lose something?"

With a deep breath, Captain Bartlow turned to see lightkeeper and son standing in a gas lantern's preternatural glow. "Uh, yes," he answered, spurned to honesty by the keeper's probing eyes. "Nothing that can't be replaced though."

"Looked like Jesse Owens the way you sprinted toward that ledge."

"Worried about…an item of mine. And the dog. Didn't want him going over."

"Looks safe to me, little riled perhaps," said the keeper, as the boy stroked Cutter's head. "You want any help searching, you just holler. I know this cove like the back of my hand."

"I'll keep that in mind."

"No, really. Be my pleasure to help you boys out."

"Heard you the first time. Thanks, but no. Go on about your business."

In the lantern's gleam, the keeper's face was indecipherable.

"Go on!" Bartlow shoved the words over a dry, distended tongue.

"I'll be completing my rounds, sir." The keeper patted his son's back with one hand, swung the lantern with the other. Across the grass and up the stairs they went.

Bartlow drew in cold air. Another ragged cough. A spike of pain through his abdomen. Despite fog clinging to the house, the half-dozen spokes of Heceta Head's light hewed the gloom and alerted him to a shape at the window: the lady from the truck. Had she witnessed the fiasco leading to the canister's loss?

Even as curtains floated back down, he saw the calculating curve of her mouth and knew he had erred by involving himself in these matters.

Too late to backtrack now. The shipment had reached American shores.

A violent retching almost drove the captain to his knees. His lungs wheezed. A tinge of green passed over his eyes, and as blindness became complete, he cried out for assistance. He stumbled. The waves alone answered, rushing to meet him as he took one false step over the cliff's gnarled brow.

Part One

No need to brood
on what tomorrow may bring....
Tomorrow will be certain to bring worse than today....
The board is set.

The Return of the King by J. R. R. Tolkien

I pray that your hearts
will be flooded with light...
that you will begin to understand.

Ephesians 1:18-19

1

Choose Your Poison

Willamette Valley, October 2003

Josee discovered the canister while seeking firewood in the thicket. A chance encounter, nothing more. The odds of finding it here beneath a sword fern were slim, she knew that, but long ago she had retreated from belief in a grand design. She'd been down that slope before.

In her hands, the object pleaded for purpose. For significance.

She shook her head. Nope. A random occurrence—that's all this was.

Prompted by sporadic raindrops on leaves overhead, Josee Walker built her campfire, blowing at kindling and newsprint until flames rose with half-hearted applause. Satisfied, she returned to her discovery. Weighed the canister in her hands, noted water spots and rust stains. Scratch marks, too. She polished it with the sleeve of her sweatshirt and found her face reflected in the metal surface.

That's me? After two days without a mirror, the sight was disturbing. *Don't even look like myself. I look so...wasted. Out of it.*

Josee rotated the object and found a skull-and-crossbones symbol. Stenciled in black, it made her shudder as she rolled the canister into her bedroll.

Rocks shifted nearby.

"Hey." She raised her voice above the patter of rain. "That you, Scoot?"

"Who else? I scare you?"

"Not even. Just making sure."

Josee's friend wheeled his bike down the railway embankment. His dread-knotted hair hung like soggy pretzels from his hood and funneled water down the front of his poncho. Moisture clung to his thin beard.

"Quick, hon," said Josee, "get in here."

"Think I'm frozen to the bone."

"I started a campfire for us using the classifieds. How's that for irony, considering we have no place to stay?" As Scooter dropped his daypack onto the ground, Josee heard his chattering teeth. "Scoot, you poor thing."

"You don't have to mother me. And what, this place isn't good enough?"

"Oh, cork it." She kissed him on the cheek. "What'd you get us?"

"Dinner. Found some bread and fish fillets at the old Safeway in Corvallis."

She studied the expiration dates. "Hmm, should be okay. Only a day late, looks like." The fillets were actually fish sticks that she knew he'd collected from the Dumpster by the store.

"They're fine," Scooter said. "Let's eat."

She pushed back a tuft of hair. "Better watch it, mister. Might find yourself traveling alone."

"Think so?"

"Know so. And you know you can't live without me. You adore me." She teased him with turquoise eyes. He couldn't resist them, she was certain of that. Part of her survival gear. Multifunctional. With a twinkle of these eyes she often masked her real thoughts from others; her feelings, too.

Right now I feel far away—that's what I feel. Detached.

"You ask me," Scooter was muttering, "beggars can't be choosers."

"You mean the food? Beggars, artists—we're all in the same boat. Yep, have to take what we can get."

"Money's a security blanket. That's all it is, Josee. People goin' through the motions for another paycheck, selling their souls for a slice of suburban heaven—"

"Or suburban hell." She watched the sputtering fire.

"Load of crock. You and I know better."

"Uh-huh."

"Babe, you okay?"

Josee peeked from beneath her pierced eyebrow and black hair, started to answer, then with a flick of her wrist waved him off while fanning at eye-burning smoke and memories. Her past was a vandalized scrapbook: pages torn, photos scratched, facts rubbed out. The book's coverage of her child-hood was a mess.

Yeah, there were a few unsullied years, beginning with her adoption at age nine. Before the darker days of teenage angst, of reproachful encounters.

Events she preferred not to speak about.

Give them credit, her adoptive parents had tried to provide an atmos-phere of acceptance in which she could open up, but she felt nothing. It was useless. They would never understand, and she refused to risk further rejec-tion. Already she had developed an effective coping mechanism: Josee Walker trusted no one but herself. After making life miserable for everyone in the house—and feeling guilty for it—she had taken advantage of her newly earned driver's license and moved into a friend's converted garage. Never bothered to look back. The past was the past, she told herself. Best to let it go.

That was six years ago.

"What're you thinking?" Scooter prodded.

"That it'd be nice to stop thinking."

"Tomorrow you get to meet your birth mother. That's a good thing, right?"

Josee grimaced. "I hope she's ready for it."

"For what?"

"For me. She might expect her daughter to be, I don't know, more…frilly."

Scooter's grin sparked amid his facial hair. "You sent her a picture, didn't you? Don't worry, she'll like you just the way you are. If not? Her loss." He dug into his poncho. "Here, Josee, little somethin' I picked up. Nothing big."

She accepted a case of charcoals and pencils. "Where'd you get this, or do I want to know?"

"Worked out a deal. Hated to see you scratching away with that stubby pencil of yours."

She paused and listened to the rain. "Where's your Discman?"

His hands pushed into his pockets, jacking up his shoulders.

Josee pawed through his pack. "You hocked it to pay for this?"

"Listen, we gonna eat or what?"

She opened the art case, found that fingering the colorful implements recharged her imagination. Too wet out to do any sketches, but later she'd get a chance. "Thanks," she said, nudging him. Her throat tightened. She clicked the case shut and busied herself with her bedroll until confident her voice was steady. "Something I wanted to show you, too," she said. "Look what I found while gathering wood." She hefted the canister. "Sort of spooky, don't you think?"

In a dank basement studio, canvases draped the concrete walls. Shades of scarlet and ebony dominated, splashed across cubist artwork. Spanning floor to ceiling, the collection's centerpiece depicted a white chess queen against a stark background. She was losing her balance on a castle parapet, her silent scream exaggerated, lances poised below to skewer her.

The Lady in Dread.

Karl Stahlherz frowned at the picture. Since its completion, he'd been unable to paint, despite his gnawing appetite for distinction. He knew the art was good; his mother had fostered his gift, and in statewide galleries his pieces had sold for respectable and increasing amounts. Never under his own name though. Payments filtered through an art institute called the House of Ubelhaar, and the only means of identifying his work was his signature saffron streak across the lower right-hand corner.

He remained an unknown. Barely a footnote in federal government files.

Soon that would be rectified.

Stahlherz slipped an audio book into his newly acquired Discman. Taking only cash or trade, he supplemented his income with the sale of art supplies. The kid who'd stopped in earlier had telephoned first, asked for a specific item for his girlfriend. Stahlherz had waited on the porch's uneven stone steps, nervous, tapping his fingers against the air until the kid arrived astride a rusty bike. Most likely another college dropout—scrawny, hair tickling his chin, multiple pockets down the baggy pant legs.

The kid handed over the Discman. "Works great. Check it out for yourself."

Testing the player's components, Stahlherz fumbled and almost dropped it. "Appears functional," he managed. He relinquished the art case, tried to look his customer in the eye. "Keep me in mind the next time you need supplies. Without the overhead, I can underbid most shops around Corvallis."

"Thanks, but I'm from out of state."

"Your girlfriend—"

"Doesn't live here either, not anymore. Ran across your number on a flier."

"Shipping's inexpensive," Stahlherz pressed. "With an address, I could add you to my files and send you quarterly fliers. Or e-mail if you're online."

The kid kicked at a foot pedal. "Nothing against you, but I pretty much keep to myself. I try to stay off those kinds of lists, to avoid the eyes of Big Brother. Fly under the radar, low as I can go."

Stahlherz bobbed his head. Despite the twenty or thirty years that separated them, he could relate to this kid. "Your views sound vaguely anarchistic."

"Might say that."

"You're not the only one with such ideas. This region's gained a share of notoriety for similar leanings. In fact, I could put you in contact with others who—"

"Nah, that's all right. You know how it is… Girlfriend's waiting."

Watching the kid ride into the drizzle, Stahlherz felt he had mishandled a potential recruit. Never mind. As a mentor to many, a sower of discord and activism, Stahlherz could visualize his objectives at last. He and his recruits would soon mete out justice to this cancerous culture in which they'd been bred.

Chemo treatments, as it were. To purge society's disease, bring it to its knees.

In the basement, Stahlherz rotated in his desk chair and drew inspiration from his canvases. He focused on *The Lady in Dread*. Pain, he mused, was the great equalizer. None were beyond its reach, and he had harnessed his mind to see into such mysteries. He could control his intellect. Guide its mighty surges.

As if to mock his thoughts, a rook squawked from the cage above his desk. Black wings beat the bars, and feathers lighted on Stahlherz's onyx chess table. Insolence filled the bird's sable eyes. A single talon, a polished spike, poked between the bars.

"Now, now," Stahlherz reprimanded. "You'll have your chance to roam."

Logged on to the Internet, he sent his first summons. He signed it: Mr. Steele.

━━

"What is that?" Scooter was pointing at the cylinder's base.

Josee traced a hand over the skull and crossbones. "Nothing."

"Maybe you should put it back where you found it."

"Maybe I'm a big girl and can do what I want." She braced herself, hoping for Scooter's opposition, which would confirm her sense of foreboding.

"Your call," was all he said. "Let's get this food cooking."

"That's your big response?"

"You got a hungry man sittin' here."

"Why do you do that? Why do you back off?"

"What, you'd rather fight?"

"Well, you spout off at everyone else like you're the man of the hour, but when it comes to me, you back away. Don't you have an opinion at least?"

Scooter shrunk into the thicket's shadows, arms crossed beneath his poncho. His introspective nature had drawn Josee to him, yet his lack of assertiveness annoyed her. All the loyalty she tried to give… *And he just grunts when it comes to choosing sides?*

"Figure it's up to you, Josee." His fingers twisted at his moonstone ring. "I'd leave the thing alone, but that's just me."

"Hey, if we disagree on something, it's not like I'm going to bite your head off. You should realize that by now, Scoot. I care about you. Any reason you should doubt that? Am I doing something wrong?"

"No."

"'Cause sometimes it sure seems like I'm doing something wrong."

"It's been a while," Scooter ventured. "A long time actually."

"Since?"

"Since…you know what I'm talkin' about. You gonna make me spell it out? I'm lucky to even sneak a kiss anymore."

"We've already talked about this. You said you understood."

"I do, in the cerebral sense. Up here. Not trying to complain, but"—he tapped his chest—"in here it still feels like you're pushing me away. Am I blowin' hot air? Am I making any sense?"

"There's more to love, hon, than just getting it on. Plenty of people do that without an ounce of real feeling for each other. Look at Josh and Heather— perfect example. Already told you, just need to work through some stuff."

"You think it's wrong, babe? Is that it? Like some kind of moral issue?"

"No. Yes. Heck, I don't know, Scooter. Yeah, we jumped in too quickly. There's a part of me that says to hold off. It brings up thoughts of the past I don't want attached to our relationship."

"So I'm the one who gets robbed."

"No, don't give me that. I'm not your property, never have been."

His eyes caught hers with the look of a wounded animal. "I've never thought of you that way."

Josee lifted the canister and heard herself growl, "Dang it, why do you make me feel guilty? How'd we even get on this subject? When're you going to start standing up for yourself? That was my original point. What's so stinkin' hard to understand about that?"

"Listen, I'm not trying to—"

"Not trying? Hey, you said it, mister, not me."

"Josee—"

"Wait, I didn't mean that."

He pulled his knees to his chest. Although Josee wanted to reach out, she distrusted her ability to do so in the aftermath of indignation. She had a real knack for lighting sticks of dynamite around those she loved. *Dynamite...and love.* A poem idea swam through her head, but she held it under.

Scooter nodded at their meager food pile. "Chow time yet?" His teeth still chattered as he rubbed his hands together.

Josee resorted to routine. "Should take only a few minutes. Know how you feel. I'm hungry too." Before taking out a battered frypan, she set down her discovery and gave it a maternal glance. "I'm keeping this thing," she said. When he failed again to retort, she added, "Finders keepers, isn't that the way it works? Belongs to me."

Creepy. Or was it just her imagination? The skull and crossbones seemed to be taunting her with a cold, black grin. She fidgeted. Tried to ignore it.

Throughout the meal, the hollow eyes continued to stare right through her.

~

"Whasit gonna be? Choose your poison."

Beau saw the countergirl's brow lift over sequined glasses, and he scratched his chest. He felt like a moron. Café Zerachio's whole vibe was wrong, and he couldn't figure out why Mr. Steele had summoned him here. The overhead menu was a blur of neon chalk curlicues, and the sound of grinding espresso beans had Beau grinding his teeth.

"What about just straight coffee?" he tried. "Got anything like that?"

The girl pointed to the coffeepots behind her. "House blend?"

"Perfect," Steele broke in. "And I'll take a short double cap. Make it dry."

With his part-time tractor repair job, Beau made okay money, but he was glad to see his mentor pay the bill. Not that it mattered much. As of tonight, Beau knew that his life was going to change.

Mr. Steele was leading the way to a corner alcove, chin down, a sack slung over hunched shoulders. Smarter than smart, the middle-aged guy wasn't much of a people person. Had salt-and-pepper hair, eyes that darted this way and that, fingers that tickled the air when that brain of his started revving.

Geniuses were like that, Beau had been told. Always ten moves ahead.

"You see the way that girl looked at me?" Beau touched coffee beans strung along the wall. "Real snooty."

"Don't let it irritate you, my friend. Let's say nothing foolhardy."

"Foolhardy?"

The girl approached with their drinks, nodded at Steele. "Thasit?"

"Should do the trick." From beneath graying brows, Steele's eyes tracked her retreat. His body rocked in his seat.

Beau carried on, his interest in the coffee diluted by the sting of his mentor's words. "You're wrong there, boss. You watch, I'll do everything as planned."

"I have been watching, and soon you'll have the chance to prove yourself. Within the next twenty-four hours, the girl should be arriving in town, may even be here now." Steele savored his cappuccino. "Mmm, won't she be in for a surprise?"

Beau cast a glance around the empty café. Although his heart raced in anticipation of the task, he was afraid of messing things up. His father's face flashed before him, but he knew nothing would ever impress that fool. Beau had tried—oh, how he'd tried. Forget it though. Eight months ago he'd torn a flier from a bulletin board at Fred Meyer's supermarket and found a legitimate shot at approval.

ICV...*In Cauda Venenum.*

The group had nabbed Beau with its ad for artistic outsiders. It fit him to a tee. Before dropping out of school, he had earned nothing but trouble from teachers and disrespect from classmates for his cartooning. "Wasting your time," a senior had once told him, with a finger thump against his latest sketch. "Your artwork's a joke." Others had done more than ridicule; Beau would always hate those high school locker rooms.

Mr. Steele was the one who'd given him new ambition. He and the members of ICV recognized Beau's value.

And the Professor won him over for good.

At secretive gatherings, the Professor hammered out their goals in that hushed tone that masked tough-as-nails determination. *You can, you will, you must obey to find the way...* It was one of the Professor's credos. Inspiring. Providing purpose. And Beau soaked it up like a rag stuffed into a gas tank's spout.

"Okay, cough it up," he said. "What's my next move?"

Steele shifted his eyes, then clasped Beau's wrists. The fingers were anchors dropped into soft skin. Beau tried to withstand the pain, looked toward the counter where the girl swayed to soft drums over whale song. He curled his toes. Chose to shut down. Focused on the last ICV meeting and the support he'd sensed in the Professor's eyes. *I must obey to find the way...*

Steele's grip tightened, testing the anchor's hold. "Beau, this will be your chance to leave your mark. Do you believe that? Are you ready to pay the price?"

He hardened his gaze. "Yes, I'm up for it."

"As I understand it, you've worked before on the machinery at Addison Ridge Vineyards. I assume, therefore, that you're familiar with Ridge Road.

Starting this evening, we need you posted there on surveillance. When this girl of ours arrives, she expects to meet with her mother. You'll make certain such a reunion never occurs."

"You betcha, boss. For the good of the network."

"In cauda venenum."

Energized, Beau echoed the phrase. A literal reference to the sting of a scorpion's tail; it was a name wrapped within a warning. For as long as he'd been shoved aside, he'd looked forward to making others suffer. This was his big chance.

Scooter was in the tent as the campfire burned low. She needed a few minutes to herself, Josee had told him. In the slivered moonlight beneath the branches, she found their canteen. From a vial she kept on braided twine around her neck, she extracted a red capsule and washed it down with water.

Daily routine. Doctor's orders. Through the years it'd become second nature.

She heard Scooter shifting in his sleeping bag, felt a tug of remorse. Words that flowed so easily from her fingers could stab so sharply from her mouth. Dynamite…and love. Her manner of delivery seemed to have pushed him farther away.

"Scoot? You still awake?"

His breathing skipped, then turned heavy. No reply.

She slipped a pencil from her new case and, by firelight, wrote:

> who will discover the gold in me
> without the use of dynamite?

A pause. A nibble on the eraser.

> dreams and hopes, buried alive
> beneath the rubble of strife

Josee slapped at a mosquito, then crouched to ensure that the canister was still in her bedroll. With her sleeping bag removed and situated in the tent, the metal object felt cold and unyielding against her hand. A chill crawled along her skin. She hurried to cinch and knot the cord with all the strength her small fingers could muster.

2

Black Feather

Kara was out here, eluding him. Although pillars blocked Marsh Addison's view as he descended the flared brick entryway, he could hear his wife's footsteps on the gravel and could smell her perfume through the late-October mist.

"Now what?" he called. "Talk to me. Let's try to work this out."

Inside, supper plates cooled on the formal dining table. Maybe he should go back in and finish without her. Baked salmon and Brie, last year's Pinot Gris harvested on their own estate… To let such delicacies go to waste bordered on sacrilege. Food was his religion, wine his personal sacrament. He'd been raised here at Addison Ridge Vineyards, guided like a trellised grapevine into his role as master vintner.

"Kara."

No response.

"Come on, stop playing games with me."

Beneath the portico he loosened his tie and listened to the rain. Considering his recent rise in wine-growing circles, he was still perplexed by his miscues in the marital department. Not that he had much to go by. His father had died while he was an infant, and his mother still held to her widowed status. Marsh's relational approach reflected his ties with his mother—cordial and steadfast, yet aloof. After twenty-plus years with Kara, he was aware he had a few edges left to smooth. More than a few perhaps.

But haven't I been trying? Haven't I gone the extra mile?

No pun intended, he thought. Across the water-soaked gravel, the white BMW Z3 was testimony to his efforts. A birthday gift for his wife. One sweet machine.

"Honey," he tried again. "Please, can't we talk this out? Come back inside before the salmon gets cold." He just wanted some resolution here—and his meal.

Which she was quick to note. "Have mine, too, Marsh, if that's what you're after."

Definitely from his left. He took a step that direction, but the diesel equipment clattering between the trellises disrupted his senses. "Okay, I give in. Where are you?"

"Not now, Marsh. I haven't the energy for verbal warfare with you."

"A war?" Two additional steps, zeroing in. "That's hardly fair."

"The way you undermine me, I simply can't deal with that right now."

"How can we carry on a conversation when I can't even look at you?"

"You haven't seen me in months, not really."

He found her seated at the base of a pillar. "It's the marketing campaign," he said, "not you. National distributors, European connections... I know it's been hectic around here, but we're exceeding our goals. We're taking it to the next level. Do you realize what this could do for the vineyard? For my father's legacy? For us?"

"Since when have I been part of this?"

He sighed. "What do you want from me?"

She stood and swatted dust from her derrière. "I want you to meet your daughter. Is that so horrible a thing?" Wine was sloshing over the rim of the glass in her hand. Her eyes, too, were brimming.

"We've already discussed this. More than once, I might add."

"Because you won't listen, Marshall."

"This is pointless."

"See, that's what I'm talking about."

"Kara—"

"The way you tune me out as though I'm not even here. Try to tell you something, and you...you're a million miles away, reading wine reviews, thumbing through the day's receipts. Remember the way we used to actually talk over dinner?"

Marsh did remember. They'd survived the mistakes of those early years, but his stock as a husband had since gone into a prolonged tailspin. He couldn't pinpoint the moment things had turned. Couldn't specify the cause. He provided shelter, security, a shopping budget—not to mention annual excursions to the Caymans—yet the distance between them continued to widen. Through it all, Kara's gentle disposition was the glue that refused to let go, and Marsh was grateful for that. He really was. But her expectations seemed unrealistic. It just wasn't…it wasn't normal that he should have to carry the onus of intimacy upon his shoulders.

Men aren't wired for romance. How many times have I tried to explain that?

Kara, seeming to catch the bitterness in his gaze, looked away. The glass tilted in her grip, dribbled amber liquid onto the drive. "Marsh, I'm planning to meet her, with or without you."

"Without."

"She's our baby—"

"You know that as a fact?"

"*Our* daughter."

"Either way, we gave her up for a reason. Do we have to replay that discussion? We made a decision, a tough decision that cost us many sleepless nights. You know that as well as I do. Now, just when it seems it's all behind us…no, it's back again."

"*She's* back. Her name's Josee."

"You've had too much to drink. Please, honey, maybe we should discuss this later."

"Why won't you do this? Your refusal to meet her can do nothing but—"

"But what? Hurt a relationship we've never even had? It's been two decades, Kara. She wants nothing to do with me, and I can't blame her."

"She knows you're not interested—that's why. She's just afraid."

"Well, then—"

"You both are."

"Wrong!" Marsh felt his pulse pounding in his neck. "This is nothing more than a silly delusion. Do you understand that? You think you're going to restore things with one magical meeting, but—I hate to break it to you—it doesn't happen that way."

"You don't know that."

"I do know it. Josee knows it. Apparently, you're the one blind to the truth. We have it good here, and now you're going to jeopardize all that." Marsh gestured to the slopes of Addison Ridge, where Chardonnay and Pinot Noir grapes shimmered in necklaces of rain. His father, Chauncey Addison, had carved this business from the ground; his mother, Virginia, had fought to maintain it; and Marsh had acquired it like a mandate from the grave. Transformed it into a viable business too—with a lot of sweat and panache, thank you very much.

"I need some time to think," Kara said. "Without all the trappings."

"Whatever works."

"Marsh," she spoke in a quavering voice, "do you suppose there's a reason they call them *trappings?*" She did an about-face and took one limping step.

"Wait." He set a hand on her arm, combed a golden strand from her shoulder. She teetered on high heels and turned back. He touched her teardrop-diamond earrings—another of his gifts. Or didn't they count for anything? "Kara, I'm not trying to sound harsh. You're working through a lot of emotions, I know that, but I'm not sure you've weighed the consequences. Are you sure you want to go through with this?"

"It's what she wants, Marshall. It's what I want." She brushed the lapel of his jacket. "Please, darling, I can't turn her down. What kind of mother would that make me? It's been three weeks since Josee first called…my daughter, my *baby.* Every hour of every day I've had her running through my thoughts. She's gone to the trouble of tracking us down, and as her parents, we at least owe her an explanation."

"Her parents?" Marsh huffed as residual doubts gripped him.

"Darling, when will you believe me that I—"

"Listen." He mounted the brick steps. "You just do what you have to do, okay?"

When she rejoined him at the dining table, neither said a word. Marsh admired the way her disheveled hair framed her petite face and downturned caramel eyes. After all this time, still so attractive. Still so hard to read. True, he knew a few of her secrets, but perhaps his attempts to forget them had blinded him to her current state.

Of course, his family bore secrets as well.

Insinuations. Shame. Matters best kept tucked away.

In light of the vineyard's recent successes, Marsh marveled that in a lavish home with a desirable wife his future could be so imperiled by one door into the past.

—

"I'm all over it, Mr. Steele. I'm there."

"That's good to hear." Stahlherz removed his clenched fingers, watched Beau flex his wrists. He said, "Go ahead and drink up. We need you fully cognizant. You do understand that if you're captured, you know nothing about me."

Beau sipped from the cup. "Never heard the name Steele in my life."

"It's not an uncommon name. Even if you say something, they may suspect you've made it up."

"But I already know—"

"Know what?"

Beau leaned in. "That it's not your real name. Gotta protect your own backside."

"You, my friend, are one of the sharper tools in the shed," said Stahlherz. "Don't be mistaken though. If you do reveal any details of our purposes, I'll personally drop you where you stand—in a prison cell, a witness stand, wherever. I will not hesitate."

"Fair's fair." Beau slugged down a mouthful of coffee, and Stahlherz saw a twitch run down the recruit's arm. "We're all expendable. You taught me that yourself."

Amused, Stahlherz finished the cappuccino and let his gaze drift up the alcove walls. He had difficulty locking eyes with his recruits. Some of them interpreted this as insecurity, yet that wasn't it at all. Truth be told, he feared they would see his disdain.

Pawns, that's all these kids are. To be shifted about, exploited, and sacrificed.

"Beau," he said, "you're certain that imprisonment will not deter you?"

"Not even." Beau's words became muddled. "This one guy—he and I overhauled an entire engine at a farm in Philomath—he says the slammer's not bad so long as you keep to yourself. Bring it on. I'll take the rap."

"Have you talked to him about us? We're resting our hopes on you, my friend."

Beau shook his head, choked down the last of his coffee. His movements were growing jittery; his eyes were glazing over. "You made it clear: No runnin' off at the mouth." The kid's rambling grew louder. "I swear my lips're sealed. I wanna be part of what's goin' down."

Stahlherz lifted a canvas sack onto his lap and located the zipper. "And what, precisely, do you believe is 'goin' down'?"

"Like you always say, it's for you to know and me to find out."

"Actually I say that it's on a need-to-know basis."

"Yeah, that's it. That's exactly what I told him."

"Told whom?"

"Uh, no, what I meant was—"

Stahlherz slashed his fingers across his recruit's shoulder and hooked them into a pressure point. The boy's words crumbled into a moan while Stahlherz continued digging into skin and nerve tissue. After retracting his fingers, he unloaded from his sack a worn denim jacket. Certain that the pockets contained the requisite items, he wrapped it across Beau's back, then beckoned his sedated rook from the sack.

"Your turn," he directed. "I told you your chance would come."

With glassy eyes reflecting the bar's neon light, the bird clawed his arm, a fiend rising from the darkness. Stahlherz jerked. A talon—breaking his skin!

"Careful there. You do as you're told."

Ka-kaw-reech! A paroxysm rippled through the creature's muscles.

Stahlherz mouthed an injunction: "Rook captures pawn."

The bird hovered over the table, then, in a shuffle of feathers and talons, settled on Beau's shoulder. *Kee-reech-reach-insiiide!* It spoke into the boy's ear, the tip of the beak dipping into the orifice like a pen into an inkwell. Beau's lips parted in a gasp, seeming to repeat his earlier comments as statements of acquiescence: *We're all expendable... Bring it on. I'll take the rap.*

Without further fanfare, the rook disappeared.

Stahlherz stood and wiped at his wound with a napkin, then plucked at the single black feather now protruding from his recruit's ear. The girl lowered her magazine to the counter and peeked over her glasses at Beau's immobile figure.

"He'll come around," Stahlherz said, slipping currency onto the magazine. "A bit disoriented, but he'll be ready for his assignment. Fifty dollars? I think that'll cover the extra 'shot' you put in his drink. *Audentes fortuna juvat.*"

"Fortune favors the daring," she repeated in English. Then pocketed the cash.

Stahlherz had intended for his words to seal her loyalty, yet as he shuffled out the door, he was annoyed by the lackadaisical shrug of her shoulders. "You live your life. I'll live mine..." It seemed to be this generation's motto. Though it served his and the Professor's needs for privacy, it made motivating their recruits laborious.

Is there no one willing to fight? Are there only pawns on this board of life?

Stahlherz challenged the night. "A fight to the death—that's what I want. Come now, Mr. Addison, surely there are easier ways to get the job done, but let's you and me make a game of it."

3

What You Cannot See

Josee Walker emerged at dawn from the tent. Her muscles felt like damp ropes strapped across her back, and her hips creaked like old fence slats. *I'm falling apart,* she thought. Defective merchandise. She snugged a coat over her Seattle Mariners sweatshirt.

Across the firepit, Scooter was perched on a decaying log. "You sleep okay?"

She shrugged. "How long've you been up?"

"A while, I guess. Didn't sleep much."

"Me neither."

Her mind had been mulling over today's reunion. Wednesday, October 29. For the first time since birth, she would see her mother. One o'clock at Avery Park. No big deal, but she'd go through with it for her own peace of mind, then move on. As for her father, Marsh Addison? According to Kara, he was "conflicted and confused." He'd opted out. *Typical dirt bag. Had his thrills, but wants zero responsibility. Like I care.*

Scooter leaned back on the log. "Whaddya say? Should we turn this thing in?" He rolled up his poncho, rubbed the canister he'd concealed on his lap. "Could be some cold, hard cash in it for us, a reward. You never know."

"Scooter!" Last night's fears returned in a rush. "What're you doing with that?"

"S'okay, babe. Just checkin' things out."

"Could be dangerous."

"It says: Gift."

"Gift?" She snatched the object away, drew her finger over a row of faded numbers and letters. "G-I-F-T. I didn't even notice that in the dark. Well, there's some twisted humor for you. Looks more like an old artillery shell."

"The grand spankin' mother of all bullets."

"What if," she theorized, "it's from World War II? You know, Oregon's the only state that had war-related casualties on her own soil during the war. Soldiers used to train near here at Camp Adair. Every once in a while a farmer'll dig up some old armament and get his picture in the paper. Think that's what this is?"

"Don't know. Is that really true—what you said about Oregon, I mean?"

"It's not like Puget Sound's the only place things happen."

"It's where you and I hooked up, isn't it?"

"Ooh, good answer. Might have to give you a point for that one."

Three years ago they had met and formed an immediate bond that carried over into friendship, art, and love. Josee had been a freshman and Scooter, a sophomore at the University of Washington. They'd dropped out the following summer, however, convinced that college was a diploma mill devised by corporate greed to raise a working class of loan-imprisoned drones. Nope, that wasn't for them.

They'd formed an artists' colony in a travel trailer on his grandmother's lakeshore property. Word got around. Soon budding artists and musicians arrived, yearning for expression and connection, for the sense of family of which most had been deprived. Josee spent hours in the living room, leaning against the rattan couch, filling a journal with poetry and pencil sketches. Behind the trailer, Scooter crafted metal sculptures in a shed pieced together with scrap aluminum siding and two-by-fours. When his creations were complete, Josee gave them titles. Often she matched them with one of her poems. As a team, she and Scooter sought out spots to display each welded image— on the porch, on a stump facing the lake, among the trees shading the pitted drive. Together, they sold their work at local galleries and cafés. The minimal cash flow was enough to keep them afloat.

Scooter edged forward on his perch. "Think you've got a point, Josee. Looks like it could be GI: government issue. Like a war relic or something. Be careful with it."

"Excuse me? I can take care of myself."

"You're a hundred and ten pounds."

"And all muscle—don't you forget it." Though she tried to sound lighthearted, she found herself twiddling her eyebrow ring between two fingers. She considered the canister, feeling torn between the threat of the unknown and the allure of the forbidden.

"Josee?"

"Huh?"

"You with me? You okay?"

"Yep."

"You look like you're off somewhere else."

"Did I ever tell you about my grandfather? He died a few years after World War II, or so Kara told me on the phone. Never knew him, never even met the man." Another page, Josee brooded, missing from her scrapbook. "She sent me his picture, thought I might be interested."

"Yeah, you showed me, remember?"

"But I don't even know what killed him. Isn't that weird? I mean, I should know something like that, shouldn't I?"

"Maybe it's better you don't."

"Better?"

Scooter scratched at his bearded chin. "Sometimes the truth hurts, that's all I'm saying."

"Well, thank you. Why do men feel like they have to protect me, like I need their help? I think I can handle the truth. 'The truth shall set you free,' isn't that what the Bible says? Heard that somewhere, way back when."

"Wouldn't know. Sorry. You ask me, it's better to free your mind. Little somethin' to take the edge off, if you hear what I'm sayin'. Less pain that way."

"That's it, just tune out altogether? That can't be the answer."

"Comes highly recommended."

"Not gonna happen. I'd rather feel pain and at least know I'm alive. Aren't you even a little curious about things? There are so many unknowns, things that just don't add up. Maybe it's a part of being adopted…looking for, I don't know…identity."

"Least you've got this link with your mom. Today's the big day, right?"

Josee rolled her neck. "One get-together's not going to erase twenty-two years of separation. Maybe I shouldn't have come."

"Hey, don't think like that. I know what this means to you. We didn't thumb it a coupla hundred miles to see you skip the big event. This is connection at a root level."

"Yeah, yeah."

"Good stuff, think about it. Kara's your blood, your family. From what you've told me, she sounded nice enough on the phone. If she's even a little bit like you, she'll be good by me."

"Now you're getting sappy on me, Scoot."

"What, who me? Must've been in a daze. Scratch every word. Lies, all lies."

"That's more like it." She smiled and reached to squeeze his hand.

"Okay, Josee, so what about that?" He indicated the canister. "You got me curious. See any buttons or latches, see a way to open the thing up?"

"Nothing obvious." She looked down to find the skull's same chilling stare from last night. And what was that smell? Sweet but spicy, with a bite to it. "Maybe you were right," she confided. "Maybe we should leave it alone."

He brushed it with his hand. "C'mon, don't leave me hangin'."

"Forget it. Don't mess with this thing, okay?"

"If you say so."

"I mean it."

"Sure, babe. Hands off." Yet his fingers tarried, and Josee would've sworn that his moonstone ring surged with a pallid gray glow.

———

After generic cornflakes and powdered milk, Josee took hold of Scooter's bike. "That little market's just up the road, right? I'm gonna ride over and give my mother a call, make sure everything's still a go."

"Got change for the phone? I'm all out."

"I'll figure a way. It's this feeling, I guess, like I need to see what's going on."

"Worried she'll cancel, huh?"

"No." Josee disengaged the kickstand. "Just wanna touch base."

"You are worried."

"No, I'm not."

"Be careful, babe. Road's narrow out there."

The bike was a symphony of squeaks and sighs. Two days earlier Scooter had haggled for it at a local garage sale. Josee's feet just touched the pedals, and by the time she reached the market, the sun was winking hello through trees thick as lush lashes. A scene worth drawing. She wiped the sweat from her chin and thought how good it was to be back in Oregon—her birthplace.

Inside the market, by a rattling ice machine, she saw a flier tacked to a corkboard. Some institute, the House of Ubelhaar, advertised art lessons and supplies as the pathway to fulfillment. Probably where Scooter got her case.

"Morning," said the cashier, whose thighs hid the seat of her stool.

Josee mumbled a reply. So much for flirting with a guy clerk for a chance to use the phone. "Think I can make a call?" she asked. "It's local."

"Pay phone's out front." The woman's eyes never left the television behind the register.

"Yep, I know, but see, I'm out of change. Not a dime on me."

"Sorry. Store policy."

She stared past the woman at rows of locked cigarette cartons. "It's a Corvallis number, I promise. Please, I'm trying to get ahold of my mother."

"I don't make the rules."

"And you won't bend them, not even to help someone in need?"

"Geez, okay." The cashier dragged a rotary phone into view. "I'll have to do the talking for you, pass on a message or whatnot. Gimme the number."

Sitting in a van parked among the pine trees off Ridge Road, Beau shivered. He swallowed a yawn, then wiggled his toes under the blanket wrapped around his legs. What was he doing here? His brain felt disconnected from his surroundings. Maybe that's what the cold did to you—like hypothermia. During the night he'd run the engine a few times to get the heat flowing again, but Mr. Steele had warned him to keep the lights off. Not like anybody'd see him back here.

Skreech!

The wind clawed branches across the rooftop, a sound that set his teeth on edge. Or maybe his ears had caught the far-off shrill of a bird.

Ske-reeech!

He winced at the ache in his temples and wondered where he'd picked up this headache. Pounding again, worse than last night. Had to keep on task. Stay dialed in. Yesterday's meeting in the café was a little fuzzy, but as Steele had promised, Beau was now wearing a denim jacket with specific items in the pockets.

Yeah, buddy, the details were coming together.

When the Motorola cordless chimed at his side, Beau answered and confirmed his position. The signal might come at any minute, he was told. He was to sit tight and keep from nodding off. Committed to this task, he loosened his jacket and spread his arms like wings to welcome the morning chill. Anything to keep awake.

Lonely out here. Still, it felt like something was hovering over him.

Through gritted teeth, to boost his courage, he stole a villain's line from half of the cheap DVDs he'd watched at home. "Let the games begin," he said.

———

"Babe?" Scooter wrapped an arm around her. "What happened?"

"Let's get out of here."

"Did you talk to her?"

"What do you think?" Josee appreciated Scooter's concern but pulled away when he tried to touch her cheek. "She stinkin' bailed on me. Stood me up."

"Kara called it off?"

"Well, not exactly. Guess some housekeeper lady answered, said there'd been a disruption and I'd have to call again tomorrow. Not like I'm going to waste my time."

"Don't let it mess with you, babe. Didn't Kara warn you this could happen?"

"She said that if it didn't work out, we could try again for the day or two after. What does she think, that I'm going to just sit around and wait? Like I have nothing better to do? 'Oh sorry, Josee, today doesn't exactly work either. How 'bout the day after next or—'"

"No hurry, we got time on our hands."

"Or how about never!" Josee regurgitated the events from the market for him, then tossed back her head and dragged both hands through her cropped black hair.

"But you didn't even talk to her," said Scooter. "Not in person. What, you're gonna believe some cow behind the counter? Just call back *mañana*. It'll work out." He tried to meet her eyes, produced a pack of cigarettes, and dropped it in her lap. "That's it—the last of our stuff."

"Thanks, hon." She lit one and leaned back to expel smoke over her shoulder. "I just keep getting this bad feeling. Why should I even expect her to care after all these years? Maybe she's like my father, having second thoughts."

"Sucks, I admit, but she wouldn't agree for you to come down unless she meant it. Here, want some croissants? Stale, but better than nothing." When she shook her head, he added, "Sorry about the limited menu. You deserve better."

"It's fine, Scoot. Upset tummy, that's all. Nerves." Her eyes scanned the thicket. "Speaking of which, where'd that thing go?"

"The canister thingamajig?" Scooter moved to the tent's edge and lifted the object from behind the flap. "Thar she blows. Thing was giving me the creeps, so I stashed it away."

"What happened?"

"It was gettin' hot to the touch, like there was somethin' inside."

Josee took it and ran her hands over the metal. The burnished surface seemed warmer than was natural.

"See what I'm sayin'?" he said. "Bizarre, isn't it? Like it's—"

"I told you not to—"

"Like it's alive."

She challenged him with a look and tapped her cigarette over the pit. "You're not worried, are you?" By aiming the fear at him, she could pretend it wasn't her own.

"Josee, you're the one who said it was sort of spooky, and you're the one who knows this stuff, right? Like with my sculptures, you've always got the words that fit."

True, Scooter had always given her the liberty to christen his work. Now, in her hands, the canister begged to be christened as well. It weighed upon her, its corporeal need for attention draining her even as its title made itself known.

In cauda venenum…

The Latin words scrolled across Josee's mind, remnants from some first-period lecture. As she plumbed her memory for a translation, fingertips of anxiety brushed her neck. Literally, it meant "In the tail is the poison." Referring to a scorpion's whiplike tail, the words were loosely paraphrased "Beware of what you cannot see."

She sniffed along the cylinder's seam. "Whoa, hold on a sec. You smell that?" She thought she detected spiced cinnamon sticks. Or stove-cooked applesauce. Or the holiday potpourri the workers used to spread out at the group home the weeks before Christmas. She'd pronounced it "pot-pour-ee" just to bug them.

That's when it grabbed her.

Pain seized her chest, squeezing until she dropped the cigarette. Her eyes bulged. She dry-heaved. Tears boiled along her eyelids, blurring the pine needles at her feet.

"Babe, what's wrong?"

She coughed through a mouth full of cotton, spit into the coals. Spit again.

"Tell me you're kidding," Scooter said. "This isn't funny."

Josee gulped, rubbed her face and neck. Fever heat scorched her ears, and the shaft of pain that had spiked between her ribs felt permanently lodged there. She dropped her head between her knees and tried to see beyond the swirling flecks of light.

"Was it the food last night?" Scooter grasped for an explanation. "You checked the dates, yeah? The fish wasn't overdue, was it?"

"Only a day." Her voice was hoarse. "But it's not that."

"Should've known better and just left the fillets where they were."

"You did your best, Scoot. Not your fault. It's that…that freakin' canister." As though identifying the problem was a remedy of sorts, she felt warmth settle over and coat her with a sense of protection. Oxygen rushed back into her lungs, and her eyes began to clear.

The canister... *Oh, no! Where'd it go?*

Josee scanned the carpet of roots, leaves, and twigs. She must've dropped the thing when the pain grabbed her. There—it had made a half circle around the firepit and bumped into Scooter's feet.

He scooped it up. "See, what'd I tell you? This thing's hotter than sin."

"No, don't! Put that down!"

4

The Opening

Turquoise eyes watched him from a five-by-seven framed picture. Chaffed by this manipulation, Marsh dropped the photo facedown on the vanity countertop. Kara should've known better than to try such a tactic. Asinine, that's what it was.

"Maybe I went too far," she had admitted. "I hoped only that it might touch something inside you. Thought it might find a soft spot."

"You thought wrong."

Though he'd been tempted to slam the master-bedroom door, he had let it click into place instead. Restrained anger. Always more effective. He'd discovered that certain business maneuvers paid dividends here on the domestic front. Of course, when Kara had pulled on jeans and a sweater and threatened to leave, he hadn't taken her seriously. She'd insisted that his mood would not contaminate this momentous day and had stridden out to the car. Strapped herself into the Z3's cockpit. Lifted her chin.

And she actually did it, actually left!

It'd been years since Kara had done such a thing; he could almost respect her for that.

The brass frame sparked his ire anew. To prove his immunity to it, he flipped the photo back up beside the faucet and pondered the young lady's face. Unfamiliar, yes, but he knew who this was. She had Kara's chin, petite and strong, eyes the same shape, set wider and deeper. On her eyebrow, a silver hoop clung like a question mark that refused to go away.

Josee Walker...

Her likeness was supposed to twist some emotional knob, but that just wasn't going to happen. As though to convince the man staring back at him in the mirror, he shook his head and combed through his wavy black hair.

For crying out loud, Josee, I have questions too. You're not the only one.

From the sunken shower enclosure, the sweet scent of Kara's Shalimar lingered in Marsh's nostrils. He'd been hard on her, maybe too hard. Didn't she see, though, the folly of traipsing back into the past? She was not only driving a wedge between them, she was gambling her daughter's stability.

Within the photo's gaze, Marsh ran a triple-bladed razor over his stubble and swirled the residue down the drain. He slipped into gray slacks and Arin Mundazi loafers, buttoned his shirt, draped over his chest a silk J. Dunlary tie.

Almost seven o'clock. Only minutes till his daily chess match.

His tie fit the chess motif, with random white squares against a field of black.

In his study he stood waiting at the window as a tangerine dawn squeezed over Addison Ridge. Below, in the brick-encircled parking area, Japanese maples swayed in the breeze. Within the hour the manor and vineyards would stir with activity; migratory grape pickers and machine operators would clock in; Rosamund, the Addisons' lone live-in employee, would manage the daytime kitchen and custodial staff. At the moment, however, the estate lay subdued. Marsh was sure that, aside from Rosie downstairs, he was alone.

Alone? Well, that was Kara's choice, wasn't it? Not his.

He punched the intercom button. "Rosie, you there?"

"Sir?"

"Bring my breakfast up to the study. Buzz to get in."

"The usual?"

After a string of capricious personnel, he had hired Rosamund Yeager for her European efficiency and attention to details. At seventy-six years old, beneath honey-tinted hair and powdered wrinkles, she remained unflagging, meticulous, attentive to his patterns. To keep her on her toes, he said, "Throw in an egg overeasy—salt, pepper, and a dash of paprika."

"I'll bring it up myself, sir. And will your wife be joining you?"

"She's not here."

"Oh? Is she…keeping an appointment? Should I prepare her meal in advance?"

"Appointment?" Marsh watched a repair truck pull up the drive. "Yeah, set something aside. Why not? Of course you know what she likes."

"I'll see to it, Mr. Addison. You're certain she'll be back?"

"She'll be back."

Marsh hoped that Kara's morning away would give her fresh perspective. She'd saunter in, sporting independence like some imitation fashion design, but experience assured him that she would return. That much he could count on.

———

"She's making her move."

"I'm all over it." Beau jutted his chin, rolled his eyes like marbles in their sockets. "How do you chess masters say it? 'Guard your queen'?"

"A superfluous warning. A worthy player has no need for it."

"Was just a comment, Mr. Steele."

"Keep those eyes peeled. That's your priority."

Beau folded his arms over the van's steering wheel and studied Ridge Road. Nothing yet. The cold had constricted his hands into talons as they gripped the Motorola. He gnawed on the rubber antenna and wondered how Steele maintained his cool. With patience and a plan—those were the keys.

Ske-skereech!

That stupid bird. Still shrieking. Why didn't the thing shut up?

As sunlight sliced through the trees, Beau blocked the rays with outstretched hands. His fingernails turned deep orange, as though he'd scratched at the burning sphere and got its rinds beneath his nails. Even dropped into his lap, the fingers retained a numinous glow that empowered him.

Enabling. Enervating… Ha, there was a big word for ya! In cauda venenum.

Still no sign of the queen. Where was she?

———

At the foot of the vineyard's curved drive, beneath the stucco archway, Kara sat in her Z3 and let the sun run its fingers through her hair. The light caressed her face, soothing and warm. She looked back to ensure that she was out of sight of the manor, out of sight of Marsh's study on the second floor.

She needed this. A moment of peace before facing Josee this afternoon.

With head tilted against the headrest, she looked at herself in the mirror.

Despite the fashion sense she displayed at social events and the airy demeanor she pasted on during winetastings, she felt timid. Did others see through the facade? Did they detect her insecurities?

Look at me. I can't even work up the will to leave the property.

She watched the day advance while whispering prayers to stifle her ebb and flow of emotion. She smeared a tear from her cheek and laughed. Was this the plight of the female species: slavery to estrogen and to men who did not understand?

As if we enjoy such fluctuations. What nonsense.

It was true that the mere suggestion of a reunion with Josee had caused Kara's emotions to spike. And the questions had returned with new vigor. Phantoms. Plaguing her sleep, skirting the edges of her daily activities, always haunting her.

Indeed, what sort of mother would surrender her child at birth?

How had Marshall been able to erode her intention of keeping the baby?

Why had she caved to the pressure of her own father who, as a respected deacon, told her he would be shamed? What hypocrisy! She'd been tempted to accept the money he offered, but amid 1981's conflicts between choice and life, she had settled on adoption.

Had selfishness caused Kara and Marsh to shirk the burden of a sick child?

And for all these years, what questions had chased through Josee's head?

"I'm so sorry. Josee, forgive me." Kara's hands wrung the steering wheel. The words sounded hollow, but with only hours until their reunion she hoped beyond hope that her daughter would look past facades and recognize her mother for the woman she was—and the woman she wasn't.

"Help her to understand the battles I've fought. Please, God," Kara begged, "open her eyes."

⸺

Seven o'clock sharp. Time for war.

On the study's chess table, crystal soldiers faced each other, glittering and poised for the day's first sortie. Marsh heard the computer turn itself on. The task launcher was taking him to the online gaming zone where his opponent would be waiting. A battle to the death would ensue.

The zone's slogan read like a rallying cry: "Chess…sixty-four squares, thirty-two pieces, one winner! No weak-kneed pseudojocks allowed."

For years, to prime himself for entrepreneurial challenges, Marsh had wrestled the same adversary routinely on the Internet, a person who played under the user name Steele Knight. Marsh knew little of the opponent's background, physical appearance, or location. These topics were taboo, as though to discuss such details would provide an edge. Through combat alone, he had learned the intricacies of his opponent's mind-set.

And vice versa, no doubt.

Torch-lit and cavernous, the gaming zone materialized. Steele Knight wandered into view, a brown-robed entity wielding an iron mace.

Marsh felt his pulse quicken. Time to sharpen the senses. With the mouse, he clicked Play Game and watched the entrance of his own virtual persona: a blank-eyed mannequin plastered with quartered black and yellow circles. The two players were sequestered to a dungeonlike room.

"You're white." The opponent's words scrolled along the screen in Old English letters. "Make your move, CCD."

Crash-Chess-Dummy—Marsh's user name.

Typically, before settling on a move, Marsh liked to work out his ideas on the glass board behind him, but this was a no-brainer. He advanced his king pawn.

Steele Knight keyed in, "Predictable, CCD. As always."

"Take your best shot. I've won the last three days in a row."

The robed figure rose from the dungeon table, pounded a gauntlet against his chest. "All for a reason, my friend. Today the strategy shifts."

"You mean you have a strategy?"

"Aah, very funny."

This verbal posturing was normal, a little trash talk to raise the stakes.

"Now," Marsh responded, "the real fun begins."

He pushed forward his king's bishop pawn…the King's Gambit. Although business decisions required a more methodical approach, chess granted him some swashbuckling swagger. By offering a pawn for a positional advantage, this opening magnified the importance of each move upon the chessboard.

Marsh jiggled the pointer on the monitor, tapped his loafers beneath the desk. Would his opponent accept the challenge? Or play strategically and safe?

Steele Knight seized the pawn and typed, "Next, I'm coming after your queen."

———

Bzz-bzz-bzzzhhh…

"Who is it?" Marsh snapped at the sound of the buzzer. He pushed away from the computer, head thick with tactical ideas. He punched in the key code, and the study door slid open.

"Your food, sir."

"Almost forgot." His stomach rumbled as he eyed the tray. "Thanks, Rosie."

"And I thought you might like to know that Mrs. Addison has returned."

"As I predicted."

"She's packing her things."

"Packing?" He looked from the steaming coffee, to the computer, down into his household manager's gaze. With squared shoulders and a grunt, he decided Steele Knight could hold his horses while he checked on his wife. One game at a time. He waved for Rosie to set down the tray, then brushed past her as he walked toward the bedroom.

Marsh found Kara at the foot of their fourposter.

"And where," Marsh demanded, "are you going?"

"You sound concerned."

"I'd like an explanation. I think you owe me that."

"Do I have to check in and out? Am I under some sort of obligation here?"

He'd anticipated the show of independence, yet the open suitcase ignited his concern. "We're married, Kara. Of course we have obligations."

"Marshall, Marshall…relax, it's not what it seems."

"What is it then?"

"Just some silly notion of mine. Thought it might be fun to take Josee to the beach house for the night. We can share some quality time that way, and it'll free you from any expectations."

"Does she know about this?"

"Not yet, but she's traveled this far, and I'm sure we can make arrangements. Please, I don't need your surliness to spoil our fun." Kara held up a sundress, then opted for a burgundy, lace-sleeved affair. "You think Josee would like LeSerre? Their food is *fabulous*. Perhaps a night on the town. You think she'd enjoy something along those lines?"

"In Yachats? Wouldn't call that much of a nightlife."

"Or perhaps a stroll along the beach? A chance to catch up."

"Pardon me if I can't share in the excitement, but you know how I feel about it."

Kara's caramel eyes petitioned him. "Your support, darling—that's all I'm after."

"Is that all Josee's after?" Marsh moved to the bed, almost tripped over a set of cream-colored pumps. "Here we are, pulling in significant profits for the first time in years, and look who should appear. You must admit that the timing is suspicious."

"Nonsense." Kara shook her head. Her expulsion of disbelief almost muted the sound of a telephone.

"You think I'm joking? If this girl—"

"Our daughter."

"If this girl's able to prove she's related to us, it could grant her some legal portion of our estate. That's a possibility. She could be an opportunist, taking advantage of the latest state measures. Now that Oregon's opened its files to all adoptees, you can bet there are scam artists out there rubbing their hands with glee."

"The audacity, Marsh. Have you even considered the alternative, that perhaps business is prospering so we *can* put together a family again? It seems as if, on some level, there's a bigger plan here. As if God's hand is reaching down."

"Right. Pull out the heavy artillery."

"Why do you always ridicule my beliefs?"

"Okay, so that religious stuff works for you. Guess I'm programmed differently."

"Somewhere in that heart of yours I know you believe."

"Well, if God is out there, he's too big to be concerned with our measly problems."

"Or so big that he *can* be concerned."

"I just don't think we can count on his doing us any favors. Kara, you care a lot for other people—and that's commendable, don't get me wrong—but it doesn't win you brownie points with God. You still have to face things on your own. You can't lean on anyone else."

"Not even my own husband?"

"When it comes down to it, all of us are alone. Each and every person."

"Well. That's nicely stated. Certainly sets my mind at ease."

Over the bedroom intercom, Rosie informed them of a call on the private line.

"Rosamund, if it's not business," Marsh vented, "it can wait. Tell them to call back tomorrow. For heaven's sake, can't we even argue in peace?" He released the Speak button and continued his tirade. "This vineyard was my father's dream, Kara. He worked this land, named that ridge out there, and hoped his one son would carry this on…his dying wish. I'm not about to go and risk it all now."

"I understand that. Your dad would've been so proud, darling. You've met his hopes—exceeded them!—and I respect your hard work. There are other things in life too. That's all I want you to see."

"I'm not as ignorant as that."

"Perhaps," Kara said, "losing the vineyard isn't what you're afraid of."

Marsh stalked to the bedroom's picture window. His eyes raked the landscape. Didn't she understand his dilemma? Sure, Josee's photo in the bathroom breathed wistful hints in his ear, but a reunion was out of the question. Where did a man acquire guidelines for such an encounter? Boardroom strategies would be of limited use.

There it is. I grew up without a father, and I don't have a clue how to be a dad.

His jaw pointed back at Kara as he considered sharing this fear, then he thought of how she would try to allay his concerns. She'd snuggle against him.

Speak encouraging words. Look into his face and spot the self-doubts that roamed behind his eyes.

Worst of all, she would understand. He would be naked before her. Vulnerable.

He faced the window again. "How much longer?"

"Till?"

"You leave."

"Is it so awful to have me around?"

"There's work to be done, my morning routine. I'm ready to be alone." Marsh imagined Steele Knight's impatience in the online dungeon. Ironic, he thought, how chess hostilities seemed safer than human interaction.

He heard her move up behind him. In the window, the troubled expression on Kara's face matched the sincerity of her prayer, so soft that he almost missed it.

"Please, God," she said, "open his eyes."

Fixed like statues at the window, Marsh and Kara faced their joint reflection, a couple in tableau against the wind-tossed landscape. Outside, the wind skimmed over Addison Ridge Vineyards. Coming and going without warning, it tugged at the tails of early mist, nudged beneath a blanket of foliage, then roared upward in a column of fiery leaves. White pebbles scattered as the gust rushed the manor, and Marsh could feel its grip through the double-paned glass.

Kara shivered too. In the reflection, in their nebulous union, he watched her curl closer to touch his cheek with one hand and smooth the ends of his tie with the other. He closed his eyes, wished that Kara would go. He did not want to feel. Did not want to see. Was that so hard to understand?

Then she was jerking away. Her warmth vanished from his side.

"Marsh!" A ragged gasp.

In the windowpane, he viewed his wife's eyes rounded with pain. Her face was turning blue with the effort of breathing; her neck was swollen, pinched by a strip of cloth knotted against her windpipe. He pivoted to look down.

What the heck?

His hands were reaching for her throat.

5

Eyes of Flame

"Scoot, don't mess with that thing. We're not alone."

"Oh no, the girl's goin' schizo on me."

"I'm not kidding." Josee eyed the canister. Earlier, despite warning bells that had jangled in her subconscious, she'd been blindsided by an attack. One whiff had triggered the pain. In this brief span of time, though, something had shifted; now, in vivid color, her pupils registered a hostile entity.

Creeping. Green. Oozing into view.

Across the coals, Scooter was cradling the canister as though enraptured with a newborn. "What'd you smell?" he wanted to know. He put his face near the surface. "I can't smell a thing. Yeah, yeah, okay, now I can, sorta."

An aftershock spasmed through Josee's torso. Scrapbook pages from the past: glaring lights, distant voices, a sharp needle prick…and her red gel capsules.

"Scoot, just do what I ask."

"Hey, it's all good."

"No," she told him, "it's not."

"Things're cool, Josee. No need to stress. Check this out. My ring starts glowing when it gets close to this thing." He stretched out his arm, brought it in again, while the moonstone throbbed. "Man, you see that?"

"Please, hon, this is no joke."

"S'okay. What's the problemo?"

From the canister's seam, a neon green vapor emerged. Scooter seemed blind to it as it twined up his arm. Josee, on the other hand, witnessed the movement in lucid detail. Coils, shifting and sliding. Fangs, curved and transparent, gathering substance from the emerald wisps.

"You can run," he said, "but you can't hide."

Alongside Highway 99, Sergeant Vince Turney sat in his police cruiser and tried with thick fingers to fetch peanut M&M's from the bag between his legs. He nabbed a morsel. Yellow, his favorite.

He didn't deny he could lose a few pounds around the middle, but he'd wolfed down an early breakfast and was feeling the urge to nibble again. He crunched on the candy, dug for more.

Fuel, he told himself. To keep his body going.

Before her passing, his fiancée had teased him that he'd be hitting thirty before she did. In his memory, her voice had lost its humor. "Two or three years, Vince, and you'll be on the downward slope, slip-sliding away. As for me? I'll still be young and perky. Just trying to warn you that you're gonna need more sleep and exercise, not to mention those longevity supplement drinks." Milly had winked, and Turney had wisecracked that she couldn't handle any more man than she was already getting.

Of course, after she'd left for her shift at Key Bank, he'd rushed out to the garage to hide his stack of Sobe beverage elixirs.

Not that it mattered. Milly was gone long before his thirtieth milestone.

A teenage driver fiddling with a CD... A twist of the wheel... A median overrun...

For nearly three years, Milly Svenson's gravestone had graced a hillside cemetery outside of Junction City. Near her parents. At peace and with God.

Here Turney was, still plugging along the career path of law enforcement. Had he missed a turn? Misread the signs? Chief Braddock's old-school leadership grated against Turney's sensibilities, as did the job's brushes with human depravity.

Best to stick to my duties, that's the thing—to serve and to protect.

On the Corvallis outskirts, he adjusted his weight in the driver's seat, fished for another M&M, and waited for a bike to reemerge over the rail embankment. He'd seen a rider disappear near this spot, and he knew there was nothing over yonder but trees and ferns and poison oak.

Some hobo most likely. Or a harmless bum. He'd seen the type before.

Although riding the rails held a certain appeal for Sergeant Turney, he knew his job suggested that he'd better check this out, for the sake of all law-abiding citizens. He radioed in his location, then lumbered from the car, tucking in his shirt and swinging at flying insects on his way through tall ryegrass.

That's when he heard a scream.

———

Josee could do nothing but watch as the vapor coiled up Scooter's arm to his neck. It brushed over his beard, fondled his locks in a licentious caress, then rushed down the other arm to his ring. Scooter's eyes fixed upon the moonstone, and the being struck. Snakelike, the vapor thrust itself forward. Jaws unhinged and rear fangs extended toward him.

"Scooter!"

He whipped his head toward her so that the fangs missed his eyes and clamped instead onto his cheek, where they pumped midnight blue venom into tissue. Within seconds, his face became a mask of repulsive calm. Subservient and accepting of his fate? Or reveling in the experience?

Josee couldn't tell. Strange. Maybe both.

As the fangs retracted, blood glazed over Scooter's eyes. He showed no response, zilch, as droplets spilled from his eyelids onto his poncho.

Shame filled Josee. She'd felt the threat, seen the clues, yet she'd let the speed of the attack keep her from responding. As if she could've. She, too, had frozen in position while a cloak of leaden incompetence weighed upon her back.

Lead: metallic blue gray, the color of a bullet, of a sinker on a line.

The color of her helplessness.

Old snapshots flipped into focus: the time a kitten was swept down the Long Tom River; the day a stuttering classmate endured insults at the back of the school bus; the night her foster mother absorbed blows from the same drunken jerk who'd locked Josee in the basement…

Josee's emotion now swelled into outrage. Blue gray turned red.

Can't just sit here. I have to do something!

"Leave him alone!"

She erupted from her seat, casting off the leaden cloak. She armed herself with a branch and kicked at the leaves. "Get away!" She cranked the limb and took a swing; bark sizzled through the wispy form. In the serpentine coils, Scooter's body remained limp, and the complacency on his face incensed her. *Typical,* she thought.

"Fight!" she commanded him. "Do something."

The vapor turned its gaze her direction.

"Why don't you leave us alone?"

No more than a foot away, the being's tongue flapped forward to read her heat fluctuations. Sizing her up. The miasmic mouth wielded fangs, and the eyes turned into flame. Searing. Dancing with aggression. She knew instinctively that she would never find a snake like this in the Portland Zoo's reptile house.

Josee stepped back. What was she doing? This was insane.

But this creature had no right! A righteous indignation rose within her— from the soil of her childhood vows, from the withered seed of a child's faith.

Along the coils, a twitter of muscle cocked back the serpent's head as it prepared to strike, finalizing its coordinates. Only seconds left, milliseconds. Josee's heart pounded against the spike of pain between her ribs and seemed to drive it deeper with each blow. Deeper. *Clanggg!* Deeper.

Why hadn't she reacted sooner? Where had she gone wrong?

The clanging spike resurrected a vision of torture. A crucifixion. In one of her foster homes, the scene had been depicted in a wall hanging. She was sickened by it, yet comforted by the Savior's kind gaze. There, amid that household's iniquity, it was the only comfort she'd received.

Josee cringed. Another hammer blow.

And the serpent stalled; its fiery stare flickered. Was it teasing her, playing a cruel game? No, it seemed repulsed by something.

By a withered seed...

Josee fought the tightness in her throat. "Get away!" She was vibrating with fury and horror. "Go! Leave us alone!"

In a burst of green, the being darted toward her. Scooter rotated once, remaining upright as the coils unwound. Razor-sharp scimitars arched down toward Josee's eyes, and orbs of poison that looked the size of billiard balls clung to the fangs.

"God!" she cried out like a terrified child. She awaited impact. "God, no."

The serpent froze. Venom spilled and burned holes in the forest ground cover.

Josee emitted a thin cry of faith. "Please, Jesus…save us."

A mustard seed…

The eyes of flame faltered once, twice, and then, in an explosion of color that rent the air with the odor of decay, the being came apart and evaporated into the thicket's shadows. Without ceremony, Scooter landed on the ground. Lying there, vulnerable, he reminded Josee of a prey numbed, yet alive, heart still beating to provide fresh sustenance on demand.

Stahlherz faced the computer that had become his bane. Here at this machine he had hoped to instill terror in the heart of his opponent, yet two moves into it, Marsh Addison had abandoned their chess match.

Crash-Chess-Dummy—the man's user name said it all. *Oh, isn't he witty?*

Of course, Stahlherz knew the sting of Addison rejection. From a photograph on the shelf over his desk, a man seemed to smirk at him. The man had one hand hooked into a loop of his Wranglers, the other dangled over the handle of a plow.

Chauncey Addison…Chance…Marsh's father.

Stahlherz dusted the frame with his thumb. Yes, here was the responsible party, this maggot feeder of a man. He had tossed Stahlherz aside. Left him for dead. Stahlherz's rage dug its talons into his temples, stirred the acids in his stomach.

Bad blood? Now there, my friends, is an understatement.

Outfitted in a slate gray corduroy jacket with elbow patches, Stahlherz slipped from his basement lair. His false ID was in his pocket, along with his sheathed dagger. The park was only blocks away, but he stopped to load his Discman with an audio book, John Le Carré's *The Little Drummer Girl.* Full of artistic types and terrorists, the novel mixed politics and the antiestablishment fringe in a heady dose of mayhem.

A classic. An injection of inspiration. ICV would prevail.

Karl Stahlherz held his chin up, striding in defiance of the aches in his back, the arthritic tightness in his legs. He entered the park from the east, alert for the Professor's presence. Within their network, no one knew of his and the Professor's blood ties. True identities were guarded fiercely. As a safety precaution, ICV operated in small, independent cells.

Stahlherz ran gray eyes over the red-stone path. Envisioning his chess table, he moved fingers in midair as though coordinating troops upon his onyx board. Plans were in motion, the waiting nearly over. Moving into position, the chess pieces were mirroring the actions of his physical troops.

ICV—their network of young men and women. Trained and ready.

Over the years he and the Professor had recruited these members from the soil of disillusionment. Mere kids, really, seedlings of desire that had been watered with a will to survive, to shape their world, to cast off the lies of the preceding generation.

Let the social commentators sneer; the power of a unifying vision was not to be denied. Generation X, Y, or Z? Make no mistake, they would make their mark.

He followed the park path, kicked at a loose rock. Tomorrow he'd have another shot at Mr. Marshall Addison. He'd been using the gaming zone confrontations to evaluate the man's psychological makeup. Used other means, as well. But chess… Ah yes, chess: informer, inquisitor, impartial judge, and jury.

Steele Knight loved the royal game. Exhibiting more justice than life itself, it pitted equal forces upon a balanced battlefield in a fight to the death. There were hidden motives, to be sure, but no hidden moves. Oversights, yes, but no true secrets.

Real life was not so tidy. On the plains of human conflict, one secret remained.

The secret of Chance Addison's journal.

In his mind's eye, Stahlherz twirled his dark bishop like the chamber of a loaded gun. "You, Chance, you are the one to blame. You may be gone, but after what you did to me, I'll burn in hell before letting you finish this game that you started. Your family will not go unpunished."

Did she dare look? She folded her arms, quivering. Sweat trickled along her ribs. With a tentative glance, Josee saw Scooter's chest rising and falling with the congested rattle in his throat.

What's wrong with him? Jesus, please don't let him die.

Expressed without a sound, her words called up long-suppressed affections—as well as deep-seated doubts. One part of her longed to renew her bonds of faith, while another feared thunderous rejection. She set her chin. Looking upward through damp leaves, she challenged the skies to rain down acceptance.

"Howdy. Anybody down here?"

Josee spun her head to the side and, between the branches, saw a heavy-set police officer descending the embankment. With rotating lights at his back, he ducked into the thicket, spotted Scooter on the ground.

"Morning. I'm Sergeant Turney."

The man's insignia marked him as a City of Corvallis public servant. Set between fleshy skin, his eyes were Hershey's chocolate kisses melted deep into cookie dough, and Josee detected empathy there. Actual concern.

"Heard you hollerin'. You two in some sorta trouble?"

"I don't know what's wrong with him."

The officer knelt beside Scooter. His trained hands checked for vital signs.

"It happened so fast." She paused to steady her voice. "I mean, I'm not even sure what just… Can you tell if he's okay?"

"Hard to say right off."

"He's breathing, isn't he? Tell me he's breathing."

"Barely. We're gonna need some paramedics down here. His pulse is weak, and it looks for the life of me as though your partner here's bleedin' from the eyes." Sergeant Turney turned his gaze to the branch in Josee's hand. "Got any ideas why?"

She let the branch fall with a muffled thud.

6

Drum Roll

Kara's mouth was open, her pain an arrow shooting from her pupils with such force that Marsh recoiled. "What's going on?" He fumbled with the silken material at her throat. "Tell me what to do!"

"Marsh, I can't—"

His fingers found a tangled seam. He tugged.

"I'm…choking!"

"How'd you get this around your neck?"

The entreaty in her eyes told him that explanations could wait. *Prioritize,* he told himself. *Get her free of this thing.* Funneling his attention to the cloth noose, he felt a reciprocal tightness in his own larynx; her gasps—and his— were thin and muted. He grappled with the material. Where'd the knot begin and end? He tugged again. Heard a despairing moan. Tried it the other way and whipped the cloth away with the relief of a bullfighter dodging a charge.

"Honey, you okay? What happened!"

Kara coughed. "Why'd you do that?"

Marsh was dumbfounded. "That thing was strangling you."

"You're scaring me."

"I was trying to help."

"Help? But you almost…" Her eyes turned away. "You're right. I should go."

Was she accusing him? "It was this," he said, shaking the material in his hand. "I have no clue how it got around your neck, but it got knotted up somehow. I had nothing to do with it."

Contrasted by black silk, the designer signature caught his attention.

J. Dunlary. It was there in plain sight.

Marsh's free hand clutched at his chest, and he stared down, realizing that his tie was missing from around his neck. He had wrapped it over his shoulders, with no intention of tying it until his boardroom powwow with Henri Esprit, the vineyard's esteemed winemaker. Kara had been running her fingers over the silk. Had she nabbed the tie and playfully slipped it on? She must've. Nothing else made sense.

Nevertheless, the picture of his hands at her throat refused to fade.

———

Marsh had unnerved her. He'd pawed at her, catatonic with fear; he'd thrown his tie to the floor, as though wrestling a creature. And with the conjuring of some crazy scenario, he had brought their conversation to a halt.

His intention most likely. He did nothing without a plan.

Tears stung Kara's eyes as she hobbled with her sports bag down the stairs, out the brick entryway, and to the Z3 convertible. Marshall's gift for her fortieth birthday, the car was an attempt to manufacture intimacy with a chunk of pricey metal. He meant well.

Against the vehicle, the sun beat her shadow into a form without identity.

Marsh called to her from the portico. "Still hours until your mother-daughter reunion. What's the hurry?"

"Shouldn't matter to you," she said. "You might as well sign me out like a piece of your equipment, mark me down in case I don't show back up."

"What's that supposed to mean?"

"Fairly obvious, I'd think. You don't want me around."

She fired the engine, felt raw power purr throughout her body. She thought that this must be why men loved their cars. Her understanding stopped there. She was befuddled by a husband so dedicated to his work, to his father's memory, to a sense of justice that he erected walls between himself and those closest to him. Didn't he see the potential rewards of Josee's return into their lives? Of Kara's place as his life partner?

No, his staunch objectivity blinded him to such things.

With the Z3's top down, she corralled her hair in a chiffon scarf and felt the knot settle like a butterfly in the cleft of her throat. She wouldn't let Marsh's actions dictate her emotions. This was a day of reunion. Reconciliation. She'd think on that.

The driveway carried her from the manor. On Ridge Road, Kara hugged the corners, followed the dotted yellow line where it zipped through stands of evergreens and moss-bearded outcroppings. She let the wind and speed shred her troubles.

I'm going to see my daughter. Today. Finally!

She tossed up an uncharacteristic yell.

Entering an S-curve, she downshifted into the descent. Like an apparition, a van appeared in the crisscrossed shadows. The driver was young and...

I've seen that face before. A repair guy up at the estate. He was—

He was flagging her down. No time to stop.

Her arms stiffened, hands clamped on the wheel, and she pumped the brakes to avoid a collision. To her left, sunlight glanced off a guardrail at the lip of a gulch and speared her eyes. She flinched. Colors danced. Kara Addison felt the wheels slide, and in the chaos of the moment, her scream melded with the squeal of rubber as the roadster ripped a hole in the air over the ravine.

＊

Dust whirled behind her vanishing sports car. Marsh had tried to explain what he'd seen with the necktie, but she wouldn't hear of it. Beneath the portico, he drew a Montblanc pen from his pocket and fired an imaginary shot in Kara's direction. Women. They were like firecrackers—always good for a burst of excitement, but you never knew when one might blow up in your hand.

And you'd think by now I could defuse at least one of them.

He marched up to his study and punched in the code to open the door.

At the computer, Steele Knight was gone. No surprise. Marsh had lost focus anyway. Rattled by the happenings in the bedroom, he consoled himself with thoughts of a rousing game the following morning.

For the next two hours, Marsh sifted through Wednesday's paperwork, made phone calls, sketched out an agenda. Finally, with the boardroom pow-wow ten minutes from starting, he turned to the black tie. Time to don the proper attire. His thumb traced the checkered motif, and he lifted the J. Dunlary over his head. Then paused. The bewilderment he'd been squelching now threatened once more, and he fought a reluctance to noose the silk around his neck.

I don't trust the darn thing. How crazy does that sound?

The mystery remained. What had gone on at their bedroom window? Kara's rounded eyes…his hands…the knotted cloth. Figments of imagination? No. The tie was tangible, silken and smooth. Given the proper facts, he was sure he could sort this matter out, but sharpness of dress was less vital than sharpness of mind, and with the latter in jeopardy, he considered ditching the article in the laundry hamper to let Rosie deal with it.

As if a good dry cleaning could exorcise it? Wait, this is ridiculous. This thing's not going to get the best of me.

He hoisted the material again, worked it into a tapered Windsor knot. Then, as he started to cinch it, the feeling of horror returned, and Marsh cast off the tie for good.

—

"You're loosening up, I see."

"Come again?"

"Dress shirt and slacks, but"—the wiry winemaker tapped Marsh's collarbone—"no tie. How long've I been trying to convince you it was unnecessary?"

"It's only temporary."

"And so are the protocols of business fashion. Take a deep breath, Marshall. Taste the winds of freedom." In the corridor, Henri Esprit spread his hands, closed his eyes, and inflated his barrel lungs as though partaking in reverent ritual.

Marsh hid a smile. "You've been sampling the late harvest grapes again."

"Sampling, yes. Imbibing, no."

"For work purposes?"

"Naturally, and of course." Esprit produced a hand-corked bottle, a reserve of their best Pinot Noir. He decanted and proffered a glass. "Try some yourself. You'll be impressed."

About to protest, Marsh found himself wooed by the wine's bouquet. One sip, and the velvet fruitiness gave way to a waltz of tannins upon his tongue. "Wow. Double wow." Forget the pretentious blather; this was religious release.

"Winds of freedom." Esprit's eyes sparkled. "They only add to the delectation."

Although his tenure dated back to Virginia Addison's days at the helm, Henri Esprit continued to bring unique expression to his position. He revered the vineyard's winemaking techniques, and despite a palate sensitive to the fruit's complexities, he never overindulged—a man in unity with his abilities and the results. Although Marsh held him in high regard, he'd avoided Esprit during his own formative years. With Virginia's fancying Esprit as something of a male role model for her son, Marsh had resisted.

Time was eroding that barrier. He was turning to Esprit more and more.

Marsh glanced at his watch, a sapphire-faced Bulgari. "Let's get in there."

"What's on the agenda?"

"A number of items: vineyard purchase options, minimum wage increases, overseas tariff hikes. With my trip to Europe on Saturday, I might need a bit of coaching for the scheduled negotiations."

"Or I could simply go along."

"Oh, you wish."

"My language skills are more polished than yours. You know it's true. My French alone could save you tens of thousands of francs."

"But this place wouldn't survive a day without you, Esprit."

"I'll keep asking. You know that I will. May as well invite me along."

"Come on. We're late to a meeting."

"All in good time. You mustn't let work drag you through life by the throat."

The throat? Marsh steadied himself against a barrage of images.

"Thank you, O wise one. I'll keep that in mind." He started toward double oak doors inscribed with the initials ARV woven among curled autumn leaves. Without a tie, he felt naked for a boardroom skirmish. "Glad to have you joining me, Esprit. I believe that our board members await."

"Bored members, indeed." Esprit feigned a yawn. "On a serious note…"

Marsh grunted.

"What's bothering you, Marshall? There's something wrong. I can see it in your eyes."

"I'm fine. Nothing a little sleep can't fix." He was glad that Kara and he had kept her intended reunion with Josee to themselves. No need for the prying eyes of vineyard staff and acquaintances. "Enough with the questions," he said. "Let's get on with business."

———

On a park bench hugged by hydrangeas, Stahlherz skipped to the audio conclusion of *The Little Drummer Girl*. He now had his own drummer girl in town. Time was his ally, and after his years of searching, she'd presented herself—so unwittingly.

The week had started well and was shaping up for the grand finale.

Check and mate.

In his pocket, the vibration of his phone alerted him to a new message. He entered the security code and heard Beau's voice. The kid—that ignorant, bumbling pawn!—had already deviated from the plan. He was supposed to have forced the Addison lady at gunpoint to drive them to the hiding spot. Her car would be the perfect cover. Instead, he had caused her to ram the BMW into the guardrail. Loose ends, plans unraveling. Stahlherz loathed this. Chess consisted of precision and timing, and even one set of transposed moves could unravel the finest strategy.

How'd I end up in this cesspool of incompetence?

First things first. The Professor had arrived.

A vintage Studebaker rolled into a space at the walkway's edge. The engine's anguished snarl was that of an old tomcat, stirring rooks from among the trees. The birds beat the air with their wings, silhouettes against a gloomy sky.

Stahlherz approached the vehicle. "Audentes fortuna juvat."

The Professor's Latin put him to shame. "Audentes fortuna juvat. My son, you're two days from the national stage. Surely you could do with a haircut."

"More important things on my mind," he snapped. "Is it true that she's here?"

"True indeed. Her name's Josee Walker." The cracked window and the sound of rustling trees could not hide the tremor in the Professor's voice.

He said, "Mmm, after all this time. Where is she now?"

"That's the odd thing. Although details are sketchy, we know that she and Kara planned to rendezvous soon. Instead, according to a dependable source, Josee has been picked up by police and taken to Good Samaritan."

"Hurt?"

"Not that I'm aware of. However, the young man she was accompanying has suffered an injury resembling a snakebite." Touching a hand to an old wound, the Professor cringed. "I believe it has returned. It has found me one last time."

"You're certain? Any proof that this man was envenomed?"

A tired shake of the head. "Doctors'll know soon enough. We can only hope."

"That's a positive thing, isn't it? Confirmation that the end game is upon us."

"Either way, Stahli, the plans have been set in motion. Tell me, has Kara Addison been removed from the board?"

"She has. Even Beau's miscues cannot set us back."

"Miscues?" Aggravation twitched across the Professor's visage.

"I'm setting things right," Stahlherz said. "I've taken crisp countermeasures."

The Professor allowed him to explain, then, unimpressed, extended and waggled a forearm to entice a loitering blackbird. The rook touched down and received a directive before rising again on strong wings to advance across the cloud-checkered sky. "Be careful, Son. I know that you fancy yourself a grand master, but you're not so impregnable as all that. Anger is a tool, yet you swing it like a weapon."

"It is a weapon."

"A clumsy one at best. You're liable to injure yourself."

Stahlherz pushed arthritic fingers along his brow. He was a scolded child, revisiting isolation and inadequacy. Why did parents undermine their offspring's greatest gifts? Envy? Regret? Wasn't the scope of his anger his to control?

No one will impose limits on me. Not even you, esteemed Professor.

"Stahli? Are you listening? Your job now is to get to the hospital and ensure that the facts are spun to our benefit. With our ICV members in position, that shouldn't be difficult. And you'll pay the victim a visit, I assume? Outstanding. We'll use every possible resource to keep tabs on Josee Walker."

"Her every move," he agreed. "Attack and defend, with no fear and no regrets."

"So long as the task is accomplished, my son. You'll make me proud yet."

As they went their separate ways, he wondered if that was possible.

—

In the van's mirror, Beau checked the blanketed bundle on the floor. The Addison woman—she deserved what she had got. She was pretty, all right. But so what? She drove that flashy Beemer just to flaunt her money, just to taunt people like him. And those earrings? Well, diamonds didn't make her better than anybody else. When would the world get that through its thick skull?

Never, according to the Professor. Such hopes were wasted. That's why the cancer had to be cut away, piece by piece.

Stay cool, guy. Don't go drawing attention to yourself.

One by one he lifted clenched fingers from the steering wheel and stretched. He eased his foot from the gas. Sixty-seven miles an hour? He couldn't risk being pulled over. The cops would see, and they would know. Wasn't time for that yet.

Ke-reech…

Scrapes on his knees were scabbing over with dirt and dried blood. His descent into the ravine had cost him time and energy, but Mr. Steele had insisted. All part of the plan—even if it was Plan B, even if Beau had flubbed up. "Crisp countermeasures"—that's what Steele had called them.

Lost in his thoughts, Beau entered a graded curve. The van tilted, and the bundle behind him rotated, pounding an uneven beat against the metal floor, a drum roll played with elbows and kneecaps.

Snip-a-snip-a-snappp!

Ooh, that had to hurt.

The curve shot the van back onto a straightaway, and the bundle rolled back to its original position. Beau noticed more angles in the shape now, which meant more hassles for him. He still had to carry her down into the cellar. He fought off an urge to puke. He'd never physically hurt a woman before today. What'd taken over him?

He clawed his fingers along his neck and told himself to get a grip. *Just do what you gotta do,* he ordered himself. *I must obey to find the way...*

7

Sparring Partners

On their way down from Washington three days ago, Josee and Scooter had been dropped off at Champoeg State Park by a rancher in an old pickup with a bumper sticker that read "Compost happens."

The words summed up her feelings now. She was sweaty. Dazed. Uneasy.

"Any news, Sarge? Tell me he's gonna be okay."

Sergeant Turney trudged from the nurses' station, splashing coffee from two cups. "They'll let us know soon as they hear somethin'. You sound concerned."

"Wouldn't you be?" Josee collapsed into a waiting-room chair, tucked her bedroll behind her legs, then adjusted her damp sweatshirt over no-name jeans. The scents of antiseptics and tonics infiltrated the space. Medics rushed a gurney up the corridor, and at the sight of a child beneath a shiny thermal blanket, Josee imagined Scooter's ordeal. He'd been in Good Samaritan's ER for over two hours.

I'm here, Scoot. Hang in there.

She said, "Hospitals give me the creeps."

"You and me both." Turney extended a hand. "Ready for a cup o' joe?"

"Styrofoam."

"Say what?"

Josee pointed. "Styrofoam. Haven't you heard of the ozone layer?"

"So that's your shtick. Well, kiddo, it won't hurt ya to drop the environmental martyr act and pour a little warmth into that skinny belly of yours." To prove the liquid was harmless, he took a gulp. Sputtered. "Sakes alive, that'll put hair on your chest."

"Smells burnt." She cast her words like bait. "Is that the way *real* men like it?"

He ignored the question, examined the drink.

"What now? Something wrong with the cup?" She underlined the question with arms crossed beneath her breasts—small, yes, but all natural. She felt no need to conform to the silicon standards. She could still provoke a lascivious response when necessary, and at this moment she wanted Turney to snap at the bait so she could cement her resentment of him. Holsters and badges. Desire. Derision. She and Scoot had faced their share of power-hungry cops.

"Doesn't taste that bad." He looked up. "Got a kick to it, that's all. Go ahead and drink up. Either that, or I'll hafta book you for resisting an officer."

"Ooh, getting rough now."

"Just don't wanna see you shivering for the rest of the day."

To Josee's surprise, the sergeant's eyes glowed with a clean, bright fire. Whereas most men's eyes—even Scooter's—burned like soot-stained lanterns, his revealed nothing dirty or disturbing. A hint of sorrow maybe. Nothing lecherous.

"Fine, have it your way."

She took the cup, placed it against her cheek. The heat was nice. Champoeg State Park had provided her last shower, and she knew her clothes were growing musty. She thought of thanking the officer but decided against it. She popped a daily gel capsule into her mouth, then let the vial dangle back around her neck. Beside her, Turney wedged himself into a chair with a copy of *Field & Stream,* his belly parting his shirt at the lowest button.

"So, how long do we have to sit here?"

He flipped a page. "Long as it takes 'em."

"I'm a big girl. I'm good here on my own if you have work to do."

"Actually, I'm waitin' on Chief Braddock. Should be here soon enough, poking his nose into matters." Turney fiddled with his badge. "Not to mention, you and I've got some questions to go over, to establish what went on out there. Was it a case of self-defense? Had you been in some sorta argument?"

"It wasn't like that."

"When I walked up, you were standing over him. Did you happen to hit him with your hands or with that stick?"

"This is so lame. Why would I want to hurt him?"

"Is Scooter your boyfriend?"

"Friend, boyfriend. Whatever. We've hung together almost three years."

The sagging magazine in Turney's lap seemed to match the gloom that tugged at his face. "A lot can happen in three years."

"Am I a suspect, Sarge? Is that what you're getting at?"

Turney sucked in his lips until his heavy jowls puckered. "Josee, if his wounds indicate your involvement, you could be looking at an assault-four. What with the APA and all—the Assault Prevention Act—we'd have to separate the two of you. Is that what you want? Please work with me here."

"I…did…not…hit…him. There, you satisfied?"

She rebuked herself for lowering her guard earlier. Turney was a freakin' bacon strip. She knew better than to trust a cop, particularly one with Y chromosomes.

Stahlherz named the hospital as their next destination. Darius complied with a turn of the steering wheel. His nut brown hair, tied back over his shoulders, matched the Aerostar van's nondescript exterior.

"A reasonable speed, please. No need to draw attention our way."

"Hey, Steele-man, be cool. I've done the driver's-ed thing. Passed every test they could throw this boy's direction. You be safe with me."

"I be safe? Well, you be careful."

"Shazaam."

Stahlherz knew the minced lingo belied his driver's intelligence. He liked the kid and compensated him—in cash, nontaxed—for mileage and road hours. Thus motivated, Darius bore his cell phone at all times, responsive to his employer's whims. Saving up for filmmaking classes, Darius confided. Here in town at Oregon State University.

Well, well, this boy was driving his way to the stars.

Not that Stahlherz was unable to operate a vehicle. Please, he was not that incapable. To steer clear of governmental records, he'd chosen to forgo a driver's license. Footpaths and bike lanes, drivers, and CTS bus passes purchased at the Rite-Aid—he made do. It'd be incomprehensible to risk exposure for the sake of speedier transport. Too much at stake.

To Darius, he'd told a different story. "A leg injury—that's what impedes me. Bone spurs suffered in a city-league soccer match." Truth be told, arthritic aches and worsening migraines had forced him from the team. Further evidence that his genius was leeching off his body's resources.

He removed and reapplied the Band-Aid over the talon wound on his forearm. That insolent beast. Always trying to wrest control from him. Last night's memory made his scalp twitch like the lid on a boiling pot. Bitterness rose in his gullet. *No, I'm the one in control! Rationing myself. Not much longer to go.*

Allhallows Eve…

Two nights hence, while others paraded in ghoulish costumes, he would peel away the mask for all to see. Karl Stahlherz would become a household name. The forsaken one no longer. He imagined that somewhere in the raging flames of his own mind an effigy of Chance Addison was burning.

—

Long ago chessboard rooks had been fashioned after soaring castles, and as Good Samaritan Regional Medical Center loomed ahead, Stahlherz decided that this structure was a modern incarnation of the medieval fortress. Situated on a hill, with towering walls and an imposing entrance, it gazed upon the city below. Spoke of sanctuary and hope within. An empty hope for many.

Without insurance or wealth, the peons still groveled outside the castle gates. And society's cancer continued to spread. The time had come to storm the walls.

"Never been in thurr." Darius propped a leg on the dash. "Sick people smell."

Stahlherz loosened his seat belt. "It's been ages for me, the early '80s."

The last time he'd stalked through this hospital lobby he had carried a gun. He'd confronted Marsh Addison and his fiancée, Kara, but failed at his task. Parental castigation was the result. The Professor demoted him to his basement existence—alone with turpentine and oils, cages and rooks. Art and warfare molded him there. In solitude. Then the dawn of the Internet brought reconnection, granting access to the mind-set of the human animal. Feeble beings. Far from their evolutionary apex. Pandering and lonely, they allowed a plethora of addictions to rule them.

"Yo, Steele-man, you gonna jump out, or's I gotta kick you out?"

"I'm paying you, aren't I?"

"Don't have all afternoon, brah. Got's me a date. A brunette."

Stahlherz stepped from the van, then slipped a fifty-dollar bill across the dashboard. "Here, Darius, a bonus. Enjoy the time you have…before it's gone."

He faced the hospital entryway. Josee Walker was in there. She was the key. For now, though, others would monitor the little drummer girl's movements. He had additional factors and players to consider before she could unlock the final combination for him.

Combination. The definition was known to any true disciple of the game of chess: a series of forced moves, often initiated by sacrifice, that lead to a winning advantage.

—

"Listen, Josee, I need details. Gimme some facts to work with."

"Why should you buy anything I tell you? Just some drifter's take on things."

"Is that what you are, you and Scooter?" Sergeant Turney adjusted his uniform.

"What if it is? Scoot and I, we refuse to be pawns in some capitalistic kingdom. Look at our cities, cushy little incubators growing babies with dollar signs in their eyes." The waiting area magnified her voice. "No thanks! If that makes us drifters, so be it."

"'Not all those who wander are lost.'"

Josee lifted an eyebrow. "That's Tolkien. Are you a fan?"

"Not much of a reader, to be honest. Think I saw it on a bumper sticker." She hid her amusement by digging through her pockets. "You smoke?"

"Nosiree." He gripped his belly. "Already got this to deal with. And none of your wisecracks, please. Not a day goes by that I don't have someone tryin' to feed me horse manure in shovel loads." The sergeant cinched up a pant leg. "Can get pretty deep, if you know what I mean."

"Yeah? Must explain the smell."

"Want me to round you up a pair o' hip waders?"

"Funny."

"Put it to you this way, kiddo. I consider myself a decent judge of character, and I see somethin' in that face of yours. Behind the anger and fear and attitude, you seem to be an honest woman."

"Which is it? Woman or kiddo?"

Turney laughed and scraped a hand over his blond crew cut. "You got me there. Here's the thing. I just wanna nail down the truth for my report. Already Mirandized you back by the railroad tracks, so you've got a choice to speak up or keep quiet."

"The truth? You know, it might not be what you expect."

"Even in a city this small, nothing surprises me anymore."

"I didn't do it, bottom line."

"Then who did?"

Who? Or what? She quivered, recalling curved fangs and dripping venom. "You'll think I'm blowin' smoke. You may as well cuff me now, book me, and print me. Like I care. Just promise me that the doctors'll take care of Scooter in there."

"He's in good hands. They hounded me about the lack of insurance, but I've been in this city long enough to pull a few strings. That's a good thing." His voice trailed off as though a number of bad things had risen to challenge his claim.

"What've they told you? You're keeping something from me, aren't you?"

Turney closed the magazine. "Do yourself a favor, Josee, and remember who you're talking to. My job's to uphold the law. Is that clear? Some o' my partners, they'd take one look at you and judge you before ya got a word out. That's not me. So why don't you cut me some slack and show a little trust here, a little faith."

Trust? Faith? One prolonged hardy-har-har to those concepts. In Josee's experience, they were brainwashing terms used to shape the weak-minded.

She said, "I'll believe it when I see it."

"That's fair, since you hardly know me. But you oughta know that faith is...well, faith is believing in somethin' you cannot see. Goes beyond the human level."

"A spiritual thing—that what you mean? You think I should send up a prayer?"

"Not that it's my place to say, but, yeah, it couldn't hurt."

Josee pushed back a lock of hair. "Already tried it, Sarge, out there in the thicket. And look where I'm sitting now."

"You prayed in the woods? Why?"

She huffed. "I was afraid, I guess. Desperate."

"Afraid of what? Tell me what you saw."

Although she shook her head at the picture of fangs pumping venom into Scooter's cheek, the image held fast. Exasperated, she fixed her eyes like drill bits on the sergeant, but instead of bracing himself with frustration or indignation, he let his eyes melt into hers—Hershey's chocolate kisses. Josee sensed something melancholic about him. No, not his weight. She could look past that. Something in his posture. In his face. As if he'd witnessed his own demise and left behind a shell to carry on the functions of life.

Survival mode. I know it well.

"Okay, fine," said Josee. "You wanna know what happened? I'll tell you."

"I'd be appreciative." He stood and gestured at her. "C'mon, though, let's take it to the cafeteria, where I can fatten you up while priming you for answers."

"Not me, not hungry."

"My tab, Josee. The department'll reimburse me if need be."

"Do I look like I need a handout?"

"Who are you foolin'? Bet you haven't had a decent meal all week."

Turney turned his broad back and walked away. Josee stammered. Decided to stay put. Changed her mind, grabbed her belongings, and followed. Turney was right. She was starved.

In her rush through the lobby, she collided with a man who groaned and turned as though ready to vociferate. Instead, he stared. His shoulders were hunched in the manner of many tall men, gray hair streaked his black mane, and a thin nose sliced vertically the way his lips did horizontally. Aside from patches at the elbows—how '70s was that!—his corduroy jacket matched the slate gray eyes that now riveted her.

"Got a problem?" Josee demanded. "Watch where you're going."

He rocked forward, fingers plucking at the air.

"Stare hard, retard." Feeling juvenile even as she said the words, she shook off his predatory gaze and continued to the cafeteria with its round, white tables.

—

Josee shoved a plastic tray down the cafeteria bar. Eating with a cop didn't fit into her antiauthority framework, but that deli vegetarian sandwich did look good. So did the Sun Chips. She took swigs of iced tea so that her mouth was too full to protest each time Sergeant Turney added another item to her tray.

The clerk at the register seemed to know the sergeant. She waved him on.

He paid anyway, nabbing the receipt.

At a table overlooking a courtyard, Josee plopped into the seat across from him. She didn't want this guy thinking he controlled her. Absolutely not. Yet she did find a certain calm in his presence. Turney had been the first on the scene, the one to radio for help, and—shocker of all shockers—the only man in a long time to avoid making a pass at her when given the opportunity.

What is it about him? Not that we click, but it's like... Oh, forget it!

After light chatter and fervent eating, Turney wrestled pad and pen from his pocket. "Feelin' better already. Now, let's start this off with your name, first and last."

"Josee Walker."

"J-O-S-I-E?"

"Two *e*'s, no *i*," she replied through a bite of macaroni salad.

"Place of birth?"

"Corvallis, Oregon. Right here at Good Samaritan."

"A small world. Bet you remember it like it was yesterday."

She played along. "Mm-hmm, every detail. Actually, I was given up for adoption. Haven't seen my birth parents since day one."

"Hope things've worked out for you."

She lifted her shoulders. Sucked on a sliced dill pickle.

"Back to my ruthless interrogation. Your age?"

"Twenty-two."

"I've got a good nine years on you. Date of birth?"

"July 4, 1981."

The sergeant gave a puzzled look.

"Stinkin' Fourth of July," Josee reiterated. "And you can hold the jokes, please. Got teased enough in school. 'Were you born with only a fourth of a brain?' 'Miss Independence.' Seems silly, but it irritated the crud out of me back then."

"Kids can be cruel. Believe me"—he rubbed his stomach—"I've heard it all."

"You're packing lead, all right." A quick thrust to regain her advantage.

"Lard's more like it. So, kiddo…uh, Josee, you got any birthmarks, tattoos, or other identifying features?"

"Excuse me? What's that got to do with anything?"

"I'll mark down the piercing. How 'bout that?"

"Which one?"

"Uh…" He faltered, made a note on the pad. "The eyebrow. There, that'll do."

"Wanna see my newest tat?"

"Tattoo? Nope, nope, we're good."

With a quick gulp of Pepsi, he regained his composure and suggested that she proceed with her account. She peered out the window and gave it to him straight. He scribbled away, never looking up or contradicting her; by the end, however, she felt his demeanor shifting. Was he doubting her? He rubbed his eyes with a large fist and closed his notepad upon his knee.

"So," he said, "you're sure that's how it happened? You'd testify to it under oath?"

"I knew you'd write me off." Josee bounded to her feet, slung her bedroll over her shoulder. "Never should have opened my mouth in the first place."

"But I'm buyin'," he cajoled. "Every word of it."

She planted a hand on her hip.

"Looky here." The sergeant began rolling up the left sleeve of his blue uniform. He looked like a heavyweight boxer preparing to throw a punch. A prizefighter. With every jab Josee had thrown, Turney had ducked or parried with equal force. Although in need of conditioning, he seemed to have a few good rounds left in him.

"Josee, you all right? Hello? Anybody home?"

Without realizing it, she'd again locked on to his gaze—those warm eyes.

"Yeah," she said, "just thinking." She was thinking that it wasn't weakness that had softened his brown eyes; it was empathy gained by ordeals endured. Turney, too, had a scrapbook of shredded pages and photographs. She could sense it. See it. If she observed him long enough, she thought she might even identify his pain.

Oh, this is crazy. Like I can trust this guy? Nope, not gonna go there.

Turney's sleeve was now rolled to the shoulder, and he was pointing to a biceps wasted beneath a layer of flab. "True, these arms ain't what they used to be. Back in my prizefightin' days, though, I even won myself a purse or two."

"I was just thinking how you reminded me of a boxer."

"I was a big kid. Thunder Turney—that's what the gym rats called me."

"Has a ring to it," she ribbed him. "You know, as in, a boxing ring?"

"Yuk, yuk." He flexed his arm. "C'mon and take a closer look."

"Just a joke. Please don't hurt me, mister." She dipped her head for a peek and nearly choked. "Wait! This can't be coincidence. Are those what I think they are?"

"They're fang marks." Spaced two inches apart on his freckled biceps, pale green scar tissue capped wounds that had once oozed blood and pus for weeks. Or so Turney claimed. He said the marks were twenty-two years old. "You were just a little thing, Josee," he kidded, but his eyes watched hers, intent on her reaction.

"So now you're a math whiz. Good for you, Sarge."

"Easy to figure, really. Happened on the day you were born."

"Fourth of July? Okay, that's freakin' weird."

She studied his arm, recognized the bite pattern. Same as Scooter's. The scars confirmed her instinct to come clean with this cop. Yep, he must've been testing her, determining the things she had seen and what she attributed them to. Sergeant Turney might even have a clue as to what had gone on out there in the woods.

Or maybe… Maybe he's still looking for answers himself.

Either way, she sensed an opportunity for a connection. Sparring partners. Training for what, the big match? Against a stinkin' vapor, a serpent being? Things were getting fuzzy, as though she'd taken one blow too many to the head. Maybe she should hang up the gloves before things got worse. Best thing to do was get Scooter out of here and return to the original plan. She'd call to see her birth mother Thursday afternoon, play the part of long-lost daughter, then head back to Puget Sound.

In other words, get far away from here, get on with life.

Turney was tapping his scars. "I told ya I believed every word. So, Josee, you wanna hear how I got these buggers?"

She was a statue in her seat. Afraid to know. Afraid not to.

The arrival of Chief Braddock stole that decision from her.

8

Empty Space

Marsh crossed the parking area to the winetasting room. The meeting had gone well. Routine was taking over. While Kara pursued her pipe dreams, he'd continue with the day's demands. Let her do her thing, go to the beach house, whatever.

Mark me down in case I don't show back up…

Her words ran through his mind. And that sadness on her face.

He'd been harsh; he could admit that. Offering sparse sympathy. Shutting her off. How though, he wondered, could he show her that he did care? What would be meaningful to her?

"Afternoon, Mr. Addison." Straddling a tractor, a mechanic greeted him.

Marsh nodded, then pushed through huge doors into an area lined with oak barrels. Bottles in wine racks wore gold medals around their necks; T-shirts and etched glasses displayed the Addison Ridge name. In the warehouse things also looked presentable, and he spent an hour monitoring fermentation levels. He thought of calling Kara, even hit speed dial on his cell phone, then rejected the notion for fear of being coerced into a conversation with Josee.

What would he say, for heaven's sake? After two decades, words were cheap.

As he entered the manor, an idea struck him.

The parlor… Stodgy and staid, his mother's Hepplewhite antiques and dour-faced daguerreotypes lined the room. Kara's additions, inherited from her grandmother, were perfunctory: velvet drapes, ruby-colored carpet that begged admiration but offered only minimal functionality, and the *pièce de résistance,* a walnut-grained organ that was polished more often than played.

Why not clear the room? Create a parlor suited to Kara's interests?

Harebrained, but I like it. Maybe Kara will too.

With a phone call, he enlisted help. Before dinner, the space was emptied, the bric-a-brac transferred to a downtown storage unit, the carpets and drapes stripped away, the organ covered and preserved by a specialist who fawned over the craftsmanship. There was no doubt in Marsh's mind that his mother would lament the removal of her "precious heirlooms," but Virginia had moved into a coastal retirement community, and for over two decades this had been his and Kara's home.

So be it. Till death do us part.

In the late afternoon, he saw Rosie arrive from town in the vineyard's company van. After directing the unloading of kitchen supplies, she followed him into the parlor and scanned the space without comment. When he took a broom to the baseboards, she shooed him away and took over. Later Marsh found her heading down the hall into the two-room area she occupied with her dachshund. She had started her duties early and, as scheduled, was now ready to retire for the evening.

"Rosie, thanks for your help."

"All in a day's work, sir."

"I'm putting together an idea for Kara," he said, fishing for female feedback.

"As I've observed."

"Yeah. I think the room'll look better, more Kara's style."

"Rather sparse, if I might be candid."

"I've got some ideas, stuff that she'll appreciate. Or maybe I should wait until she gets back and let her choose for herself."

"She's mentioned on more than one occasion how she loves the piano."

"Really? But the organ, she never even played it while it was here."

"Hardly the same thing, sir. The piano's more whimsical, don't you think, in keeping with Kara's temperament."

"Hmm, not a bad idea."

"Will that be all?"

"Sure. Thanks, Rosie. Have a good night."

With her inimitable style, she turned down the hall.

Marsh slipped into his study at the top of the grand staircase. Thunderclouds were gathering over the Cascade foothills, and he watched claw-footed lightning shred the night. Behind him the door slid closed, and a beep signaled the activation of the electronic lock. Henri Esprit was the only other person with access to this room. For security reasons, the keypad was repro-grammed on a quarterly basis.

Marsh went over the previous week's spreadsheets on his desk while his father's picture gazed down from a bookshelf. Chauncey Addison. His dream lived on.

"Chance…Dad. I'm taking this place up a notch. Wish you could be here."

As he pulled his eyes from the photo, a discrepancy demanded attention. Here, where he orchestrated his affairs with precision, here, where he knew the position of each Escher original on the walls and the precise formation of combatants upon the chess table, something was amiss.

His frosted glass queen… She had vanished from the board.

For crying out loud, why couldn't people leave things alone? His father, as a young infantryman, had purchased this chess set more than five decades ago in the weeks following the Nazi surrender. The set was irreplaceable. The fact it had arrived on American soil without a mark was testimony to its value.

Now a piece was gone. The inner sanctum had been violated. The question was, who had been in his office? Rosie, Kara, Henri Esprit…

Someone else? Or…something else?

He admonished himself for irrational suppositions. Time to get a grip.

After a thorough check of the carpet and the space under the furniture, he plunked down on the black leather sofa. Moonlight sparkled amid the chessboard regiments, but the queen's space remained empty and dark. Kara's parting words played once more in his ears. Had she been trying to tell him something? No, he was reading too much into this. Of course she would show back up. Always did.

He changed into swim trunks, grabbed a towel and a Black Butte Porter, then headed for the back deck Jacuzzi.

The Tattered Feather Gallery specialized in Native American art. Suzette Bishop owned the shop on SW Second, and though she carried other items—sand candles, myrtlewood clocks, Mount St. Helens ash-carved statuettes—it was the tribal imagery that connected her to the beating heart of mother earth. She told customers she had Nez Percé blood, and she'd begun to believe it herself.

Hadn't she smoked peyote in college? That made her one of them. In her haze, she'd felt the brush of feathers on her skin, heard the scream of a soaring eagle.

Thus, her self-given native name: *Tattered Feather.*

Through dream catchers strung along the gallery window, Suzette watched the sun complete its circuit. With closing time at seven, she had just over an hour to go.

A sharp tone sounded at the entrance, and tree shadows leaped through the opening shop door.

"Still open?"

"Why, yes, yes, absolutely. Come on in."

A stooped, middle-aged man entered, toting a paper-wrapped canvas as large as himself. Suzette retreated behind a long glass display case. A premonition? She wasn't certain. What had the electric eye seen that made it cry out so?

"How's your evening? Any questions I can answer for you?"

"I'm an artist."

"Wonderful, that's wonderful."

The man ran his hand along the paper, up and down, up and down, while his eyes scanned the showroom. "Didn't mean to startle you. My apologies."

"Oh, no, no, not at all."

"Audentes fortuna juvat," he said.

She pulled a hand to her chest and wrinkled her mouth. It'd been weeks since her last meeting with ICV. She loved the Pacific Northwest for its natural resources, and this group claimed to fight for environmental concerns. They gathered and inspired artists, taught awareness, and collected and donated funds. More recently, however, they'd segued into anarchist activity under the guise of civil disobedience.

In her last meeting, she'd seen one recruit—only one—decry such means.

ICV's retaliation was swift. Anything but civil. And she hadn't gone back.

"Ma'am, I know it's been a while. I'm seeking your help, hoping to sell my newest work on consignment." The man stripped away the paper to reveal a white chess queen upon her castle walls. She was reaching for something, losing her balance. Concealed among thorns in a cubist foreground, a book was open, pages flapping. Was this the object of interest? A saffron streak marked the painting's edge.

"My, my, my. Very original. Is this yours?"

The artist gave a nod, his aura draping him like a buffalo blanket.

"Striking. And quite good." Suzette Bishop's misgivings crumbled before her passion for creative expression. "I *like* its brooding magnetism. I'll *make* a space."

The man looked her in the eye for the first time. "Sounds trivial, I'm sure, but do you make deliveries of purchased works? That's been my understanding."

"Why, on occasion I've made such arrangements."

"With a piece this large, it might be a necessity. My asking price is $3,999."

She propped the canvas beside a shelf of amulets and bear-claw necklaces, mentally calculating her commission. If it sold quickly, she could attend the upcoming psychic fair. All was coming into alignment. Tattered Feather would have a chance to fly. "I can guarantee delivery," she told the artist. "Not to worry, not at all."

"Thank you, ma'am. In cauda venenum."

"In cauda venenum." The phrase spilled so smoothly through Suzette's lips.

With the porter thick on his tongue and chlorine heavy in the air, Marsh let a waterjet drill at the tension in his back. Tomorrow he'd start fresh. He had hurt Kara with his words, but he would make it up to her. With any luck, she'd be happy with the changes in the parlor. He would let her tell of her encounter with Josee, and then maybe she would calm her hormones, and the kitchen staff could serve them a candlelight dinner in the dining hall, and they'd laugh and act as they had during their engagement in his junior year at Oregon State.

Before the pregnancy. And the doctor's grim prognosis.

Before his mother's enigmatic warning that had served as precursor to both…

"Son, I cannot tell you everything. Wish that I could, but Chance wouldn't want it that way." In his memories, Virginia's voice was always shakier than in real life, as though the decades-old conversation were taped and wearing thin. "You need to know, though, a few things at least. Now that you and Kara are considering marriage, I'm obligated to issue a caution."

"A caution?" Marsh snorted. "About what? You make it sound so ominous."

She pushed ahead. "Marshall, you may be unfit for fatherhood."

"Unfit?" He forced a laugh. "Who said anything about kids?"

"Your risk's high. You've been contaminated, and it'd be wise to have a doctor—"

"What crazy talk is this, Mother? What're you going on about?"

She screwed her eyes tight as if to block a chimera of horror. "One day you'll see."

"I'll see? Oh, very cryptic! And helpful, I might add."

"One day it'll make sense. We can only pray that such a day never comes, that perhaps you'll be spared. It's a matter your father involved himself in at the end of the war, something bound to endanger your offspring."

"My father was a good man."

Virginia sniffled. "Duty called him into military aspects of chemical research. Son, you need to understand this. Please don't disregard it."

"What's the point here?"

"Contamination. Your father suffered from his work. Only later did he realize the long-term effects."

"What? Was there an accident? A chemical leak? What're you trying to say?"

"It was no accident." Virginia clenched her fingers in her lap. "I'm trying to protect you from a portion of the pain that I've gone through."

"Yeah? That's something every parent says. You ask me, this is insane."

"We must break the chain."

"You bet, Mom. I'll start working on it right away."

Infuriated by his mother's gall, he had refused to broach the subject again.

He wouldn't yield himself to this curse she had tried to drop at his feet. Later, however, when Kara's obstetrician announced the ailing status of her unborn daughter, Marsh stewed in uncertain blame. The tiny baby did not deserve this. A blood disorder. An unknown form of hemophilia threatening her very life? He did not need this encumbrance on his time and finances. Surely he was not responsible for her sickness. Or was he? Had his own father passed along a genetic anomaly? What had actually happened at the end of the war?

Maybe his mother's words were true; maybe he had afflicted a child with his own defective genes.

Unfit, indeed.

Stretched out in the hot tub, he felt a droplet of sweat sting his eye. He blinked twice. In his peripheral vision, he thought he saw a figure at the end of the cedar deck, and he shot up from the water. Called out in warning. Armed himself with a beer bottle and prowled the planks till he was convinced he was alone. Whatever it was, it had vanished.

9

Scars and Stripes

"Oh, brother," Chief Braddock chided. "Not this story again."

Turney bristled. His superior had arrived with measured strides, keys swinging in rhythm from his belt. Although white hair showed at his red temples and wrinkles carved his rawhide cheeks, he moved like a younger man. Turney stood and let his sleeve drop back over his arm. "Hello, Chief."

"Tell me, Sarge, whose ears are you twisting this time?"

Shoving in his shirt, Turney felt his cheeks grow hot. He'd faced ridicule before, learned to keep his trap shut, but with Josee at his side he felt an urge to defend himself—an urge he hadn't experienced this strongly since before his fiancée's passing.

Milly. Josee. Different in lots of ways, but both had that feisty streak.

Time to speak up. He opened his mouth. Stood there like a confounded fool.

"Full of the usual wit, I see." Braddock turned. "And you must be Josee." His eyes flashed reproach, then dalliance as they roved from her attire to cheekbones to upturned eyes. "Josee Walker?"

"Maybe. Who are you?"

"Don't tell me you're buying Sarge's drivel."

"You know, we were having a private conversation here."

Sergeant Turney gave a silent hurrah. He knew what it was like to be on the other side of Josee's attitude. *Let him have it, kiddo.*

The chief rested his hand on a belt buckle where shiny flint letters spelled *Big Juan.* "I'm Chief Braddock. You know what that means? It means I come and go as I see fit. I've been around this area a long time, and nothing's private, not to me, not in this city." He spun a chair and straddled it.

Turney said, "Josee and I were just finishin' up a report."

"That so? Looked to me like you were about to launch into one of your stories. Let me guess, the one about the snake?"

"Actually, she—"

"Listen, he's yanking your chain, Josee." Braddock wagged a censuring finger. "Sarge tells a good story. Don't get me wrong. But he'd be better off saving his ideas for some campy late night TV show, *X-Files* or somethin'."

"TV?" Josee gibed. "I yanked the plug on the great surrogate mother years ago."

"Surrogate mother?"

"Yep. Baby-sitting America's kids, telling them how to look, how to act, how to—"

"As I was saying…" Careful to leave his badge visible and gleaming, the chief folded his arms and flicked aside her interruption like lint from his starched uniform. "Years ago the famous Thunder Turney met his match in a hospital corridor. This very place, in fact. He was just a kid, you understand, but he couldn't hold his own. Ever since, he's fabricated these stories to salve his conscience. Truth be told, a woman was shot, and her newborn baby was lost. Unfortunate. Wasn't his responsibility though. You'd think he'd move on and let it rest, but, oh no, not our boy Vince."

Josee said, "Bet you just love belittling people."

Braddock's laughter was a stone skipping over the cafeteria tables.

Turney bit his lip. Jabbed at the crust of his hamburger bun.

The chief said, "Now don't get your shorts in a wad, Sarge. We've got work to do. I've just come from the Rotary Club, and I'm meeting with the hospital administrator shortly, but in the meantime I'll keep Miss Walker here company. As for you—"

"Josee hasn't seen her friend, sir. She's worried. I was plannin' to take her—"

"Just told you the plan. I'll make sure she gets her visitation time. Now you've got paperwork to go through at the station. Need you to set up next week's swing-shift schedule and have Rita post it today. And while you're at it, if you'd be so kind as to arrange tonight's lodgings for the young lady here, I'm sure she'd appreciate it."

"Don't need it," Josee piped up. "I'll sack out here in the waiting room."

"It'd be better if—"

"I'm not leaving, not till I see Scooter."

"You'll see him. Then you gotta trust the sergeant to set you up. That clear?"

Josee massaged her earlobe. "Sure, I guess I can trust him."

"Well, well, score one for Sarge."

Turney looked straight ahead, his heart slowing to a stop.

"So," Josee carried on, "why don't *you* trust your own officer to stay here and take care of business? He seems like a good guy, despite the junk you're flinging at him. I'd rather we just keep things the way they are."

Braddock dragged a hand over his sun-wizened cheeks, fixed his eyes on a fluorescent light overhead. "Girl, I'm going out of my way for you as it is. I've even requisitioned benevolence vouchers for you, something to tide you over while your friend's healing up. Am I wrong in assuming that you're strapped for cash? Take what's offered, and knock that chip off your shoulder."

"But I can't help it," Josee said, her words dripping with sincerity. "It's an extra appendage. Had it since my day of birth."

"Then maybe, just maybe, you need to go back and start over."

"Maybe that's exactly what I'm trying to do! What do you know anyway?"

Turney placed his hand close to Josee's tray. He could see her leg jittering beneath the table. He hated to admit it, but the chief's brusque manner couldn't hide the truth in his words. Turney said, "Josee, things'll be all right. You just sit tight, do as the chief says, and we'll get you a place to lay your head for the night."

"What's wrong with staying here?"

"First off, the hospital's not real wild about runnin' a hotel. Through the department, we've got a list of homes ready to open up whenever we need a bed."

"You mean whenever someone like *me* needs a bed."

"These're kindhearted people. They're not judging you. Neither am I."

"So Josee," Braddock broke in, "you ready for some news on this Scooter kid?"

Her eyes batted in coy machination. "Pretty please, Chief, with a cherry on top."

"Knew that'd please you. You girls're always easy to figure."

Turney held his breath for fear of what he might say.

"Hold tight, you two," Chief Braddock directed, "and I'll be right back."

—

Josee watched the chief plow between tables and chairs. "What a jerk."

"That's the man's style—always gotta stay on top."

She turned and saw Turney's eyes sinking deeper into cookie dough, melting in the heat of his self-reproach. "Tell me what happened. What did he mean about the lady and her baby?"

The sergeant dropped his head, clasped his hands in back of his neck. "I lost the kid. I was there and tried to stop it, and I failed. The baby disappeared, and that was that. Don't know if it was a kidnapping or what. Maybe some child-custody thing."

"But you were just a kid yourself, right? Why are you to blame? I don't get it."

"Neither do I. Just one o' those things I can't get outta my mind."

"Does this have anything to do with those fang marks?"

With a sigh, Turney met her questioning eyes. "See, Josee, I'd been up the whole evening with a coupla my school buddies. I'm talkin' fourth grade here. My mom was gone—that was pretty normal—at some Independence Day party, and we'd gotten into her liquor cabinet. Drunk ourselves silly. I'd once heard my mom's friends talk about poppin' pills and stuff, and being a dumb kid, I figured I'd swallow a few aspirin to impress the guys. When I went comatose on 'em, one of them panicked. Called the paramedics. Next thing I knew I was laid up in a hospital bed."

"Here? This hospital?"

"Ain't life funny."

"Where does the baby come in? I'm lost."

"It was gettin' late, and my mom was finally on her way. She'd talked to me on the phone. Not a real happy camper, considering the cops had tracked her down and given her flak about leavin' us kids on our own."

"Sounds like one or two of my foster homes."

"If you can survive childhood, you can survive anything."

"Mm-hmm." Josee stared into her lap.

"So this lady on the next floor—the nurses were talkin' about her, saying how she was real pregnant, ready to pop any minute, and they wondered if her baby was okay. They had reason to be concerned. Guess a coupla hours earlier someone had shot at the lady while she was pacing up and down the stairwell. Cops were swarmin', talking about how a bullet had gone clear through her left hip. Missed the baby by six inches…two inches…a millimeter. Story got better every time they told it. Strange thing was the administrator had found this note on his desk, unsigned, that vowed this lady's baby wouldn't live to see the light o' day. The nurses were abuzz. 'You hear about the note? Strangest thing. Says to beware of what you cannot see. How spooky is that?'"

Josee flinched. In cauda venenum. The canister whipped across her vision.

"That's messed up," she said.

"Tell me about it. There are some certifiable sleazeballs roamin' our streets."

"Was there a motive? Did the note explain?"

"Not that I know of. I was only going by what I could overhear. My mom still hadn't showed, so I wandered up a floor, thought I might peek in on this brave lady, see a real-life bullet wound, what have you. I was only nine, okay."

"I'm listening."

"There was a cop posted outside her door, drinkin' a cup o' joe, reading an Edgar Rice Burroughs book. I told him how I wasn't much for reading, but I loved the Tarzan series. While he showed me the pictures, I heard a baby's cry from that room, which just made me even more curious. Silly boy stuff. Always wanted to be a hero ever since I can remember. Before I could weasel my way in there though, the cop and I both heard somethin' moving down the hall. Turned and saw a doctor's jacket flutter around the corner, then this silver canister—ring any bells?—came bumpin' up against our feet. Knocked over the cop's coffee mug, made a big ol' mess."

"Let me guess. It had a skull and crossbones on it."

"Bingo. Stenciled in black."

"Any writing?"

"Writing? Not that I recall."

"The one this morning had *Gift* written across it."

"Well, this was no gift, let me tell you. Not that I had time to study it real close. Soon as I reached to pick it up, it came alive in my hands." Turney's jowls sagged. "I found myself holdin' on to a monster."

Josee twisted her eyebrow ring like a dial to calm her nerves.

Turney went on. "I don't think the cop saw what I saw. Should've listened to him in the first place. Might've saved myself a lotta trouble. Might've saved the baby."

"What'd he say?"

"He told me to hand it over, said it might be a tear-gas canister, a diversion to get at the woman in the room. That baby was crying again, like it was trying to scream and just couldn't muster enough sound. And then…*bam!* Smoke started curlin' out of the canister, like a living, breathing creature that'd been locked inside. Wrapped around me, gave me the heebie-jeebies. I froze, looked down, and this thing was just staring at me. To this day, I'd testify under oath that it was a snake. And a big one! It was like a stare down before a fight. I'd been boxing at the gym since third grade—to keep me outta trouble, according to my mom—and what with my big arms they were already callin' me Thunder Turney, like I told ya. Well, I'd never blinked first in a stare down. Never. This time around, though, I lost it, and soon as I showed fear, the thing struck. Hard and fast."

"And it bit you."

"You kiddin' me? Felt like red-hot railroad spikes rammed clear through my arm. My head started spinning, and I dropped like lead. The cop was on the ground beside me, eyes rolled back in his head, coughin' and spittin'. Later, they said his coffee'd been poisoned, found residue in the mug."

"But you didn't drink the coffee. What about you?"

"They said I made it all up. For attention. Pointed to the trouble I'd gotten myself into, fooling around with my mom's liquor, and discounted everything I tried to tell 'em."

"What about the scars? They couldn't explain those away."

"Sure they could." Turney pressed his hand over the sergeant stripes on his sleeve. "Chief Braddock was a detective at the time. He said that I must've slipped on the coffee and landed on the cop's mug, the two ends of that broken handle puncturin' my arm. 'End o' story. No questions asked. Go on with your life, boy.' Come to think of it, Josee, you might be the first one's ever heard me all the way through."

Josee met his gaze. "And this is why the chief mocks you."

"Any excuse'll do."

"Then let it go, Sarge. You were a kid. It wasn't your fault."

"Easy to say. Thing is, when I came to, that baby was gone. Some hero, eh?"

"Who knows what went on? Least you're still around. This morning that thing would've killed Scooter if I hadn't jumped in. It was out for blood, I'm convinced."

"Whoa now, Josee. You don't think it was you that saved him, do you?"

"I must've done something. I was out there all alone."

"Were you?"

"I guess. No, not exactly. But if I hadn't—"

"Hadn't what? You gonna try telling me you fought it off with your smarts and bravery? Or your good looks? No, it was the same thing that saved me: prayer. From down the hall, this nurse rushed right to me and hit her knees. Can still hear her cryin' out, 'Deliver him, Lord. He's one of yours. Oh, please keep him safe in your arms.'"

"Well, glad it helped. Just not sure I buy into that stuff anymore."

"Not exactly somethin' you buy into. When it's real, it's free."

"For a small monthly donation."

Turney's gaze tipped her way, a scale weighing its verdict. "Okay then, what stopped that serpent inches from your face? Soon as you called out, it froze. Ain't that what you told me? Sounds to me like an answer to prayer."

"I don't know, Sarge. Everything happened so fast."

"Whoo boy, now it's gettin' deep in here. Up to your eyeballs in excuses."

"Just not sure what to think. I used to be, you know, hard-core into all that stuff. That was a long time ago."

"Afraid to trust again. I know just how ya feel. Never too late to turn back, you know?" He leaned forward with his elbows on his table. "You mind if I set aside my position here for a moment to tell you a verse I read? From the Bible?"

"If it makes you feel better."

"Well, it says"—Turney cleared his throat—"says we're allowed to make U-turns every now and then, says God's mercies are new every morning." He let his words trail away as though they'd caught even him by surprise. "Anyhow, that's the way I read it. Only tellin' you as a friend, you understand."

"We're friends now?"

"Just sharing what's been a comfort to me. See, about three years ago I lost someone close to me...my fiancée. Be three years on the eighth of November."

Josee slunk in her chair, struck by how myopic her own misery had become—childhood garbage, teenage scars, the horror of today. She wasn't the only one carrying unseen weights. "Sorry," she said. "Man, must've been a nightmare for you."

"I'm still working, still breathing. You move on. A day at a time."

"Dang, we're quite a pair, aren't we?" She tried to produce a chuckle, but thoughts of the thicket slithered down her back and clamped around her waist. She could see that canister's frosty black grin. The table began to wobble beneath her elbows. The lights flickered.

"Whoa, now." Turney's hand was on her arm. "You all right? Guess it'd be best if I just kept my mouth shut, what with all you've been through today."

Josee pushed herself up. His hand—this man's hand—was warm, strong. Her instincts told her to take off, yet an inward echo of her childhood vows told her it was time to identify the threat, time to stand firm. Through her skull, the morning's images swarmed in an attempt to smother her belief. She drew her fists to her chest, tried to hold herself together.

"Please, Sarge," she implored, "tell me more of your story. I want to hear it."

"Josee, you are one tough woman."

So much for her gallant facade. Although she tried to dam the flood of her fear and emotion, she felt the color in her eyes stir into liquid motion until it seemed to be spilling across the white table toward Sergeant Turney. Caught in the current, her words washed forth. "Sarge, I know this sounds crazy, but what do I do? That thing, that creature, whatever it is—it's gonna come back for me. I can feel it. I don't know why it came after me and Scooter. Just seems like everything's hit the fan at once. It's not like me to fall apart like this, to turn to someone else like I'm some charity case, to blabber on and on like an idiot, but please…I need your help."

"S'all right, kiddo. Been hopin' you would ask."

It was late afternoon when Chief Braddock escorted Josee to the refuge of a nurses' lounge. Turney had been dispatched, and, as promised, the chief had taken her to see Scooter. Despite the doctors' confidence that they had nullified the poison before it became fatal, they remained tight-lipped as to its cause. Scoot was groggy. An IV was hooked to his arm. Still, with gauze covering half his face, he gave a faint smile when she entered the room.

Their meeting was short. Anticlimactic. He needed his rest.

At least he's still here. I thought you were a goner, Scoot.

In the lounge, Josee burrowed through her bedroll for her art case. She ignored the droning of the water fountain's condenser and the snoring from the nurse on the love seat. Time to draw. To drain the poison. Others often mistook her sketches as dark fantasies; they failed to understand her need to excise the gloom from her mind.

Her pencil emptied shapes onto paper. Serpentine contours. Beads of blood on twisted thorns. Tilted initials…ICV. In burnt sienna, she covered the letters with reptilian scales. Set fangs over them.

Then she shredded the paper and cast the accursed images into the garbage.

Beware of what you cannot see?

It was the things she had seen that frightened her. Behind her pupils, deep within her retinas, something had shifted so that realms invisible had become real. Battles…and evil's face…Scooter's body landing on the ground, fresh sustenance. Words to another poem began to form. Not now, maybe later.

She spent the next twenty minutes reorganizing her bedroll, folding and stuffing in her mildewed clothing. She rolled her art supplies in a brushed-cotton blanket. Pushed down the frypan and tin utensils. Finally, from a Ziploc bag, she extracted her birth certificate. Her umbilical cord. A lifeline. So what if her friends mocked this bureaucratic waste of paper? To her, it was a symbol. She was connected by blood, by genes and DNA, to a woman named Kara Addison. Today's plan had been to reunite. Okay, so that had gone down the flusher, but tomorrow they'd make it happen.

Don't bail on me, please. Wherever you are, Kara, I hope you're okay.

She found herself praying for her mother's safety while she tucked the document back into the bag and zipped it tight.

~

The van floor flexed hot and hard beneath her, the ribs of a carnivorous creature that had swallowed her whole. Kara Addison's bones ached. She moaned, then scolded herself for announcing her pain to the driver up front. She couldn't see him—he had blindfolded her. She couldn't move on her own accord—he had trussed her arms and legs together behind her back and wrapped her in this itchy wool cocoon.

Lord, be with me. Where is he taking me? Why's he doing this?

Kara's motherly instincts spoke fearful things in her ears. Did her abduction have to do with Josee, with their reunion? The timing suggested so. What would her daughter think when she failed to show up? They'd made the arrangements on the phone; they'd started to reconnect their torn bonds through hesitant stories and chuckles; they'd exchanged photos.

If it weren't for her indignant dread, Kara was sure she would cry.

A screech tore through the van's interior.

Why does it keep doing that? Goodness, I wish whatever it is would shut up!

This time she was unable to stop her whimpers. They welled from her throat, sputtered between bruised lips. The cords were cutting into her wrists. Her back was knotted, and cramps twanged through her calf muscles. She could still taste the blood from her attacker's blows.

Seconds after she had skidded across Ridge Road and careened into the guardrail, the kid she recognized had raced toward her. She'd thought he was coming to help. In shock, she had watched steam billow from the hood of the BMW and wondered what had just happened.

Moments before she'd been celebrating the day, and the next thing she knew this kid was there trying to wave her down, standing in her way, and she knew his face from the work he'd done at the vineyard, and she didn't want to hurt anyone, so she pumped the brakes the way Marsh had taught her to do when it rained hard or snowed, but he said this car had antilock brakes so she didn't have to worry about it now, and the scarf flapped at her throat where Marsh had wrestled with her earlier, and all this was going through her mind when she slid into the rail, and she sure hoped he had insured the car, which was a ridiculous concern since Marsh always saw to such things, but he'd be upset anyway, and she didn't know how she would explain it to him…

Ka-baaam!

Leaning into the Z3's cockpit, the kid had struck her with such force that she thought her head would twist off her shoulders. Through a veil of steam and shattered light, she watched him walk around the car. Ranting. Slamming down a fist. Pleading into a cell phone. Then injecting her with something that made everything fade.

How long had they been driving now? Kara had no idea. The van was dark, yet the blindfold's cloth allowed her to see shapes and shadows. Gravel crunched beneath the tires. A slight curve in the road tilted her over so that her hip banged against the wheel hub.

Owww! Her left hip. The one still tender from an old bullet wound.

Two slow turns and the van coasted to a stop. What would come next? Hope and terror fought for space in her head.

God, don't let him violate me in any way. Guard me, please! Oh, Lord, why did you let this happen? I don't understand. I was going to see my baby girl today.

Before departing the estate, Kara had tucked a commemorative item into the pocket of her jeans. She'd dressed down so as not to intimidate Josee. Now Kara begged God that her attacker wouldn't search her well enough to discover the item. It would mean nothing to him. It meant everything to her.

She found strength in her will to see Josee, comfort in her knowledge that Marshall would search for her and do everything in his power to see that the wrongdoers received justice. True, he was not adept at sharing emotion; true, he had acted peculiar this morning. But he was a trusted provider and protector.

He'll come for me. Somehow.

As the rear doors opened, Kara's hope faded with the realization that her husband would not even suspect anything until she failed to show up sometime Thursday. As far as Marsh Addison was concerned, she and Josee were spending the night at the Yachats beach house. For a few hours at least, she was on her own.

Sergeant Turney returned in the early evening, and Josee suppressed her desire to bound from her seat. That friendly face. His kind eyes. He'd been making arrangements—for her. Though she felt guilty leaving Scooter alone at the hospital, she longed for the embrace of a real bed. How long had it been? Almost a week?

"You're gonna like these folks," Turney promised her. "Real down-to-earth."

"They don't mind? It seems like—"

"Not in the slightest. The Van der Bruegges have got big hearts and a house to match. John's a music instructor out at Linn-Benton. His wife, Kris, is a retired elementary school teacher. With two kids off at college and the other one married, they miss warm bodies in their home. In fact, they're even settin' up a room for Scooter. Doctor says he's stabilizing and should be released by noon tomorrow." Turney handed her an envelope. "Here's the vouchers, like the chief told ya. Good as cash. Should get ya through the next few days."

She was speechless. Couldn't even get a thank-you through her lips.

Within fifteen minutes they arrived at the Van der Bruegges' brick and timber two-story home. Along the landscaped yard, a row of potted evergreens guarded the sidewalk. Turney made introductions, then left Josee in their care.

Quick to recognize her exhaustion, John and Kris showed her to her room. On the dresser, a towel with a bar of Dove. On the bed, a peach-and-cream comforter with extra pillows at the headboard. Shaded lamps on matching nightstands. And a bottle of McKenzie Mist artesian water.

"Let us know if you need anything, Josee," said Kris Van der Bruegge.

"Omelets and waffles for breakfast," John said. "You prefer coffee or tea?"

"Uh." Josee was overwhelmed. "Anything's good. More of a coffee drinker."

Mrs. Van der Bruegge tried to gather her into an embrace, but when Josee stiffened, the lady switched to a soft pat on Josee's shoulder and followed it with a shushing sound. "Go on then, Josee. Don't let us keep you. I hear those pillows calling your name."

Through the night Josee Walker remained atop the comforter, afraid to mess up the bed.

PART TWO

The Enemy...
is about to open his full game.
And pawns are likely to see as much of it as any....
Sharpen your blade!

The Return of the King by J. R. R. Tolkien

~

The mighty prince of the power of the air...
is the spirit at work in the hearts
of those who refuse to obey God.

Ephesians 2:2

10

Be Prepared

He needed results. No time to waste. Before the bombardment of the alarm's Top 40 cacophony, Marsh Addison jumped from bed, wrapped himself in his bathrobe, straightened his side of the comforter, and ignored his wife's unruffled portion. No doubt Kara and Josee had stayed up late into the night, swapping memories, catching up, doing that heart-to-heart thing girls did so well.

Well, more power to them, but he had his own concerns. Such as online piano shopping. Oh, that dreaded *S* word. He must really love her to make the sacrifice to shop—so much easier to let Rosie or someone else do it. But no, he wanted to make this gift his own.

The black leather chair squeaked as he took a seat in his study. It'd been a while since he'd felt this twinge of excitement. Had to get this just right. Something to match Kara's style. Shopping wasn't his thing; perhaps, though, if he placed a computer order through a local place, he could have a piano selected and paid for and delivered before her return. With the recent growth of Addison Ridge Vineyards, he could afford something nice. She deserved it. Plus, the piano might figure nicely in next month's photo shoot for *Wine Spectator*'s feature on Oregon wineries. He grinned. Perhaps a stem glass and a grape cluster perched on a baby grand...

A Google search stirred his anxiety again.

Steinway? Kawai? Grand or upright? Ebony polish? Mahogany or white?

Narrow the options—that was the best strategy. As if he had a clue to Kara's preferences here. They hadn't talked about this stuff recently. Hadn't talked much, period. She'd been right about that.

When Rosie buzzed at the door with his breakfast tray, Marsh keyed the release from the button at his desk and continued perusing the onscreen choices. It took him a moment to realize she was asking him a question. About Kara's whereabouts. Was this going to be a pattern, Rosie wanted to know. And, if he didn't object, could she call to confirm the day's schedule with the lady of the house?

"Sure." He waved a hand. "Whatever you like. She's probably still at the coast."

"The house in Yachats? I'll try her there."

The aroma of Guatemalan coffee turned his head. "Rosie."

"Sir?"

"Is Marlena in today? Is she baking up any muffins?"

"Orange walnut, made fresh on the premises."

"I'm sold." He tamped down his ego, decided to elicit her opinion. "Hey, take a look at this, and tell me what you think. Kara likes white, and I'm leaning toward a baby grand, but my knowledge of brand reliability is limited at best."

Rosie moved behind him, started to respond, then her voice caught.

He glanced back to find her staring. He gathered his robe around his legs. "There a problem?"

"Are you feeling well, sir?"

"Fine. Should've dressed, I know, but I was anxious to get this taken care of."

"Have you visited the washroom yet?"

"What? Why're you delving into—"

"Your face, sir. It looks as though you've been injured."

"Injured?"

"Should I ring someone?"

Though Marsh tried to dismiss her concern, grave eyes fixed him in place as she balled a cloth and dabbed at his cheek. "Hold it, Rosie. What're you doing?"

She studied the material in her hand and said, "It looks like…blood." Her tone was as wispy as her hair, her slightest movement lifting strands from her forehead. Her fingers ran along his jaw. "And it's…oh my, it's in the shape of a question mark."

"A question *what?* Okay, Rosie, go on. I can take care of myself."

"Mr. Addison, I think it'd be wise to—"

From down the hall, the phone summoned.

"Better get that," Marsh said. "I'll be fine."

With a handful of Kleenex, he wiped away the remaining smear and considered himself in the vanity's glow. He ran his hands through his wavy hair and sighed. Nothing sticky or bruised or injured. That was a relief. His face, too, was okay. No wounds, not even a razor nick along his sometimes treacherous cheekbones.

"Okay"—he dropped the tissues in the toilet bowl—"what gives?"

Although he'd slept alone last night, he was sure the blood was not his own. Then whose? Goose bumps lifted along his arms. Pinpricks of guilt? Had he—

Hold it. Standing barefoot on this cold floor—it's no wonder I've got the chills.

See, one mystery solved. He refused to waste any more time fitting together these puzzles with missing pieces. Not that he'd forget them entirely; for now, however, they'd go into his need-more-hard-facts file. He'd blame the blood on a nocturnal spider bite. Why not? Stranger things had happened. He needed to get on with his day.

Battle positions. Nearing the seven o'clock hour.

Buttoning slacks and a brown denim shirt with the vineyard's emblem on the pocket, Marsh cut back into the study. He slipped his feet into his Arin Mundazis and waited for the task launcher to pit him once more against his foe. In moments Steele Knight and Crash-Chess-Dummy would rumble. The royal game, may it reign, would whisk his thoughts from yesterday's unfathomable events.

He called Rosie to assuage her concerns. "Sorry if I worried you earlier. Figure I must've cut myself shaving." He forced out a laugh.

"Was a bit startling, sir. Forgive my intrusion."

"Not at all. Thanks for caring. Guess things get dangerous when you leave me and a razor alone before the break of dawn." Watching the intercom light fade, he felt shaken. He'd lied only for lack of solid answers.

He crouched to the floor. At his back, the computer stirred to life while he made a quick search of the carpet, certain he would locate the glass queen he'd noticed was missing last night from the chess table. He must've overlooked her in the dark.

Swish…

"Rosamund?" Surely the muffins weren't already done.

Squeak…

The sound of leather creaked through the room.

Whew. What was that smell? A rank odor permeated the space and settled like a mildewed tarp over his back.

Still in a crouch, Marsh had the feeling that he was not alone. He gripped the crystal chess table and clenched his teeth. His heart drove a blow into his chest, then retreated as a hollow ache settled over him. Again that image of Kara's porcelain neck, his black and white tie. The squares of the chessboard melded with his thoughts, gripping him with a sense of guilt.

Which he rejected. He wasn't the only one with secrets in this house.

Please, God, Kara had called out, *open his eyes…*

What had she meant by that?

This is silly, he told himself. *Turn around and play your chess match.*

Instead, he shut down his external senses and tried to perceive something—or someone—on a level he rarely explored. Events had propelled him toward this. The unexpected. The otherworldly.

No! What was he thinking? He didn't believe in that stuff. With a splash of cold logic, he jarred himself back to his domain, the concrete world, which he scheduled, comprehended, controlled. Time to take charge. He gritted his jaw in combat mode, stiffened his hands into chopping implements. He dug his loafers into the rug, rose, and swiveled back toward his desk. Prepared for anything.

Well, almost anything.

———

Be prepared…

His father's eagle scout motto tramped through Marsh's head as he turned toward his chair in the study. From boyhood, Marsh had striven to follow those words, to be prepared—like his father. He had no memory of Chance Addison, knew only what his mother told him of a tall, proud man who had spoken sparingly and, after the war, laughed far too infrequently.

One day, arriving home early from middle school, Marsh had found his mother in the sitting room sifting through a box of memorabilia.

"What're those?"

"Photos," said Virginia. "Some of your father's things."

"Why don't you ever talk about him?"

"Don't see a need. Nothing more you should know for now."

"Shoot, Mom, I'm thirteen. Old enough to know something at least."

"There's nothing to say that'll change things. Won't bring him back now, will it?" Virginia Addison handed him a photo in a silver frame. "That's him. Nineteen years old and not much bigger than you, Son." Angled in the sunlight, the picture showed Chance's thumbs hitched into Wrangler belt loops as an elbow steadied him against a plow handle. In the background, fingers of clouds combed the ridge that would later bear his name.

"Wish my dad was still here."

"That was just after he bought this place," Virginia said. "He was feeling mighty proud of himself there."

In the spring of 1941, she told him, Chance had received a modest inheritance from an aunt and purchased this colonial home on a hillside north of Corvallis. His dream was to cultivate one of Oregon's first commercial vineyards. Instead, following the December attack at Pearl Harbor, he found himself training at nearby Camp Adair, where he met and eventually married Virginia Drake.

"I was just a farm girl. Made regular milk deliveries to the mess hall."

"And the sparks flew, huh?"

"What do you know about that sort of thing?" She brushed off a humble wedding album, thumbed through the pages. "Sad thing is, your father and I never did have a proper honeymoon."

"Ooh, yuck. Don't wanna hear any of that romance junk anyway."

His mother's head was shrouded in memories. "Chance always said we'd take one after the war, but we never did. The vineyard was his focus. Things to be done, work on the ridge to be kept up."

"Still is."

"You do your fair share, Marsh. Yes, you do." She took the photo from him. "Your father was a patriotic man. He loved his country, without a doubt, but his dreams were always here on Addison Ridge. It pained him to leave it behind. He'd have done anything to get this place off the ground, but the dreams had to wait."

Soon after their wedding, she explained, a train took Chance far from his vineyard aspirations to complete his training in the deserts of eastern Oregon, Arizona, and California. In the fall of '44, he and the "Timberwolves" of the 104th Infantry Division had entered the conflict on European shores. Within a year, they'd fed over six thousand of their members to the voracious belly of the war, and they were but one of Camp Adair's four divisions.

After the armistice, First Lieutenant Chance Addison was transferred to CIC (Counterintelligence Corps) on special assignment at Kransberg Castle. Near Frankfurt, Germany. His letter writing became more sporadic. He claimed his work was top-secret, that there was little he could divulge. In late '45, having dutifully completed his task, Chance caught a cargo plane back to American soil.

Alive, yes. The same person, no.

Despite his emotional reticence, the homecoming resulted in Virginia's pregnancy, but after nine months of numerous difficulties, the son she'd nurtured in her womb died during delivery. Umbilical cord around his neck, the army doctor told her, and the tiny body was rushed out of her sight.

She became hysterical. A male nurse gave her an injection that provided only temporary relief. When she awoke, she was alone in a heartless room beneath lights and metal mirrors.

Not even for a moment had she been allowed to hold her son.

"You never told me about this! Why?" Cross-legged in the sitting room, Marsh was overwhelmed. "I'm a teenager now, old enough to know this stuff. You mean I would've had a brother? What would his name have been?"

"He's gone. Doesn't much matter now, does it?"

"Why can't you tell me? By this time he'd have been in college, I bet."

Virginia rose to her knees and fluffed her calico dress. "'Course he would've. Now shush. I'll go on if you'll keep quiet and help set these things back in the box."

In 1947, after a period of grieving their firstborn son, Chance and Virginia began cultivating their small vineyard. They buried their memories beneath the tilled and fertilized soil, beneath the hours of labor and sweat poured into their grape arbors: Rieslings and Chardonnays, Gewürztraminers and fruity Müller-Thurgaus.

Children? There were none. The Addisons kept themselves occupied.

As the vineyard expanded, its reputation did likewise. Over the next decade, social events became commonplace, luring merchants, investors, Napa Valley winemakers, and county officials, plus Chance's golfing buddies and Virginia's bridge-playing friends with their competing bouffant hairdos. Smiles sparkled like artificial diamonds. Periodically, genuine laughter flitted through the Addison manor—though it always departed with the last guest to leave.

In 1959, coming as a surprise to all, Virginia conceived again.

Was she ready for this? A child? She and Chance were in their late thirties. How would this affect their lifestyle, schedules, social circles? Would it disrupt Addison Ridge Vineyard's promising growth?

Most pressing, would the baby survive?

Virginia's guilt from losing the first child weighed even heavier than the new life inside. As her belly expanded, so did her depression; she was convinced her efforts would be for naught, the pounds gained for nothing. Per doctor's orders, she spent the last trimester on bed rest.

Then in November, following eighteen hours of labor, Marshall Ray Addison entered the world headfirst. The doctor placed the boy in his mother's exhausted arms, and she blubbered sweet nothings to him through a grin that wouldn't quit.

She had her baby. At last.

"And regretted every minute of it."

"Shush, Marsh, not true, not true at all." Virginia was sorting a stack of yearbooks. "Could never have kept this place up without you. 'Course, I never expected that we'd be on our own. I expected your doggone father to stick around longer than he did. Wasn't meant to be, I s'pose."

"Wasn't there something the doctors could've done? Some kind of treatment?"

"Nothing that lasted. Too little too late."

Soon after Marsh's birth, she explained, Chance Addison started to fade.

And quickly. For years, Chance had suffered from migraines and bleeding from his ears and eyes. The army physician blamed the symptoms on his war wounds. Fifteen years earlier, in the Rhineland, Chance had scrambled through a trench to snatch up and heave away an enemy grenade, thus saving a fellow soldier's life, but the resulting explosion had smashed him into the dirt, rendering him unconscious and temporarily deaf. The physician explained that the residual scar tissue in his ears was now tearing and rehealing—or some such nonsense. Though worried sick, Virginia was placated by the medical jargon and by government checks that appeared monthly at the post office.

But Chance knew better. His guilt demanded an outlet, and as he wasted away beneath the muddled diagnoses, he spilled his secrets onto the pages of a journal.

Marsh sat up. "What secrets?" He was almost done organizing the box.

"Secrets."

"Come on, Mom, you're talking about my father."

"Things from the war." Virginia gazed off through the sitting room window. "Certain things are between a man and wife and no one else. That's it. That's all I've got to say about it."

"Where's his journal? Let me at least read that."

"It'd be about useless to you. That journal's so faded, so scribbled—looks like the tattered remains of an old pirate's map."

Marsh rummaged through the box of memorabilia.

"It's not there," she told him. "It's not anywhere, as far as you're concerned. That's the way your father wanted it. His instructions were specific that you should not read it. Until…"

"Until what?"

"Until… Gracious, I can only hope that time never comes."

"What're you talking about? Come on."

"A sure waste of your energy, Marsh. Hogwash, most likely. On his deathbed, your father became delusional, spouting more than a few things that defied common sense. No man should have to go through that…that sort of pain. Blood seeping from his eyes, pooling in his ears. I watched him. I…" Virginia's voice dissipated.

Marsh was not to be deterred. "If you're not gonna tell me, why'd you even bring it up? I hate it when you do this to me."

"One day, Marsh. One day."

"What about this?" He'd located another object as consolation, a yellowed newspaper photo. "This from his funeral?"

"Where'd you find that?"

"Stuck in the pages of this yearbook."

Marsh scrutinized the picture. Captured from across his father's flag-draped casket, the photo showed his mom cloaked in black and holding his own infant form in her arms. Virginia's eyes were distant, despairing, full of a bitterness that made little sense to Marsh. What secrets had etched that look into her face? Only later did he come to recognize that look for what it was: the look of a woman betrayed.

—

The same look now shaded his own wife's face.

Charged for action, Marsh turned on his study carpet and found Kara seated in his desk chair. Profiled against the computer's online chessboard, she was a queen trapped upon the battlefield. Her hair was liquid gold, melting down the black leather headrest. Her eyes were leveled into his.

Another arrow of pain shot clear through to his retina.

"Kara?" His voice came out in a raspy croak. "I thought you were in Yachats."

She said nothing. She was bound and gagged.

Behind her, on the screen, Steele Knight was waiting.

11

Room 223

This silverware was heavy, unlike the cheap utensils she and Scooter used. Per Kris Van der Bruegge's instructions, Josee smoothed the lace tablecloth and distributed four place settings for breakfast. Felt good. The routine of family life. Though Kris and John seemed decent enough, she was relieved to know Sergeant Turney would be joining them.

In uniform? He'll probably have to loosen a button for that tummy of his.

"Morning, sleepyhead," John greeted her. "Bet you're hungry."

"Mm-hmm."

"We get going early around here. I have a first-period class to teach out at Linn-Benton Community College." John handed Josee a platter of butter-drenched waffles, then as she took possession, he reached to tousle her spiked hair in a fatherly manner.

She backed away. "Excuse me? The hair's not public property."

Kris arrived from the kitchen with pitchers of maple and blueberry syrup and a carafe of fresh orange juice. "Would you look at that scowl. Just like our baby girl, Annalise."

"Baby? She's twenty-four," John amended. "Senior at Gonzaga. She's no longer a little girl."

"I miss her. Why'd she have to move so far away, I ask?"

For some stinkin' breathing room. Josee set down the platter. *Big shocker.*

"You'll have to forgive us, Josee," Kris said, watching her. "We've always been a demonstrative household. We mean no harm. One day you'll understand when you have kids of your own."

"Kids? Nope, not the mothering type."

"Neither was I. I blame it on this rascal here." Kris wagged a finger at John.

He whispered loud enough for Josee to hear, "All I can say, Krissy, is that I'm keeping an eye on this girl. She's liable to bite off your hand, and I thought

Annalise was bad." He backpedaled from the room in exaggerated slow motion.

Josee tried to ignore his antics. Felt a grin slip out.

"Gotcha," he said, then continued through the archway for coffee and cream.

Sergeant Vince Turney tugged up his uniform trousers, sucked in his pale gut, and strained his belt to the last notch. Had he looked this dumpy at age twenty-two? He was only nine years older than the girl he'd helped out yesterday. Josee Walker. She was a tough nut, all right, but she had opened up. Just a little. A crack.

The thought still warmed him. He was a cop, yessir, but he was also a man. And a sad example of one, according to his full-length mirror.

He'd always been big boned, learned to live with it; after Milly's accident, however, the pounds had started creeping up on him. He'd beaten down the old patterns of alcohol abuse—hadn't bought a Red Dog in years—but the substitute was now taking its toll. For three years sugar had served as his sweetheart. Sugar. And deep-fried foods. And super-sized caffeinated soft drinks. Turney used this sweetheart to hold other relationships at arm's length. He'd lost one love, but this one would always be around.

Around? He swung his belly away from the mirror. Gosh, that's not funny.

Eight minutes till breakfast at the Van der Bruegges.

Lowering himself into the police cruiser in his driveway, he wondered why he kept beating himself up over his size. Not that a trimmer physique would help. Three dates. In three years. Three strikeouts. He'd stopped looking for that one, good, God-fearing woman who could handle his weight along with his job's brutal doses of reality. Most churchwomen were a bit too sheltered. Or too syrupy. Or too old.

He pushed back his seat, slurped at a forty-four-ounce Dr Pepper in the cup holder. Tasted flat. He'd bought it…when, a day or two ago? He took another sip.

—

Turney extended the platter. "Last one's yours, Josee."

"I'm good. You want it, I can tell."

"C'mon, it's calling your name. Mmm, catch a whiff o' that."

"Full already. My tank's smaller than yours, you know."

"A low blow. Ouch."

"Nothing personal, Sarge. This country's freakin' obsessed with weight and looks, thanks to the whip-cracking fashion gurus. To be in shape? Nothing wrong with that. But this drive for perfection at all costs? It's twisted."

"Not like you hafta worry."

"Oh, thanks."

"About the weight, I mean." Turney drizzled syrup over the remaining waffle. "Here ya go. It's got your initial on it."

Josee watched the blue-tinted J seep into the dough and felt the warmth of this place settling over her as well. Breakfast had been nice. Normal. John and Kris had refused her help with the cleanup duties, insisting that she and the sergeant relax.

"So what do ya think of 'em?"

She hitched a shoulder. "John and Kris? They're not bad."

Turney nodded. "From you, I'll count that as a roar of approval."

The Van der Bruegges—okay, so they were too touchy-feely for her taste, but she could survive that as long as she knew it was heartfelt. Josee could even deal with the nature photography on the walls, the sort that displayed character attributes in bold letters with trite slogans underneath. Usually such platitudes pushed her buttons. On more than one occasion she'd heard them spouted from the mouths of self-righteous phonies. She knew the type well—dress the part, talk the part, act the part. One big show. With a crank of the thermostat, she could turn their religious stage makeup into cracked and splotchy messes.

This couple though? Their beliefs seemed more than skin-deep. Josee's past had taught her to recognize genuine from bogus, and these people were the real deal.

It worried her. Their disarming candor might further pry her open.

The grandfather clock chimed seven o'clock. In another hour she'd call her mother. Turney had agreed to drop Josee at the hospital to visit Scooter and further promised to return on his lunch break to shuttle Josee to Avery Park for her one o'clock rendezvous.

Today's reunion had to work. Kara couldn't keep stringing her along.

On the way to the hospital, Josee felt awkward in the cruiser's front seat; during her teen years, cop cars had represented the enemy. Samaritan Drive swept them between saplings arrayed in autumn splendor and past a rescue chopper on a helipad. The dips in the road amplified the hissing for nicotine in Josee's temples.

Good-bye to family life. Back to the real world.

Sergeant Turney let her off at the hospital's circular drive. "Josee?"

She dipped her chin and looked back over her shoulder.

"You take care. Meet ya back 'round twelve-thirty."

She gave a thumbs-up, then, choosing to save her vouchers, hurried in past the gift shop and her craving for a cigarette. Wouldn't that be some nifty economics: They sell you the cancer sticks, then sell the chemotherapy. Despite the lobby's placid expanse, she sensed a lingering disquiet. Or maybe it was just another flashback ripped from her childhood scrapbook.

At the information counter a nurse was fixated on the tilt of her own head and the gloss of her blond hair. Josee hitched the sleeve of her oversize knit sweater and, resting an elbow on the counter, asked for quick confirmation of a room number. She despised the fact that her friend had suffered an entire night hooked to an intravenous drip.

"Like, what was the name again?"

"It's Scooter," Josee said.

"That a first name? Nickname? Ah, it doesn't matter. I remember the one, kid with the long brown hair? Yeah, okay, heeeere we go." The nurse stretched out the word like chewed gum. "He's been moved. Room 223 looks like."

"Second floor? Okay, got it."

Josee hit the elevator button, shifted from foot to foot, then took the stairs instead.

—

"She's here, Mr. Steele." The young nurse's voice was full of verve. "Like, I was just doing my job, then she walked up. Same girl you pointed out yesterday."

"Thank you, Nurse."

"Thought you'd want to know. In cauda venenum."

In the basement studio's October chill, Stahlherz set down the phone. He looked to his laptop where the online gaming zone flickered. For the second day in a row, Crash-Chess-Dummy had left the game unfinished. CCD, a.k.a. Marsh Addison, had abandoned him.

Like father, like son!

Yes, Stahlherz trusted that Kara's abduction was now secure, and he had reason to believe his delivery was on its way, but he had counted on the grand platform of this morning's chess match to shake his opponent's world. Ah, well.

Soon you'll understand, Marsh. Soon you'll get the picture.

The day now required his energies elsewhere, and Stahlherz turned with the intensity of an Oriental tea-leaf reader to divine the future from his onyx chessboard. Amid slashing bishops and stalwart pawns, Steele Knight could picture the outworking of ICV's schemes. Pieces girding themselves for the Allhallows Eve assault.

To his surprise, an enemy knight shifted.

"Who are you?" Stahlherz touched the chiseled stallion's mane and nostrils. "Where do you think you're going?"

Previously stagnant on the perimeter, the horseman was sliding from the side toward the center. From the muck into the fray. Reining back against Stahlherz's hand, he came to life, and although his movements lacked a toned warrior's sharpness, there was no denying his resolve.

"Now, now," Stahlherz said, "I did not anticipate this. Tell me. Who are you?"

Behind the pewter helmet, the horseman remained silent. Out of shape as he might be, he seemed determined to do his part.

Never mind. Stahlherz shook off his consternation and chose to accelerate the day's plans. He knew well that a tempo gained on the chessboard was a step toward victory. He entered the garage through a gap in the concrete wall, rapped on the van window. "Darius, my friend. Time to go, time to make the circuit."

The kid behind the wheel lifted an eyelid. "You gots to be kidding me, brah."

"Not in the least."

"It's…shoot, it's way friggin' early."

"Precisely. Let's go."

Stahlherz's thoughts flashed to circuit riders of yore, men and women who rode on horseback to minister to far-flung congregations. He, in much the same way, would ride circuit through the Willamette Valley to stir his sep-arate ICV cells, to invoke irreverent action along the I-5 corridor where mil-lions lived and breathed.

His driver brought him back to reality.

"If you thinks I'm gonna last behind this wheel, Steele-man, you must be on somethin'. This calls for some serious caffeination. Here's the deal…" Darius rubbed his fingers together, denoting his need for cash. "I fly, you buy."

"One quick stop," Stahlherz capitulated. "And that's it."

"Yeeeah, now you speaka my language."

Steele Knight turned to a garage door opener on the wall. The unit had been programmed with additional functions that would work only if the garage door was lowered. He and the Professor alone knew the code sequence. He shielded the unit with his body, tapped twice at the door lock while depressing the Open key, counted to three, then removed his hand. A red light blinked. In a whoosh of air and an exhalation of mist, a panel slid open to reveal a refrigerated compartment sunk into the earth beneath the house above. In three rows of four, silver canisters stood like overgrown bullet cas-ings. Beneath skeins of frost, they seemed to be watching, waiting, for a sig-nal established long ago.

"Brrrr! That be some scary stuff."

"Scary? No, for the time being"—Stahlherz slapped work gloves into his driver's hands—"that be some harmless stuff. As you've heard, we must be 'wary as snakes and harmless as doves.'" He issued his corruption of the biblical passage with tittering amusement. "The time is upon us, my friend. Let's bring these creatures to life."

—

From the nurses' station, a familiar voice hooked Josee's curiosity. She edged from the stairwell, caught a glimpse of Chief Braddock and a white-jacketed doctor. Friction laced their dialogue. Pretending to peruse a financial donors plaque on the wall, Josee angled herself out of sight, yet within earshot.

"So Scooter's doing better? Poor kid had a heckuva time there."

"He's resting in his room as we speak, Chief. An acute case of food poisoning."

"Food poisoning?" Braddock's voice echoed Josee's surprise. "Dr. Dunning, shoot straight with me here. I saw this Scooter kid myself. His lymph glands were swollen. He was convulsing, bleeding, muttering that he was dizzy and could taste nails in his mouth. I'll admit we don't see many rattlesnake bites past August, not here in the valley, but he had the symptoms of one. Or something like it."

"Snakebite? Doubtful."

"Weren't those bite marks on his cheek?"

"Preexisting abrasions. His thinned blood simply found the path of least resistance. Our pathologist is taking a look. Blood typing, urinalysis, and a CBC should provide a more detailed picture. Nevertheless, I stand by my diagnosis."

"You're certain it wasn't a bite?"

Josee heard the doctor's clipboard hit the counter. "I'll admit, Chief, that envenomation can be tricky to assess. For rapid and accurate treatment, it's always best to have a witness."

"A girl was with him."

"I should've spoken with her."

"One of my sergeants interviewed her but reported nothing along those lines. At first we thought we were dealing with a violent assault case."

"Then you, too, understand the difficulty of coming up with an accurate picture. Snake venoms are complex protein mixtures, and it is possible, as

you've suggested, that enzymes interacting with specific chemical and physio-
logical receptor sites caused the manifestations you described. Seems unlikely
though. Acute food poisoning can produce similar symptoms."

"What's Scooter say about it, Dr. Dunning? I'd like to speak with him."
Josee was hanging on every word.

"The patient? Oh," the doctor said in a temperate tone, "he's wary of our
questions and remains disoriented, but he did confirm that he ingested tainted
fish. Pulled from the Willamette, if I had to guess. He was camped out in the
woods, correct? Well, I don't have to tell you that river's been coughing up a high
number of contaminants, which is certainly consistent with my findings."

"Still trying to convince yourself, sounds like to me."

"Chief, if a bite releases histamines or serotonin, it can hinder diagnosis.
For this reason, we've continued to monitor our patient's progress, but at this
point I can say with confidence that he's well on the road to recovery. He's
received the best possible care. Yesterday the EMTs administered epinephrine
in the ambulance, and soon after his arrival I ordered fresh plasma to counter
any prothrombin deficiencies. He's responded favorably, recovering with
remarkable speed."

"He'll be ready to answer my questions then?"

"Don't see why not. Less than an hour ago an orderly gave Scooter a protein injection. We'll see how he does with that, but his blood should be clotting normally again. If all goes well, he'll soon be ambulatory and ready for
outpatient care." Dr. Dunning cleared his throat. "So then, let's stick with my
diagnosis, shall we, Chief? Food poisoning covers a lot of ground. *E. coli,* bot-
ulism, even anthrax can be traced to contaminated foods."

"You know your stuff. I'll leave you to your job."

Josee had heard enough. She didn't want the chief to find her standing
here. She turned and followed the room numbers, letting their gibberish fade
behind her. It was comforting to know that Sergeant Turney had kept her
secrets.

As she passed the stairwell door, she thought she heard it click shut.

Just jumpy, she told herself. *Room 215, 217…*

"Josee?" Chief Braddock had sighted her. "Hold up. I need to talk at
you."

She waved him off. She had to see Scooter, had to know he was healthy and things would be fine. Her foreboding became a weight around her ankles, slowing her steps. *Room 219, 221…* She slipped through the door into Room 223.

"Scoot? It's Josee." She let her eyes adjust to the sun-sliced shadows.

The bed, however, was empty. Peeled back like a wrinkled eyelid, the blanket revealed the lifeless white glare of the sheets.

12

The Arrivals

"Kara!"

Marsh lifted his hands in astonishment and expelled a volley of expletives. A scan of the study revealed no sign of intrusion or forced entry. Over his wife's shoulder, his online foe awaited their customary chess match, but that was the least of his concerns.

He rushed to the desk to loosen her restraints. The cord felt…furry?

"Who did this to you, Kara! You okay? How'd this happen?"

She appeared unharmed—her cheeks were smooth, her lips soft and parted—yet betrayal and trepidation formed dark circles around her eyes. Her hair was tousled. Her perfume was a welcome substitute for the study's earlier rank smell. She was muttering through the leather gag, and as he stripped it away and tossed it to the carpet in disgust, she said, "Thank you. I could scarcely breathe."

"How'd you get in here!" He held her shoulders, steadying himself as much as her. Fury crackled along his skin. "Did they hurt you? Tell me who's responsible, and I swear I'll—"

"You don't know?"

"No, I don't know! How would I know? I thought you were at the coast."

"You *should* know." She massaged her wrists.

"What's going on?" He removed his hands, sensing yesterday's suspicions hanging again over his head. "You think I had something to do with this? I don't even know how you got in here."

She pulled her arms to her chest.

He said, "That door's electronically locked. The keypad combo's supposed to keep out intruders, and I know for a fact I closed it behind me. Whoever did this is—"

"You're right. You did close it. Closing me out the way you always do."

"Oh, come on. You know how many valuables're in this office, and I—"

"Marshall, Marshall…how can someone who knows so much see so little?"

There it was again, her tedious refrain: *Please, God, open his eyes.*

He punched the desk intercom button. "Rosamund, come upstairs ASAP."

"The muffins, sir, they're—"

"Forget the muffins and get up here!" He turned back to his wife. "Rosie helped you, didn't she? She was the last one I let in here. I had my back turned, and she was able to sneak you in so that you could rig this masquerade. To gain my sympathy, I presume? Well, the joke's backfired. I'm not laughing. You know what it's like to find your spouse tied up and gagged like this? You scared the hell out of me!"

"That was the point."

"Ah, so you admit it."

"Time we stood together. Isn't it God's plan that man and wife function as one?"

"Now it's making sense." Marsh nodded, shifting the puzzle pieces into place. "The tie, that was part of your scheme too, wasn't it? Another ploy to shake me up. Well, whatever you're up to, I don't appreciate it. You want to talk? Great, let's talk. But enough with your attempts to manipulate my emotions—the picture on the vanity, the tie around your neck, this! You know, certain things should be off-limits."

"You keep nearly everything off-limits."

"For a reason."

"Even yourself, darling."

"Now you're not making any sense. You're changing the subject."

Kara stretched the stiffness from her limbs. "No, I'm focusing on the issue, the manner in which you've excluded me from every corner of your life."

"Not like you're Ms. Innocent here. You have a conveniently short memory."

"Short? It's been over twenty years. But you won't let me be free of that, will you?" Her voice was fading. Losing substance. "This isn't what you think it is, Marsh. I didn't set this up, and I promise that Rosie didn't sneak me in here."

Marsh dropped his head and leaned against the desk. Across his monitor, a message caught his attention. "CCD, I've captured your queen... Wish to resign?" Resign? The game hadn't even started—the sheer arrogance! Steele Knight must be fuming after two mornings of interruption.

He turned his back to the screen. "Then who did tie you up, Kara? Answer that for me."

"Does it matter? You care only about proving a point, being right at all costs."

"I care about the facts. Facts are power—even the power to care, if needed."

Caramel eyes were pooling with tears. "The power to care, Marsh, is the power to change."

"Then I'm on the right track, aren't I?" he said smugly. "Takes two to tango."

"So you'll meet with Josee?"

"Oh, for heaven's sake, not back to this subject. No! I don't want to see her. Far as I'm concerned, Josee's your deal. Is that not clear enough? This is one door to the past that's better left unopened. You want me to step in as the father figure, but what do I know about playing a role that was never modeled for me? I'll pass, thanks."

She was silent. Sinking. Disappearing into the black chair.

He strode toward the door. "Where is that woman? If Rosie didn't tie you up, then I'd like to know who did."

"Darling, think about it. You should know the answer."

What a waste of time. Thursday was his alleged day off, the time he spent schmoozing: wining and dining, courting and golfing with potential investors, peptalking local publications about the vineyard's weekend activities. Truth was, Thursdays always found him working the business angles. A day off, ha. He'd have time to rest in the grave.

The intercom sounded. Even as Marsh reached to respond, Kara threw out a final question. "Whose blood was that on your face this morning?"

He froze in his tracks, and a wave of black hair surged over his eye. He brushed it back and said through a granite-carved smile, "You're trying to torment me, aren't you?" The intercom sounded again. "I bet you were here all night, spying on me, toying with me. Have to admit, you had me going. What'd you do? Prick a finger and wipe the blood on my cheek? A question

mark... Very funny. I knew there was a logical explanation behind all this."
He keyed the intercom, paused, got no response.

"You honestly think I tiptoed through the night just to play with your mind?"

"Wouldn't put it past you. Or Rosie maybe."

The entry chime sounded.

"About time." Marsh hit the release key, and the door slid open. "Okay,
Rosie, let's hear it. This better be good."

"Sir?" The household manager tilted her head, her honey-tinted curls
budging not an inch from their austere arrangement. She looked around his
shoulder, eyes registering nothing. She brushed by to set a platter on an ebony
side table. "Orange walnut muffins and a dollop of butter."

"Rosamund. What'd I tell you? I couldn't care less about that right now."

She tucked her hands into her apron and bent her head in supplication.
"Pardon my delay. These officers arrived moments ago, two fine young
gentlemen expressing an urgency to speak with you. I tried to inform you over
the intercom but got no response."

"Officers?"

"Apologize for the inconvenience, Mr. Addison." A pair of policemen
stepped through the door, and Rosie bowed on her way back down the hall.
"Officer Lansky," the older cop introduced himself. The rigidity of his stance
and handshake implied embarrassment at being here. "And my partner,
Officer Graham. With the Corvallis Police Department. It's regarding your
wife, Kara. Did I say that right? *Care-uh?*"

"That's right."

"Have a couple of questions to ask you."

"Oh, she can speak for herself. Believe me"—Marsh lifted his eyebrows,
trying to solicit male empathy with such matters—"sometimes you can't keep
her quiet."

"That so?" The officers exchanged a glance.

Graham hoisted a soiled Ralph Lauren sports bag. "We found this earlier
this morning, Mr. Addison, with your wife's ID inside." His trimmed mus-
tache was stiff despite the movement of his mouth.

"Looks like Kara's. Where was it?"

"We were dispatched," Lansky cut in, "at 5:45 AM to mile-marker four on

Ridge Road. Down the hill from here. Half-mile from the Dari-Mart. A motorist called the station on his cell, said there was a vehicle in the ravine and that it looked like it'd jumped the guardrail."

"The Z3?"

"A convertible BMW, that's correct. Ran the plates. Came up registered in your wife's name."

Marsh threw up his hands. "I purchased that car just last month."

"I trust you have good insurance, Mr. Addison. We arrived on the scene about 5:55. It appeared the vehicle had lost control at the bend and flipped over the rail. The engine was cold. We're still searching for the vehicle's operator, hoping for the best."

Graham added, "The sports bag was thrown from the vehicle, along with a number of other items. You say it's hers. Are you sure?" From the bag in his hand, a wet leaf fluttered to the carpet. "Has your wife attempted to contact you?"

"It's the first I've heard anything about it."

"We understand that you may be concerned, sir, but your wife's probably fine. Remember, we haven't found a body."

A body? What the—

Lansky cut in to cover his partner's impropriety. "Any idea where Kara might be, sir? Any way that we can contact her?"

Marsh Addison, incredulous, was staring at Graham. "So tell me, are you fresh from the academy? Of course, you haven't found a body. If this is your version of tact, it's a good thing I don't need comforting, isn't it?" He turned to confront Kara seated at his desk. "I can't even believe this. You know that car's worth a—"

The chair was empty.

On the black leather upholstery, circles of blood demanded an explanation.

⌐

Marsh was stunned. Was he losing his mind? Hadn't he talked to his wife in this chair only moments ago? He stalked the study's confines but found no trace of her. Where had she gone? File this one under don't-let-your-spouse-out-of-your-sight. He'd bought her some sweet wheels of her own, given her room to run, and look where it'd gotten him. Kara must be nearby, breathing easy, no doubt laughing at his discomfort amid the abundance of evidence.

The bloodstains—if they were hers, he was sunk.

The knotted cord—he recognized it now as the strap from his bathrobe.

The leather gag—one of his own belts? What was it doing here?

Judging by their expressions, the same chain of reasoning was rattling through the officers' minds, lowering the portcullis between the keepers of justice and the lone, suspicious husband. With no defense against the flaming arrows of inquiry fired from their castle walls, Marsh knew he must guard his words and actions.

To humor the watching officers, to divert attention, he made a show of trying to contact his wife. He placed a call to Kara's cell phone. No answer. He dialed the house in Yachats. And left a message. He could visualize the answering machine, propped on a beige laminated counter beneath a calendar of Pacific Coast lighthouses. He tried to imagine Kara there, reading on the couch or slicing chanterelle mushrooms that she had picked on a nature hike or playing Parcheesi with Josee.

He hung up the phone. "Not there. She could be out on the beach."

"Doubt it," said Lansky. "Storm coming in, according to last night's news."

"Kara loves the ocean right before a storm." How long, he wondered, had it been since they'd walked barefoot through the sand? Months? Years? He wasn't sure.

Why was Kara doing this to him? What was going on?

Darling, think about it. You should know the answer... Her words, spoken from his chair only minutes ago. *How can someone who knows so much see so little?*

"We spoke with your housekeeper lady," Officer Graham broke in. "At the door."

"Rosamund?"

"She told us how you cleaned out the parlor yesterday, how you were creating a space for your wife. She admitted that tensions've been running high the past week or so. Said she hadn't seen Kara since before noon yesterday. Is that accurate?"

"Sir," Lansky confided, "these things happen in the best of marriages. I speak from personal experience. I'm wearing the same ball and chain. No shame in admitting to a squabble now and then. You two had any recent alter-cations, verbal or otherwise? When was the last time you saw your wife?"

An instant replay: Marsh aiming his Montblanc at Kara's disappearing form and triggering the pen like a gun. For the first time, he questioned his own innocence here. He glanced back at the bloodstained chair. Who was it he had talked to? Sure looked and sounded like his wife. At the monitor, Steele Knight was gone, as was his message: *I've captured your queen... Wish to resign?* The screen had returned to the gaming zone's foyer where losing players sought rematches by distorted torchlight.

I'm the one losing here. Losing my wife. My grip on reality.

Marsh steadied his voice. "Listen, my car's ruined, my wife's...gone. I'm going to need some time to absorb this. Thank you, Officer Lansky, Officer Graham, for bringing me into the loop. I'll make some more calls, see if I can't locate Kara. You have a number where I can reach you?"

Lansky looked up. "Are you asking us to leave? Or may we conduct a brief search?"

"You're being a bit premature, aren't you? I'm sure this is all a big mistake. Knowing Kara, I bet she loaned the keys to a friend, probably doesn't even know what's happened yet."

"She'd loan out her brand-new BMW?"

"Kara? She's generous that way. Always has been. Twenty-two years of marriage, I think I should know."

"All good and well, Mr. Addison, but if you have an explanation for the blood there on the chair, I'm still waiting to hear it. Otherwise, I say we've got a potential crime scene on our hands. In fact, Graham, I'd like you to go down to the patrol car, get on the radio with downtown, connect the dots for them between the car in the ravine and what we've found here, see if we can't obtain a telephonic warrant from the judge. When that's done, bring the yellow tape on up, and we'll establish a perimeter."

Graham trotted off.

"Now, Mr. Addison… Is it okay if I call you Marsh?"

"Let's stick to formalities."

"If that's how you want it."

"Some nerve you have, coming into my home and throwing out accusations."

"No one's accusing anyone. Just seeking answers—all part of my job. For your protection. If, and I repeat, if a crime's been committed here, you wouldn't want to find yourself falsely accused because you had contaminated the scene, would you? Graham'll tape it off, the crime team'll do their thing, and with a little luck we'll be out of your hair pronto. By tomorrow, if things go smoothly."

"I have a business to run. Today was my day off, you might like to know."

"Should those be your biggest concerns at this moment?"

"Listen, Officer, I'm as perplexed by all this as you are, and I understand it paints me as the bad guy, but you're wrong. That's not how this happened."

"How did it happen, sir? I'm all ears."

"Do you think I'm guilty of something? Give it to me straight."

"All I'm saying is, I hope there's a plausible explanation behind all this."

"Then that makes two of us, doesn't it?"

In a voice coated with professional concern, Lansky proposed that Mr. Addison accompany them down to the station to fill out a report, handle a few questions, sort things out. "Could be a logical explanation we're overlooking here," he added.

"Don't you need to read me my rights?"

Graham jogged back up the grand staircase, police tape and warrant secured. Thus fortified, his senior partner rattled off the words in a monotone. "Mr. Addison, you have the right to remain silent. Anything you say…"

Moisture beaded on the cellar walls, and spider webs hung thick with dust, like brown yarn spooled and unraveling between the overhead beams. The cement floor was cold. Steps rose to a trapdoor where cracks of gray afforded dim visibility.

Kara's eyes kept going back to the trapdoor.

When would that kid be back? She knew him. He'd worked on their machinery at the estate. A normal-seeming kid, just doing his job.

Why this? What does he want with me?

She cried through the gag and the oil rag stuffed into her mouth, imploring God's protection over Josee. Kara had spent one freezing night alone, tied to this chair in this hellhole, but at least the kid had left—without touching her, without searching her front pocket. Simply dumped her down here. Tied her up, removed the blindfold, and left. Was he still up there? She realized that she might die in this dark spot. How long till anyone found her? The thought left her shaking. She bit down on her panic. She didn't want to die, not like this, not without her husband knowing what had happened.

Not without seeing her daughter.

Let me see her, just once, and then I'll accept whatever happens. Please, Lord.

———

At the foot of the grand staircase, the officers stopped. The parlor doors were open.

"What have we here?" Lansky's boots clicked across the parlor's hardwood floor toward a painting on the east wall. A vision of surreal drama and color, the canvas ruled the room. With hands on hips, Lansky peered at the engraved plate on the gilded frame. *"The Lady in Dread,"* he intoned. "Did you choose this yourself, Mr. Addison, a gift for your wife's new surroundings? Creating some sort of shrine, is that it?"

Marsh knew the words were meant to provoke him but reacted nonetheless.

"A shrine? Hey now! I didn't buy that, don't know anything about it." Marsh regretted that he had delayed ordering a piano. But this? Where had it come from?

"Like the bloodstains," Graham said. "You just don't know."

"That's correct!" Marsh saw Rosie enter the room, felt bolstered by her elderly face. "Maybe she knows what it's doing here."

"Why, it arrived soon after these gentlemen," she told him. "Delivered by a woman in a station wagon with the backseats folded down and, if memory serves, the logo of an art gallery emblazoned on the door. A delightful girl. Sweet-faced. She showed me an invoice verifying a delivery to this address, scheduled for today's date."

"And you signed for it? Without checking with me?"

"It was ordered and paid for in your name, sir. What was I to do?" She surrendered an ivory envelope. "The girl presented this as well, said it contained the painting's certificate of authenticity and a note of appreciation for purchasing through her gallery. A commendable touch, I thought. It's not yet been opened. The writing's beautiful, don't you think?"

Marsh weighed the parchment in his hands and admired his name in calligraphy. Then he noticed the subtext, nestled within a swooped tail of ink.

Three letters: CCD.

13

Without a Sound

"Scooter?" He was here somewhere. Had to be.

Josee rechecked the number on the hospital-room door, then considered the possibilities. Her head became a cave of reverberating doubts and concerns. Why had she left him on his own? Had that creature found him here? She envisioned him helpless in the bed with his bandaged face. Scooter was vulnerable at this time, no better than fresh meat—*fresh sustenance on demand.*

She stepped deeper into the room's bars of sunlight. She needed answers.

"*Hola.*"

She jolted. Where had the voice come from?

"You Josee?" A short Hispanic nurse with hair gathered into a tight knot entered from the attached bathroom.

"That's me."

"He no here," said the nurse, with a finger pointed at the bed.

Josee met the woman's sympathetic eyes. She took a step. "Where is he?"

"He say, tell you to meet him."

"Scooter? You've seen him? He's okay?"

"*Sí.* He no look the same. He—"

Chief Braddock, flushed with anger, flung open the door. "What do you think you're doing, making me chase you down the hall? Don't you run from me, Josee. Don't you abuse the charity I've shown."

While he assessed the situation, the nurse's eyes fell to her work. She took a stack of towels into the bathroom, busied herself with straightening and restocking. To Josee, her movements appeared fluid and unhampered by those watching her; she seemed used to the notion of blending in unseen.

"Where'd he go?" Braddock approached the bed, gripped the sheets, and peeled them to the foot of the mattress as if to unmask a threat. "You hear me? You understand me, nurse?"

"*Serpiente* here," she told him as she refilled a soap dispenser.

"A snake? You saw a snake?"

"Sí, *señor. Verde*—green. By window."

"Green?"

"With fire eyes. *El diablo.*" She kissed the crucifix around her neck. "*Jesús Cristo,* have mercy."

"Okay, I can see this is going nowhere. What about the patient? Where'd he go?"

"Sí. He go."

"Where?"

The nurse wadded a towel, stuffed it into a laundry bag. "He no here. *No aquí.*"

"'No aquí.' Gee, thanks, that's a lot of help." Braddock wrung the bedsheets in his fist, flung them down. He mumbled, "What planet do these people come from? Doesn't anyone in this country speak American anymore?" He looked under the bed, checked the closet, the bathroom. Josee heard shower curtain rings jangle on the rod before he reappeared and fired an order at her. "You wait here," he said. "No, I can't force you, but I'm asking you not to budge, you hear me? I'm gonna go find out what the devil's going on."

As the door swung shut behind him, the nurse signaled to Josee. Her tone was hushed. "Diablo, sí. Serpiente—it want your man. This no good."

"Did he say anything else to you?"

"Scooter? Sí. He want me give you message, *comprende?*"

"Comprende, yes." Josee shored her foot against the door. "Quick. Please tell me before the chief gets back. What's the message? What'd he say?"

"You meet him. Afternoon. He say you know where."

"Scooter told you that?"

"Sí."

"But I don't know where. That's all he said? You're sure?" Despite the nurse's nod, Josee saw misgiving brim in the wide brown eyes. "Why'd he leave?" Josee wanted to know. "*Porqué?*"

"Diablo...serpiente. It watch him by window."

"You saw it? With your own eyes?"

"Sí, *en pleno día.* It make sound...*hsss!* I try to help, but your man much afraid."

"You said he doesn't look the same. Why? Did he get bit again?"

"Bit? How you know this? Doctor say food poison."

"That's not true, not totally. We did eat some fish sticks that were a day past due, but he was attacked after that. Saw it happen myself."

"You speak truth." Touching the corners of her own eyes, the nurse said, "I see he have wounds. But doctor—he no want to worry the people."

"Maybe they *should* be worried."

"Sí, *señorita.* Fire eyes. Scooter needs help. You also." The nurse rummaged in the laundry bag. "Aquí. This why your man no look the same." Gathered in the wadded towel that she'd brought from the bathroom, locks of nut-brown hair spoke of Scooter's last-minute desperation. Thin facial hair topped the pile. "I bring him…razor. Other clothings."

"He cut his hair? And his beard? Omigosh, Scoot, you must've been scared out of your mind. So," she asked the nurse, "where did the snake go? El serpiente?"

"It go"—the nurse rubbed her fingertips together, then let her hands spring open—"go *rápido.* Sí, Josee, you be careful. Poison *muy fuerte.*" She placed a hand on her own heart. "Scooter—he in trouble, I think."

"I have to find him."

"You hear me, *por favor. Ten cuidado…*be careful."

"I hear you. Okay, I got it."

The nurse removed her crucifix, pressed the object into Josee's hand. "You take. Remind you about Jesús Cristo."

"For me?"

"Sí, for you." A soft hand moved to Josee's cheek.

She drew back, but the gesture felt sincere, and warmth radiated from the nurse's bronze skin. "Just a reaction," Josee said in meager apology. "Thanks, you know, for the necklace. *Gracias.*" She let the leather cord fall through her fingers, touched the rugged figure carved from myrtlewood. Though the Savior's half-clothed body was twisted on the cross, stretched on the archaic instrument of agony, his eyes, even on this small scale, seemed to radiate compassion. "Listen, this is yours. I can't take it from you. I mean, it's nice of you…" She looked up. "Hello? Hola?"

Mystified, she wandered into the bathroom and out, but there was no sign of the nurse. Grasping the myrtlewood cross, Josee surveyed the room and saw that she was alone with towels bunched at her feet and sheets mounded on the bed.

Without a sound, the woman had vanished.

Over the years Josee Walker had met her share of accusers. They'd take one hard look at her, point sanctimonious fingers, then turn their backs while she fought off the loneliness that scorched her cheeks and charred the corners of her eyes.

Black: the color of an old skillet. The color of her loneliness.

She knew Jesus wasn't the type to write her off, to put a gun to her head and demand perfection as a family prerequisite. She also knew she was a sinner—didn't take a genius to figure that out. Didn't everyone have faults? As a girl, she had confessed and asked forgiveness, choosing to join God's family of love. She didn't know what to expect from a family, but anything would beat the bits and pieces she'd experienced. Torn photos and memories. Closets and angry words.

God's family, she discovered, could be just as cruel.

She soon felt as if…well, as if she'd been put up for adoption. Again.

Now, in the stillness of Room 223, Josee gripped the myrtlewood cross to her chest and looked skyward. "I want to believe you're here," she breathed.

Josee, I never left you. The voice was still, small. Felt, rather than heard.

Armed with a fusillade of old accusations, she started to challenge this claim. Then her mind replayed yesterday's encounter—the serpentine vapor and those eyes of flame exploding and evaporating into the thicket's thin air.

Something had stopped it. Or someone.

"Thanks," she whispered. "Guess I owe you that."

She wished she could thank the nurse as well.

In the Corvallis Public Library on this quiet Thursday morning, Beau waited at the computers for an e-mail. Could be a while, he'd been warned. Maybe all day. He had his thoughts to keep him company. That Addison lady, she wasn't bad lookin'—except for the swollen lip he'd given her. He could still see her look of shock, the brave little thing biting back her tears. Well, she might not be feeling so high and mighty now, stuck in the dark, no way to take a whiz. She'd smell like a bum by the end of the day.

"Serves you right. You think your diamonds'll save ya?"

In his hand, her earrings sparkled. A pair of teardrops.

Beau glanced over the partitions to make sure no one was watching. Per instructions, he had ditched the van at a condemned shack on the outskirts of Philomath and ridden the bus back into Corvallis. Had anyone missed him over the last thirty-six hours? Yeah, right. His father was away on business; his mother was on her third marriage and living in central California; his high school friends were trapped in classrooms and looking forward to tomorrow night when they could stockpile Halloween candy and egg their teachers' houses and stay up late watching horror flicks.

Not that he'd be with them. Not one of them had invited him to a party. *Skee-reeech!*

Well, he'd have the last laugh. Ha! If ICV's plan pulled together, his former classmates would be watching his face on the news instead. Yeah, buddy, he could hear them now. "Isn't that Beau Connors?" "You ever suspect he'd do something like this?" "Isn't he the one those jocks messed up and threw into a locker, found him the next morning sniveling like a baby?"

Pressure exploded in Beau's head. His arms whipped back like broad wings and threw him back in the library chair so violently that he hit the floor and turned heads. He ground his palms against the high-pitched squawks in his ears.

"Sir, do you need me to call someone? Are you all right?"

On his knees, he scrambled from the librarian's touch. Pocketed the earrings.

"Maybe you should step outside, get some fresh air."

"Leave me alone!"

Beau staggered down the library's front steps, fleeing curious eyes but wanting to stay close so he could recheck his e-mail. Mr. Steele's instructions might arrive at any time. One of two phrases: "Game Adjourned" or "Pawn

Sacrifice." If he was told to sacrifice, Beau would walk into the police station tonight and turn himself in for Kara Addison's kidnapping. When they matched the ravine's evidence with his jacket and shoes, when he waved these teardrop earrings, they'd go ape wild.

Who'll be sniveling then, huh? Tell me that much. Who?

—

Chief Braddock held the elevator door so Josee could come aboard. Once they were closed in together, he turned toward her.

She edged back. "Hey, keep your distance."

"You're an uptight kid, you know that?"

"Scooter's missing, and I hold you responsible. You let him escape."

"Why don't you zip it? I came to do a welfare check of your friend, make sure it was safe for him to be moving about, and he goes AWOL on me. We've searched this hospital thoroughly. No sign of your pal, so don't blame me. Maybe you had a part in—"

"It's my fault again?" Josee shoved past him with an elbow. "Stay away from me. You want me to scream bloody murder when these doors open?"

"Breathe easy, girl." His eyes wandered over the front of her knit sweater before snapping back up. "I'm not here to let you stir up trouble for me. As a young man, I made my share of mistakes, but those days are behind me. We clear? You can smile big, try to look pretty, what have you. But this is business, police business."

She faced the door, convinced this elevator wasn't big enough for the two of them. "I'd rather deal with Sergeant Turney, if you don't mind. Supposed to meet him here soon."

"Obviously you have the big fella eating out of your hand."

"Least he listens. You know, with those two things on the sides of his head."

The chief followed her through the lobby to the patient drop-off zone beneath an overhang. Josee marched up and down the white-painted curb, watching for Turney. Or maybe she'd spot Scooter. Could he be out here? Without any clues, she wasn't sure where to start looking.

Chief Braddock was facing her. "Okay, I'm listening. What brought you here? Why'd you and your boyfriend choose to pass through Corvallis?"

"Personal matters."

"Personal. Ah. To see your mother, you mean?"

Josee tilted her head, threw him a blank gaze. Her mother? While the hospital was being searched, she'd made three calls to Kara Addison and had gotten an answering machine each time. So much for that. Josee knew when she was being avoided.

"What has she told you, Josee?"

"Zippo. Zilch. *Nada.*"

"Why'd you come then?" Braddock got no response. "What about your father? What do you know about him?"

"Is there a point to this, Chief? I mean, my family's none of your concern."

"I'm a public servant." Braddock's smile was irritating. "How 'bout ICV?"

"Icy what?"

"In cauda venenum. The name ring any bells?"

Josee stiffened. To hear those words verbalized brought her fears back to life. She scrounged for an answer.

"ICV," Braddock elucidated, "is a group of local anarchists, active mostly here in Oregon but Washington, too. Like to cause trouble. They've instigated a riot or two, stirred up dissent on college campuses. Been keeping an eye out for their activities recently, but they're slippery. You know zip about them—that's your answer?"

"Never heard of it…them, whatever."

"What about your friend? Is he connected with them?"

"Man, why're you jumping all over me? I just want to see Scooter and ditch this town. I've done nothing wrong. Is that so hard to believe? Should never have come back in the first place. Big mistake."

"You have lots of history here."

"Got that right."

"Is that why you've returned? What about the key? Do you have it?"

"Key?"

"It belonged to your grandfather."

This detour rattled her. What did Braddock know about her family and her past? "You must have the wrong chick. Must've got your signals crossed, Chief."

"Girl, you've got quite the attitude—"

"Couple of piercings and a tattoo don't make me a criminal."

"And a mouth on you that won't quit."

"Call it a gender attribute."

"That's rich. You and Turney make quite a pair. Let's see what he does now that I'm giving him some leash to run with. We'll see how long it takes."

She touched a finger to her eyebrow ring. "Takes? For what?"

"For him to hang himself with it." Braddock nodded at the police cruiser curling into the drive. "Here he is. Don't get me wrong, I like the guy. Sad thing is, he's let that one incident back in '81—he was just a kid, for Pete's sake!—lock him up inside. Guilt is a horrible thing, no matter how misplaced. Best to let it go. That's my policy."

"But it can still come back and bite you."

"Sounds like something Sarge'd say. Tell you what, he'll be stuck forever if he doesn't deal with this psychological weakness. Don't you do like he's done. The very night Sarge should've been celebrating his freedom was the night he chained it down—Independence Day. What do you think of that? Life's a funny thing."

Josee wasn't laughing. With the car door open, she met Turney's eyes.

July 4, 1981. They'd both been here. At Good Samaritan. A baby going up for adoption and a nine-year-old boy coming down off a mixture of pills and alcohol.

With a flurry of ideas and emotions chasing questions through her head, she admitted that she had ignored these correlations. Too much. Too bizarre. She remembered Turney's quizzical reaction to her birth date. His retelling of the snakebite. His guilt over the lady who'd been shot and the vanished baby.

Could it be? Josee's heart beat like a jackhammer. *How-can-I-know-how-can-I-know-how-can-I-know?*

There was one way: If her birth mother could show her a bullet scar in her hip.

Fat chance. Wherever Kara was, she'd obviously lost interest in their happy little reunion.

14

A Glimpse of Pain

"Show and tell," said Officer Graham. "Let's see it."

The patrol car was at the foot of the estate, passing through the stucco archway. Behind the divider, Marsh was uncertain about the ivory envelope. The initials made this personal. CCD? Only zone players knew his user name, and Steele Knight alone addressed him by those initials. Reasoning told Marsh this note was important. He had not ordered that painting in the parlor; therefore, this thank-you note was one of two things: a mistake...or a message.

So as not to arouse Graham's suspicion, Marsh obliged. The same fingers that had fumbled with Kara's restraints dipped into the slit and produced a handwritten note. Then he tucked in the flap fastidiously and turned the envelope back over on the seat.

Twice he read the note. Tried to show bafflement on his face.

"Well? If you didn't order the painting, as you claim, what does the note say?"

"I'm lost. Here, read it for yourself." As Marsh handed it through the divider, he theorized, "Maybe it's a gift from one of my investors. The vineyard's been doing well of late."

Graham read the note aloud, as though pronouncing a courtroom verdict.

Mr. Addison, thank you, thank you, a million times over for your patronage. This piece boasts startling originality. This artist is brilliant in his use of color, pulling drama from every hue. One institute, the House of Ubelhaar, reviewed it thus: "The artist draws the viewer into the queen's dilemma and leaves him asking: Does she fall? Is she impaled on the waiting spears? Where is her protector, the king, in all this? There is a true sense of urgency. And, if one is attentive to the cubist touches, he will note the hidden journal in the rampart's thorny foreground. Was this the object of the queen's attention? Was this the cause of her misstep along the ramparts? Perhaps, one wonders, the king might've saved her by offering up the mysterious pages."

Obviously, Mr. Addison, you share our belief that this art piece has poignant significance. May it inspire you to search for and share your own set of life mysteries.

Again, thank you.

Tattered Feather Art Gallery.

"Your own set of life mysteries?" Officer Lansky repeated from behind the wheel.

"My wife's missing," Marsh said. "That's more mystery than I want."

As pines soared along Ridge Road and the temperature dropped, Marsh replayed Steele Knight's gaming zone messages. Yesterday, October 29: *Next, I'm coming after your queen.* This morning: *I've captured your queen... Wish to resign?* Now, in his own home, a canvas of a threatened queen raised related questions. He wasn't sure how or why, but he was convinced that his longtime opponent had now shifted from prosaic online skirmishes to the battlefield of flesh and blood.

Was the explanation inside that envelope?

With a herculean effort, he ignored the object on the seat. A sense of purpose had permeated the words of the official note. What more was written on that thinner scrap of paper he had spotted and left inside?

—

The car was a mess. Marsh peered over the tangled guardrail at the white convertible Z3, a snagged shark stretched upon the stones below. The engine cooling vents were the gills, the coolant and transmission fluid were the entrails bleeding from the torn belly. Thankfully, the shark's belly—the cockpit—was empty.

Where are you, Kara? No one could've survived this.

Beneath towering Douglas firs, he waited in stunned silence. When Officer Lansky had opened the rear door for him, Marsh had slid from the seat while slipping the envelope into his waistband. Graham had circled to the front of the car and stood watching, as though he expected Marsh's actions to betray culpability in the day's events.

"This is it, mile-marker four," said Lansky. "Here's where she went over."

"Thought your partner said there was no body."

"I meant the car, Mr. Addison. Sorry. She jumped the rail right there—see the dent and the paint chips?—and bounced down into the ravine." The officer swung his leg over the yellow tape along the rail and lowered himself through clumps of fern. "Wanna take a look? Might catch a clue we wouldn't expect."

"She's not down there? You're positive?"

"No guarantees. The brush does get pretty thick. We did conduct a preliminary spiral check earlier—covering, I figure, a forty-foot circumference—but contacting you was the next logical step since you were just up the road." Police boots sent stones clinking into the gully. "We were hoping your wife'd be home with a ready explanation."

Marsh's usual business-quick responses had fled him.

Had Kara been in his study? Had she been in the car when it went over?

A cold sweat broke out around his collar. Surely, after years of benign Internet chess, there was no reason for his online adversary to intrude upon his marriage. True, Steele Knight's name sounded ominous, but so did most of the zone's monikers. Money—was that the motive? A hefty ransom? Or was it more base than that? Was his opponent some sicko hoping for a little—

Okay, that's enough. For all I know, this guy lives in the Midwest or Boston or Venezuela. Chess is our only connection.

But the official note had alluded to the threatened queen... His wife?

It had also mentioned an absent king, and a hidden journal.

The journal! My father's journal!

"Mr. Addison?" Officer Lansky was staring up at him from a spit of stone.

"Yes, I'm right here," he said. "I'm coming down."

While Graham watched him from the patrol car above, Marsh clutched tap-roots and muddy rocks and descended twenty feet into the ravine. By the time he joined the policeman next to the mangled wreckage, his loafers were ruined, and his hands were smeared with the earth's gritty scent.

"Warned you it wasn't pretty."

Marsh took a deep breath. "I need to know what went on here."

Nearby, a stream played over polished gray rocks. Marsh ventured a closer look, saw the Z3's front window frame jutting out like a dorsal fin while the oval snout pointed into the water. The shark wanted back in its element.

Funny, the things that go through your mind at a time like this.

He moved to the cockpit. Yes, same tannin red dash and interior, same chrome accents. On Kara's sheepskin seat covers her initials—KDA—were handstitched. He could still see her on her birthday four weeks ago at the sales lot in Eugene. From the driver's seat, she had tossed back golden hair and gazed over her shades at him with lighthearted passion. His response? He'd whipped out the checkbook and marched to the sales office, buying her favor in the manner he knew best.

Here, staring into the wreckage, he felt a surge of anger. It seemed that some cosmic force was out there laughing it up, relishing his discomfort, branding his efforts with a big stamp of disapproval.

Kara's unknown whereabouts and the details of this accident dropped into his stomach. He doubled over. Growled. Slammed down his hand on the tilted chassis.

"What now?" said Officer Lansky, with a surreptitious glance.

"Who is behind this? You have any ideas, any at all?"

"Still weighing possibilities. It is her car, isn't it?"

Marsh nudged aside a half-deflated air bag. From a jumble of papers spilling from the glove box, he retrieved a pumpkin-colored flier that an-nounced a community Thanksgiving dinner and named his wife as the co-ordinator. News to him. How would he write it off at year's end if she didn't keep him in the loop?

Stop. Business can wait.

He rolled the paper in his hand and looked up. "It's hers, no question."

The officer cleared his throat, tossed a glance up the cliff where his partner stood ready at the guardrail. "Any reason she might've done this of her
own volition?"

"Done what?"

"This. The accident."

"Are you… What're you asking me exactly? Cut through the bull."

"Was she experiencing any depression, taking any medication?"

"Suicide, Officer? Is that what you're getting at?"

"Simply covering all the bases, sir."

"Who do you think you are? You have some nerve, you know that?"
Marsh's broad frame led him back around the car where he aimed the rolled
flier at the policeman's chest. "Did you bring me down here to see if I'd crack,
to pressure me into spilling some dirty little secret? Sorry to disappoint you,
but I'm in the dark here, same as you, and it's my wife who's missing. That
make even one iota of sense to you?"

"Back off, Mr. Addison." On the rocks above, Graham stood with legs
apart, a hand on his holster.

"Listen," said Lansky. "We want to find your wife, same as you. At this
point we're treating it as a routine accident investigation. But there are some
curious facts we need to face."

"I deal in facts. Lay it all out. Go on. What do they tell us?"

Lansky ticked them off. "First, based on the info at our disposal, we could
have a straightforward accident here, driver not yet located or identified.
Could be a suicide attempt—now hear me out on this—and the body may
have washed downstream. Another possibility's a life insurance scam. Not
uncommon. She might've hoped the car would catch fire, destroying any evidence. Looks good on television."

"You're kidding, right?"

"It's been tried more than once."

"Okay, fine, the facts could lead to several possibilities. I know my wife
though, and Kara's not a destructive person." He handed over the flier.
"There, that's more her style. I'm forty-four years old, I've known her over half
my life, and I've never seen her try to hurt anyone—not physically, not intentionally. Believe me, it's not her nature."

"I'm sure that's the case, sir. Of course, there're other theories linked to the scene in your study, which you have yet to explain."

"Well, I sure wish someone would explain them to *me*. You know, I don't give a rip about your insinuations. I have the right to remain silent, remember?" Marsh knelt by the stream and scrubbed his hands in the rippling water. Was she out here somewhere? Dead or injured?

"Kara," he called out.

The stream's draft carried her name through a tunnel of overhanging limbs and foliage. On the opposing bank, a squirrel darted across a fallen hemlock; in the trees, a rook called out, then took flight. Where was she? Who was it he'd talked to in the study? Had to be her, of course, but that didn't explain the accident. With his own eyes, he'd seen her leave in the Z3 yesterday. Had she survived and returned to the manor on her own? Was she down here somewhere?

Or had someone taken her? Steele Knight?

"Kara," he cried out again. "If you can hear me, say something."

A voice. Weak, but distinct. Whispering from the stream. "Marshall…"

"Is that you! Kara, honey, speak louder."

He was skeptical; she couldn't have survived a crash such as this.

From high above, winged seedlings fell in lazy helicopter spins. Against the October sky, it looked to Marsh as though they formed black and white links that came looping around his neck. He winced and, lowering his eyes, strained to hear his wife's voice. He thought of all the times he had tuned her out.

"Over here, Marshall," the stream whispered again.

"I'm here. Where are you? Talk to me."

"Here. Please, don't leave. Please."

⌇

Stahlherz clambered up the stairs to a two-bedroom apartment over a Chinese restaurant. Though the Golden Dragon would not open for another hour and a half, scents of broccoli and ginger filled the single-light-bulb stairway.

He reached the landing, cursing his mortality and the tightness in his limbs. The talon wound on his forearm throbbed, a reminder of his feathered friend and its burst of unruliness in Café Zerachio. Stahlherz had never allowed his rooks to seize control. An isolated incident. Yet, like an isolated pawn in a game, he felt weakened.

In the apartment, three recruits were gathered: two men, one woman. A Trailblazers blanket was tacked over the main window, lending the apartment a dark, crimson hue.

"Fortune favors the daring," the trio chanted.

Stahlherz reciprocated, then drew back an edge of the blanket to verify Darius's position in the lot below. His driver was wired and happy, a sentinel armed with a quad-shot white mocha. The girl at the drive-through espresso booth had taken his order with a flirtatious smile that said she was impressed—in more ways than one.

"Is the Professor coming?" the woman recruit asked Stahlherz.

"No." He dropped the blanket. "Is that a problem? Am I incapable of delineating your task?" He tried to fix each individual with a stare; instead, with the flaring of his social anxieties, he blinked. No, no, no. Control. He must guide these pawns, exhibit strength. "Thank you for gathering on short notice, my friends. The time is upon us."

From far-flung Roseburg, Astoria, and Umatilla, these three political dreamers had converged upon the city of Salem with the pillars of the capitol in their eyes. The years, however, had picked apart their ideals, and at their first *tête-à-tête* he had instructed them: "Don't try to remove the splinter from your friend's eye. First remove the pillar from your own. Here in Salem, as you've discovered, that pillar is the system. It has blinded you. Or tried to. You must pluck it away, with no fear and no regrets."

They'd hung on every word. Ulcerating in the bosom of the political monster.

In cauda venenum!

From his carpetbag, Stahlherz removed a canister and set it on the coffee table. "Don't let its simplicity disappoint you. This vessel is a means of storage and dispersion, nothing more. Tomorrow evening you will bring it with you to the site I've designated. From that point, then, you understand your instructions?"

The woman said, "Of course. We've been reconnoitering for the past year."

The older man said, "Will it be safe, Mr. Steele? For us, I mean."

"Safe? Did you learn that word from brown-nosing politicos? Radical change comes by veering from the path of comfort and security. It's time to strike before being struck, don't you think? Only last month a handful of al-Qaeda sympathizers confessed their guilt before a judge in Portland. Did they accomplish their goals beforehand? I think not. Will you, too, shrink from the dangers inherent?"

"We wouldn't be here if that was the case, sir."

"You—we—are threads in the garment of revolt." Stahlherz warmed to his oratory. "Here are some samples from history's tapestry: 1940…the Japanese start an outbreak of the bubonic plague by dropping ceramic pots of contaminated rice and fleas on China's Cheking Province—"

"That does it for me, no more meals downstairs."

"In 1763, the English give smallpox-laden blankets to those Indians loyal to the French. In 1346, in what is now modern Ukraine, the Tartars attack a seaport by catapulting diseased carcasses over the city walls in hopes of starting an epidemic. Finally, and particularly apropos, is the story of Hannibal in 184 B.C. While fighting a naval battle in Pergamum, he orders earthen pots to be hurled onto the decks of the enemy ships."

"Pots? What was in 'em?"

"An ancient evil. A creature known to spark fear and enmity."

"Snakes?"

Stahlherz grinned. "He made sure they were filled with 'serpents of every kind' so that his enemies caught a glimpse of the pain they had coming."

"Not to question your plan, Mr. Steele, but a couple of snakes?" The oldest recruit frowned. "Honestly, how many does this canister hold? Am I missing something?"

Marsh saw nothing at first. A gust of wind wrenched the Z3's chassis against the river rock. Between boulders, the stream narrowed and gurgled, then fanned into a pool that reflected iron-bellied clouds and protruding tree limbs.

"Kara?"

"Sir, what're you doing?"

He kicked off loafers and dress socks. Ignoring Officer Lansky's inquiry, he stepped into the water. "I'm right here, Kara." He waded to his knees. Wetness crept up his pant legs as he picked his way over moss-coated slabs. A crayfish raised its pincers, then spurted out of sight.

"Here, Marsh." A thin cry of pain.

A splash of color arrested his attention, and he reached for it, gathered chiffon material from the tugging nubs of a tree. Kara's scarf. He remembered her tying it on before her departure on Wednesday morning.

"Here...over here."

"Coming."

He ducked his shoulders beneath a canopy of branches and found himself enveloped by shaded silence. And there she was. Kara was a shimmering butterfly, emerging from the stream's watery cocoon onto an extruding rock. Her arms were like wings, beaded with drops of water as they tried to stretch. She was created for flight; she was struggling to position herself.

"Kara! What happened? Are you okay?" Marsh steeled his emotions, surveyed the scene. "You must've lost it on the curve. The car's ruined."

She pulled herself another foot from the water and struggled for a secure purchase, for a point of takeoff. For her first—her final?—flight.

Marsh splashed toward her, and as he set a big hand on her shoulder, she moaned under the weight. He told himself he'd have to be the strong one. She needed him, needed his poise at this moment. To his astonishment, there wasn't any visible blood; the branches must've somehow cushioned her fall into the stream. To this point, she'd survived. But he had no delusions. She would need immediate medical attention.

"Can you move your legs?" he asked. Was it safe to lift her?

She shook her head.

"Anything broken?"

"Don't think so. But...not sure that I'm...going to make it."

15

The Elements

Josee watched Sergeant Turney brush a Burger King wrapper and a dog-eared manual from the seat to the floor. He said, "Sorry 'bout the mess. Are you gettin' in?"

"Scooter's gone."

"Chief told me over the radio."

"He left a message with this nurse lady, said I'd know where to meet him." She stood frozen at the open door. "As if I have a stinkin' clue."

"What've you got in your hand there?"

"Jesús Cristo," she mouthed in Spanish, her pinkie tracing the figure on the wooden crucifix in her palm. She slipped the object over her spiked hair onto her neck and tucked it beneath her sweater so that it hung between her breasts. "Nurse gave it me."

The cross and her vial of gel capsules. Nestled together above her heart.

Turney's brown eyes watched her.

"What're *you* staring at, mister?"

There she went again, tossing out her sticks of dynamite. She was such an idiot. This man had been so kind yesterday, sharing not only his own self-doubts but an understanding that they were battling something unusual and unnatural. Supernatural? Most likely. How long, though, had it been since she'd entrusted another person with her well-being? And a cop, of all people. Dangerous ground. She'd been lured before into positions of trust and had them melt away like quicksand beneath her feet.

Turney checked the dash clock. "Concerned about you, Josee, that's all. Let's find Scooter, then get you over to Avery Park to meet your mother. You get ahold of her?"

"Nope. Listen, it's your lunch break. Don't let me waste all your time."

"Chief's freed me to do what needs to be done. He wants the best for you too."

"Oh, right. Just enough leash to hang ourselves."

"What?"

"Forget it." She dropped into the seat. "Just wish I knew where Scooter was."

"How 'bout the park? He knew you planned to meet your mother, right?"

"Worth a try, I guess."

She guessed wrong. By one-twenty, Avery Park still showed no sign of her missing friend or her mother. Not that Josee expected any different. Despite the Subway sandwiches they had picked up, her stomach was knotted. She used Turney's cell to place a fourth and a fifth call to the Addisons, left two messages, then put her head against the window. On their way back to the Van der Bruegges, the sergeant suggested they stop by the police station downtown to pick up Scooter's bike and belongings that had been stored since yesterday.

"Maybe you'll find somethin', get an idea where he's run off to."

"You mean go scrounging through other people's stuff? Excuse me, Sarge, but I have a little respect. Scoot's stuff—I don't touch it." Actually, she had reached for his backpack once and been startled by Scooter's harsh rebuke.

Turney pursed his lips. "Hmm. Blame it on my cop instincts. I'm shameless as they come." He turned into the station parking lot. "You comin' in? Can't leave you in the car unattended. Nothin' personal. Just strict guidelines."

"I'll sit outside. Need some time to think. Some air."

Ten minutes later Turney wrestled the rusty bike and Scooter's pack into the trunk. He grunted and grabbed a hand to his biceps as a flash of pain crossed his face. With an apology, he headed back into the station. Said he'd be right back.

One minute later she heard the noise.

Tunka-tunk-tunk...hsss!

⌒

Turney's knee struck a wayward chair in his glass-partitioned office, his feet slipped on old newspapers and Snickers wrappers, and he scrambled for balance. An empty Dr Pepper can clinked against the desk leg. He fell into his seat. One hand clutched at his arm; the other waved away a fly.

How many years had it been? This hadn't happened since he was a kid. "Lord, don't leave me now."

On the wall, certificates and plaques offered vain praise. More fitting, Turney thought, was the Weekend Warrior poster that fellow officers had given him on his last birthday. The Warrior cradled a bag of chips and a six-pack, a fishing pole and net, and boasted a cartoon belly that distended an old wrinkled T-shirt. His eyes were apathetic.

Turney related. In this job he tried to sympathize. Tried to care. "The job's a struggle for me," he'd told his minister. "Sometimes it's easier to just apathize."

"Apathize? Is that a word?"

"It is now."

From boyhood, Turney had wanted to help others. Wanted to save the day. Be a hero. He'd worked out in the ring. Read Tarzan books beneath the bedcovers. With a little help from his mom's liquor cabinet, he'd even found a way to feel larger than life. But when push came to shove, he had failed in his role. Let that snake stare him down. Lost a baby. He should've pulled that cop's gun and stood guard. Stopped anyone from steppin' foot through that hospital-room door.

And as a grown man, where had he been when Milly needed him?

He'd earned his badge and the privilege of driving a car with a siren and spinning lights, but it did her little good. Maybe if he'd been there at the scene...

"Daydreaming again?"

"Chief." Turney straightened in his seat.

Chief Braddock stiff-armed the door shut, rattling partitions on three sides. "You drop off that Josee girl back at the Van der Bruegges?"

"Not yet. Swung by here to pick up her friend's stuff." Turney hid a grimace.

"Well, let's talk about her, shall we?"

"Can it wait, sir? I've got her sittin' out by the car."

"You know who she is, don't you? Don't tell me you haven't put two and two together. You wrote the report. You marked down her birth date. This is your big chance. The girl's here in town again, and look whose arms she's come running to."

"Jumpin' to conclusions. That's not the way it's been."

"Oh, it's not? Listen, Sarge"—the chief hooked his thumbs into his belt buckle—"I'm happy for you. Don't you back off the way you usually do. No. Let fate play its hand here and get back in the ring. Let's see ol' Thunder Turney go a couple of rounds. Put this behind you, grow up, and maybe you'll have a shot at taking my position someday. 'Chief Turney.' You'd love to see me retire. Don't tell me you wouldn't."

"Sir, what makes you so sure that Josee's the same kid?"

"Besides the obvious? Well, let's tick off the facts—"

"Can we play this game later?" Turney pushed himself from his desk. Cupped his arm. "If you don't mind, I gotta get out there."

"Katherine Davies. Remember that name?"

Turney lurched. The lady who'd been shot years ago. The baby's mother.

"You want confirmation of Josee's identity? Well, there it is. I'm handing it to you on a platter. Ask her the name of her birth mother. Then, while you're at it, ask her what her mother's married name is now. The lady's shortened her first name, but you'll recognize it. She's a prominent philanthropist, a respected community member."

"Chief—"

"Ms. Davies got married soon after that ugly incident. Did you know that? Or doesn't a nine-year-old kid read the wedding announcements? Ms. Davies is now Mrs. Kara Davies Addison."

"As in Addison Ridge Vineyards? Those Addisons? They don't have children."

"Why do you think Josee's here, Sarge? A reunion—that's what it is. Except we have a problem. Lansky and Graham found Kara Addison's vehicle this morning, a heap of metal at the bottom of a ravine. No sign of her. They're pulling in Mr. Addison to ask some questions." Braddock dropped a file on the desk. "Read all about it."

Turney shook his head. "Hold up. Why drag me into this?"

"Thought you'd like to keep abreast so you can mull it over with that imagination of yours. As for our little friend outside, I'll leave it to you to break the news."

~~~

Cross-legged on a strip of lawn beside the cruiser, Josee was filling her lungs with the scent of approaching rain. Even the blades of grass, infused with emerald luminescence, seemed to breathe it in. A seagull floated across the darkening sky, and Josee decided a squall must be headed inland; as a girl, she'd learned that gulls in the valley indicated stormy weather from the Pacific.

Hope you're somewhere safe, Scoot. Somewhere nice and warm.

Time for her prescription. As good a time as any.

With a saved chunk of Subway bread to help it down, she tapped a red capsule into her hand. She noted her vial was running low. Refill orders were shipped special delivery to her through a medical courier. This month's order had failed to arrive before her trip south. Would it be there when she went back to Washington? Without it, something as minor as a bruised heel could have serious consequences. She would bleed internally. She could bleed to death.

Tunka-tunk-tunk...hsss!

Behind her, a horn blared and tires squealed. Had someone blown a tire? She whipped around. Cars were streaming through a yellow signal, and an elderly couple in a Dodge Duster sat trapped in the intersection, afraid to turn, afraid to reverse.

Tunka-hsss...tunka-tunk-tunk.

The noise irritated Josee. She saw no sign of a damaged tire or collision, no explanation for the sound that seemed within arm's reach.

In the warmth of her palm, the gel capsule was turning soft.

Ignore the noise. Just stick to your routine.

Josee had hemophilia. She had read of others with similar conditions; nearly a century ago, young Alexei, the son of Russian Czar Nicholas II, had almost died from a standard nosebleed. Josee knew that her particular type of disorder had stumped the professionals. As with the other four hundred hemophiliac babies born each year across the country, her blood lacked essential clotting proteins. To further complicate her condition, she had developed inhibitors in utero that blocked the activities of clotting treatments such as recombinant factor VIII.

The doctors had tried everything. Only with constant blood transfusions had she been able to function with some safety and normalcy. State funds and foster homes handed her around like the damaged material she knew she was.

Then, after her ninth birthday, a local specialist had offered her and her newly adoptive parents an experimental treatment—one final transfusion plus concentrated capsules to regenerate daily the protein-rich blood that would pump through her veins.

Just like that, a new world had opened before her.

For the first time, Josee Walker was able to affix fresh pages in her vandalized scrapbook of memories, writing new captions to cover the past. Lights and needles, probes and scalpels—they were history. She felt big and reborn, no longer a damaged child with blood that ran thin as water through her veins, no longer a mistake rejected by nature, by biological parents and foster homes, by twisted fate. She was a girl who could now play with kids who had always been bigger, stronger, and less likely to bruise and bleed to death. She was a very grown-up nine-year-old with a vial of gel capsules that tasted like metal-tinged blood.

"Just one pill?" she had confirmed. "That's all?"

"One each day, Josee." Her adoptive father had smiled at her wonderment. "Take it with some bread, something to absorb it and ease your tummy. Soon it'll be second nature. But of course we'll be here to remind you."

"Do I have to go, you know, back to that place anymore?"

"The clinic? Your days there are over."

"No more transfusions?"

"No more. Nope, Josee, that was it."

With arms stiff at her sides, she leaned into his embrace and let tears spread over his shirt. She tried to lift her arms around his middle, but her arms had never learned that maneuver. Hugs were not part of her repertoire. Maybe with time.

Now on the grass, amid traffic sounds and exhaust fumes, Josee clutched the capsule in her hand and hoped her adoptive parents weren't too worried about her. She'd given them more than their share of grief. Wasn't really their fault she left when she did—she knew that at this point, accepted responsibility—but it'd broken their hearts. She'd seen it in their eyes, heard it in their voices.

The prescription. *One each day, Josee… We'll be here to remind you.*

She reached for the bread crust, lifted the capsule. These were her elements of survival. Like the elements of communion, the Lord's Table… His broken body. His spilled blood.

That sound again, very close. *Tunka-tunk-tunk…hsss!*

She chewed through the bread, set the gel capsule on her tongue.

Tunka-tunk-tunkkk! Tunka-tunk-tunkkk…hsssssss!

The movement beside her arrested her attention. First, noting how Turney's vehicle swayed on its struts, she thought passing cars were causing the disturbance. Then, decimating that theory, the trunk's side panel began bulging as though giant knuckles were rapping against the metal. Something was in there, and it seemed to want out. Seemed to want her.

—

"Whaddya doin'? I told you I'd be right back."

Josee looked straight into Turney's chocolate-kiss eyes. She said nothing.

"Josee. What is it? What'd you see?"

She shoved her hands into the rose-embroidered pockets of her jeans. They were standing inside the station's entryway. She felt so awkward here. This was the last place she would ever find Scooter; she was sure of that.

"Don't you hold out on me." Turney's voice was raised. "Talk to me. Tell me what's eatin' at ya."

She pressed her eyes shut and leaned into the cold wall. Into the ropes. Sparring partners? No, she had to keep up her guard and ride out Turney's flurry of questions. Here it came—the suspicion and judgments he had harbored all along. The prizefighter was back in the ring. Prancing. Swinging.

"Josee!"

That's right, big boy, throw a punch.

"Don't do this, please. Don't box yourself in."

Box? Yeah, you know what's going on here.

"Josee, are you listenin' to me? Best to talk these things out."

Bring it on. This girl can take it.

"I need to know. Did it do somethin'? Did it try to hurt you?" He touched her arm, and she opened her eyes. He softened his tone. "Sorry I'm so riled, but I should've warned you. Somethin' in Scooter's pack, I could just feel it. Could hear it hissing. By the time I got it into the trunk, my old scars were swollen like ticks and oozing again. Hurried back in there to clean it up best I could, but it wasn't much use." The sergeant removed his hand to reveal the pus and blood that had matted beneath the chevron on his sleeve.

Josee's fear robbed the air from her lungs. A convulsion shook her body.

God! I need you here. Where are you? Where's Kara? Where's Scoot? Did I come down here for nothing? Do something to let me know you're here. I want to believe! Please, help me believe.

She wanted to look back at Turney, but he would see right through her. His soft eyes might cause another meltdown. She wouldn't let that happen; tears would do no good. She swung her gaze and noticed a clump of people near the main entry. Two police officers stepped away so that she found herself facing the person they had brought in.

There was something familiar…

16

Seeing Ghosts

Marsh could see Kara shivering. Her usually gleaming hair was plastered to her face and neck, and her torso was twisted toward him. Beneath the torn fabric of her blouse, a wound went to the bone, colored blue-purple by the frigid stream. Had a branch punctured her chest? Or a piece of metal? In the cavity, her pulse throbbed.

"Marsh," she said, "can you...just hold me?"

"We need to get you some help. We don't have—"

"Please. I just want...to have you near. You understand?"

"Later, honey. Right now, I need to—"

"Wait. Where're you going?"

"I'm right here."

She must be hallucinating; he wasn't going anywhere. A stew of emotion rose in his throat. He tried to fight his panic. So this—he tried to prepare himself—was how it would end, with a tragic finale in the shadows of this gully. Sure, they'd had occasional problems but nothing they couldn't work out. Even an amicable divorce, if such a thing existed, would be a better ending than this.

Or was this the way she wanted it? Had she driven off the road intentionally?

Refusing to accept that scenario, he urged her to stay with him, to keep talking. "Tell me," he said, "where it hurts most. We'll get an ambulance here ASAP. We'll fill them in over the radio, get you all the help you need."

"I told you...before. Told you already." Kara's voice was feeble. Fading.

"Told me what?"

She'd told him nothing, not a lousy thing. Great, she really was hallucinating. Not surprising, considering she'd been out here through the night. If only she could provide some solid info—to empower him, to help him care for her. Isn't that how it worked? How many times had he tried to get through to her?

"Stay with me, Kara. Don't give up now."

"It's...no use. You're not hearing me."

"I hear you fine."

"No, darling. You're not...listening." Her light lashes closed, squeezed out droplets that ran from her cheekbones into her ears. "Marsh, just hold me. I don't need...your answers or solutions or...any advice. I need you to be here...with me."

Stretched over the rock, the butterfly stopped struggling.

Gotta hurry. No time to lose!

"Don't let go, Kara. Hey, I found you. There's a reason for that, right? Don't give up. I'm going to get help." Water splashed around his legs as he turned to head back. Knowing that her chances for survival were in his hands galvanized him.

"Hold it right there, mister." Officer Lansky's command broke through the canopied stillness. "Where do you think you're going?"

"She needs help. Looks serious."

"Who?"

"I found her, found Kara."

"Your wife?"

"Who else?" Marsh displayed the chiffon scarf.

Lansky stretched to take the evidence. "Where? I don't see her."

"Back here." Annoyance filled Marsh's voice as he maneuvered the uneven streambed. "We have to hurry." With numb feet, he stumbled forward, threw his arms out for balance.

"Stop right there! Back off a step." A drawn pepper-spray canister prompted obedience. "What're you blabbering about?"

"Kara. She's right here."

"Is that so?"

Lansky waved him to the side and sloshed ahead, boots stirring silt and pebbles. Marsh followed the officer's eyes to the rock where Kara had been. She was gone! In her place, on the flat stone, lay a frosted glass chess piece, the queen that was missing from his study. Sparkling and wet, the figurine bore a deep crack in her side.

"Am I mistaken, Mr. Addison, or is that a piece from your own chess set? Did you bring it along in the patrol car? For your sake, I hope this isn't some psychotic gesture, some sick version of a confession."

Marsh broke his astonished stare from the stone and lurched barefoot toward his accuser. "You *pathetic* wannabe! Tell me where my wife is!"

Their eyes locked. Lansky's fists tightened.

A sudden movement forced both men to duck. In the trees overhead, a wind gust scattered leaves, and a black-winged rook swooped down like the Grim Reaper's sickle, seizing the sparkling queen in its beak. As swiftly as it had appeared, it cut upward into the forest's tangled fabric and vanished into shadow.

The rook's cries, to Marsh's disbelieving ears, formed syllables as they faded away. *Kaw—kaa—ka—kar—kara—Kara!*

—

Four towns left to visit. Springfield was next.

In the Aerostar van, Stahlherz shifted his cramped muscles and bones. He felt drained by the human interaction at each stop and the miles between. He preferred the buffered contact of the Internet, yet the Professor had stipulated that he meet his recruits face to face. *No better way to motivate them, my son.*

At the wheel, Darius was alert. His third white mocha was in hand, his eyes wide and jumpy. By permission, he was tuned to the U of O's independent radio station.

Stahlherz consoled himself with the obvious. Although Crash-Chess-Dummy had deserted today's match, he had joined Steele Knight in a much larger game, one put in motion by Marsh's own birth in 1959. Fifty-nine...a superlative wine?

Marshall, I'll pour you out like the inferior vintage you are.

As if to hasten the day's inexorable march toward victory, a shape crossed the window and hovered along the van's passenger side.

Tappity, tap, tap...

"You've been absent since last night," Stahlherz said. "Thought you might never return." He reached to lower the window, but flapping wings curtailed this action. Beak first, a rook materialized through the glass, a primal force conquering the laws of physics and nature. The window remained closed.

"Steele-man," exclaimed Darius, "you see that? Time to lower my java dosage."

"Eyes on the road," Stahlherz said.

The rook's ebony beak was clutching a small, glittering object.

"What do you have there?" said Stahlherz. "A gift for me?" Black wings brushed the air, caressing his sunken cheeks before receding in descent. The bird surrendered its captive to his beckoning hand.

Kaw-kaw-reech!

Stahlherz smiled. "Job well done. Look at this magnificent queen." He studied the chess piece and, with his sleeve, wiped away the moisture from the creek.

Surely Marsh had been stunned to find her in the ravine. Placed by Beau, as part of their countermeasures, the piece had been waiting. The rook had also waited to confirm Marsh's encounter before swiping the queen back. Pleased, Stahlherz turned the figurine with a jeweler's attention to detail. Using the dagger from his pocket, he picked at the crack in her side. "Is this your doing, Marsh?" He clicked his tongue, then dug the dagger deeper so that chips of glass fell like frozen tears to the van floor.

Kaw-kaw-kaa...

"Yes, my friend. This queen represents Mrs. Kara Addison." Stahlherz corralled the rook in his hands. "Now you must wait for your next task."

The blackbird clamped its beak onto a handy finger, and Stahlherz yelped. Fluttering in a smoky haze, the creature flew into a tantrum of feathers, sparking eyes, and curved claws.

"You little devil!"

Scrrreech!

"I'm the one choosing the moves," Stahlherz said. Fumbling for the automatic window switch, he snatched at the bird and scooped it from the van. He choked down the bilious substance in his throat and dropped the glass queen into his jacket pocket.

Four more canisters to go.

He speed-dialed his cell phone. The display read: Crash-Chess-Dummy.

⸺

Kara must be dead.

Based on the accident scene, based on her unaccountable appearances and disappearances in his study and the ravine, it made the most sense.

In the patrol car's caged backseat, Marsh was miserable. His feet and pants were wet and muddy; his head was spinning; his chest was pounding like a drum. In the whirl of questions, he latched on to the one thing he trusted most: his intellect. With cold logic—or was it shock now moving through his thoughts?—he faced the finality of the moment.

Earlier, while awaiting the crime team back at the manor, Lansky and Graham had allowed him to make inquiring phone calls, and not one of Kara's friends or acquaintances had seemed to know where she was. They'd all promised to call with any news, but according to the team now monitoring the message machines at his estate, there'd still been no word.

So this was it. Death. A fact of life.

Kara: *Sign me out like a piece of your equipment.... You don't want me around.*

Had she seen it coming? She must've died in the crash, thrown from the Z3. Out there somewhere. On his fingertips, Marsh could still feel the chiffon scarf, an indication that she'd been in the car when it went over. Only a matter of time before they located the...before they found her. Would he be required to identify her? Would they suspect him of foul play? What would this do to the vineyard's recent growth?

So who had he seen in the study? In the stream?

A ghost, he decided. Kara was dead, and he'd been visited by her departed spirit or whatever you called such things. He wasn't sure how to classify this. He'd never bought into the idea of nirvana or some secondary existence as a soaring eagle in the vast Alaskan wilderness. Nice concepts, sure—concocted to shelter and sedate the masses. No. When he was gone, he was gone. He could accept that.

But now Kara might be gone.

How could that be? What about heaven? Did it promise something different? A scene of final judgment sat well with Marsh. This life had its demands, and people should reap what they had sown. One life, one shot. Cash in your chips.

What had Marshall Addison sown?

Lots of grapes. Some darn good wine. Enjoyment to others around the country. He supported Kara's charity work. He gave. He paid fair wages, always on time.

Please, God, open his eyes…

He echoed Kara's words for himself. He could use a little help here. He believed there could be a God out there somewhere, omnipotent but removed. Did the Big Guy ever get involved? Did he make exceptions?

Please, God, open his eyes…

Perhaps, in some inexplicable way, Kara's words had triggered within him a psychosomatic reaction. Perhaps the mind, with its untapped powers, was fabricating these incidents. Interesting theory. But it had gaps. How could he catalogue the physical evidence? The knotted J. Dunlary tie, the question mark of blood, the online messages, the missing glass queen, the bloodstains on his chair, the thieving blackbird that had swooped down at the stream, the painting in the parlor, and the note…

The note!

Officers Lansky and Graham were talking in the front seat. The downtown Corvallis police station was nearing. Marsh set his jaw. Eased his fingers into his waistband. Pretended to adjust in the backseat. With the envelope now slipped under his leg, he tugged the small scrap from within.

> Our imperiled queen, isn't she lovely?
> I'll call with the details of our transaction.
> Let's see how you play the real life game.
>   Steele Knight

Marsh's first reaction was relief. Kara must be alive! Whatever was wanted, he would get it. Anything to bring her back. He discarded the notion of police assistance as quickly as it came. On the chessboard, Steele Knight didn't succumb to flimsy traps and swindles; in real time he would be no less cautious.

Plus, Marsh had reasons for distrusting the local force. Personal reasons.

———

The policemen flanked Marsh from the car into the station, then paused at a desk to secure an unoccupied interview room. Before they could go any farther, a sharply dressed, manicured attorney rose from the orange chairs along the wall and strode toward them with all the confidence of a promo for the newest Grisham flick.

Over a handshake, she said, "Your message found me at the country club, Marshall. Didn't even tee up. Changed and shot right over."

"You are on retainer, Casey. I'd expect nothing less."

"I'll charge my green fees to your account."

"Been a long morning," he offered as an apology. "Appreciate your getting over here. I'm sure you'll straighten out these boys in blue."

"Afternoon, gentlemen." Defense attorney Casey Wilcox faced the officers. "Are you charging my client with an offense?"

Lansky eyed her with distaste.

Graham piped in, "Shouldn't take long, ma'am. Just a couple things to clear up."

"You're new, am I correct?"

"I'm a trained officer of the law. But, yes, my first year full-time."

Wilcox gave him a deprecatory wink. "Read up. Your job's done here. Unless you're actually charging my client, you'll have to practice your good-cop–bad-cop routine somewhere else. Let's go, Marshall." Her Stanford class of '87 ring threw ruby flecks of light at the lawmen's eyes as she gestured to the exit. "*Ciao* for now, boys. Why don't you go drum up some legitimate work for me? I'm sure it's out there."

Marsh prodded her. "I need a time frame."

"Time frame?"

"When do I get back the house and my Tahoe?"

"Officers? Could it be that you're searching my client's living quarters? And what about his vehicle? I hope, for your sakes, you can produce a warrant."

Lansky assured her that proper procedures had been followed and suggested the crime team could be cleared out by Saturday, possibly tomorrow if all went well.

"Should hope so, since you won't be covering Mr. Addison's lodging expenses or his business losses. Call my practice as soon as you get the all clear." Wilcox reached into a pocket of her fitted suit and, from a monogrammed holder, presented Lansky her card.

He used it to dig beneath a fingernail. "Will do, Mrs. Wilcox."

She dismissed him and turned to Marsh. "You need a ride, *mon cher?* I'll take you wherever you need to go."

"Have any sage advice, lawyer lady?"

"Corporate and criminal law—I practice both. But let's keep them separated in our relationship, shall we? Don't make me party to anything illegal."

"Have I ever before?"

"Nothing more tawdry than land disputes and workman's comp claims, but don't think for a moment I'll choose you over my job. Job's numero uno, and I mean that."

"Relax, Casey. I know you play by the men's rules. You always have."

She rubbed the back of her neck. "Let's see, we need to find you a hotel…"

To Marsh Addison, her words became side chatter. He looked across the lobby. For years, Josee had been a blur that haunted his mind; this morning, in a brass frame on his vanity, she had taken on substance and form. Here, compared to the photo, Josee looked older, more womanly. He was shaken by her presence less than twenty feet from him. What was she doing in the police station? Would she know who he was?

Do I want her to?

"Marshall?"

"Uh."

"You look like you've seen a ghost."

"I should talk to that girl over there."

"You know her? Your ghost have a name?"

"Ghost is right. I haven't seen her since… Well, let's just say it's been a long time. Doubt she'd even recognize my voice. Her name's Josee. Don't know what she's doing here, but I intend to find out. She may be the last person to have seen my wife."

PART THREE

One piece...
I greatly desire to find....
I must go...and learn what I can.
But the Enemy has the move.

The Return of the King by J. R. R. Tolkien

As you read what I have written,
you will understand...about this plan....
So please don't despair.

Ephesians 3:4,13

17

Deadline

"Josee." His clipped tenor voice wavered. "Did I get it right?"

She felt her insides melt away. Two weeks ago she and her mother had exchanged photos through the mail in order to recognize each other at the park. In one photo, this very man was digging through an ice chest on a pier, while Kara smiled thinly from the yacht behind him. In another, he was strolling along a fairway, a golf club tucked under his arm. Wavy black hair. Strong nose and jaw. Sun-bronzed wrinkles.

"Who wants to know?"

"I'm Marsh. Marshall Addison."

Beside her, Sergeant Turney's quiet presence gave Josee courage to scrutinize Mr. Addison's eyes. She ran her routine lantern check. Soot stains? Cracked glass? What kind of fire burned within? Storm gray and intense, the eyes were steady.

"You do know who I am, right? My wife's Kara. Your mother."

"Thought you didn't want to see me."

"I didn't," he said. "Nothing personal."

Nothing personal? Oh, that's priceless.

"I believe in moving forward," he clarified. "Life's too short to live in the past."

"Hey, you don't have to rationalize it for me. Do what you want." Her flippant rejoinder did nothing to hide her wounds. His words were sharp. She redirected the conversation. "Who's the lady over there?"

"Ms. Wilcox? She's my attorney."

"Hmm. Well, why hasn't anyone answered my calls? Is Kara avoiding me? You talked her out of it, didn't you?"

"Out of what? Meeting with you?"

Josee tilted her head and raised her eyebrows.

"I tried, Josee, I'll admit that. But she wouldn't budge. This reunion is all she's thought about for the last two weeks."

"Then why's she ignoring me? First, it was the housekeeper lady, then the answering machine. Hitchhiked all the way down here, and all I get is the shaft."

Sergeant Turney stepped forward. "Josee, somethin' I need to tell you—"

"So"—Marsh cut him off, his eyes still on Josee—"you haven't seen her?"

Turney persisted. "Josee, you gotta hear this—"

"Wait a sec."

"It's about your mother."

Josee wasn't registering his words. She was fixed on Marsh. "You know, I'm a grown girl now. If Kara was going to write me off again, she could've told me straight up. I'm big enough to handle it. Mind at least telling me how I can reach her?"

"I was hoping you could tell me the same thing."

Josee stared. Saw the storm gather in Marsh's eyes.

"Kara left yesterday," he said, "with plans for taking you to our beach house. Until this morning I thought you two were together. After everything else that's happened, I was surprised to find you here."

"Everything else?" Josee took one step back.

"She's disappeared."

"Kara? When?"

"Cops found her car this morning at the bottom of a ravine. No sign of her."

"If this is some scheme to—"

Turney said, "He's telling the truth, Josee. That's what I've been tryin' to tell ya. Just got word of it myself."

"No. No. See, that doesn't make sense. I just freakin' talked to her a few days ago." Josee aimed her anger at Marsh. "Maybe she ran out on you. What about that?"

"That's not what happened."

"How do you know?" Josee's mind refused to process the alternatives.

"Not her style. She's not the type."

"They never are. Never thought my own birth parents would throw me to the system. And before Scoot, every guy I went out with performed a disappearing act. What'm I saying? Now he's gone too. Nice. Very nice. In the span of two days, my entire world's been turned upside down."

"Know the feeling," said Marsh.

"This is wrong! Totally wrong." Josee moaned. "Please, God, open my eyes."

Marsh acted as though he'd been slapped. "What'd you say?"

Sergeant Turney broke in with an offer of assurance. "Keep in mind, we're doing all we can to find Mrs. Addison. Chief Braddock says that—"

"Braddock?" Marsh spat out the name. "What's he got to do with it?"

"It's his job, sir."

"He and I go way back. Don't like the guy. Don't trust him. Better if he kept his paws off this, and you can tell him I said so."

Alert to her client's change in demeanor, Ms. Wilcox pranced over on long legs in sheer nylons and rested a hand on his arm. Josee glared at her. Who did she think she was, touching Marsh in an intimate manner? Josee knew all about the game of female guile and was annoyed by this other woman so well equipped to play.

Ms. Wilcox said, "Marshall, we might want to take this conversation elsewhere. No offense to you, Sergeant—you're one of the few I respect in these hallowed halls—but my client here is all lawyered up. We're done talking. C'est la vie."

"Just tryin' to help, ma'am."

"Tell you what," she said. "Give us thirty, forty minutes. Josee and Marshall and I will grab some dessert around the corner at Barkley's. Then you can join us. A little give-and-take. Sound fair? I'd like to know on what grounds the department's chosen to turn the spotlight on Mr. Addison. He has no priors, no history of domestic abuse. You wouldn't want to stir up trouble where there's none to be found, capice?"

"Thirty minutes." Turney nodded.

Marsh said, "Coming along, Josee?"

"Is that an invitation?"

"I know I'm not your favorite person, but a cup of coffee won't hurt. I'll buy."

"Jonesin' for a cigarette."

"There's a market around the corner."

Ms. Wilcox said, "Marshall, this might not be—"

"Not asking you," he retorted. "I'm asking Josee."

Josee tugged at her earlobe, anything to occupy her hands. A rush of anxiety coursed through her. "Sure, whatever. I'll go. But I can pull my own weight, in case anyone's wondering. Something I need to know first though."

"Yes?" He dipped his chin.

"Just give it to me straight. Are you my father?"

Marsh's gray eyes wandered off. "Your guess, Josee, is as good as mine."

As they moved down the station steps, his cell phone chirped from his belt.

———

A determined voice broke through the poor cellular connection. Standing in the shade of acorn trees on a bluff over the McKenzie River, Stahlherz smiled. Time to play out this little drama between Marsh Addison and himself. Time to take the stage.

A: "Hello?"

S: "Crash-Chess-Dummy."

A: "Who is this? I don't normally answer blocked numbers."

S: *(curtains rise on a black-and-white set where two actors face off at center stage)* "This, my friend, is the voice of a longtime foe. Your deadline's just over twenty-four hours away. 4:30 PM Allhallows Eve. We'll meet at the Camp Adair monument."

A: *(soft, yet belligerent)* "What do you want? Do you know where my wife is? Is she there? Let me talk to her."

S: "I'll be seeing her shortly. Would you like me to pass on a message?"

A: "So help me, if you've done anything to—"

S: "No journal, no wifey. That's the way of it."

A: "What're you talking about?"

S: "I want your father's journal."

A: "First tell me this, what's your response when I play the King's Gambit?"

S: "King's Gambit Accepted."

A: "When I use the Sicilian Defense?"

S: "The Wing Gambit. It's my pet opening." *(a forced smile)*
"And a tricky beast to control, I'll grant you that. You're crafty,
Marsh. Well done. Now that you've tested my identity, can we
carry on?"

A: "Steele Knight." *(snarling)* "What's this about? How do you know
my name?"

S: "We're brothers in arms."

A: "You're no brother of mine! How'd you find me? Why're you doing
this? You have no right intruding into my personal life."

S: "No delays, Marsh. The end game approaches."

A: "I'm no patzer. I'll draw blood if I get the chance!"

S: *(bitter laughter, a glance at the transfixed audience)* "Chance. Funny
that you should mention him. He's the one who left me for dead,
the one who poisoned your loins, and yet you worship at his grave.
Read his journal. I'm sure it's all in there. I'm doing you a favor,
opening your eyes to the truth."

A: "What truth?"

S: "Chess…a parable of life. Study the board and learn."

A: "This isn't funny. What are you, some sort of online stalker? How'd
you track me down? How do I know you really have her? I want
proof, or I'm not doing jack for you!"

S: "Would a severed pinkie suffice?" *(a gasp from the audience)*

A: "I'm not laughing."

S: "No, I suppose it's not funny. Understand this, Marsh. I have every
right to be here, more right than you ever had. You are a usurper
born of a usurper. Question is, are you willing to face the past?"

A: "The past?"

S: "Glad to see you're paying attention."

A: *(stage left, the actor paces in thought)* "Okay, here it is. You ask Kara
where she and I are planning to go this weekend. A romantic getaway, just the two of us. You tell me the correct answer, then I'll
know you're for real. Then I'll do as you ask."

S: "I'll play along. I'll call you in a few hours with an answer. Of course, you should know to leave the police out of this."

A: "I can't avoid them. They think I'm guilty."

S: "No tricks, Marsh. I'll know the difference. Given the evidence now mounting—your bloodstained chair, for starters—it's no wonder the police suspect you in her disappearance. What'll you do when they come for you, when you stand before a jury in ankle chains, when your name's dragged through the muck by the media?"

A: "They have nothing to go on. No motive. No body."

S: "I can provide one, so don't push me. Hard to identify but irrefutably Kara Addison. Alas, after a basic match with her DNA—an object as mundane as a toothbrush can provide a sample—they'll be hounding you for answers. You'll be the prime suspect."

A: "I've done nothing wrong."

S: "You've lost sight of your queen. An unforgivable chessboard blunder. Yet I can provide you a means of escape: a man who'll not only take the blame for your wife's disappearance but will also provide evidence to reinforce his guilt."

A: "A pawn sacrifice."

S: "That's it precisely. Watch the news at eleven if you wish confirmation. In the meantime, locate that journal, or your game will be ended in mate. Stated more accurately, your mate's game will be ended."

A: "What if I can't find the journal? What's in it that is so—"

Stahlherz flipped off his phone. With this act concluded, he moved along the river bluff to his waiting van. Soon he would see Mrs. Addison for himself. An entirely different scene but no less engrossing for an audience weaned on the melodramatic.

Josee squinted through a cloud of smoke. So it wasn't the best cigarette she'd ever had—GPC brand, or, in Scooter-speak, Generic Pieces of Crap—but it did the trick. She took a final drag, crushed the end against her heel, and perched it on a brick windowsill. Waste not, want not.

"Coming in?"

Marsh held the door as Ms. Wilcox went into Barkley's to arrange seating with the hostess. His face was blank. It seemed, Josee noted, that his cell phone conversation had sucked the life from him. He hadn't said much in the market or during their stroll to this restaurant.

"You always sound so angry on the phone?" she inquired.

"My conversation a few minutes ago? What'd you hear?"

"Heard you sounding angry on the phone." She turned her eyes on him. Searchlights. "Anything wrong? Don't hold out on me. Is my mother involved?"

"Personal business," Marsh said. "Something I have to take care of."

"Right."

Josee brushed past him into the restaurant, caught a whiff of his cologne. Pine and cloves—earthy, yet urbane. An inexplicable yearning welled in her. She helped herself to a menu from the deserted podium with the piano light. At rosewood tables, business transactions were taking place over cups of Earl Grey. An easel proclaimed Viennese *Sacher torte* as the dessert of the day.

"Why'd you approach me at the station?" she asked.

"I thought you'd have answers about my wife. I shouldn't have dragged you into it. My mistake. I tried to warn Kara. Told her this was a surefire way for someone to get hurt—you go digging up the past, you're bound to get dirty—but she wouldn't listen. She's an idealist, has this rosy picture in her mind of how things'll work."

"She told me you were like this."

"Like what?"

"All heart. One big warm fuzzy."

"Josee, I'm trying to protect you." He paced, flipping a menu in his hand. "Trying to put two and two together, because whatever's going on, I don't want you mixed up in it. Might be best if we said our good-byes now."

"Have we said hellos?"

"Be safer for you this way."

"Oh, now you're worried about my safety?"

Marsh swallowed. Glanced at his polished watch face.

Josee noticed it was a Bulgari—oooh, was she supposed to be impressed?—and saw a snapshot of the life that might've been her own. Expensive fragrances. Casual elegance. NutraSweet smiles to hide the loneliness at the top. No wonder they shuttled her off at birth—just too stinkin' inconvenient, a cloud on their financial horizon.

Josee Addison? Little rich chick? As if I'd ever want that.

"You know, all I wanted," she barked at Marsh, "was one meeting, pure and simple. One moment in my life to look back on so I could say that I met my mom, that I know what she looks like. When Oregon's Measure 58 passed, I got the itch. Took me awhile to actually do it, but I thought if I could get a copy of my preadoption birth certificate, then I could track down my biological parents. Put this whole issue to rest."

"So you applied, and they sent it to you."

"Got my very own copy. Office of Vital Statistics in Portland. Had to do a little digging to find my mother. Hospital staff wouldn't give me squat, but I demanded to talk to the administrator, and then he found your name connected to the birth records, even looked up your number in the local directory for me. Could've kissed him through the phone. I just crossed my fingers, hoping I was on the right track."

Marsh said, "Are they going to seat us or not? What's taking so long?"

"Have you heard a word outta my mouth?"

He was peering back through the glass-paneled doors. Nervous.

"So you're not my father?" She knew that would snap him back. "Sure looks like your name on my certificate. Not that it proves anything, I know. But why're you so unsure? You don't remember committing the act, is that it? Not like I'm after your money. I just want an answer, that's all."

"Twenty-two years, Josee. That's a long time."

"My entire lifetime, *Dad.*" She breathed sarcasm into the final word.

"You're sensitive right now, I understand that, but let's not overstep our bounds."

From the far end of Barkley's, Ms. Wilcox shrugged and held up a finger to indicate one more minute till they could be seated.

Josee's patience was running low. "And what gives you the right to decide my bounds? Didn't you relinquish those rights when you signed the adoption release forms? Maybe you don't think you're my father, but Kara seems to have no doubt. Says you signed the same papers she did." Josee snorted. "She warned me you wouldn't want to see me. I mean, how stupid can I be? For a split second, though, back at the station…"

Marsh stopped. Looked up from the menu.

"I guess… Well, when you walked toward me, Marsh, for one tiny little moment I thought maybe something had changed."

"How so?"

"Okay." She picked at the sleeve of her sweater. "Here it is. I thought you might actually want to talk to me. Meet with me, same as Kara. Get to know each other, as if that's a crime. I hoped that—"

"Enough." The storm deepened in his eyes. "Let's stop right there. I'm sorry, but this is bad timing. Terrible, in fact. Things're going on here that can do nothing but cause trouble for you. Best thing, in my opinion, is that you go now before you get hurt. I'm saying this for your sake."

"For my sake? Unless you count my foster fathers—one of whom was a wife-beating alcoholic, a real loser!—I've spent almost half my life without a dad. Obviously, you have no clue what that's like. Zilch."

"Actually, my father died when I was five months old."

"*Your* father? Oh." She sucked air through her teeth. "I…didn't know that."

"His name was Chance. I have no more than a handful of pictures of him. He kept a journal, but my mother's never let me see it. I'm not even sure it still exists."

Ms. Wilcox was returning. The waitress in her wake wore black slacks, a white shirt, and a bolero tie. "We've cleared a quiet space in the back. Is your party ready?"

Josee said, "Maybe you're right, Marsh. Time for me to say good-bye."

She slapped her menu into his hand, snugged her sweater, then pushed out onto the sidewalk where she rescued her cigarette from the brick sill and touched it to her lighter before heading up the street. Time to go. Somewhere. Anywhere but here.

—

"Whoa now, where're you off to in such a hurry?" Sergeant Turney was surprised to find Josee strutting along the curb. "Thought you were with your father."

"Who says he's my father?"

"Kara's your mother, isn't she? They're married, so I assumed that—"

"You assumed. Know what happens when you do that, mister? You make an—"

"I know the saying. Cut me some slack, would ya? I'm not feelin' so hot." The gelatinous mass on his arm was draining him. Like a leaky spigot, it dripped from his scars. He felt depleted. With a hand rested over his belly, he said, "Now's no time to be runnin' off, Josee. Glad I caught ya out here."

"Sure, yeah. Glad to see you, too. Whoop-de-do."

He cleared his throat. "Let me talk to your…to Mr. Addison. Then I'll meet you back at the station. Ask for Rita. She'll show you into my office. Should be safe there."

"Safe? You make me sound helpless."

Turney thought of Scooter's backpack in his cruiser. "Little concerned, is all."

"Liar. I bet you're worried sick over me."

"Only this much." Turney held up two fingers that almost touched. "That's my story, and I'm stickin' to it."

"Nice to know *someone* cares. Past two days've been whacked-out. Kara's missing, Scooter's gone, and my father—or whatever you wanna call the jerk back there—refuses to claim me as his own. Like I care! Just be nice to hear the truth."

Truth? As a cop, Turney reminded himself that it was his duty to search for and defend it. In every conflict, every love scene, every birth, and every death, truth was a silver cord that bound that moment in time. Falsehood caused those cords to unwind.

"What'd Mr. Addison tell you? Does he know where his wife is?"

"Heck if I know. The man's cold-hearted. Forget him."

The sergeant rolled his wide neck, took a breath, and eased into Josee's gaze. Like a child losing his footing on a rope climb, his heart slipped. One notch. Then two. This woman… Sakes alive, was this what they meant by "chemistry"? Could it be chemistry if only one person felt it? Not that he had much to offer.

"Josee? C'mon, you gonna tell me what happened, what's got ya so riled?" She shrugged. "Nothing worth telling."

"And that's why you're poundin' the pavement."

"Did I say I wanted to talk about it?"

"Didn't say either way. Am I supposed to read your mind?"

"Like to see you try, Sarge." She set her hands on her hips.

"Oh, no you don't. See, if I could read your mind, you'd change it."

"Smart man." Her half smile boosted him up a notch. "But that's not the point, women don't want you to know what we think."

"What is the point?" Turney pretended to dig for his notepad. "Mmm, let me write it down. This could make me millions."

"Simple. We wanna know that you care. Just ask and just listen."

"Ask and listen."

"Really listen." Josee dragged a hand through her hair and left it there. "If you quote me on this, I'll deny every word, you hear me? Thing is, it's not even about reading minds, okay? Guys can be so ignorant—it's about the heart."

"Then let me ask you one more time…"

18

No Rest for the Wicked

Marsh Addison knew he had a reputation for sniffing out vulnerability. He was the king, sizing up his foes and his latest acquisitions. Whether in a boardroom or on the golf links, he could smell it like crushed grapes: tannic and tangy, with the promise of fermented surrender.

But this was different.

As he watched Josee retreat through the doors of Barkley's, he heard no call to arms. Questions swarmed in, and melancholy coated his mouth. In his chest Josee's vulnerability evoked an uncommon response. Long-submerged emotion rising from an abandoned shaft, cranked upward from deep waters, attached by a tattered rope. A water bucket. Swaying, sloshing, splashing…

And icy cold! I could drown in this stuff.

He released the crank, letting the bucket plunge. He could not indulge himself. Josee had misunderstood his reticence and, no doubt, hated him for it, but what option did he have. Anything he said would not only place her in danger but would also threaten Kara's release. Sure, Josee had made an impression. A decent kid. Sad beauty in her eyes. A wide, thin mouth that—

He touched his own lips and tucked away an observation. Not now.

With a commitment to the task at hand, he pivoted and traced Casey Wilcox's steps between the tables to a spot in back. Eased into a seat. Placed his order.

As the waitress moved on, Marsh excused himself to the men's room.

He was a man in control, a man with a plan. Time to call his mother. Hadn't she hinted at dark secrets all these years? If Virginia couldn't point him in the direction of Chance's journal, then Steele Knight would bring this game to a hasty end.

No. It's not over until I get Kara back.

"Mother, I need answers ASAP. Can you tell me where—"

"I knew you would call."

Virginia's flat response halted Marsh. He closed and locked a stall door, leaned against it with his eyes shut. "What else do you know? Now's the time to tell me everything…Dad's journal, your cryptic words over the years, everything."

"Did you try calling earlier? I was out playing tennis with Barbara."

"Don't brush me off. This is deadly serious." His thoughts thrust him back to that day as a thirteen-year-old in the drawing room, thumbing through the family keepsakes. *That journal's so faded, so scribbled—looks like the tattered remains of an old pirate's map… One day, Marsh. One day.*

He said, "I think today is the day you tried to warn me about."

"Have they contacted you?"

"Who? Mom, what is going on? Have you heard from Kara?"

"Not since she told me about her plans to see Josee. That's when I suspected."

"Suspected what?"

"They want the journal, I s'pose. Am I right about that?"

A urinal flushed. *Whooosh.* Marsh popped his head from the stall, saw that it was an automated system on a timer. He was alone in the rest room. "Do you know where it is, Mom? I need to get it. I could drive over this evening."

"The ramblings of a dying man. Hogwash, most likely." Defeat filled her words.

"You've read it! You knew this would happen, didn't you?" In the event someone should walk in, Marsh held the phone between shoulder and ear, ran the water, and slapped paper towels at his wet palms. "What's so important? Some war secret, a treasure, what?"

"I'm not so certain you're ready for it, Marsh. Chance feared this day would come and held himself accountable, but he was quite clear in his stipulations that the journal remain hidden. A last recourse and nothing less."

"Kara's gone! This is beyond worrying over a dead man's wishes."

"Marshall Ray Addison!"

He lowered his voice. "Sorry, but we're talking about Kara here. Someone's taken her, and I've gotta show up with the journal tomorrow night if I want to get her back. You never remarried, Mom. You never moved past his death. That's your business. But I'm not about to let your antiquated loyalties keep me from protecting my wife, is that clear?"

"Clear as it's always been. I shoulder my share of the blame. I used bitterness like a shield, holding even my own son at bay. For that, I owe you an apology."

"An apology?"

Marsh had never heard such words from his mother's mouth. After Chance's death in early 1960, Virginia Addison had nurtured Addison Ridge Vineyards through numerous setbacks until its grape yields carved their niche in the Oregon wine industry. She raised Marsh with all the care she could muster, his playgrounds ranging from warehouse floors to muddy vineyards to the burgundy carpet in the manor's wainscoted boardroom. She was there, albeit with little show of emotion, as his growing hands switched from Matchbox cars to Tonka trucks to John Deere farm equipment. In the early '80s, multiple hip surgeries had prompted her to relocate to a retirement community in Depoe Bay, but only recently had her emotional backbone begun to soften. Like the other war widows, her parenting years had been an amalgam of devotion and detachment.

Not that Marsh had minded. He respected her. He'd often heard her say that it was good for a kid to have a thick skin. Accordingly, he kept his own distance.

Just as she'd taught him.

"Apology accepted," he said. "Does this mean you'll help me?"

"You're not ready for this, Marsh. You don't yet know that which you face."

"I'll be ready. In a dog-eat-dog world, I'm the one they run from. Don't worry about me. What about you? What time should I come?"

In the receiver, Virginia's deep sigh was the cry of an inclement wind. "Be here around suppertime, why don't you? I'll have food on the table, and we can discuss it then, the manner in which your father's choices have returned to haunt us."

"No, Mom, my father died with honor. He was awarded posthumously."

"His journal tells the other side."

＊

Next he contacted his winemaker. "Gotta make this quick, Esprit. Can't tell you all that's going on, but it's urgent that you help me out here. You know, of course, that the police have taken over the manor. They suspect me in Kara's disappearance."

With the timed urinal flushes as their soundtrack, Marsh and Henri Esprit strategized responses to the inevitable media meddling and the potential gossip of the employees at Addison Ridge. They resolved issues regarding the vineyard's harvest schedule and suspended a number of lesser decisions.

"Our first priority, it seems, is to locate this Steele Knight character." Esprit's voice was heavy with resolve. "Let me assist you on this. I have an idea."

"I'll take all the help I can get," Marsh said. "Steele Knight's a frequent player in the gaming zone. Chesszone.com, I believe it is. Not a lot to go on, I know," Marsh said, "but it's all I've got."

"Has he done something...untoward with Kara?"

"That's what I need to find out. That's all I can say for now."

"Well, I've a nephew who might come in handy. He lives on campus at Oregon State, and if I understand the rumors, the kid's a certified computer whiz."

A father and son entered the men's room. Marsh ignored them. "A hacker?"

"Hacker, slacker, the terminology's lost on me. A good kid. I'll call him."

"Great. Okay, here's another idea. Call up the billing department at AT&T Wireless, and get today's activity on my phone, all incoming numbers. Tell them whatever. Tell them we've been getting prank calls that we don't want to be charged for, anything. You have full access to my account info, so you can act on my behalf."

"I always do, Marshall." Esprit's convivial nature could not mask his fervency. "I also act for your better half, Kara, a lady in every sense of the word. We'll bring the two of you together again if it takes every last resource at my disposal."

Highway 34 was carrying them over the coastal range toward the bay at Waldport. From there, it branched north to Newport and Tillamook, south to Yachats and Florence. Stahlherz calculated that, depending on the flow of logging trucks and motor homes, they'd arrive in an hour. Tack on a brief detour in Tidewater.

The ocean was beckoning. He could feel its damp and mystic pull.

Fifty-eight years ago—shortly before his birth—the canisters had arrived upon these very shores. The rugged Oregon coast. A fateful incident for all involved, and a moment of surrender for one young woman.

Why then had First Lieutenant Chance Addison turned against him? Stahlherz felt his mouth twist at the thought. Fatherless and nameless, he'd had his own identity tossed to the wind. Who was he really? Mr. Steele, Karl Stahlherz, Steele Knight—did any of these draw upon his true lineage? Yet he had risen above these questions; he had set forth a strategy for the network and was now implementing it, directing the pieces into position. He would channel the poison of resentment down the throats of his enemies. He would—

Kree-acckk!

A rook's cry cracked like a whip between his ears. Stahlherz ground his molars, refused to make a sound. He couldn't let his driver view his vulnerability; he was a man in control. "Darius, I'm going to rest for a bit," he said, "in the back."

"Sure thang. That be cool by me. Radio gonna bother ya?"

"Keep it in the front speakers. That's my only stipulation."

Stahlherz maneuvered to the furthest bench seat, where he stretched out on his back. As he admired his captured glass queen, he was surprised to hear strains of Mozart; perhaps young Darius was imagining a soundtrack for his first feature film.

From beneath the window's weather stripping, a breeze sliced over Stahlherz's exposed neck and bent knees. He shifted to his side. Put a hand over his throat.

As they say, no rest for the wicked.

A movement feathered over his arms and sent tremors through his body. The space above him clouded. There was something there.

A question fired through his head. *Where have you been?*

He knew the answer. He had never been alone. With a musty stench, black wings collapsed upon his face, and talons pried apart his lips. He fought against it. These beasts had been clamoring for dominion, and he would not give in. Karl Stahlherz was the authority here. He was—

"Urrra*aaggh*!

He choked on his own voice. He gulped. A thick presence descended into his throat—*the poison of resentment?*—and he hung his head over the seat to spit viscous yellow discharge into an old espresso cup. Stahlherz fixed the lid in place and set the cup on the floor.

Kee-ke-reeeacch!

Darius was rolling down his driver's window. "Yo, what that smell?"

Motionless on the bench seat, Stahlherz clenched his neck muscles and bit back on the gag reflex. Despite the classical strains from the front speakers, torturous shrieks bounced through his skull for the remainder of their coastal journey.

———

Marsh knew that Casey Wilcox was watching him with concern. Like an automaton, he ignored her and focused on his torte. One bite…chomp, chomp. Another bite. His mind was racing, fueled by thoughts of tonight's trip to his mother's place on the coast. He lifted the coffee to his mouth and saw Sergeant Turney step through Barkley's front entry.

This was the man Josee had said he could trust? A cop? Well, that was a joke to Marsh, considering what had occurred in the months before his and Kara's wedding.

Nineteen eighty-one… In wine terms, it had been a "bad year."

"Well, well," Casey greeted the cop, "if it isn't one of the blue knights."

"Knight?" The sergeant's chest swelled. "Been called worse. That'll work."

"You've already met Mr. Addison. Marshall is my client and a fine man."

Marsh felt her polished nails graze his wrist as she slid a hand along the white tablecloth. His mind, however, was on Steele Knight's warning that he not involve the police. What option did he have? If he shoved away from the table, it would make him look guilty. *Keep it short and sweet,* he told himself.

Turney looked his way. "Sorry I was runnin' late. Bumped into Josee outside."

Chomp, chomp…swig.

"She your daughter, Mr. Addison? Seems to have some of your features."

"Don't have an answer for you on that one. Why? What'd she tell you?"

"Very little of not a whole lot. Girl's heart is on overload."

Casey said, "I don't see that this has any relevance to Kara Addison's whereabouts. Is this what you came for, Sergeant?"

"Don't want to keep you from your investigation," Marsh said.

"But talkin' with you is part of that investigation, Mr. Addison. Mind if I take a load off?" Without waiting for a response, the large man lowered himself into a chair.

Marsh glanced at the door. "This might not be the best time."

Turney was perusing the dessert menu. "Mmm. All looks good."

Casey waved down their waitress, and Turney ordered the specialty. He asked for it to-go and refused Casey's offer to pay, claiming regulations. No gifts while on duty. He segued into the details of the case, doing an information dance with the attorney, both grasping for what they could without compromising their values.

A lady in jeans and a blouse passed. Golden hair brushed her shoulders, and Marsh felt his heart jump. Kara? Was she here? But when the lady turned, he saw she was a stranger. Was this how it would be, his mind toying with him at every turn?

The interplay between cop and attorney wound down. Casey turned to more practical matters. "Marshall will be needing his personal effects for the night." She tucked a strand of hair over her ear. "We'll be checking him in at the Ramada—under my name, to avoid press harassment. Would you be so good, Sergeant, as to deliver his items to the concierge?"

"Change of clothes, toiletries? Sure thing." The cop handed a card to Marsh. "There's my extension at the station. You need anything else, you can catch me there. You got somethin' to talk about, I'll answer or give ya a quick call back."

Marsh pocketed the card and fanned his gaze over the neighboring diners. *Don't even do this to yourself. She's not here. You must find that journal!*

"A few more questions for you, Mr. Addison, if you don't mind."

Casey held up a hand. "I mind. Sergeant, my client will be making a formal statement later. You and I both want the same thing here. We want justice to be served, and we want this missing woman—Marshall's spouse—to be found. He's had a long day, so let's take a breather and touch base in the morning."

"Ma'am, every minute lowers our chances of finding her."

Casey folded her napkin. "Conversation's over."

"The keys," Sergeant Turney pressed. "Did I ask you about those, Mr. Addison?"

"Keys?" Marsh was stumped.

"Down in the ravine," Turney said. "According to Officer Lansky, the ignition keys were missing. Did ya notice that? Who would've taken them and for what purpose?"

"Sergeant!" Casey interposed. "I know what you're doing, and my client has no obligation to answer. Let's extend Marshall a little time and space, *s'il vous plaît.*"

"Mr. Addison, you got my card. If you think of anything else, you let me know."

"I'll keep it in mind."

"Good-bye, Sergeant." Casey fired a warning look and rose from the table.

As if on cue, the waitress floated into the scene. "Ready for the check? Here's your dessert to-go, sir." The heavyset policeman grasped the box and stood, but in the process his hand toppled Marsh's coffee cup and sent black liquid gushing over the tablecloth.

"Hoo boy, sorry. Here, let me—"

"No problem," said Marsh. "Got it under control." He cornered the spill with his cloth napkin, and Casey stepped back to avoid staining her business suit. Sergeant Turney grumbled about his own clumsiness, apologized again, then squeezed his way through the tables of onlookers to pay his bill.

As Turney ambled through the restaurant exit, he slipped a glance over his shoulder. Marsh Addison was lifting a plate and shuffling the table's finery in search of his fork. Turney removed the borrowed utensil from the to-go box, wrapped it in a napkin, then, without fanfare, tucked it into the pocket of his uniform.

Well, looky here. Clumsiness has its rewards.

19

Double Negative

"We ain't touchin' that trunk," Turney said as he guided Josee to the cruiser.

"No argument from me."

"The Van der Bruegges have got more experience with this stuff. We'll let them take a look, but first off we're gonna make a little side trip."

Although the vehicle remained still and showed no damage to its outer panels, they circumvented the rear and hurried to the front doors. Turney set the to-go container on the seat. He reaffixed the gauze beneath his sleeve, and Josee tried not to look at the viscid green stain. This was her sparring partner; bizarre as it still seemed, she felt connected by their shared conflicts.

Josee Walker had come to Corvallis for one reason: to reunite with her birth mother. The perceived rejections over the phone yesterday and today had been bad enough, but she would've endured them ten times a minute, every minute of every hour of every day if they guaranteed Kara Addison's survival.

Her mother was gone? No wonder their reunion had been stymied.

Had Kara been thrown from her car? Abducted? Murdered?

Josee couldn't let herself imagine the possibilities. She fastened her seat belt. Earlier, for a solid thirty minutes, the sergeant's office had provided refuge—a spot to slump in a chair, fold her arms, and close her eyes—but now the presence in the trunk stirred her memories of that thicket. She knew she should feel comforted by the strength unleashed yesterday in her moment of faith...*a withered seed.*

Instead she felt weak. Shaken.

She felt like a kid with a match who, striking the pilot light of a long-dormant furnace, finds herself both scared out of her wits by the hot blast of ignition and unexpectedly filled with a sense of accomplishment.

Scared and filled. Fearful and triumphant.

Time to rekindle the fire? How long've I been keeping things at arm's length?

She clutched the myrtlewood figure around her neck. It was a symbol; that's all it was, a reminder. And right now she needed reminding. She'd always been fascinated by, even respected, spiritual power. God? Wasn't he the true source? Yep, she believed in a Creator who was bigger than herself, and she accepted the forgiveness of a Savior who had hung battered on that cross for her mistakes.

But she'd been burned by religion's heat. She'd seen others go up in flames.

Honestly, if God was the fire, why did people try to force him into man-made boxes? No wonder so many spiritual do-gooders burned out. Harnessing the heat for their proclaimed agendas. Touching the torch to their self-serving passions.

Shame burned in her eyes, for she knew firsthand the scorch of those passions.

Slumped against the window as the cruiser headed north of town on Highway 99, Josee saw how ryegrass nearly obscured the mileposts, and she was struck with the realization that she had lost her own bearings. She decided then to tell the sergeant that she couldn't carry on, that she was worn out and hungry and ready to head back to the comforts of the Van der Bruegges'. Before she could do so, he applied the brakes.

"Here we are," Turney said. Grass scraped the cruiser's underbelly as it rolled to a halt. "Didn't Scooter tell ya to meet him this afternoon? That got me to thinkin'—"

"Thinking? No wonder I smelled smoke."

"Yuk-yuk. Seriously, though, it hit me. Where would the kid go? The answer seemed clear as day. I'd bet money he's holed up right through there."

Josee followed his finger to railroad tracks and dense foliage beyond.

The thicket! No, I can't do this.

Turney checked the rearview mirror, then he wiped his sleeve across his brow, down his jowls. He forced a grin. "Almost forgot to mention, Josee... This to-go box, I picked it up at Barkley's. Some sorta dessert. Sacker torte, sucker torte—somethin' like that. Thought you might like it."

⸺

"Why here, Sarge? I don't get it." Josee slid another bite from the plastic fork. She'd lost her appetite, but the dessert delayed the inevitable journey over the railway embankment. Her toes had turned to ice.

"Why, you ask? Why not? How's that taste anyway?"

She mumbled appreciation through a creamy third bite. Tasted good. Rich chocolate and the hint of another ingredient, apricot maybe.

"To answer your question," Turney said, "it's human nature. Straight outta Proverbs. Might sound rude, don't get me wrong, but it says, 'As a dog returns to its vomit, so a fool returns to his folly.' Scooter's here. It's the obvious choice."

"You lost me. I mean, he's no glutton for punishment."

"The mind can be a devious little joker. I'm speaking from my own experience. See, years ago, I wouldn't admit I had a problem."

"Problem?"

"My drinkin'. Had friends confront me about it, but I refused to believe 'em. To prove 'em wrong, I'd abstain for days at a time. 'Course, then I'd go and reward myself for my good behavior—with another drink. I was convinced I had this monster under control, yessir. Other people needed AA, not me."

"And you kept drinking."

"Bingo."

"As a dog returns to its vomit."

"Knew you'd figure it out."

"So Scooter's going back for more. That's some twisted logic. I doubt he enjoys the feeling of venom in his veins." Josee closed the box. Tension knotted her insides.

"Well, take smokers for example—"

"Watch it, I am one."

Turney leaned forward, his tummy pressed against the steering wheel. "Look, no offense, but why keep lighting up when you know full well the things'll kill ya? Addictive behavior always spirals downward. That's the long and short of it. The very thing that makes you feel guilty is the thing you go back to when ya wanna feel better again. Which, of course, makes you feel guiltier than before, so—"

"You go back for more. Been there, done that." Josee gave a nod to Turney's belly. "Guess you're still dealing with it too."

"Whoa now, take it easy. We all have our demons to fight."

Demons?

From memory, eyes of flame ignited before her. Josee fought the urge to strike out. She had refused to address her basic fears, but now that Turney had verbalized them, she felt an instinct to fight. Her survival mode. She thought of how Scooter's friends liked to whisper about such dark things at their lakeshore trailer and of how, over the years, she had run across evidence of an otherworldly realm—good and evil, the chessboard of life. A plan at work. She didn't buy, however, the concept that she was some piece shoved around by divine decree. She had free will. She made choices and mistakes—more than her share! Yet, always hovering at the edges, forces seemed locked in a supernatural struggle. Earth's tension between heaven and hell.

And I'm caught in the middle.

But, she admitted, her eyes were now open. She couldn't act like she didn't see.

"Sarge," she spoke out, "do you know who I am?"

"Who you...what?"

She said, "Don't you think there's a plan at work? Here. Between you and me." When the sergeant dropped his head between his arms on the steering wheel, she tried a different angle. "Kara Addison's my mother, true. But you know what it says on my birth certificate? In black and white, no room for question: Katherine Davies. She gave birth to me in this city, in that hospital, in 1981. Freakin' Independence Day. And you were the boy standing outside her room—am I wrong?—trying to be a hero, but running headlong into something you knew nothing about. For some reason, you've let that drag you down and freeze you up. For some reason, I'm back, and this serpent thing's back. For some reason, Sarge, we've been thrown together. Who knows why? I don't even like cops. No offense, but it's true. Now we're stuck together, and we can't keep acting like it's all a big mistake."

"Gee shucks, we found each other." His arms muffled his words.

"I'm right, and you know it. I'm that baby. I'm the one."

"Where'd they take you, explain that. Why'd you disappear without a word?"

"Heck if I know. Way I understand it, there was this couple ready to adopt me, but after learning about my horde of medical complications, they backed out. I was this sickly thing. Had a rare form of hemophilia, some genetic anomaly. Doctors had to fight to keep me alive. Guess I just wouldn't give up."

Turney's head turned her way. "You're a scrapper, all right."

"Ah, you're just saying that."

He sat up. "So after someone attacked your mother and threatened you, the cops must've rushed you outta there, taken you to another location, kept it under wraps. Left most people scratchin' their heads. Left me thinkin' I was to blame." His fist came down on the dash. "Braddock! He must've known the truth all along."

"He's a jerk. Figures. Not that I was old enough to know, but it all seems to fit."

"So now you're tracing your biological roots. That's what brought you back."

"Something like that. When I was nine, a family up in Snohomish, Washington, adopted me for good. They're nice people, good people, but I'd already learned to keep my distance, you know. They made an effort to take care of me, help me with school, take me to church, all that. Not their fault, but I just never settled in. I was afraid to get close to them. Sounds crazy, right? But that's the way my mind worked. Then…stuff happened. From there it got ugly, and I bailed when I hit sixteen."

"Been on your own ever since?"

"Basically. Scoot and I've hung together the past three years."

"Boyfriend-girlfriend?"

"Off and on. Recently we've been sort of distant from each other."

Turney swatted away a fly. "So it is true. You are the one."

"I'm the one." Josee raised a hand. "Sounds so momentous."

"Well, you're right. This ain't no mistake."

"Double negative, Sarge."

"Exactly." His brown eyes fixed on Josee's. "I botched things once, and, God help me, I'd be a mess if I let it happen again. Double negative—that's what I'd be, all right. A zero twice over. I've lived with this long enough."

"So I'm your ticket? You want to use me to ease your conscience."

"Won't deny that I've packed my fair share of guilt—no matter how misplaced. You ever notice how logic and guilt just don't go together?" He ran a hand over his blond hair. "But I also care about you. Twenty-two years I've had you running through my thoughts, wonderin' what became of that baby. You were an unknown. A part o' me that slipped away."

"And now you've found me," Josee murmured.

"Not sure I had much to do with it. Think God's got a finger in this? He's got every hair on your head numbered, isn't that what it says?" To her surprise, his hand floated toward her. Two fingers, hovering...*ploink!*

"Hey!"

"Think he'll miss this one?" Turney held up a thin black strand. "Number four hundred and eighty-nine."

"Stay away, you wacko." Josee tossed back her head, expelled air from the side of her mouth. "You know, it was bad enough that Scooter snuck out of his room before I could get there. Not surprising really, since he despises hospitals as much as I do. But when Marsh walked up at the station and oh-so-nonchalantly tweaked my dials, that's when I felt myself starting to slide. You think I'm tough? Like you can just yank out a hair here or there? Well...I'm...I'm also a woman, okay?" She covered her face with one hand, kneaded her sweater with the other. "This isn't like me. I don't know what my problem is today."

"I'm your problem. Should've asked first, Josee. Sorry."

She saw him shift in his seat. He seemed like he wanted to set a hand on her shoulder to comfort her. The protocols of his job restricted him, no doubt.

"We're both on edge, Sarge. Let's start over." She turned her body and faced him, then added, as though any hesitation would keep her silenced forever, "You can't back away now. This is your chance, your shot at making things right. Forget what the guys at the station think, especially Braddock. It's time we do this and move on."

"Do what? I've caused enough trouble as it is."

"You said it yourself. God's mercies are new every morning, right?"

"Look at this." He pulled at his sleeve. "I'm wounded. Always have been."

She gave a slight tip of the head. "Join the club."

"Not that easy. You lose once, and you get this whole thing goin' in your head—"

"But here I am, Sarge. I need your help. You've got to fight."

"You want me to step back into the ring? Is that what you're sayin'?"

"Do I have to paint it in purple on my forehead?"

That brought a smile. Then Turney laughed. She'd never heard him give a real laugh. It was deep, rumbling from within. He threw his head back. The laughter was loud, contagious. Next thing she was giggling.

"Stop it. It wasn't even that funny."

He laughed harder.

Then, as though jealous of a joy unshared, the sounds in the trunk kicked in.

Tunka-tunk-tunk…hsss!

Josee and Turney met one another's gaze, then turned to look through the rear windshield. A pounding noise reverberated along the cruiser's chassis.

"Whoa, here we go again." Doubt was a dry riverbed soaking up Turney's mirth. He nodded, accepting the inescapable, and pulled himself from the car. "There it is, actin' up. What'd I tell you? Scooter's somewhere close."

Beau ventured back into the Corvallis library. The day had been as long and boring as those days in Mr. Rathburn's geometry class. Gotta stay cool, he told himself. He'd go in, check his e-mail again, and stroll back through the doors without a flicker of concern. What could they do to him—kick him out? His taxes paid for this place.

Okay, not *his* taxes. His dad's maybe.

At ICV meetings, Mr. Steele had instructed them on how to avoid leaving a paper trail. As an unlicensed contractor, Beau'd taken cash and never filed any forms. Government or otherwise.

Preoccupied, Beau nearly collided with an assistant librarian as he entered the computer work-station area. She was reshelving books. Cute. For a bookworm.

He pivoted like a revolving door. "Outta the lady's way. Pardon me*ee*."

She made a point of ignoring his display, and a thought ripped through his head.

I could hit her. Smash her right in the face the way I did that Kara lady.

After tapping in his password, he found the e-mail he'd been waiting on.

He checked the computer's toolbar clock. Couple more hours, then he'd send those bumbling cops into a tizzy. Would his sacrifice put a stop to the pain tearing through his temples? Sure it would. The claws were there to keep him on task, that was all.

—

Tunka-hssssss!

Turney took a step back from the car. Josee could see him in his boxing days, toned and not so heavy, crouched and dodging blows. She imagined those hefty arms counterpunching, delivering thunderous blows to an opponent's body and chin.

The sergeant winced.

"What?" Josee jumped through her door. "Something happen?"

"It's…nothing. I'm all right." Even as he spoke, he rocked back another step, clutching at his upper arm where the gauze was unraveling from the fang marks. Dripping. *Dripppp, dripppp…* His teeth were clenched. He was waving his fist.

"What can I do, Sarge?" His struggle was her own. "Let's just ditch this car."

"No." Turney batted away a ring of flies.

"Can't you call for a replacement or something? Let's not even mess with it."

"No! No, Josee, that's all we've been doing, playin' right into our enemy's hands. The intimidation factor. Not this time, no sir. Ugggh!" He shook off the pain. "No, I'm sick o' livin' with guilt and fear ruling my every move. Ugh. Time for…ughhh…time for Thunder Turney to climb back into the ring."

Josee would've cheered.

If she hadn't been so scared and worried that she might pee in her pants.

—

Kara Addison felt the warmth spread down her legs. She hadn't relieved herself since last evening in a bucket in the cellar's corner. The darkness had guarded her from her captor's stare. Now, he had been gone for hours, and she was alone with the spiders and dust and no answers. She almost wished for his return.

God, this is not what I had in mind. I thought I was going to see my daughter.

She couldn't allow herself to dwell on that. She didn't trust the words that might spill out in anguish. Her emotions dipped and rebounded. Dipped further.

I'm sitting here in my own waste! Is this your plan, Lord? I don't understand.

The smell of the urine pricked her nostrils. She felt so degraded.

At least the item in her front pocket was safe from the flow, tucked against her outer thigh. A pink knit cap. Provided by Good Samaritan for their newborns, this was Josee's original baby cap. Marsh didn't even know about this; it was Kara's secret. Her one link. She had hoped to extend it to her daughter as an offering of peace. Atonement. Evidence of Kara's long-term attachment to what might've been.

After all these years? God, I'm not strong. I can't keep up the facade.

She sobbed into her gag, letting the salt of her tears spill onto her legs and blend with the acidity of her shame.

20

Fianchetto

Marsh waved off his attorney's protests and gave his American Express card to the Ramada front desk staff. He'd also paid at Barkley's. Though Casey Wilcox tried to convince him that her firm could write it off, he insisted. Why not start an electronic trail? For years he had battled Steele Knight online. He had seen his opponent use every measure available to win and suspected that even now he was under surveillance. If Steele Knight had any intention of tracking his movements, then Marsh would counteract with strategies of his own.

Kara, wherever you are, I'm working on this. You're not alone.

He'd also utilized another tactic. Before dark he expected a return call in which Steele Knight would provide an answer to Marsh's test question: *You ask Kara where she and I are planning to go this weekend. A romantic getaway, just the two of us.*

There was no getaway. Kara knew this. Marsh had business in Paris, but he hoped Kara would catch on and provide a clue, anything to hint at her location.

"Marshall?" Casey was tapping on the counter. "You're all set for the evening."

"Good. Okay. Oh, hold on, I was hoping for one last favor, Casey."

"Last one?" She arched an eyebrow. "Better make it good, mon cher."

"Swing me by Enterprise Rent-A-Car. I need wheels of my own for tonight."

"Now there's a plan. I'm done running Wilcox's pro bono taxi service."

With suite key secured, he joined her in her luxury sedan. Overhead, blackbirds circled against swollen clouds. The meteorologists had forecast a storm, and even in a place as unpredictable as the Willamette Valley, it seemed a sure bet. For once, the weather psychics may be right. What about Kara though? Marsh stiffened at the thought. He hoped she was under a roof at least.

"Mind turning the music down?" he said.

"You want me to turn Kenny Wayne Shepherd down?"

"For crying out loud, I can't hear myself think."

"Your call. You're the client." Casey acted nonplussed. She merged into traffic. "But once I'm off the clock, Kenny's staging a comeback."

"That's one thing I like about you, Casey. You're never off the clock."

"Been known to make exceptions."

Marsh ignored her right hand now resting on his side of the dash. In the side-view mirror, he spotted an old mid-size Chevy. Was it tailing them?

"Marshall, why do I get the sense you're not telling me everything?" Polished fingernails lifted from the steering wheel, implying that Casey washed her hands of incriminating knowledge. "I'm your legal fire wall, your corporate shield. It's my duty to defend you, regardless of any misgivings I may have personally. But that's just it. On the personal level I like you, I admire you. Tell me I haven't misjudged you."

"You want me to find another attorney? There are cheaper ones out there."

"Well, *excusez-moi.* You get what you pay for."

"I didn't hurt my wife. There, is that what you're after?" Marsh added, "But I think I know who did."

"Then for mercy's sake, tell it to the police. Confide in me, if nothing else."

"After tonight I should be cleared."

"And on what basis do you say that?"

A pawn sacrifice...news at eleven. Good news or bad, if Steele Knight's words panned out, it would give Marsh a focus for his energies, a tableau on which to calculate his moves. "I'm done talking about it," he told Casey. "We'll wait and see."

"We don't have much—"

"Drop it." Marsh snugged his seat belt. "Take me to Enterprise."

"Aye, Captain," she said in her best Scottish accent. "I see, so you're going to play incommunicado with your own attorney. Give me the tools, and I'll go to work for you, but you're making that next to impossible. Very manly of you, this stonewall act. Doubtless you get some Cro-Magnon thrill watching me spin my wheels—"

"A cheap thrill, I admit."

"You're full of it, you know that?" She slapped at his shoulder. "I don't know why I put up with you. Something about a man who knows where he's going, I guess."

Knows where he's going? Considering the day's mysteries, that was debatable. *Let me be a lamp for your feet, Marsh. Let me be your vision.*

The thought came out of nowhere. A seepage of light. Marsh had to wonder if he was losing touch, talking to himself, offering inane advice in the midst of traumatic events. Or was this a remnant from his comparative religions courses, an echo of his professor's theistic leanings? Maybe one of Kara's phrases. She read from the Bible regularly but was gracious enough never to push those moments on him.

Marsh's phone rang, showing another blocked number. He braced himself for further threats from Steele Knight. Or, perhaps, a clue from his wife.

———

"Sir?"

"Rosie, your number's blocked. Where are you calling from?"

"Oh my, is it ever good to hear your voice. I'm with relatives. Investigators have been combing the manor since your…departure this morning, and we were told politely, but firmly, to vacate. An unpleasant turn of events. At my age, it's most shameful to be tossed onto the streets."

"They're desperate. Misguided but trying to do their jobs."

"Thankfully I have Li'l Corporal to keep me company."

Marsh thought of Rosie's dachshund, the way his tail wagged his tube-shaped body. She had brought Li'l Corporal along when she took the position. Like a well-meaning aunt, Rosie was a bit abstemious and old-fashioned but always attentive. He regretted, and took some blame for, the turmoil of her day.

"The team should be finished by tonight or early tomorrow," he tried to assure her. "Was Henri Esprit able to contact everyone as I instructed? How'd the staff and crew handle things? Did everyone survive the Thursday morning surprise?"

"Survive? An unseemly choice of words, sir."

"An expression."

"If I may say so, a little more caution might be in order. Before I left, the police appeared intent on uncovering something. Anything, perhaps. They were able to locate the art gallery I saw advertised on the station wagon, but the curator lady insisted she had no record of a purchase in your name."

"Isn't that what I tried to tell them?"

"Nevertheless, they wanted to twist that into an item of suspicion as well. The painting is breathtaking, but I must ask, why *did* you select that over a piano, such as we discussed?"

"I didn't buy it! Even you think I'm lying about this, Rosie?"

"No, sir, I don't believe so. But they found other items that gave me pause. The hand towel, I must mention that. The blood was still wet, and they found it where I'd set it with the laundry. I told them how you'd cut yourself. They sealed it in a bag."

"Great, just great." Marsh ran a finger along his cheekbone.

"Sir, I tried to be circumspect in my responses. I hope I haven't over-stepped my—"

"Listen, you did what you had to do, Rosie. Far as I'm concerned, I've got nothing to hide. Best to answer honestly, or it could come back to haunt me."

Haunt me? What am I saying? Those were my mother's words earlier.

"Sir?" Rosie squeaked. "I do have a request. I…well, I thought perhaps I could check the beach house for you, verify whether or not Kara ever arrived. I know there's been no answer. I tried ringing her myself. But it wouldn't hurt to look."

"Police've got it covered. Officer Lansky said they'd have a county sheriff check it out this afternoon. Not like those coastal cops have much to do."

"To be honest, sir, I do have another motive."

"What's that?"

"Well, as you're aware"—her voice cracked with an elderly woman's pride—"I've been ousted from my quarters. As it stands, there's little room here at my relatives' home. They're hosting a German exchange student, and I fear I'll only be a millstone around their necks. They've agreed to watch over Li'l Corporal, which is certainly one weight off my back, but…I suppose what I'm trying to say is that I…"

"You what, you need a place to sack out?"

"Yes, sir. Thought I could kill two birds with one stone, make myself useful."

"Sure, you're welcome to stay in Yachats." He tried not to chuckle. "You can straighten things up, give the place a good overhaul. Remember the mess it was in after we let the Brocks use it for a weekend?"

"I'll see that things are spotless."

"Good. With the bad weather, you won't have much else to do with your time anyway. You know where the key's hidden, right?"

"Knothole in the second porch post?"

"Third post. Drive safely. It's supposed to get nasty tonight."

—

"Almost there." Casey pointed to the nearing Enterprise Rent-A-Car sign. Her hand slipped to the console between them, and her voice eased into a non-work-related tone. "Hope there's nothing wrong between you and Kara. You're a busy couple, not much time alone. She does take good care of you though, I'm sure."

"She's missing, Casey! What're you talking about?"

"No reason to get defensive, Marshall. You're an attractive man."

"Not bad for a Cro-Magnon, huh?" He gave a primeval grunt.

"Speaking of which, you were a bit boorish with Josee."

"Boorish? So how would you have handled it? I offered to buy her dessert, and she refused. Stormed out. You saw her."

"She didn't want you buying off your guilt. On the witness stand—here's a pointer for you—even the innocent ones look guilty when they act cold and distant as you did. I'm sure Josee saw it that way. You looked guilty as sin."

Pinpricks of guilt? A bloody hand towel. A question mark of blood...

Marsh cast his eyes at his attorney. How much should he divulge? Anything he said could jeopardize the arrangement with Steele Knight. He could not risk that.

Casey was slowing. She hit her turn signal before the rental parking lot, and in the same moment, shadows moved over Marsh's legs and up his torso.

Feathery specters. Irritating blackbirds, like those circling at the hotel. He blinked against a spike of ice through his temples, and when he refocused, he saw a woman standing in the driveway.

Casey was turning. Going in fast.

"Watch out!"

"What?"

"You're gonna run into her!"

Marsh grabbed at Casey's arm so that the sedan hopped over the curb and skidded into the lot. The front end clipped the woman's legs and vaulted her into the air. Limbs flailed, and a head collided into the windshield. The body clung to the hood.

"Marshall!" Casey jammed the brake pedal to the floor, and the smell of burnt rubber filled the sedan. The car slid sideways to a stop. "What are you doing?"

"You hit her!" he said.

With a slow turn, the woman's face stared through the glass with frightened eyes—turquoise eyes that pierced straight through him. He stared back in disbelief. Had Josee walked here from downtown? She couldn't have known he would come to this particular rental lot.

"Hit who?" Casey pried Marsh's fingers from her arm.

"She's hurt."

"Who are you talking about?"

Dazed, Marsh watched Josee slump her head, saw her mangled body slide back off the hood and drop below the bumper. He jumped from the car and dashed to her aid. Casey joined him, crouching beside him in the hot breath of the car's radiator.

"What's going on, Marshall?"

"I swear, she was right here," he whispered. "I saw her."

"Who?"

"Where'd she go? She needs help."

"What're you saying? Are you speaking of your wife? Yes, we know she's gone but not for good. We don't know that, not yet—unless you have something to tell me."

He rubbed a hand over the pavement; tiny pebbles dug into his skin. The shape of his arm fanned back and forth across his vision. No blood. No broken glass.

Josee, was that you? Are you out here? Talk to me.

"If you know something," Casey said, "please don't hide it from me."

He looked up, uncomprehending. "Don't tell me you didn't see her."

"No, I didn't. There's no one out here."

Marsh pressed his face to the pavement, scanned the ground beneath the sedan. Nothing but oil drops, a wrinkled receipt, a black comb with a strand of knotted hair. Another apparition—was that all she'd been? A psychosomatic concoction?

Scrap it all. Why had he even reacted? He should know better by now.

See, Josee, this is what I was saying. The past gets dirty. It messes you up.

Casey was trying to console him. "Hang tough, Marshall. It's been quite a day. I suggest you get your rental car squared away, then head straight over to the Ramada. Relax, have yourself a drink. Take it easy for the rest of the night, shoot a round of golf tomorrow if you think it'll help. Perhaps I'll stop by later and check on you. Knowing you, tomorrow'll be packed full, particularly in light of your vineyard's downtime today."

"The vineyard? What about Kara?"

"They'll find her, don't you think? Explanations always seem obvious in retrospect. In no time, you two'll be back to your routine, back to meetings and winetastings and hobnobbing. As though nothing ever happened."

But something has happened. These glimpses—of Josee, of Kara.

Beneath the car's chassis, an object moved in the breeze. Caught Marsh's eye. He stretched his hand over the asphalt. "I'm sure you're right, but—"

"Of course I am. Women's intuition."

"If you're so in tune"—he lifted the object—"then tell me where this came from. Answer that one, lawyer lady."

She touched the glass figurine. "A chess piece, isn't it? A bishop?"

"Same style as the set in my study. Unavailable in the US."

"Scratched and a bit dirty, but it's exquisite nonetheless. You think it's yours?" Her green eyes locked on to his. "You do, don't you, Marshall?"

He rolled the piece in his palm, deep in thought. On the chessboard, a bishop could be hidden between pawns in a maneuver called a fianchetto. At the right time, it would slash across the board. This bishop, though… Where had it come from?

"Mine? Yes," he said. "I'm just surprised it's not broken."

As Casey drove off, Marsh tucked himself behind the wheel of a Bonneville sedan, a rental upgrade on the vineyard's account. Not much longer till dinner at his mom's place. He sat for a full minute, head swimming with the events of the past few days. He was overdue to vent on a bucket of balls at the driving range.

He merged into traffic, let the tide carry him along. In anticipation of the weekend's homecoming game against Arizona, OSU black-and-orange flags fluttered from car windows and antennas. Was that the same mid-size Chevy in his mirror?

Barkley's Restaurant appeared straight ahead.

What, he wondered, had compelled him back to this spot? What did he expect to see? Or whom? Josee was long gone. Petite in her jeans and knee-length knit sweater, she had turned away from him.

He increased the pressure on the gas pedal, and the Bonneville surged ahead.

Along the row at Trysting Tree Golf Course, golfers practiced their swings. Tempered curses followed white and yellow balls onto the driving range; intermittently, the sound of clean connection floated across the plain. With a borrowed pro-shop driver, Marsh hooked the first ball and bounced it past the two-hundred-yard marker. The second swing clanged into his bucket, sending white balls skidding through the turf.

He would've cursed on a normal day. Today was not normal.

He moved to retrieve the mess and saw that the balls had come to rest in the rough shape of a bishop. Wide at the base. Tapered. A notch at the top.

Skittering overhead, clouds pushed shadows across the range, and Marsh lifted his club in defense as he ducked. A shot of adrenaline raced through his limbs.

Okay, now you're losing it! Bye-bye, reality.

But if Kara was his queen, he mused, did that mean Josee was his bishop? His foe had told him to study the board and learn, told him chess was a parable of life. He couldn't believe how easily his life could be reduced to a game, but he was afraid not to heed the warning.

Refusing to entertain this folly further, Marsh snatched a lone ball and bent to tee it up. From his shirt slipped the exquisite bishop he'd pocketed at the parking lot. By some strange ability, it landed upright on the tee, daring him to take a swing. He felt angry. Helpless. He drew back the club.

"Ah, forget it!"

He flung the club aside, returned the chess piece to his pocket, and marched into the clubhouse for a drink.

⸺

Depoe Bay was over an hour's drive. Time to shove off.

"Good talkin' at you," said a short, balding man on a barstool. He raised a hand in farewell as Marsh headed for the clubhouse door. "We got your back."

The bartender concurred. "You take care, Marsh. Time comes, we'll be there. You'll be safer than asparagus at a fast-food convention."

"Nice visual, Don. Thanks."

"You can count on us." The bartender gave an exaggerated nod to underscore the esprit de corps Marsh had found over the years along Trysting Tree's fairways.

Tomorrow, he realized, it'd be time to cash in those chips.

From the parking lot of the golf complex, he watched a police car scream by, sirens wailing. His throat tightened, and his heart jumped. For a split second, he saw Chief Braddock handcuffing him, shoving him into a cruiser, arresting him for the murder of his wife. A common criminal. Dragged by circumstances into the gutter, hamstrung by a conspiracy that left him flatfooted in the path of small-city justice.

Not if he could help it. The game of kings was far from over.

In twenty-four hours he would face off with Steele Knight at the historical monument north of town. Camp Adair, the site of young Chance

Addison's training for war. How appropriate. Marsh knew the spot, scoped it out in his mind, and trusted that his father's journal would aid him in that encounter.

He stalked to the Bonneville, determined to bring his foe to his knees.

Headed toward the coast, he saw no signs of being tailed; nonetheless, he had the sense that his opponent was staying abreast of his every move.

Marsh asked himself, How much longer till the phone call? Till Steele Knight responded to his trick question? Had the note been a ruse? No, Kara was missing, and his opponent's knowledge was too intimate. How long had chess served as a subterfuge for this man's schemes? What motive would drive a person this far?

Every aspect of this attack felt personal.

—

"Keep the change from your white mocha," said Stahlherz. "Buy yourself *The Oregonian,* treat yourself to clam chowder—whatever suits you. We'll meet back here, but if I don't reappear by eight, check by every half-hour. We clear on that?"

"We clear." Darius took a gulp of briny sea air. "Aah, gotta love that."

"Don't wander far."

"No worries, brah." He slapped the van's hood. "This beast gonna be thirsty for the bounce back. You packin' a twenty? I can get her juiced up, ready to roll."

Stahlherz relinquished a bill, scratched at his brow. "I expect a receipt."

"You know it, Steele-man." The driver headed for a local diner.

Stahlherz walked up a path lined with dune grass. The Lincoln County sheriff approached. Had she come from the beach house? Stahlherz waved and tipped his head at her as the sheriff drove on. In the car's wake, the sand sparked like electricity on his hands and face. He paused to watch the breakers roll ashore, line upon line. Similarly, he was ready to roll with his plans of monstrous misery. He thought of his circuit along the I-5 corridor. All those lonely people.

Take a sip from the past... Tell me, how long will you last?

Swept by sand, a gravel road led him along rows of beach homes, over a dune, and into a section of fenced cottages where boats and automobiles hunkered under tarps to escape the coastal elements. His bones felt brittle in the dampness. His lower back ached. A quarter mile down he turned at a white-lettered sign.

Timberwolf Lane.

Chance Addison had given the name in honor of his 104th Infantry Division, the Timberwolves. His beach house here had been handed down to his son. How fitting that Kara should be held captive in this place, one more victim of the family sins.

21

Under a Spell

Scrambling up the railway embankment, Turney tried to ignore the sound of yesterday's yells. Josee's voice: *Go! Leave us alone!... Please, Jesus...save us.* What was he thinking, bringing her here? He wasn't exactly thrilled to be here himself.

"Hold it." Josee glanced up and down the highway. "Maybe we should wait."

"If I can drag my lard belly up here, you can do it."

She called through cupped hands, "Scooter, it's me, Josee. You there?" When no reply came, she said, "What'd I tell you? We're wasting our time."

Oh no we're not. Turney took a deep breath. *I can feel it. I can hear the hissing from the cruiser's trunk and smell the venom where it burned those holes in the ground. I've got pus oozin' hot and sticky from my old scars.*

Were those fresh prints in the gravel?

He took a step and lost his footing. His weight toppled him so that he landed on his side and speared down the embankment's backside. With boots ahead and rocks shredding the bandages on his arm, he arrived at the base in a mound of twisted legs and billowing dirt. Pebbles, soda cans, and decomposing litter cascaded down upon his wreckage.

"That was most bizarre." A male voice.

Bizarre? Rolling over, Turney moved the weight off his wounded arm.

"Man, how'd you pull off a stunt like that?"

The sergeant struggled to his feet to find a young man outfitted in a baseball cap, an unbuttoned plaid shirt over a black T-shirt, and khaki pants cinched with a cord of hemp. "Scooter. Thought ya might be out here."

"Took awhile getting here."

"Without your bike, I'm sure it did. The bike's in my trunk."

Scooter snickered. "Don't get me wrong, but that was funny as hell."

Yeah, tell me about it, kiddo. Hell laughs at our pain.

"Scooter!" Josee half ran, half stumbled down the incline. When he stayed put, she leaned into him. "Glad to see you, Scoot. You're alive. Where've you been? Don't tell me you walked all this way alone."

"Knew you'd track me down, babe. Can always count on you."

"Did you thumb it or what?" Josee smoothed his moonstone ring with her fingers. "You come out here on your own?"

"Walked, jogged part of the way, cut down the hill from the hospital. Wasn't that far really. Had to get outta that place. Bagged down for a while in an old barn."

Turney was sniffing the air. He moved closer to Scooter and detected an odor, something other than the counterculture scents of patchouli oil, sage, and humus that hovered about the young man. What was it? The smell of rot and decay? Could be anything, but he still felt troubled. A policeman's experience? A boxer's instinct? Or something else—something, for lack of a better word, from another realm?

A chill sluiced over Turney's scalp, and he found himself standing in an eye-of-the-storm calm. He'd been here before, long ago, clearheaded and seeing things from a different angle. *Okay, God, I'll try followin' your lead here.*

He looked to Scooter. "So'd you walk out here on your own?"

"What's it matter?"

"It was part of Josee's question. Should answer the lady."

"Kinda obvious, don't you think, big guy? I'm standing here with the two of you, aren't I? See anyone else around?"

"I'm just glad we found you." Josee ran her eyes over his face, over the swollen fang marks on his cheek. "You okay? Heard they operated on you, gave you a shot."

"Stuck me like a Kewpie doll. Hospitals, ack! Creepy places."

"Takin' off wasn't the best of ideas," said Turney. "Chief had a few questions for you. Plus the doctor hadn't released you yet. Left a lotta people worryin'."

"I'm all in one piece. Feel fine, see?" In mimicry of a sobriety test, Scooter took ten steps along a railroad track, hopped back down, flourished a bow.

"Could still be some delayed reactions."

"Delayed?" Scooter searched Turney's face with a hint of concern.

Josee stepped in. "Hon, your hair and your beard—I can't believe you cut them."

"Couldn't exactly stroll out the hospital doors unnoticed, so I went for a new look. Grabbed the clothes from the room next door—don't fit me right, but that's the way it goes—and the nurse gave me this." He tipped the baseball cap. "Not the Mariners, but, hey, the Angels'll do."

"Angels." Josee studied the logo. "You know, I met her. I met that nurse."

"Talk about a knee-high. She was shorter than you."

"Hardy-har."

As Turney looked on, Josee nudged Scooter and caressed his jaw. Now wasn't the time for petty envy, yet, for a flash, he wondered what her hand felt like.

"That's weird," she said. "Smooth as baby's skin."

Scooter said, "Just somethin' I had to do, Josee."

"It's different. You don't look like yourself. Guess you can always grow it back."

"Maybe it's better like this."

"Like how?"

"Not so…unclean."

"Unclean? It's not like you've had a shower anytime lately. What do you expect?"

"Don't want people to see."

"See what? People see what they wanna see. Isn't that right, Sarge?"

Turney nodded. In his head, sensors were going off, all lights and whistles. *Unclean?* That was a word you didn't hear often, except in biblical passages referring to evil spirits. *Don't back off now,* he told himself. He had to let this kid know that he was on his side but that he meant business.

"Did you come alone?" Turney persisted.

"Alone?"

"You heard me."

Scooter touched a finger to his cheek wound, and the sergeant resisted the urge to look away. With the cap's brim curled around his face, Scooter's eyes were those of an animal trapped in a cave.

Turney locked on to the kid's eyes the way he would in a boxing ring stare down. He tuned out the buzz of insects. "With God as your witness, Scooter, I need you to tell me the truth, need to hear you say it with your own mouth. You come alone or not?"

"No. There, okay, you satisfied? No one gave me a ride. I came here on foot. Is that what you're after, big guy, that what you wanna hear?"

"No one gave you a ride. But what about you? Did *you* give someone a ride?"

"Give him a break, Sarge. He just told you he hoofed it here."

Without breaking the stare, Turney raised a hand for Josee's patience. "Scooter, please answer me. You need help. That's what I'm here for."

"Don't have to answer to you." The decaying smell grew stronger.

"You're not answerin' to me, and you know it. You're answering to God."

"Maybe I can't help myself. You consider that possibility?"

"That may be the case, but we can start with the truth. One step at a time."

Beneath the afternoon's roiling clouds, Scooter's eyes were weary, and the puncture marks in his cheek were puffy and red. The stare down remained unbroken. The kid dropped his arms to his sides, ground the toe of an industrial boot into the gravel, and spoke in a voice that trembled with confusion and fear. "I'm not alone."

"Okay…" Conveying more confidence than he felt, Turney knew that he had won.

Scooter looked away and admitted: "They came with me."

"They?" Josee shuddered. She leaned away from her friend and took a step closer to Turney. "Sarge, I don't like this. What's that supposed to mean?"

⌇

Suzette's nerves were jumbled. She locked the gallery door, flipped the Closed sign around. Customers would be confused; she had never shut down early. She moved toward the rear exit, where she would set the alarm on her way out. With the lights off, the Indian bird masks took on a malevolent aspect. She gave them a wide berth, shouldering her tasseled leather purse with its intricate beadwork.

"Scoot, that's not even funny."

"Chill, babe. No harm, no foul."

At the front doors, John Van der Bruegge awaited them. A car sweater hung from his tall, thin frame. Kris joined him, buttoning her tw vest over a hunter green turtleneck. They looked so innocuous. Harmle teacher types.

"I'm outta here," said Scooter. "I'm not waitin' around for this."

"They're here to help us, hon."

"What's that supposed to mean?"

"To help us both, you know, putting us up for the night. Food and shelter."

"And why should we trust this Sarge character? Since when've we cared about some bloated old pig's opinion?"

"Wait a sec. If it wasn't for Sarge, you could be dead right now."

"You mean back in the woods at our campfire?"

Josee lashed out. "Where else?" She hated to react like this, but Scooter's attitude was unsettling, and he refused to look her in the eye.

"Blowin' it outta proportion, Josee. You say you found some canister thingamajig, but whatever it was, I don't think that's what got me. Look at me"—he lifted his arms as though submitting to a pat-down—"no missing limbs, toned abs, everything in place."

Turney rapped his knuckles against the side window. "You two comin'?"

Josee raised a finger to let him know it'd be a moment. She turned back, disbelieving her own ears. "Okay, Scoot, what about the bite marks?"

"These cuts? Is that what you're stressed over? They aren't bite marks."

"How can you say that? You watched that thing attack us, saw it happen with your own eyes. You just sat there, like you always do, and let it—"

"Time out. You don't really believe this line you're feedin' me, do you? I ate some nasty fish—that's what the doctor said—and it messed with my thinking, even made me start seeing things before it knocked me on my butt. C'mon, what do I expect when I'm out pickin' up day-old food, right? If you wanna call them bite marks, babe, that's cool by me. It's where I bit the dirt." He guffawed. "How's that work for you?"

"Since when have you trusted a doctor's opinion on anything?"

Scooter's arm tightened around her waist, and his lips brushed her neck.

"Reprehensible," she scolded herself. "Reprehensible, reprehensible."

Against her instincts, she had made a delivery and cavorted again wi
ICV. Why had she succumbed? Already the authorities were probing h
activities. She'd let that man's artwork cloud her perspective so. And t
money. Striving to make ends meet had weakened her. She'd angered the sp
its. She'd let the white man's ways overpower her Nez Percé reliance on t
blessings of the land.

Tattered Feather needed to set things right. The police would forg
her lies.

Suzette Bishop hadn't even entered the first number on the alarm whe
shape shifted from her left. Something struck her. Stars burst through
head in corncob yellows and berry reds and bone whites, and she dropped
the hardwood floor.

"Where are you going?" a voice demanded. "You think you're clever?'
She curled into a fetal position.

"Mr. Steele suspected you might take flight. Well, Tattered Feather,
time to clip your wings. Seems little birdie's feeling a tad too noble for her c
good."

In the cruiser's backseat, Josee squirmed. Scooter's arm around her waist
tated her. Why? They were together again after more than thirty-six h
apart, and she should be overjoyed to feel him beside her.

What had changed? Scooter's admission: *They came with me.*

At her back, the trunk had remained quiet throughout the journey to
Van der Bruegges, but Josee sensed a looming menace. If it weren't for
divider, she might have crawled into the front seat. At the sergeant's
seemed to be the place to be.

A cop, yeah so what? Sarge is fighting this too. The man's genuine.

"It's time." Turney killed the engine, then extricated himself from
front seat. "Time to deal with the junk in the back."

"Past four-twenty," Scooter told Josee with a nod at the digital dash
play. "Time to smoke a bowl, if you ask me."

She'd never known him without his beard, and it felt as though a stranger were forcing his affections on her. She pulled away. "You're hopeless."

"Only under your spell."

"Under a spell? Maybe. But certainly not mine."

—

Stahlherz mounted the steps to the front deck. Despite trees between here and the nearest neighbors, he knew he could be spotted. Small-town life. Everyone knew everyone. He moved like a man with nothing to hide and located the key in the post knothole—one more tidbit of information he and the Professor had accumulated over the years. He unlocked a sliding-glass door that faced the ocean, slipped inside, and relocked the door before dropping the key into his corduroy jacket. You could never be too safe.

Of course, if questioned, he would say that he and the Addisons were friends and they were letting him stay the weekend. In this town, it'd fly. Rentals and time-shares were commonplace.

"Help!"

The voice was a cry from the grave. Stifled. Flat.

Stahlherz knew from whence it came. He padded past a mammoth stone fireplace, down a hall lined with driftwood curios to the trophy room in the back. Here, stretched over the floorboards, a bearskin rug protected his prize. The captured queen.

At least Beau had managed to get this part right.

"Please, somebody help me*eee!*"

At the bar in the corner, he savored a stolen shot of Chivas Regal while rolling his glass chess piece in his palm. Marsh's liquor burned a trail down his throat, and Stahlherz hoped it would shrivel the beast within. Or slake its appetite at least.

"I'm down here! Down here!"

Stahlherz smirked. Outside, the wind howled along Timberwolf Lane.

He bent to the bearskin rug and peeled it back.

—

Josee noticed new vigor in Turney's step. Despite the dirt streaks on his pants and the sludge beneath his sleeve, he'd won a stare down.

Thunder Turney, you go. Don't let the naysayers drag you down.

As though aware of her thoughts, he turned from the steps where the Van der Bruegges waited and caught her eye. He winked. No, it must've been a twitch. He said, "You'll be well taken care of, you and Scooter. 'Course, you already know these're good folks, but Scooter doesn't look too sure."

"He'll get over it."

"Duty calls. Back to the grindstone." Turney hitched his pants.

"Wait up, Vince." Kris Van der Bruegge descended the steps with a generous slice of Amish friendship cake. The fresh-baked scent wafted over the walkway. "Sure you can't spare a minute? Coffee's brewing as we speak."

"Got work to do. Thanks for the cake though. Can't turn that down." Turney took an appreciative bite, then set the plate on the seat of the car. Josee saw him reach, almost as an afterthought, for the trunk latch. "Before I head out, we need to unload Scooter's belongings. John, I'm ready for that helpin' hand."

John gave a knowing nod and moved to the back of the vehicle.

Josee retreated to the solid brick walkway. From here she had a distant view of the trunk. She set a hand on Scooter's arm, felt a tremble course through him. She thought of the sounds she'd heard earlier, felt her blood throb in her ears with that same *tunka-tunk-tunk* rhythm.

"Go on, I'm waiting." John motioned to Turney.

"It's stuck...ooof. Yeah, won't even budge." Turney pulled at the latch again, then ran a hand over the back of his neck before circling to the trunk. He secured his bandages, winced, sorted through his keys. Josee could see his hesitation.

"Heyya," Scooter said, "take it easy everyone. What're you all so afraid of?"

A key turned in the lock, and the trunk popped open with the twang of springs.

John's sudden grin stood in contrast to Turney's puzzlement. "Is this what you expected to find, Vince?" He hefted a pair of hiking boots that were knotted together by the laces. "These must've been what you heard clunking around back here."

Scooter snagged his boots. "Mystery solved. So much for all the excitement, you guys." He pried his bedroll and bike loose and set them by the garage door.

For a second, Josee thought she detected movement. No, it was only the cinch cords of Scoot's bedroll coiling and twisting in the wind. Her imagination must be whacked. Playing tricks on her. When an ethereal moan snaked around the Van der Bruegges' home, she chose to blame it on the approaching ocean squall.

Test Tube

Strands of kelp waved in Depoe Bay's surf, and along the seawall the tide catapulted fountains of spume and water through a spouting horn in the rocks. On one side of Highway 101, onlookers taunted the elements; on the other, tourists huddled in tiny shops and cafés. Marsh considered stopping for a small gift for Virginia, something to loosen her tongue regarding his father's missing journal.

No, there was little he could get her that she didn't already have. Anyway, she'd see through that. She was no fool.

Shoot, it can't hurt.

He slipped into a parking space. It'd been a while since his last visit, and she was his mother, for heaven's sake. Let her think what she wanted. This felt nice for a change. He paid with his card, then continued to the gated retirement community.

"Marshall." She welcomed him in. "Punctual as always. What'd you bring?"

"It's nothing. Little something I picked up along the way."

"Son, what a beautiful candle. Gracious, look at these sand-dollar doves."

"Good for a stormy night like this. In case the power goes out."

"Practical to the end." She set the gift on the dining table, and her short legs carried her into the kitchen. Behind mother-of-pearl glasses, she still wore the wrinkles of sorrow and hard work. In the past year, however, Marsh had noted a serenity about her. Her countenance had softened. Her eyes, too.

"I'm glad you came," she said. "Thought you might reconsider, busy as you are."

"Mother. Don't you understand that Kara's missing?"

Virginia turned down the oven and, with seashell-patterned mitts, removed a Costco lasagna. A widow and a working woman, she had never taken to kitchen duties. Caterers and chefs had done the job. For her this was gourmet cooking, and Marsh expected nothing more. Tonight, food was a formality anyway.

"I've a number of items that need fixing around here," Virginia commented. "With my back being in the shape it is, I was hoping you might be of assistance." She pointed to a list on the fridge. "There's my honey-do list."

"Mom. Are you hearing me?"

"Hearing you just fine, Son. Are you hearing me?"

Marsh saw old patterns emerge, felt frustrations rise. "If there's time, I'll see what I can do. Come on, let's eat."

"Has to cool first. Always rushing ahead, aren't you?"

As she puttered about, Marsh moved to the living room where photo albums crouched beneath a coffee table. He studied the room. Wondered if Chance's journal was here. Flipping through an album, he saw himself in the vineyards: knee-high in mud, riding on a backhoe, cradling a basket of grapes. His mother was there too.

In the back pages of the second album, he found Chance Addison.

"Did you ever consider remarrying?" Marsh asked.

Virginia came and sat primly on the divan beneath the window. "No."

"He died over forty years ago. Why wasn't I allowed to discuss these things? Didn't you ever think about starting over?"

"Your father was enough for one lifetime."

Chance... The photo showed him grim faced and in uniform, lips pressed together in a long, narrow line, eyes looking ten yards beyond the photographer's lens.

Marsh pressed on with the issue at hand. "I know he did things that hurt you. I never wanted to think about it, but I know it's true."

"Yes." Virginia folded her hands in her lap. "Yes, there's some truth to that."

"Did he write about it in his journal? Is that why you've kept it from me?"

"His journal. Son, in the wrong hands, it could be destructive."

"Mother, you don't understand. I'm facing a determined foe. He's no fool, and he seems more than capable of hurting Kara. I can't let that happen. That journal is—"

"Lasagna's ready."

Mouth agape, Marsh stared at Virginia's retreating back. This was ridiculous. His own mother was holding hostage the journal's whereabouts. What did she want from him? What would it take to win her compliance? He calmed himself and decided to play along. One thing he had learned, Virginia never talked till she was ready.

He was deep into his third helping of lasagna—not bad, not bad at all for a store-bought meal—when she made her dramatic introductory statement: "You are ensnared in a deadly game, Son. Quite literally, a game of Chance."

Wooden beams groaned under the weight of the wind-battered house. The cellar's temperature had dropped, and the last vestiges of light had withdrawn. Cars crunched over gravel. Kara's jeans were cold and damp against her body.

Where was she?

In the dark, her senses sharpened. Through the oily gag, she tasted a hint of salt. Despite her tomb of concrete and dirt, she heard the slow-motion heartbeat of the surf. She knew that sound. A storm brewing. The sea was rising from sleep and pounding at its restraints. No wonder she hadn't heard it until now.

Ku-whumppp-whump...ku-whumppp-whump.

The ocean. The Oregon coast, most likely. Why had he brought her here?

Here in the cellar, Kara had replayed every phone conversation with Josee. She'd imagined caressing her daughter's face, touching her short black hair—black like Marsh's and thick. Why had Marsh always doubted her, his own wife? He'd closed off that section of his heart rather than face the sting of her mistakes.

She had tried to convince him.

He had climbed into a tower of stone and mortar. A self-exiled king.

God, for the millionth time, forgive me. I've hurt everyone close to me. Is this my punishment, down in this place? My father was right. I shamed him as a deacon. And you, the all-powerful God...you must be so disappointed in us. Waiting to pour out your wrath.

Ku-whumppp-whump!

Still, Kara thought, there were things her father hadn't shown her. He hadn't hiked with her along these dunes to see the stunning Pacific sunsets. He hadn't stopped at the tide pools to admire the colors of the sea anemone and starfish. God had another side, so clearly visible once she left the harsh contours of man's creation.

She loved the psalms. She even caught Marsh reading them now and then. The psalmists knew what it was like to question and struggle, yet wake to a new day beneath a fresh coat of dew.

Ku-whumppp-whump!

The psalms spoke of the Lord's fingertips on the mountaintops and his tears in the rain.

God must spend a lot of time crying—in this state anyway.

Kara was hungry. Dehydrated. Her last full meal had been Tuesday's baked salmon and Pinot Gris. That night she had fled in tears to the pillars beneath the portico because she had felt so exasperated with her husband. Now she would give anything to have him here, flaws and all.

No food, little sleep, the stink of her own body. How easily she was brought low.

Survival instincts shoved aside her other musings, and she struggled again at her restraints. With her tongue scraping against parched lips, she worked the rag from her mouth, bit by bit. The cloth ripped at her swollen wound. She tasted fresh blood. She pulled in her chin until the gag that had stretched in the wet air scraped down around her neck.

"Help!" she called out. It was a whisper actually. Her voice was weak.

"Help!"

Ku-whumpp-whump!

"Please, somebody help me*eeee!*"

To her amazement, she got a response, a foreign sound disrupting the auditory patterns of the day. She stopped. Listened. Footsteps. These were heavier than those of the kid who had carried her in. A slow shuffle.

"I'm down here! Down here!"

The trapdoor creaked open, and a middle-aged man hobbled down on stiff legs. Through the gap, Kara could see her husband's dartboard on the wall beside a poster from their '97 wine festival. Here? She had been brought to their beach house? Marsh had excavated this wine cellar but never completed it; she had poked her head in but never stepped down. Still, she felt foolish for not having recognized her location.

"You can stop yelling now, my queen. I already knew where you were."

What did that mean? Was this man here to rescue her?

He flicked on a light bulb and moved to her side. He rocked on his feet, tapping fingers at his pant leg. He pinched his nose against the stench so that he sounded like a man with nasal congestion. "What sublime timing. To think that you started calling for help even as I arrived. In cauda venenum."

With a dagger from his pocket, he plucked at her loosened gag and sliced it away.

—

Even as Marsh's hopes surged, Virginia shifted back to the mundane. She scooped her paper plate into the trash beneath the sink, then removed the lavender cellophane from her new candle. She held a match to the wick. It spit. Caught flame.

"Marsh, at my age, I s'pose it's only natural to mull one's shortcomings, but I failed you in so many ways. I showed you how to make a living, how to work hard and apply yourself, yet in the process I gave you no example for marriage."

"Twenty-two years, Mom. I think Kara and I have done just fine."

"You've made it work, yes. But you've had only the persnickety ways of a bitter old woman to draw from. You never saw the intimacy that a wife requires."

"You're a woman. You survived without it."

"Survived." She nodded. "That's an apt description." The candle sputtered. Beyond the window the October night was a sprawling black-and-blue bruise. "Survived much the same as Kara has."

"What're you saying?"

"You're distant from her. Arm's length. Have you created a space for her—"

"Yes!" He celebrated a minor victory. "I've just emptied the parlor for her so she can set up her own place. An outlet."

"I'm sure she'll appreciate the gesture—for now I'll leave aside the question of my heirlooms' whereabouts—but I'm speaking of an emotional space." She tilted the candle so that wax beaded over the edge in hardening patterns. "Son, you let your passion spill over her, but then you pull back, and she feels buried beneath your rigid designs. Kara's one of these doves. Fixed in place. Beautiful and decorative—"

"Okay, Mom, I understand the metaphor."

"But marriage isn't always meant to be tidy. Life's flames shape each relationship differently." Virginia swiveled the candle, this time allowing hot drops to roll into the sink until a sand-dollar dove floated free from its wax mooring. She caught it in her palm. "If you let yourself go, if you forget trying to preserve the outward image, your love can soften and free her. That's the sort of space she needs."

Marsh ran both hands through his hair and leaned back in his chair. The concern for his wife's survival pressed at his throat, tumorous, choking off oxygen. "Mom, I get the gist of it, okay? I see what you're trying to tell me. Do you understand that it's all pointless without handing over that journal? Kara's out there, as we speak. I've gotta get her back. Whether you think I show it or not, I do love her."

Virginia's face softened behind her mother-of-pearl glasses. "Oh, Marsh, I know that you do." She set the sputtering candle on the table and poured him a glass of water.

"Not that I'm perfect. I know I've made my share of mistakes. She's my wife. Right now, I'd do anything to find her."

"Love is a powerful weapon."

"Weapon? Guess I've never thought of it in those terms."

"Son, I've kept you from the light of understanding. In my ignorance, I hindered your view, fashioned you into a pragmatic man with goals and agendas. But there's much that you don't know. It may sound melodramatic, but hidden things are at work here. Elements that remain dark to our mortal eyes."

Dark to mortal eyes? If she only knew! How do I make sense of all this?

Marsh felt Kara's words blurt from his lips. "Please, God, open my eyes."

Virginia flinched. "Is that a prayer of your own?"

"Something I heard. Sounds crazy, but my eyes *are* opening. On some level."

"Marsh, use caution."

"Caution?"

"You may not like what you see." She changed gears. "Others have tried to find the journal, you know. I've reason to suspect that this place has been broken into on more than one occasion. The authorities have discounted my suspicions. I'm sure they have their fair share of fretting old women, but I know beyond a doubt that things've been tampered with."

"You've never told me about this."

"I s'pose not. You have your own concerns. Would you have believed me?"

"Does it still exist?" Marsh pushed. "You've hidden it somewhere else, I bet. Your heirlooms, the ones I had put in storage yesterday! Is it in one of them? That's it, isn't it, right under my nose all these years?"

"We'll have to continue this later, Son."

"Later? I drove all the way here, and you're not going to tell me?"

"My evening walk on the treadmill. Barbara and I meet at the fitness room and pace each other."

"Mom! I'm talking about Kara's life! First, you tell me that you suspected this would happen, then you ignore my requests, now you're going to leave? I need that journal. I'll tear this place apart if that's what it takes! Why be so obtuse when I need a direct answer?" Marsh could feel every nerve jangling along his arms. His wrath was a corrosive fluid eating at his thinking processes. The very idea of what might be done to his wife pumped him full of terror and rage.

"Your pent-up anger," Virginia replied, "will be nothing but a detriment. This is why I can't entrust you with it, Marsh. You're heading into a battle against an evil that you know nothing of. It will find that rage in you and use it against you. Only light can overcome darkness. Before rushing into conflict, you must first show selfless love, godly love. That'll be your best protection."

"Love?" Marsh snorted. "I've got my own scars to show from that."

"As I've said, it's also your best weapon. You can put it to use or fall back on your own sword while screaming vain threats at your enemies. I suggest the former."

"I do better with anger. I'll tear off the arms of whoever's responsible for this!"

"Your anger can never make things right in God's sight."

"I swear, if they hurt her, I could kill someone. Let God sort 'em out."

"Son, have you heard a word I've said?"

"Every word. Except for the location of Chance's journal."

That sent her scuttling down the hall. Marsh wanted to slam a hand on the table, to demand her assistance in finding the journal; he wanted to blame her for not telling him more of his father's past; he wanted to storm off before things went deeper. But he had to know the full story now. Nothing less than the truth. Her words echoed in his head: *Hidden things are at work here. Elements that remain dark to our mortal eyes.*

Marsh had both feet on the coffee table and ignored his mother's look as she returned from her bedroom in a powder blue sweat suit. He faced the antiquated RCA television that took up half a wall. Thirty seconds had passed since he'd turned on the power, and the screen still showed but a wink of life at its center.

"Why do you even hang on to this old monstrosity? Been around forever."

Virginia deflected the question with one of her own. "Do you still wonder if she's your daughter?" She held up a replica of Josee's photo. "Kara faxed it to me last week, the first time I've seen my granddaughter all grown up."

"I've seen it too. Don't need to look again."

"She's yours, Marsh. Have no doubt about it. You've made honorable decisions, and I respect you for that. I believe Josee's return is a reward for those choices."

"One photograph. Not what I'd call hard evidence. And what about you? What if someone told you that she was your child? Wouldn't you want some proof?"

Virginia stood motionless at the hall closet door. "I did lose a child."

"Mom, I'm not trying to stir that up again. Just trying to explain." Marsh spread his arms over the couch. "I saw Josee today, ran into her at the police station. Sure, when I saw her, I wanted to believe it. To have lived all these years without a daughter of my own? To imagine all I might've missed out on? It's hard to rewrite the past."

"Then you need to ask yourself"—Virginia started tying on her New Balance jogging shoes—"whether you are prepared for a revision."

"This is me you're talking to. Be prepared—it was my father's motto."

"Be back shortly. Stay as long as you like. Lock the door if you leave."

"Can't wait for long, Mother." The television was barely alive, and the idea of sitting idle was enough to drive him mad. "That journal's the reason I drove all the way over here. I'm trying to be patient, but without it I'm lost. That's my one bargaining chip."

"No promises on my end, I'm afraid. If you do stay, sure could use your help with a couple of items needing repair. If you have time. You saw the honey-do list?"

"On the fridge."

"Not going to think any less of you, but it'd sure be a blessing to me."

Marsh sighed. "What stuff are we talking about?"

"The television's the worst off. If you could fiddle with it, try to adjust it, that'd be wonderful."

He watched her depart. His first thought was to ransack the place, tear apart every room, look behind every picture. What if he sped back to Corvallis? Could he access the stored heirlooms? Would a night watchman let him in? Where, where, *where?* Why couldn't Chance Addison's ghost whisper a clue in his ear? Where!

He stood to go. Action was required.

At the sink, a sand-dollar dove perched. He thought of Kara…in his study, at the stream. Bound. Wounded. What had he done to her all these years? What had precipitated the events of the past few days? And he thought of Virginia.

Take a moment, he told himself, and think of all that your mother's endured.

Alone through the decades. Working, raising a son.

He spread open the photo album once more to consider Chance's photo. He slapped the covers together, stared across the room at the decrepit, one-eyed beast.

The old RCA stared back.

After perusing Virginia's list, he decided it wouldn't hurt to do her a favor or two. Shouldn't take long. If this was a test, he would pass with flying colors. See, he *could* care for a woman's needs; maybe this old dog *could* learn new tricks. He found spare bulbs in the pantry, replaced the burned-out ones in the hallway, reset the time on her digital clocks and VCR, adjusted the chain on the toilet flusher.

The RCA's faded picture tube. He unplugged the cord and wrestled the huge set from the wall. With a screwdriver, he removed the backing. Cobwebs and dust balls attached themselves to his sleeves, and his breath sent husks of dead spiders spinning into the cavernous innards. What'd his mother think he was, a repairman? He coughed. Poked into the darkness. Ran an exploratory hand over the outdated tube. As his fingers slid down, they brushed against fabric.

Fabric? Marsh closed his hand upon an object wrapped in oilcloth. His heart thumped. He knew already; it was Chance Addison's journal.

23

Secret Sight

"Did you enjoy that?"

"Good stuff. Moist. Never had friendship cake before."

"Glad to have you here for another night, Josee. A pleasure. Of course, the friendship cake is my daughter's favorite."

"Annalise?"

Kris said, "Yes. You remembered."

Josee had showered and changed into freshly laundered clothes. She smelled like a commercial for Bounce fabric softener. She wanted to sneeze. Without the facial hair, Scooter looked younger, goofy. He had unloaded his belongings in the room down the hall and followed John Van der Bruegge back to the family room. He shot her a look that said he was enduring this torture for her sake.

Kris answered the shrill of the teakettle and poured hot water into mugs of rich cream and cocoa. She dipped bars of dark chocolate into the concoctions, then handed one to her female guest. "Careful, Josee, it's hot. Oh, there I go again, a mother to the end."

"Smells good, what do I do with it?"

"You either stir the bar in until it melts or dip it a bite at a time."

Josee felt like royalty. This was a step above the dollar-store hot cocoa packets.

"Marshmallows?" Kris said.

"Oooh. The big fluffy ones?"

Kris produced a bag from behind her back, and Josee grinned.

The two ladies, cradling decadence in their hands, stepped down into the wood-paneled area where Scooter and John were shooting a game of pool over bottles of root beer. A far cry from the bars and pool halls Scoot had frequented in college.

Despite the Van der Bruegges' hospitality, Josee felt out of place in the spacious home, as if she might stain the carpet or soil something. In the past, she'd been yelled at for less… A rock-solid hand yanking at her arm, a work boot kicking her to the floor. *What're you doing? Get those filthy feet off my couch! What d'ya think, Josee, that you're some kinda animal? Here then, here's your dinner!* The dog's dish scraping across the floor. A hand pressing down on the back of her head. Her teeth bared, wanting to bite back. Cruel laughter.

Pages ripped from her scrapbook. The foster-home section.

"Make yourself at home," Kris invited.

"Do what?"

Josee turned her head and, as she did, tipped the mug and dumped a third of the liquid chocolate onto plush carpet. She blurted out an obscenity. In her effort to set the mug on a stool, the half-melted bar of dark chocolate collapsed over the rim and landed with a sloshy splat on the oak flooring beneath the cue rack.

"What am I doing? Such a clumsy fool!"

"It's okay, Josee. Here, I'll—"

"No, it's not stinkin' okay! What am I, some kinda idiot?"

Josee followed the self-condemning jut of her jaw into the kitchen and pulled off a handful of paper towels. She bit the inside of her cheek and punched a fist into her thigh. She marched back to the scene of the crime and mopped at the carpet the best she could. Kris provided her a spray cleaner and focused her own energy on the stained oak. To Josee's relief, the men, in atypical displays of wisdom, reestablished their interest in small talk and eightball.

"Sorry about that, Kris," Josee said, completing the cleanup. "Really, I—"

"I forgive you. Things happen, Josee. You know what, this place's been a gift to us, a true blessing. Isn't that right, John?"

"Absolutely." He gestured with his cue stick. "Five ball in the corner pocket."

"Most gifts are meant to be used," Kris said. "Nothing honorable in hoarding them for posterity's sake. In my opinion, it's the memories that increase their value."

"Yeah, but I don't think this stain's gonna—"

"That's quite enough, Josee. The gift to us is that we'll never forget you."

"Some gift."

"If I hear another word about it, you'll be assigned dinner cleanup."

"Okay, okay." Josee rolled her eyes, twisted her eyebrow ring. "I get the point."

~

"Ready for a visit to the ladies' room?" Stahlherz indicated the five-gallon paint bucket in the corner. When Kara said nothing, he moved behind her and started working the knots. He brushed aside her bedraggled hair. "I'll remove the ropes and turn my back once you're situated over there, but don't even contemplate some dimwitted escape. You're stiff as a board and no match for me."

Kara hitched her way to the corner and shot him a sulky glare.

Alert to any misconduct, he turned away at the base of the steps and, when she was done, ordered her back to the chair. He saw defiance flicker in her face. He waggled the dagger in the light. "You're scared, understandably. I don't intend to hurt you, but I'll do what I must to let you know who's making the rules."

"I have nothing to lose," Kara said in a cracked voice.

"Sit down! Now!"

"When're you going to let me go?"

"That's up to your dear hubby. Sit! I'm not going to ask again." He stabbed the dagger toward the chair, watched her ease her cramped body back into the seat.

"Wise move." He roped her back into place. "No one can hear you scream from here, and even if you slipped by me, which would be difficult in this small space, I'm more than capable of bringing you down with this knife in your back." From a grocery bag, he removed Wheat Thins, an apple, and a bottle of water. "Hungry?"

She fixed her gaze on the wall. "What do you suppose?"

Stahlherz lifted the bottle to her torn lips and let her drink until water dribbled down her chin. He wiped it away, then feathered his fingers like a black wing over the fist-sized bruise on her cheek. *Kaaw-kaw-Kara...let me care for you.* He set a cracker to her mouth, and she ate it. Fed her a couple more. Felt a smug curl on his lips. See how well he tended to her? The Professor would approve of this face-to-face contact.

"Drink," she requested.

"More water? Or"—Stahlherz toted a wine flask into view—"a little something to take the edge off? A well-earned reward for your patience here alone."

His captive shook her head.

"It'll help set you at ease." He removed the cork and put the bottle to her mouth.

After brief resistance, Kara let her lips part. She sipped. She pressed her eyes shut as though repulsed by her own decision. "That's awful. Hardly wine."

"Not as good as your husband's? Why'd you partake?"

"What's it matter? Are you after our money? What do you want?"

"Afraid Marsh won't pay up?"

"He'll do whatever it takes. He'll find me. Probably on his way as we speak."

Shree-acck! Kaw-ka-ka. Stahlherz laughed. Or thought he did. With the laughter came a bilious taste that raked his mouth and shot needles into his nasal passages. He twitched, shaking off the sense of being mocked. He would not be made a fool; he was here for a purpose and refused to be distracted.

"I'm not in this for money," he told her, bending to look her in the eyes— such round caramel eyes. Her fear charged him with excitement. She looked away. "Kara, you're the bait," he said, "for my traps."

"Traps? Please, let me go."

"Out of the question. Marsh has things that I need in order to reclaim my past, but I don't expect him to relinquish those willingly. Would rob all the fun. What's a game for but a little entertainment? Do you recognize this?" He produced the glass queen from his pocket and fondled it. "With his queen in my hands, he'll deliver what I want."

"What do you want? Why not just ask?"

"And Josee Walker will deliver what I want."

Kara's composure cracked. Her head fell forward as she released shock and fear and anguish through one heartrending cry. Stahlherz moved back.

Startled, but also drawn to provide comfort. He thought of peeling back her hair with his fingers and stanching her tears with a kiss. He had never kissed a woman other than his mother.

And that was years ago. She recoiled in repugnance. Never again!

"Let me go. Please. We can settle this somehow but not like this. Please."

Stahlherz listened. He watched Kara's neck muscles twang with tension. He did not mean to lie; that had never been his intent. But he caved to his compassionate side. "You'll see your husband and daughter tomorrow evening," he said, "and no one will be hurt. Once my conditions are met, the three of you will be together. I promise you that."

Hope returned to her eyes. A glimmer.

"Josee's safe," he said. "Don't work yourself up, my queen. You'll see your long-lost daughter. On my terms, of course, but a reunion nonetheless."

"What day is it? Thursday? I have to see her. She'll be worried."

"How noble of you, Kara. Of course, after your abandonment of her as a baby, it rings a bit hollow, don't you think? What drives a parent to do that? Answer me that, queenie. What sort of parent?" He thought of the years wasted, the privileges robbed from him. "Answer me!"

"Please. Leave me alone."

Stahlherz crouched to his prisoner's level. He tilted his head, birdlike, and stared at her. "Kara, you misunderstand. I'm here to care for you. I stopped by to see that you were fed. I'm concerned for you." He squeezed her arms. "Don't push me."

"You frighten me."

"But your rescuer, isn't he on his way? Isn't that what you told me?"

"You know where Marsh is, don't you? You know."

"At this precise moment, yes and no. I'm keeping tabs on him, shall we say." Stahlherz offered her the apple, another cracker, the wine bottle. "No reason for you to fear. See how I've fed you and made sure that you're well. I'm here for you."

"You've tied me to a chair. What sort of care is that?" She closed her eyes and winced as though expecting a blow. "Marsh takes care of me. Not you and your lousy Wheat Thins…but Marsh!"

"I'm sure you'd like to believe that. However—"

"Let me go!"

"I've already explained—"

"Let me loose. Let me out of here! Stop talking to me, you freak!" With eyes clamped tight, Kara thrashed her hair. "Get out of here! Leave me alone! Let...me...*gooooo!*" In the cold space, the crescendo of her scream moved wisps of cobwebs overhead and dislodged dust from the crevices. The sound faded, and she sat with shaking shoulders, heaving chest, and silent tears the color of breaking glass.

Frozen tears, chips of glass...alas.

Stahlherz gave a benign smile. "Take it easy now. I need to ask you a question, from your husband. He wants proof that I hold you captive."

———

After a vegetable lasagna dinner, they gathered in the living room where John situated a music stand and opened his velvet-lined oboe case. He wet the reed and began to play. Kris stretched on the chaise lounge and lost herself in the pages of an Anne Lamott book, Scooter folded himself into the recliner with all the unrest of a man trying to look restful, and Josee propped herself against the sofa.

Working on a poem. Scribbling in her sketchbook. Words taking form.

Veiled as yet, unfolding behind
Curtains of circumstance
Realms unseen, unrecognized
Players in the game of chance
Grant me this wish: revealing light
Yoke these eyes with thy secret sight

She thought about swapping *players* for *actors* but decided to leave it.

John concluded his piece. "There you have it then, a sampling of my classical stylings. My parents were first-generation Dutch. They played long ago—look at me, and you can imagine just how old they must be—in the

Amsterdam Philharmonic Orchestra. So it's hardly surprising that they wanted me to learn an instrument as a child. Now I'm a fuddy-duddy music professor. Usually I have only Kris to torture."

Scooter lifted a shoulder. "Not bad. Not exactly my thing but not bad."

"Scoot."

"No harm done." John winked at his wife and set his oboe back in its case. "A little resentment's to be expected, considering I whipped him at eightball."

Scooter fired back. "Home court advantage. Ya got lucky."

"Rematch in the morning."

"Better say your prayers, big guy."

Kris and John exchanged a subtle glance that set Josee to wondering, then Kris dropped a marker between the pages of her book. "Do either of you play an instrument?" she wanted to know.

"Me?" Scooter coughed. "I play the radio in the keys of loud and louder."

"And loudest," Josee said. "In his shop, he cranks it till the trailer shakes."

"Tell 'em what you can play, Josee. Give it up now, no holdin' out."

"Cork it." She focused on her pad.

"Do we have another musician among us?" Kris unfolded her legs and sat up on the lounge. "Aha, I had a feeling you were hiding some God-given talents."

"Count your blessings. You should be thanking him I don't have a violin nearby. My parents signed me up for lessons when I was in middle school. Played three years, just long enough to realize I knew squat. Haven't touched one in ages."

"Yeah, what's up with that, babe? Lettin' it go to waste—that's what you're doin'."

"Music's a tremendous thing," John concurred. "Has the power to touch us on many levels. According to Vince—Sergeant Turney—you two've had quite an ordeal the past few days, dealing with forces beyond your control."

Scooter shot Josee a look. She poked her tongue at him through her cheek.

"Music," John said, "has an innate ability to break into that realm."

"So go the rumors."

"What've you heard, Scooter?"

"Pink Floyd and a little acid can do wonders. Know that one firsthand.

You ever been to OMSI's laser-light show? What a trip, man. Far out." He flashed the peace sign to enhance the hippie lingo.

John chuckled. "Not quite what I meant, but you obviously know what I'm talking about. That's one way of tapping into the realm of the spirit. Although some try to divide physical and spiritual, it's not easily done. Like Kris's friendship cake. You mix up the ingredients and bake them, and then it's nearly impossible to separate them. They are one."

"So," Scooter scoffed, "we got a buncha little fruitcakes runnin' around."

"Friendship cakes. That was the analogy."

"My bad."

John laughed. "Sore loser. Should've banked that last shot instead of trying to slip it by the seven."

"You shouldn't have been wiggling your thumb near the pocket. Threw me off."

"Boys, boys." Kris held up a hand. "The testosterone's getting thick in here."

John waved his sheet music as a sign of a truce. He and Scooter smiled at each other. Then he said, "We do need to be careful when we encounter this other realm. A battle rages. Not all that we encounter will be pleasant."

"Scoot, doesn't that sound like something Sierra would say?" Josee felt a need to understand. "This friend of ours says that when she's been, you know, doing drugs, she's seen demons and ghosts, the Grim Reaper, some way-out-there sort of stuff."

"Nah, she just says that for attention."

"But some of the guys in your gaming group, they've said the same thing."

Kris nodded. "Doesn't surprise me in the least, Josee. Imagine the spiritual realm as a house. If you jump over the back wall, you're bound to land in the proverbial doo-doo, whereas the front door ushers you in with a welcoming light, a holy light."

Scooter flicked his fingers against the recliner's arm. "Here it comes."

"Let's hear her out."

"The truth is," Kris said, "many sorts of spiritual trespassing have been devised. Most of them are readily available, but none of them without repercussions."

"In both realms," John underlined.

"There're many paths to God. That's what I think."

"Sure, Scooter," John said, "Kris and I won't argue that. But once those paths lead you to his destination, you still have to knock on the door. Jesus alone claimed to be that door, and that's where people balk. They want God on their own terms."

"Hey, whatever works for you."

"Well, Jesus was either delusional, deceitful, or deity. Take your pick."

Josee added another touch to her sketchbook. She could feel a chill emanating from the friend beside her. She wanted to say more, to hear more, but his tension weighed upon her. *Hon, what's going on here? You're scaring me.* Sure, this was Scooter sitting behind her, but he wasn't himself. Something had changed. Something had him under its spell—*I'm not alone... They came with me*—and it was warring for expression on his face. He looked like a man in conflict.

Like a man who hated what he was about to do.

24

Games of Chance

Drawing nostalgic warmth from his father's handwriting, Marsh chased the story through the frail, tattered pages. He reminded himself to breathe as he plunged into each section. These were the words and thoughts of Chauncey Addison—a man he cherished but had never known.

The excitement fizzled as First Lieutenant Addison's war history came to light.

How much has my mother read of this?

From training at Camp Adair north of Corvallis, to harrowing accounts of battle, to grisly descriptions of Nazi prison camps and experiments discovered in process, the lieutenant pinpointed events and individuals that had shaped him throughout the conflict. He wrote of a beautiful young woman, a German in her teens, who had coaxed him into providing her a ticket to freedom…and much more.

As the war wound down and year's end drew nigh, I found myself conducting interviews at an internment camp, at Kransberg Castle outside Frankfurt. This camp was one of three for German POWs who claimed military or scientific expertise. Like poker players, these prisoners played their hands in hopes of finding pardon and a ticket into the US war machine. Indeed, to snub their skills was to pass them freely to the Russians. That was unacceptable!

Tabun, sarin—most of the Nazi gases were pesticide derivatives applied to human subjects, Jews primarily. With my training in wine-making and its corollary of pesticides, I interviewed those claiming to be Hitler's chemical warfare experts and weeded out those who, under pretenses, hoped to escape the judgments of Nuremberg.

Called "Operation Paperclip," our task was to identify and recruit the Nazi men and women who might benefit us in our opposition of

the Communists who now loomed on our horizon. A forerunner in
our efforts, Werner von Braun would go on as a catalyst in the
American rocket program. And so it was that, in our striving for the
"balance of peace," we plundered German mines and castles, recovering over 500 tons of military secrets and weapons research—much of
which lies in a Virginia warehouse to this day. But I digress. Perhaps I
shrink from the details of my own part in the drama.

My interviews took place in a cold castle room with a lone
table and chairs. There, on a sunny October day that stands firmly
in my memory, I encountered Gertrude Ubelhaar, the daughter of a
Bavarian chemist. Trudi. She preferred the shortened name, and I
obliged her. A striking young woman and a prisoner no less! To an
able-bodied man, Trudi was no easy creature to ignore, and I had
been without female affection for the three years in which combat
had been my taskmaster. I take no pride in my subsequent choices;
indeed, I suspect they are at the root of that which now overtakes me.

Marsh rubbed the back of his neck, thrashing at the surface of this deep
lake of facts. *Stay afloat and hold on,* he instructed himself. *File this under too-
deep-to-dive and you-must-first-adjust-to-the-cold.* But as he read on, the cold
only got colder.

Alone, on foreign soil, I found physical and emotional solace in
the arms of this eighteen-year-old woman. A means of personal survival, I told myself. Oh, the heart is a deceitful thing!

Trudi, too, had been ravaged by the war. Honored for her beauty
and pure Aryan blood, she submitted herself to der Führer's cause by
enlisting in the Nazi breeding program. Her duty: to birth offspring
for the purification of the Fatherland. Yet, when she proved barren, she
suffered for it at the hands of the SS men who had been her lovers.
They violated her. They taunted her about her infertility as they continued their domination of her.

Most horrific of all, her biochemist father did nothing. Turning his head and thus toeing the party line, Doktor Ubelhaar said nary a word. He buried his nose in formulas and binary experiments, quietly carrying on with his abominable work. His silence, however, produced disturbing results. He fell victim to an accident. Officially, his death was attributed to the bite of an African boomslang, a species of snake he often milked for experimentation with its potent hemotoxins. Unofficially, he had been murdered.

How, one may ask, do I have knowledge of these matters? During an interview with me, Trudi confessed her guilt. Without first warning the Doktor, she had released the snakes in his lab. Her patriotic father had betrayed her trust, abandoned her to the abuse of the SS. She left it to the gods to decide his fate.

On the sofa, Marsh let the words sink in. The tempest pounded away outside, the sounds of surf and wind and thunder tearing through his mother's house. He was a seasick man on a lurching ship. The weather confirmed the queasy knot in his stomach. When his cell phone rang, he let it forward to voice mail while he read on.

Appalled as I was, the story of Trudi Ubelhaar's trampled trust bound me to her in unholy obligation. Her father had turned his back. So had her Fatherland. She explained how she had been found guilty by association, imprisoned at Kransberg Castle for her affiliation with the godforsaken breeding program. The injustice was obvious. Thereafter, she and I met in utmost confidentiality, joined by a loneliness and heartache that fueled our desire. Conditions in the camp were poor, and among the US troops that stood guard, anti-German tensions ran high. Our trysts were fraught with risk.

Then I came upon a means to assist her. The Pentagon, without President Truman's endorsement, would soon begin shipping validated Nazi recruits to American soil, listing them as cargo to avoid the violation of international agreements. At its apex, Operation Paperclip would house and employ hundreds of Germans at government facilities around the United States, tapping them for knowledge and deadly expertise. Of these "assets," many had been involved directly in the wholesale slaughter of the Jewish people.

Based on Trudi's respectable knowledge of chemistry—she was quite the understudy to her father—I marked her file "no derogatory information," and, one among many, she was transported across the sea as part of this operation. This, I thought, would be the bittersweet conclusion to a relationship rooted in betrayal. I was a married man. Already I wondered how I could return to my young bride with joy.

Marsh huffed in disbelief. Did Virginia know about this? Of course she did. The weight of lies and disloyalty dragged him beneath the surface and flooded his lungs. He read on. Took gulps between paragraphs.

Though Trudi's arrival was without fanfare, it caught me unawares. In the cold of November 1945, she arrived by ship upon Oregon shores. At the expense of the US Army, she was to be housed in Benton County, Washington, and employed at a chemical facility across the Oregon border. With minimal fuss, however, she worked herself into the good graces of an army doctor and had her papers altered so that a train dropped her instead at Camp Adair in Benton County, Oregon. My very own backyard.

The error would soon be corrected, but taking advantage, she sent the doctor to inform me of her arrival. She demanded a rendezvous. Having made it clear while still in Germany that our relationship was cordially concluded, I was loath to accommodate her. Yet, in fear that she might thus break our oath of silence and threaten my marriage, I proceeded against my better judgment. A harmless compromise, it seemed. With the perspective of the past at my side, I see now that I should've heeded the lightkeeper's warnings. A crusty ol' man such as he? He was there on the night she arrived. He saw things. But I scorned his words, to my own detriment.

In short order, Trudi petitioned me to renew our bond and went so far as to promise she would deliver to me a child. This, in light of her treatment at the hands of the SS, was beyond her physical ability to fulfill, and I convinced her that she must find a new life here in America.

Though slow to accept this, she eventually vowed to maintain our secrets and, in an act of good faith and "as a parting gift of love," gave me a single canister appropriated from the shipment of her father's top secret chemical supplies. As a pesticide, she insisted, it would rid my property of undesirable insects and ensure success in my winemaking ventures. Cognizant of the remarkable results produced by these pesticides in the vineyards of Germany's Rhone Valley, long before Hitler's henchmen decided to try them on human "vermin," I had secretly hoped for such an opportunity. Trudi, to alleviate any remaining concerns, explained that the contents of this canister were essentially harmless. It was a binary weapon, created to maximize the boomslang venom's effect when mixed with a chemical accelerant. But it was inert. To further my hopes at Addison Ridge, I accepted the gift.

"Gift." In German, it means "poison." I should've taken note. Blinded as I was by the flattery of lurid memories, I pressed forward with my vineyard aspirations. Perhaps, I reasoned, this was an opportunity to pursue the dreams I believed I had lost during the war. Perhaps it was a gift from above, honoring my return to my wife by marriage, for, indeed, Virginia remains the woman I love, and I harbor deep regrets for my indiscretions. Imagine my relief when she became heavy with child. I assumed that my sins had been pardoned and the heavens once more were smiling down.

Two factors swayed my thoughts in the opposite direction. The first was the loss of our firstborn son. From the waiting room, I detected a flurry of activity that did not bode well, but I was unable to determine the cause until a nurse was dispatched to inform me of the news: Our son had died with the umbilical cord about his neck. A burden beyond comprehension! Virginia took it hard, and I suffered beneath the burden of guilt. I was paying for my sins. I suppose I always will.

Mesmerized, Marsh turned a brittle page and continued.

The second factor, and one I fear is related to my own blind ambition, is my declining health. Despite the doctor's attempts to placate Virginia, I know something is inexplicably wrong. As I compare my symptoms with the records of Doktor Ubelhaar's chemical experiments, I realize that his daughter has vindicated herself upon me in much the same manner she killed her own father. The pesticide Trudi presented was nothing less than the poisonous mixture her father had used upon Jewish subjects, wherein, from the glass-confined safety of his laboratory, he chronicled their internal bleeding and eye-bulging pain, their diarrheic writhing and delusional screams. Now, in a diluted state, the poison allows Trudi to watch me die a slow and painful death. The details of this infirmity are not ones to be committed to paper, but I must make their source known—for my wife's sake and for the sake of the grandchildren that may come someday from the loins of our newborn son, Marshall Ray.

Trudi Ubelhaar—at the time of this writing, a chemist and consultant on payroll at the Umatilla Army Depot—has insidiously destroyed my life. She is a woman racked by hate and motivated by her delusions of grandeur at the helm of the Third Reich. She told me many times of her personal meeting with Adolf Hitler at her initiation into the breeding program, how his hand tarried in her then-seventeen-year-old palm, how he said she would be vital to the Reich's success.

I presumed these to be the mumblings of a star-struck young woman. Oh, how wrong I was! She fancies herself a chosen vessel, an agent commissioned to carry on the madness that Hitler himself was unable to complete. She longs to mete out judgment on the masses by way of her father's stolen formula. I suspect, even, that she may have had a hand in its genesis.

According to the papers confiscated from Doktor Ubelhaar's laboratories, this poison, designated Gift 12, created a curious pattern during the experimentation period lasting from the early thirties to the end of the war: In mice and in the few surviving Jews, it skipped generations, inflicting itself upon one while remaining dormant in the other. In the documented second-generation cases, the subjects generally survived with debilitating blood and circulation anomalies. I fear my own grandchildren will be similarly handicapped.

To visit this accursed affliction upon me, via the canister, was not enough. Trudi also threatened Virginia's life. Who knows what other contemptible plots nest in that tainted soul of hers? I must act, but what recourse do I have? To expose Trudi Ubelhaar is to expose my own infidelities, my own betrayals before country and kin. No, that is not permissible! Instead, to save my wife's life, I've parried Trudi's threats with a game of my own.

Taking advantage of my clearance at the chemical depot, I exchanged the only remaining vials of her father's experimental accelerant with vials of harmless organic solutions. The actual venom vials now rest in an undisclosed safe-deposit box, and Trudi understands that her only hope of laying hands on them is linked directly to Virginia's continued health. A bribe, yes, to protect my wife.

But what could I offer in exchange for Trudi's restraint? Perforce, I divulged that the seed of my offspring alone will have access to the vials she covets. Instructions at the bank allow Marshall's firstborn and no other to open the safe-deposit box—with its enclosed poison. Only this firstborn will bring Trudi her opportunity to wreak the widespread havoc that burns like a fire in her breast. My hope is that she will not live long enough to see this through. Or—forgive me!—that my afflicted grandchild will not survive to provide Trudi her opportunity. For what choice do I have? Do I lose my wife, whom I love? Or my grandchild, yet unknown to me? I am sowing the evil of my ways. This game of chance, oh, it has become a curse to all involved!

A curse, indeed. Now, at last, Marsh understood Josee's involvement: She was the key to the safe-deposit box, to the vials of boomslang hemotoxin. On the grand chessboard, she was the bishop, alone capable of slicing to the coveted object. His daughter? Chance's grandchild? A living bribe.

Marsh walked into the bathroom and heaved into the sink. His throat stung.

Back on the sofa, with a glass of milk, he thought of Josee's vulnerable turquoise eyes. Defiance and pain bordered her pupils. And—dare he admit it?—he was on some level responsible. He had inflicted damage on those around him. He had followed in his father's footsteps and made choices that cut deep into his family.

Family? What family? I pushed Josee away.

Filtered through Virginia's hurt, Chance's betrayals had infused Marsh's life on every level. How could he be purified of this evil? The way looked dim.

Marsh, I have numerous regrets. In many ways, I've failed to attain even my lowest ambitions. I fear the possibility's slim that I'll live to speak these words to your comprehending ears. You're merely an infant. Yet, in the likelihood that Trudi or her accomplices attempt to foist this horror upon your family as well, I leave my journal as a guide toward understanding. I will not be there to partner with you— against this obstacle or any other. Truly, I'll miss watching the transformation of my son into a man.

A section addressed to him? Marsh was caught off guard. He had learned to be strong beneath his mother's hand, but these intimate words struck deep. Sorrow and anger and regret crashed over him. The same feelings Josee must be contending with.

She must hate me! And I told her to leave, to say good-bye.

The sins of the fathers had heaped pain on all involved.

The journal shall remain in your mother's possession—oh, this woman who's so faithfully stood beside me! Virginia knows some of the story, not all. She knows I've been untrue, and I've begged her forgiveness. What more can I do? I've asked her to hide this journal until the day comes that you might require it. Only in such an event do I release these confessions and thus knowingly tarnish my name before my own progeny. As for the canister, I've returned it to Trudi. And good riddance! It's useless to me. It's done its foul deeds.

In a final gesture, I've enlisted the help of one other, a man committed to the protection of my family. I saved his father's life; perhaps he'll have an opportunity to return the favor before all is done. I believe that by remaining anonymous he'll be safe from Trudi's ploys. I can only hope he remains faithful to this task. I've provided financial incentives to encourage him in this endeavor.

Marsh, my betrayals and follies are many and have resulted in much pain—for me and for those I cherish. Please don't repeat my mistakes. In life I've involved myself in a dangerous game. In death and in disclosure I hope to bring this to a close.

May God have mercy on my soul,

Chance Addison

P.S. For what it's worth…Bank of the Dunes, Florence, Box No. 89

Wrinkled packing tape held a brown envelope to the journal's inside cover. A key, with its number filed away, slipped from the decades-old resting place.

25

The Questions

Her need for nicotine drove her to the back porch, where trees whipped in the gale. The yard was dark. Josee was alone, by request, and Scooter had joined John Van der Bruegge for a rematch at the pool table.

So this trip had been a waste and a failure, a lesson in futility. The disappointment jabbed deeper than Josee had anticipated.

At least she had found Scooter again. That was a good thing, wasn't it?

But Kara Addison. She was missing.

As for Marsh, his fatherhood was still debatable. He seemed like a straight-up guy, not exactly in touch with his feminine side, not exactly dripping with sympathy and emotion, but honest. Josee knew that when it came to women, what she saw was what they wanted her to see. With men, what she saw was what she got.

Testosterone may run shallow, but at least I know what I'm diving into.

Marsh Addison had made it clear: No Diving Allowed.

At the house's edge, the wind moaned as it had throughout the late afternoon. Josee flicked fingers at the hip of her jeans. A trail of heat seemed to spiral up her leg. Warm. Itchy. She brushed a hand against her pocket, but there was nothing there.

Through exhaled smoke, she admired the moon that skirted behind the clouds—

Dang it, what is that?

Again she felt something contract and twitch from her heel and up along her thigh. Wool-stockinged feet tensed to the point of cramping in her leather sandals. She coughed and almost discarded her cigarette, but the rolled paper seemed superglued to her fingertips. She took another puff.

As she turned to go back in, she saw coiled in the yellow pool of the porch light a small snake. Had it been there when she came out? Had she stepped right over it? Or perhaps it had arrived while she was smoking and had watched her with interest.

The thing was laughable really. She could crush it with ease. One good stomp.

Kris Van der Bruegge opened the door, and the snake slithered between the porch slats into the dark below.

"Josee? Sorry to interrupt your alone time, but you have a phone call."

~

Rosie nosed her vintage car down Timberwolf Lane. The Pacific's frigid blasts buffeted the vehicle and found their way through the windows. She quivered. She would be inside in a moment, but she reveled in the ocean's brawny might and the dunes' sensual curves. Unfortunately, her years in the drier climate of eastern Oregon had left her susceptible to this damp cold, and her visits here had been curtailed.

She dialed Marsh's cell number but reached his voice mail.

"Sir," she said through static, "this is Rosie. I've arrived safely in Yachats. Again, thank you for allowing me the use of the beach house. Things've been difficult for you the past two days, but take heart, I trust that all will come to light. Please ring me when the investigators have departed and my services are needed back at the manor. Until then, I'll be seeing to my duties here. Good night."

She parked in the gravel drive and carried her carpetbag up the front steps.

~

Turney flicked a finger at a fly, then drew up his uniform sleeve to find his scars pressing through the skin. A pair of green marbles. Between the scars, trails of goop connected the freckles like a dot-to-dot. This thing was getting uglier by the hour. He applied an antiseptic cream and wrapped it in fresh gauze.

"Here goes nothing." He grabbed the phone, reached the Van der Bruegges, got Josee on the line. He was off-duty, but in his years with the department, he'd discovered that certain cases thumbed their noses at individual schedules.

"Good news. We think Kara Addison's alive," he told her.

"My mother? You found her?"

"No, but a kid stumbled into the station a few minutes ago. Does the name Beau Connors ring any bells? He was holding his head, said he'd done work up at a vineyard and started obsessin' over a lady there, so he cooked up a plan to kidnap her. Now that he's got her, he's riddled with guilt and worried he'll be put away for a long time. Doesn't want her to die, or so he claims. Says that was never his plan."

"Is she okay? What'd he do to her?"

"He's afraid. Disoriented. Won't tell us where she is."

"Maybe he's full of it."

"His facts're too specific," Turney said. "We haven't made any public statements yet about her disappearance—least nothing that's been aired before the news later tonight—but Beau knows details about the car in the ravine. The workers up at Addison Ridge have been sent home for the weekend, so they know bits and pieces, but we've kept things quiet otherwise."

"But he did work up there too. You just said that, Sarge."

"Diesel repair, contract work, nothing steady. I think this kid's the full-meal deal. Plus, he's got physical evidence." The line grew quiet. "Still there?"

"Do I want to hear this?"

Turney paced in front of his desk, kicked an old box of Fiddle Faddle. "Josee, the good news here is that she's alive. If it were any different, I'd have come over in person. Not gonna lie to you, won't sugarcoat it, but we do have reasonable hope of gettin' information outta this kid."

"So what kind of evidence are you talking about?"

"The keys to the car. Plus a pair of Kara's earrings."

"How can that be proof? He could've made copies of the keys. And the earrings? How hard would it be to pick something out at the same store?"

"Josee, we've called staff members from the Addison place to corroborate his claims. The first showed up a few minutes ago, took one look at the earrings, and started cryin'. Mexican lady. Marlena. Poor thing's shaken up real bad. How 'bout you? You okay?"

"You know me."

"I'm beginning to think I do." Turney scrambled back to safe ground. "The force is working on this hard and fast. Tracking down the kid's address, a list of his buddies, teachers, schools, bosses, stompin' grounds, et cetera. Couple of other things that we're keepin' close to the chest for now. Story hits the news at eleven, if you wanna catch my ugly mug. KMTR…channel 16."

"Sarge, you ever sleep?"

"During the news? All the time. Seriously, my segment was taped earlier."

"Okay, but you've been on this since what time this morning?"

"Mmm, who knows? Point is, I'm back in the ring. Full ten rounds."

"So what do you think? Did he hurt her? Is my mother safe? If this kid's turned himself in, why doesn't he tell where she is? Could be a wacko playing a prank, looking for his fifteen minutes of fame."

"Might've nailed it on the head, Josee. He says he'll give us her whereabouts and sign a confession so long as we broadcast a live statement. Kid wants to see his face on the news. We're still battin' around the best way to approach this."

"Let him, if it means finding out where my mother is."

"That'll be the chief's decision."

"Oh, yippee. You know, Braddock was asking me personal questions at the hospital this morning. Don't know what business it is of his."

"He's got me workin' with you on this, so he's probably keeping tabs."

"How can you trust a boss like that, Sarge? A stinkin' control freak."

"Wanna know somethin'? Chief paid for Milly's memorial service."

"Your fiancée?"

"Uh-huh. Took up donations around town and covered the whole thing. Her parents died years and years ago, and she had no life insurance, nothing. I was scrapin' at the time, so things weren't looking good. Until he stepped in." Turney thrummed his fingers down the venetian blinds in his office. Talking about Milly hurt but in a good way—like a wound being lanced of its poison. "Josee, I know how tough things are for ya. Hang in there. Everything hit the fan after Milly's passing, and I had to tell my heart to keep beatin'. Didn't understand where the Lord was in the middle of it all, and next thing, I'd stopped doing the Sunday morning routine. Never stopped lovin' him, not deep down, just couldn't stomach any more of the baloney."

"Don't you mean the—" Josee substituted her own expletive.

"Blue-collar word for it. Fits, I guess. You like tryin' to trip me up, don't you?"

"Sometimes."

"Why?"

"Why not?"

"Doesn't it get tiring?"

"Is that what you do, try to avoid all the unknowns? That's a lame excuse for existence." Josee expelled a breath of frustration. "Bet you don't even question it."

"Question it all the time. Lotsa questions and not many answers."

"Least you admit it. Am I off base, Sarge? Is it so wrong to question?"

"Not in my book."

"I mean, didn't God give us minds to use?"

"Listen, if Jesus is the answer, there's no need to be afraid of the questions."

"Exactly. Thank you."

After exhausting the updated info, Sergeant Turney said good-bye, and Josee told him that she'd be watching channel 16 for her favorite new television star. The comment enlivened him. Using humor was a good sign on her part. A tough little cookie, she'd had a lot to deal with in a short span. He did note, however, that during their conversation she had never mentioned her mother by name. Was Josee Walker disengaging herself? Going back into survival mode?

$$\sim$$

Kara had given him an answer. Time to pass it on to Marsh.

Despite his captive's entreaties, Stahlherz refitted a gag around her mouth. He lifted her hair so it wouldn't snag in the folds of cloth, then brushed it back down, soft as a feather, with his hands. Holding the crude handrail, he closed his ears to her pleas, turned off the light, and walked up the cellar steps.

Actors in position! Stage lights and props.

He speed-dialed for another scene in the drama.

S: "Crash-Chess-Dummy. I've spoken with your wife and have an answer regarding your weekend getaway."

A: "Tell me then, where are we headed?"

S: "Your lovely lady says Black Butte Ranch, the resort in central Oregon. I'm afraid that's all she would reveal. Are you pleased? Have I passed the test? I've upheld my end. Time for you to follow through on yours."

A: "Yes. But first I have a request."

S: "Hold on, now. That's not in the rules of chess, my friend."

A: "Do you want the journal or not? The request is simply this: When we meet tomorrow evening, please bring along Kara's headscarf. She was wearing it when she left yesterday. It's multicolored, hard to miss."

S: *(turns to audience and thinks aloud with finger on chin)* "A sly maneuver, Crash-Chess-Dummy. Very sly." *(wheeling to face opponent)* "She wasn't wearing one that I recall. I suppose you thought you would stump me on that one?"

A: "Just tell me that you'll release her as promised."

S: "Absolutely, so long as you provide me with Chance's journal. In no time, the news will be on to verify my pawn sacrifice. You'll be free from suspicion. If there's any trouble whatsoever, though, I'll discredit his role, and you'll rot away in a state penitentiary, defecating five feet from where you lay your head to sleep. Everyone suspects the husband in these cases. They'll all want to believe that you did it. Much cozier than accepting that persons such as myself walk the streets."

A: "You're scum! If you do anything to harm her, you'll spend the rest of your days looking over your shoulder because I won't be far behind. I'll hound you to the grave."

S: "You just be there at four-thirty. Oh, one last thing..."

A: *(apprehensive)* "What is it?"

S: "Don't grow too fond of young Josee Walker. One way or the other, this'll be the last game she plays on your side of the board." *(bursts out in maniacal glee)* "For both your sakes, it'd be better if she had never found you."
(end of scene)

Karl Stahlherz relished the drama of it all. He was at the mammoth stone fireplace in the Addisons' beach house, the queen was in his possession, and the king was beholden to locate that journal. The tactics played out so effortlessly.

He was heading for the door when he heard footsteps on the front deck.

The Lincoln County sheriff? Had she returned, baiting him even as she had passed by him on the lane, waiting to catch him red-handed?

His fingers wrapped around the dagger in the pocket of his corduroy jacket. He inched toward the sliding-glass door. One part of him resented this complication, while another welcomed it. At the chessboard, these were the things that stimulated him—the-edge-of-your-seat awareness that a game may be won or lost on the finesse of a simple pawn maneuver, something unexpected yet obvious.

Scritchh, scritchh… Footsteps scraped over the sand-dusted wood.

Stahlherz paused, his nostrils piqued by the odor of his traveling companion, the intrusive rook. With the hiss of a steam-pressure valve, the black presence lifted his arms, tugged at his extremities. He felt a desire to lift and lower his arms, lift and lower, then to open his lips and release the shriek of this proud beast.

No! Don't distract me now, you fool. Stay where you belong.

Outside, on the planks, the feet ceased their shuffling.

Stahlherz felt his breathing stop. Then in a movement beyond his control, he cracked his hand to his forehead in the manner of a salute. No! Must harness it. He clamped the hand back to his side, determined to master this creature that had become far too unruly. Fuming, Stahlherz shook the thoughts from his head and drew his dagger. Poised to deliver a blow.

He watched a figure move toward the door handle, heard a meek voice call out.

"Hello, is anyone here? Hello, it's me…Rosie."

Stahlherz slid the door open, gripped Rosie's hand, and pulled her in from the porch.

"Oh, my!" she exclaimed, grasping a carpetbag to her stomach. "Show an old woman a little respect. You startled me."

He closed the door and edged her toward the monstrous fireplace. Safe from outside detection, he helped her with her coat. "I didn't expect you so soon. Glad you arrived unharmed."

"Thank you, Stahli," she said without fear. "Audentes fortuna juvat."

"Yes, Professor," he responded. "Fortune favors the daring."

PART FOUR

We may stand, if only on one leg,
or at least...upon our knees....
A pawn? Perhaps;
but on the wrong chessboard.

The Return of the King by J. R. R. Tolkien

"Don't sin by letting anger
gain control over you."...
Anger gives a mighty foothold to the Devil.

Ephesians 4:26-27

26

Matriarchs

Marsh Addison's mind was a raging pyre. Confusion, anger, fear, betrayal—they were bundles of straw tossed onto the flames. The balls of his feet burned in his Mundazi loafers, and a sheen of perspiration lay across his forehead.

Yes, his discovery of the journal had offered hope, but it torched everything he'd grown to believe about his father.

The call from Steele Knight had further stirred his turmoil. Marsh wanted to snap the man's neck; he wanted to strike vengeful blows that would stray far from the love Virginia spoke of.

If I could just get my hands on that bag of scum... One minute, that's all I'd need!

Marsh paced the hallway in his mother's seaside condo. From the kitchen, the sand candle's light brushed the walls in gold. He thought of Virginia's assertions: *Your love can soften and free her.... Your pent-up anger...will be nothing but a detriment.*

The words were all backward. His world was upside down.

The thought came to him that perhaps he'd been studying this whole mess from the wrong angle. From board level, the chess pieces were a mob of motion; from above, however, they were parts of an intricate overall strategy. Josee, the bishop—drawn into battle by the hopes of meeting her mother. Kara, the queen—used as a hostage so he would track down and relinquish the journal. Marsh, the king—dictating the counterattack, yet helpless at so many points.

And Sergeant Turney—he was part of this. What had Casey called him? *Blue knight.*

"Marsh?" The front door opened, and a blustery wind chased Virginia inside. Her cheeks were red with exertion. She bent to loosen her shoelaces. "Oh, my feet. They're swollen like balloons."

"Why'd you make me jump through hoops?" Marsh interrogated.

"The journal. You found it."

"Might not have! Might've headed home without it and put Kara at greater risk."

"Had to know your heart first, to know that you're ready to face what's ahead."

"So I passed the test. You think I'm ready now, huh?"

"No. But neither do you. That's really the whole point, don't you see?"

"Mother! You're speaking in riddles—"

"My way of life," she said. "Has been for far too long."

In sweats and jogging shoes, Virginia appeared to shrink. She was no longer the iron-girded matriarch who had raised him with aloof affection, no longer a dedicated entrepreneur dragging her son in her wake. She was, Marsh recognized, a woman and a mother but also a wife who'd been dishonored by the husband of her youth. For the first time, her graveside photo came into focus for him. *The look of a woman betrayed.*

He stepped toward her. Enfolded her in his arms.

"Mom," he said. And he could say nothing more.

When he pulled away, she told him he was welcome to stay. He told her it was time for him to return to Corvallis and take care of business.

"The vineyard?"

"No." He shook his head. "Family business. Time to be the father I never had."

Over wet and treacherous roads, the rental car carried Marsh back toward the Ramada Inn. The journal and the key sat wrapped in the glove box. His mental gears whirred. Josee Walker, his biological daughter? Inflicted with his defective genes?

But I want proof. I need it.

His enemy seemed convinced. Steele Knight had synchronized his schemes with Josee's arrival in town. Josee had sole access to the safe-deposit box at the coastal bank, and she had a birth certificate to satisfy the bank's needs for identification. With the number and location of the box, with Josee as the key, Steele Knight could seize the Nazi-crafted poison. No wonder he was desperate for the journal.

But what did the man intend to do with the venom vials?

Marsh squinted through the high beams of a nearing car, then found himself alone again on the dreary road. He thought of the warning: *Don't grow too fond of young Josee Walker…it'd be better if she had never found you.* Something stirred within; strategies began to form. He could not leave her to be picked off by his foe.

Twenty hours. Counting down to the exchange at the Camp Adair monument.

In chess terminology, it was time to begin prophylactic maneuvers, to open his anticipate-and-aggravate-your-opponent's-every-move file.

Crash-Chess-Dummy vs. Steele Knight.

—

Stahlherz looked his mother over. Rosamund Yeager, known to ICV conscripts as the Professor, was standing here beneath the vaulted rafters of the Addison beach house while Kara sat roped and gagged in the cellar down the hall. The irony did not slip by.

The drama of it all—worthy of a canvas, of a stage. The chessboard of life.

"Did I surprise you?" Rosie said. "Forgive me, Stahli."

"Things're proceeding, Professor. So far, so good."

Stahlherz's voice was cool. Even here without witnesses he felt compelled to address her formally. Within the network, he and Rosie seldom displayed affection or forsook titles; in fact, for the sake of security, they avoided appearing together. Yesterday's meeting in the park had been their first in weeks. True, she was his mother, but she was also the Professor—a woman to be revered, a woman with a plan. The cell members had bestowed the title upon her, looking to her for instruction and advice as well as motivation. She was their catalyst.

Yes, all fine and well. But he was due some respect too. Didn't she see that?

"How's Mrs. Addison faring?"

"Still lively," Stahlherz said. "Bladder relieved and belly filled."

"She's not to be harmed, you understand. She's our means of reeling in Josee and Mr. Addison—and, at all costs, the lost journal. Please, I don't want Kara to know I'm here. If anything goes awry, she must not be able to identify me."

"Imagine her shock to discover her housekeeper-turned-kidnapper."

"A misnomer, my son." Rosie wagged a finger and settled onto a settee with her carpetbag in her lap. Light honey hair played over her ears. "Actually, I'm the kidnapper-turned-housekeeper."

"You didn't kidnap me. You rescued me."

Rosie's head bowed in contrition. "Try convincing the authorities of that."

"Well, our secret, of course. But you saved my life. You raised me as your own. That's to be rewarded, not punished."

"I did what had to be done, Stahli. To think that anyone could abandon a child." Rosie slipped off her shoes and began massaging aged feet. "Oh, my. Seventy-six years and these bones have taken a pounding. I feel perpetually cold to the marrow, and my joints grow stiffer by the day. The price of an old woman's musings, I guess."

He knelt and touched her shin. "Let me ease your bitterness, Professor."

She pulled away. "Too late for that."

Kre-aaack! Why do you shrink from me? Don't I make you proud?

"You're wrong," he said. "Even now the network is maneuvering into position. Soon you'll have hundreds hailing you as their leader, their ideological matriarch. Soon thousands will taste from the roots of your pain. You will be avenged."

Rosie patted his shoulder. "You're kind, even to an old woman."

In deference, Stahlherz kissed the age-marked hand. He thought of the photo over his desk and the combatants on his onyx chessboard. He forced his eyes open, knowing that to close them would be to amplify the crackling in his head. Despite this attempt, the agony continued. Feathers, black as sin, flapped ceaselessly in his skull.

Vengeance. Hold on till tomorrow… To endure is the cure.

As the wind bent the trees outside, Rosie and Stahlherz rehearsed their plans, coordinated schedules, arranged for contingencies.

"So tell me," Stahlherz said at last. "What're you hiding in the bag?"

"Hiding?" Rosie smoothed her carpetbag in a simulation of innocence. "This? Oh, very well then, I suppose I should share the good news. It seems, Stahli, that Josee Walker's not only reappeared at a propitious time, she's also managed to stumble upon another long-lost item of mine. Or, in a far likelier scenario, the item threw itself in her path." Excitement seemed to fill the elderly woman's hair with electricity, lifting and separating it strand by strand. She said, "It has that power, I assure you."

Kaw-ka-screech! I have power too, you understand.

"Please, Professor," Stahlherz said. "Tell me, what do you have?"

From the carpetbag, Rosie withdrew a metal canister.

In Corvallis, he stopped at Kinko's to copy his father's journal. He placed the original and the copy in protective envelopes, stamped the original, and dropped it at the post office in the indoor receptacle. He carried the copy to the hotel and instructed the concierge to put it in a safe. At the front desk, he found that Sergeant Turney had delivered his belongings as promised.

Bolstered by a pot of hotel coffee, Marsh picked up his phone. Rosie was safe in Yachats; others wished him well; but no one—not the fitness club owner or the BP gas attendants or her friends or relatives—had seen or heard from Kara today.

Conversely, Henri Esprit was full of steadfast assurance.

"Marshall, I spoke with my nephew—his name's Nick—and he's enthused about the chance to utilize his skills. He's logging into the gaming zone, dragging the Internet to see if he can't 'get a byte.'" Esprit chuckled. "That bit of his humor I picked up on, though, in general, his jargon leaves me scratching my balding head. Nick tells me he's also contacting the Webmaster to see if he can't get a list of game users registered under the last name of Steele."

"Good thinking. I like this nephew of yours already."

"He did warn that the Webmaster is under no compulsion to provide such a list, and even if he does acquiesce, the users are under no obligation to verify their Web-site registrations. Steele, therefore, could be an alias."

"Figured as much. Any help from customer service at AT&T? Were you able to use my info and get a log of my phone calls?"

"Incoming and outgoing. Numbers, yes. No names though."

Marsh took down the numbers that fell within the timespan of his conversation with Steele Knight. If only he could pinpoint the person behind that blocked number. In all likelihood, the person paying the bills on the account was the one holding his wife.

He thought of Sergeant Turney and the help he could provide here.

"Listen, Esprit, this guy could be from anywhere on the globe, I know that. But the circumstances imply someone local. In state, at least. Do me a favor and check with the authorities, see if they have a record of any registered sex offenders by the last name of Steele. Narrow it to Lane, Linn, and Benton counties. If I'm not mistaken, the information's available to the public, even the offenders' addresses."

"Marshall, some advice. Not that you've ever been inclined to listen to this doddering old man, but I'll say it anyway. Maybe now's the time to let the police in on this. You've remained ambiguous about all that's going on, but I can only assume it involves Kara. For her sake—"

"For her sake, I can't."

"Perhaps there's a way."

"Drop it, Esprit. I'll handle it, okay? Let me know what you find out."

Marsh disconnected and dropped into the bedside armchair. He glanced at the clock.

God, if you're out there, somewhere, would it hurt you to get involved here?

Killing time until the eleven o'clock news, he flipped through the cable lineup. His mind went blank; his heart tapped its regular rhythm against his chest. Monster trucks, classic movies, CNN, VH-1... Nothing of interest.

A face flashed by, and he went back to fawn over an actress with Kara's looks.

What had she meant by her clue, Black Butte Ranch? Or was it a clue? Had she misunderstood Marsh's attempt to trick her abductor and thrown out her answer in sarcasm or wishful thinking? Surely, he reasoned, she was not actually in their time-share condo at the ranch resort. If so, Steele Knight would never have passed on the message. No, on some level, she must have weighed Marsh's question against his scheduled departure for Europe and played along with the subterfuge. Otherwise, she would have told the truth, that they hadn't made romantic plans. Hadn't in ages.

Black Butte Ranch...

B. B. R. Were the initials the clue? Maybe she was near a butte. A ranch.

Of course, and Marsh hated to admit this, it could be she had no idea where she was and had thrown out an answer to avoid punishment from her abductor.

Tired and testy, he removed his shoes at the foot of the bed and emptied his pockets onto the nightstand. Marsh glimpsed the sergeant's card and thought of Turney's invitation to call anytime. But hadn't Steele Knight warned him against any police intervention?

He turned off the light and, in the television's glow, stripped down to silk boxers.

A knock startled him.

Through the peephole, he saw a slightly distorted Casey Wilcox in a cream-colored dress, her legs streaming down to black braided pumps. He poked his head through the door, met a cold wind. Casey was clutching a black purse with a pearl-lined flap that matched the string around her neck. Earrings nuzzled in her brunette hair. Marsh said, "What's going on?"

"Marshall. Thought you might want some company."

"You thought wrong."

"Raining like crazy, *brrrr.*" Casey stepped past him. "Don't you believe in lamps, or are you just sitting here in the dark?" She clicked on the bedside light.

"Thinking things over."

"In your boxers?"

"I was about to take a shower. It's getting late, if you don't mind."

"Marshall, don't pretend you don't want me here. You know that you do."

"Not in much of a joking mood, Casey. Why don't we talk tomorrow?"

She fingered her string of pearls and laughed. "Who said anything about talking?"

27

Trick or Treat

Kris Van der Bruegge turned back a pink bedspread, fluffed the pillows, and set a towel and a new bar of soap on the bureau. Outlining a full-length mirror, faded stickers stood as mementos of Annalise's childhood. "I miss that girl," Kris told Josee and Scooter as they watched from the doorway. She touched the stickers. Drops of rain pelted the window. "Thanksgiving this year won't be the same without her."

"What about Halloween?" said Scooter. "Tomorrow's the day."

"She'll miss that, too. No goodies for her, I guess."

"Halloween can get downright bizarre around our place," Josee said. "Past few years Scoot and his friends've dressed up in medieval garb and sacked out all night at our trailer for role-playing games. Me? I stay as far away as I can. With all the sugar and herbs flowing through their veins, they start bouncing off the walls."

"Herbs?"

"Yeah." Scooter shot Josee a stern look as a roll of thunder shook the house. "You know, supplements…ginkgo biloba, guarana, ephedra. Nothing man-made. All natural for us. We slug down Sobe and Red Bull like water."

Josee stuck out her tongue. "All sugar water, if you ask me."

"You two lost me at the medieval garb," Kris said. "Anyway, you're all set for the night, Josee. As for you, Scooter, you know where your room is. You'll have to share the bathroom in between. Just let me know if either of you needs anything."

Josee nudged Scooter. "See you in the morning, hon."

He kissed her lightly, his breath moving cold and stale over her lips. "Night."

Touching the corner of her mouth, she watched him tread down the hall. Her fingers moved to her eyebrow ring. She said, "Kris, thanks for, you know, letting us use your place."

"Our pleasure."

"And I really didn't mean to spill that hot cocoa—"

"Uh-uh. I warned you not to bring it up again."

"Yes, ma'am."

Kris pointed to a CD system by the corner armchair. "You're welcome to listen to music if you like. Annalise left most of her collection here. A moderate volume, that's all we ask. John's already asleep upstairs since he has first period in the morning. And, Josee?"

"Yeah."

"You're allowed to sleep under the covers."

"I know."

"Annalise used to thrash and turn till every corner was untucked. It's okay."

Josee rubbed her chin against her shoulder.

"Sarge explained to me what happened to you out in the thicket," Kris said from the doorway. "Not to make light of it, but I have confidence that you're going to pull through this. You'll be all right. Remember what we talked about earlier? Music's a powerful tool. Go ahead. You might find something there that'll touch you."

Josee squatted to look over the CD titles. "Art and music've always touched me. You think that's God? I mean, it's like his fingerprints are there if you just look from the right angle. Scooter thinks I'm crazy when I talk like this."

"Granted, it's not *always* a divine touch. But God's always willing to reach out."

Josee withdrew a CD. *I want to feel you, Lord, the way I used to. Sometimes, it's just too stinkin' scary. Been touched in all the wrong ways.*

"You need your rest, Josee. I'll leave you with one last thing. Of course, you know the story of David and Goliath. Well, David knew how to fight with more than a slingshot. He was summoned a number of times to play music in the king's court. An evil spirit was tormenting the king, but each time David played, the spirit left, and the king was appeased. The music, by God's grace, drove the darkness away."

"Vaguely remember that from somewhere way back."

."But the fix was only temporary," Kris pointed out.

"Temporary?"

"The king never gave up his free will. He could still let the spirit come back—and he did! One day, under its evil influence, the king took a spear and tried to pin David to the wall."

Josee shivered, recalling her boyfriend's stale breath on her lips. "Scooter," she whispered. The storm outside matched her mood.

"Yes."

"Yes what?"

"I know that you care for Scooter. He's a charmer. Be careful though. He has something hanging on, something hooked into him that he can't quite shake. That poison's still moving through him. Forget the pushy and greedy religious institutions you've seen. God's a gentleman—persistent, but a gentleman. Although he won't force himself on people, demonic forces will. No manners at all. You give them a foothold, and they'll try storming the walls."

"Speak English. Straight up, what're you telling me here?"

"I'm telling you that Scooter's mind is a castle under siege."

As the video cameras rolled, Turney watched Beau's posture change. Erect and proud, a product of the entertainment generation, he stared into the soulless lens, ready to perform for Mother. America's "surrogate mother." Wasn't that Josee's line?

Beau straightened on the stool. "This'll air tonight, right?"

"Up to the folks at the station," Turney said. "It's their newscast."

"Tonight. No ifs, ands, or buts. That's the way it's gotta be, or Mrs. Addison won't be comin' back. Not ever."

"Eleven o'clock news, kid. We'll do our best to run a clip."

Beau's earlier confession to abduction would be broadcast along with the news of Kara Addison's disappearance. But this? Nosiree, no suspect was gonna jerk them around. With a little digital manipulation, they'd loop a segment into the newscast and feed it through the holding cell's television. Beau would be none the wiser.

The Record light gave a wink of encouragement. From that moment until the moment it blinked off in satisfaction, Beau Connors's eyes stayed glued to Mother's. His syntax and diction changed, as though some erudite entity had inhabited his body. He decried the government's abuse of power, the evils of globalization, and the "war on our rights to freely express ourselves." He insisted that the public was not ready to make a stand for freedom and, by default, was making a stand for complacency. Having thus sided with the oppressors, the inhabitants of Oregon would reap the consequences.

Turney stiffened. The rants had turned to threats.

"That's right," Beau mocked. "Allhallows Eve."

Then his shoulders began to sag. He collapsed forward, spent, nothing more than a truant teenager in need of attention. Like a startled flock of birds, his pedantic ramblings left him, and he coughed out a last warning. "You wanna know what sorta trouble I'm talkin' about? Go find the van I ditched in Philomath. Yeah, buddy, you'll be dirtyin' your diapers on the spot. Trick or treat."

Turney was on his radio before the cameras stopped taping.

Cuffed, Beau stepped down from the heat of the stage lights. Turney led him through doors to the cruiser that would return the suspect to his cell. He wanted to shake sense into this ruffian, demand answers, throw a blow if need be.

Yet something in the kid's manner begged for sympathy. What was the word?

He's malleable, that's it. Just one more soul lookin' for love by means of hate.

From the backseat, Beau said, "You think I did all right? My speech?"

"Think ya just dug yourself a deep hole. That's what I think. If I were you, I'd spit out Kara's location before this comes down hard on you."

"Uh-uh. I say one thing, and he's gonna come after me."

"Who's he?"

"Say what?"

"Think ya just goofed, kid. Somethin' you wanna tell me?"

Beau drew inward. "Can't make me talk, Sarge. Got rights, you know."

Back in his office, Turney mulled the evidence and starting making phone calls.

Karl Stahlherz could hear the Pacific's pounding. Out there, cutting the waves, a vessel loaded with military munitions had followed this coastline to safe harbor in Florence. On a November night in 1945, the Professor had found passage to America.

Now, decades later, the culmination of her plans was upon them.

In the night sky the winds were scraping away the last remnants of clouds, and a cratered disk appeared over the treetops. The moonlight turned Rosie's powdered cheeks ashen as she fondled the canister with a quaint giggle.

"This is the one?" said Stahlherz. "The one you lost?"

"Yes." Her eyes glowed. "This canister was my constant companion. On the succession of boats from the Fatherland, I kept it close by my side. I knew that eventually it would be taken from me, along with the other canisters, but I determined to channel my, uh…shall we say, my energies into this particular one."

"How do you know this is it?"

Rosie turned her attention to the canister's scarred surface. With a linen handkerchief, she buffed the metal to highlight the skull-and-crossbones symbol and the black letters underneath. "Recognize this word?" she tested him.

"Says 'Gift,' if I'm not mistaken."

"Which in German means…"

"Means 'poison,' doesn't it?"

"That's correct. High marks for you," said the Professor. "It was the only canister so inscribed. Unfortunately, it felt the need to escape—for lack of a better word. While coastguardsmen were unloading the munitions at the lighthouse, one of the men tripped over a silly watchdog, and the canister fell from his hands. Ended up going over the cliff. At the time I felt that I was directing the beasts within to make their escape. I watched at the window, fully intending to fetch it later."

"But it had vanished."

"Allow me to tell the story, would you, Son? The trouble was that men died that night. As the canister rolled along the lawn, it left a trail of poison. A captain died. And that watchdog, who deserved it for his impudence. Two others. Remarkably, the lightkeeper and son survived. I suppose the brisk breeze had cleared the air by the time they arrived on the cliff top."

"Did you make any attempt to find the canister?"

Lost in the memory, she polished the metal with her hands. A wisp of green clung to her skin. "Under the cover of nightfall, yes, I made my way down to the beach. My young legs fared well. Already, though, men had combed the shore for their fallen captain, and I feared they had recovered my canister as well. No sight of the thing. I was convinced it would respond to my bidding, yet it refused to recognize my authority. A rascally beast then…and now."

As though conjured by an Indian snake charmer, a neon vapor spiraled from the canister's base and rose before the Professor. The vapor split in two, then split again exponentially until the settee was buried beneath sinuous shadows.

Stahlherz watched with an emotion akin to admiration. But he was shaking.

"I thought I was in control," Rosie said, "for I simply did not understand. I now know we are powerless always until the moment we give them control."

"Them?"

She nodded. "The scene's so clear in my mind. The search party had retired, and standing in the gloom on the lip of the sea, I relinquished myself. In seconds, the canister propelled itself forward on the crest of a wave and slid up onto the sand at my feet. I had been chosen. I knew this deep in my bones. I've known it since the day Herr Hitler took my hand in his and prophesied great things."

Over Rosie's head, the glowing tendrils settled into a wreath of green that emitted a sickly sweet odor: cinnamon sticks, an apple burning over an open flame. A pair of fangs protruded thornlike from the nebulous mass.

"Professor. Mother!"

"Don't stop them, Stahli. There's no need to fear. Only as you stop fighting does the pain dissipate." Her words slithered away as the fangs found purchase in pearl-white skin. Her thin hair threaded throughout the wreath, becoming one with it, and her eyes narrowed into moist slits. A look of subservient revelry.

Stahlherz felt his stomach lurch.

"All a question of surrender," she purred. "Of giving up control."

Kaww-kontroll! Stahlherz bit his lip and tried to ignore the screeching in his ears. *Who do you think you are, you putrid beast? Heave-ho… Back in your hole.*

"These creatures always aim to rule," said Rosie. "From that moment in my father's laboratory when I locked him in with the boomslangs, from the moment I gave in to the rage and tempted the gods to parcel out justice, I allowed these fiends access. Willingly so. I craved their power. I longed for the chance to bring glory to the Third Reich by bringing down our enemies. Long live der Führer!"

"But, Professor—"

"Heil Hitler! Aha!"

"I don't understand. Hitler is…no longer with us."

"*Das ist wahr.* True, he was a man, a mere mortal. He refused to trust in these very forces that had led him to success. As a corporal in the First World War, he suffered a mustard-gas attack that blinded him temporarily, and thereafter he feared the use of such weapons. He began listening to the counsel of fools, spineless generals who turned from the unseen powers and trusted instead in the wisdom of men. Men!" The collection of fangs pulsed, deepening their hold in the Professor's thoughts. "But I…oh, yes, I saw the true potential. And as a woman, I was less susceptible to the inhibiting logic of the male species. I know men. I know where they attempt to store their strength. They are weak. Their meager thrusts are nothing compared to the creative power of a woman."

"In cauda venenum!" Stahlherz's salute produced a smile of contentment on the Professor's powdered face. "I'm still confused though. How did Josee and her friend stumble across the canister? What was it doing out in the woods?"

"Been there for ages, I can only assume. After Chance Addison discovered the danger of this gift, he returned it to me and begged that I leave him and his wife alone. In exchange, he offered me an opportunity to spread the poison much farther. This part you already know. It's why we tried to steal Josee when she was only minutes old. She alone has access to my father's stolen venom vials. She is the key. And yet, without Chance's journal, none of us knows where this bank-deposit box lies."

"Marsh will find the journal. He'll bring it in exchange for his dear wifey."

"And you are sure he'll comply?"

"I've studied him at the chessboard. He's predictable. He likes symmetry and order."

"Chance was much the same," Rosie said. "Like father, like son."

The beak pecked and tore at his skull. Stahlherz grimaced, then focused on the strategy before them. "You, too, have noted his predictability. You're the one who's provided all the information I could need—mother's maiden name, Social Security number. If necessary, you could no doubt tell me his brand of briefs and the way he likes them folded. With one toll-free call, I can follow his movements by means of his latest American Express transactions. If he eats out, purchases gas, goes to a ball game, we'll know where he's been."

"A fine plan, Son."

"I hoped you would think so."

"But all this…this silliness could've been avoided years ago if you had squelched your rage. Instead, you—"

"My rage? You blame me for—"

"Son, do not interrupt." Rosie slid a hand through her vaporous wreath. "There in Good Samaritan your task was to unleash the canister—nothing more, nothing less. Instead, you allowed your desire for vengeance to supersede your commitment to my plan. You resorted to violence, attacking Marsh and his fiancée there in the hospital stairwell. A gunshot. In close quarters. And yet you managed only to strike Kara in the hip? You might've put the bullet to better use and done yourself in, for all the good you accomplished. Our strategies were waylaid by your reckless emotion."

"And you punish me still for my mistakes. How long, Mother? Don't you value my productivity in the years since? ICV is my brainchild. My gift of reconciliation."

"Think as you will." Rosie smiled from behind the curled tail of a viper. Stahlherz blinked.

"You've been a good son, don't misunderstand. But your impetuousness polluted the canister. Why do you think it failed to capture newborn Josee that night? You think the bumbling of some nine-year-old child gave Kara and Josee time to make an escape? That fool, Sergeant Turney! He could no more protect them than he could say no to a chocolate eclair! A worthless boy who got in the way, nothing more."

"So you blame me for the canister's disappearance."

"It vanished from the carnage at the hospital. Yes, Stahli, I believe it took on a mind of its own and went into hiding. Storing up wrath. Waiting."

"Until Josee stumbled across it a few days ago."

"A lovely scenario." The rear-fanged jaws gave another spasm. "When the hospital administrator called with news of Scooter's unusual symptoms, news which you then passed on to me, I knew I was being beckoned for a final time. The administrator provided the location from the ambulance log, and I hurried to the spot."

"Where you reacquired the canister."

"Initially, no. When my search of the brush and fallen logs proved fruitless, I feared the police might've taken possession of it. Of course"—her thin lips turned up in amusement as her eyelids drooped—"it's more probable *it* would've taken possession of *them*. But, yes, once again I surrendered myself, and once again the canister showed itself. Imagine. All these years it's been up the road, dormant, awaiting this moment of destiny. As I opened myself up, it appeared and took control."

Stahlherz opened his mouth to reply, but a pointed shape clogged his throat.

"Son, why are you moaning? You don't sound well."

"Ka-*kawwff*."

"You sound hoarse and muffled. Are you fighting something?"

He shook his head. Side to side, side to side. "*Kaa-aaawf!*"

"Stahli," she said, "you really should take something for that cough."

~

In the pink lampshade's glow, Josee leaned against the headboard and let the sounds of U2 wash through the room. The fears of the day and the worries of tomorrow played through her head, giving way to ethereal guitar tones and soulful vocals. She felt peace settle over her, and her eyelids grew heavy. Tonight she would even take Kris up on her offer and wrap herself within the luxurious blankets.

Josee turned on her side with her back to the lamp. Yep, she was ready to sleep, but there was no way that light was going off.

Twenty-five minutes later her eyes shot open as the room went black.

28

Noose of Pearls

Marsh shook his head and draped his towel over his shoulder. "Been a long day, Casey. I'm in no mood for company at the moment. Listen, the vineyard'll lose money if my name gets smeared, and having you here dressed like that won't help. I'm under police suspicion, if not actual investigation, *and* my wife is missing. I love her."

"You don't know where she is? You've considered all the options?"

"Racked my brain, believe me."

Casey seated herself on the edge of the bed. "There's a possibility you and I've not discussed. *Pardonnez-moi,* but do you have any reason to believe Kara might've run out on you?"

"No! None whatsoever."

"A secret lover perhaps? You're a busy man with a lot on your plate. Maybe she's needed more attention, a little more romance in her life."

"That's ridiculous," Marsh said without conviction.

"Has anything happened in the past? Either one of you ever been unfaithful?"

"Hey, what are you, my attorney or my psychiatrist? Back off."

But, he added, yes, there had been indiscretions. As he stared across the hotel room, things long buried came rushing to the surface, and he found himself delivering a monologue that started with his knowledge of Kara's pregnancy in early 1981.

—

Soon after New Year's, classes had recommenced on the OSU campus, and Marsh Addison and Katherine "Kara" Davies had discovered the news: A baby was on the way. Considering the nuisance of contraceptives, and religious upbringings that had prohibited such methods, the pregnancy was no surprise. They shoved aside the idea that they had been involved in moral failure and planned an August wedding.

It was the doctor's grim prognosis that changed everything.

Kara turned inward. Helpless, Marsh watched it happen. Her effervescence faded, and her grades suffered. She drank less, partied less, talked less. His fiancée was a flower folding in on itself.

"I should've told you," she confessed that evening on the sofa. Her tummy had a slight swell, barely noticeable. Marsh had his arm around her, but his eyes were following *Quincy, M.E.* on the television. "It's my fault, I think. A punishment."

"Your fault for what?" He grinned in an attempt to lighten her mood. "Have you been a bad girl? You need a spanking?" He realized later that she had been about to divulge her darkest secret, and he was cracking jokes.

"I was drinking. I shouldn't have drunk that much."

"When?" he asked.

"At that party a few months back. The one Jerry invited us to."

"At Phi Beta Upsilon?"

"Why didn't I just quit and walk away? Now our baby's being punished for it." Kara dissolved into tears, and as he stroked her hair that was fresh with the scent of strawberry shampoo, the words locked within her burst forth in confession. "I knew I was getting bombed, and I asked for another one. Another one! What was I thinking? I could hardly talk, much less stay on my feet. It's my fault. I should've known this would happen. I'm the one to blame."

"Stop it. I doubt one night at a party caused this."

"I'm being punished. It's my punishment, and I deserve it."

"What're you babbling on about? Nobody deserves it. Tragic things happen, and that's the way it goes. It's all part of life. The baby'll be okay."

"God's punishing me."

"He's punishing all of us. Look at Ethiopia. You think they deserve what's happening over there? He gets off on these little power trips, reminding us who's in charge."

Kara was shaking her head. "I don't believe that. He's not that way."

"Oh, yeah? But he can punish you personally. He's that way, huh?"

"Darling, we're not even married yet."

"Testing the waters first. Nothing wrong with that. Isn't God into love?"

"But we're engaged."

"Exactly. Practically the same thing. Not like a signature on a piece of paper proves anything. If the Big Guy's all-knowing, then he knows we're about to be hitched. He's cool with that. Shoot, he made us this way. What does he expect?"

"He expects us to be faithful."

Marsh watched the flicker of the television. "Listen, I know I can be a flirt—a big flirt, I guess—but that's just my style, the way I am. Doesn't mean that I'm going to—"

"It was me."

Marsh's hair-stroking hand stopped.

Kara pressed her head into his chest as though hoping for absolution from the guilt that weighed upon her. "At the party…" She paused, seeming to brace for a reaction. Her words continued, hot and moist against his shirt. "You were out back, you might remember, on that porch swing with that old girlfriend of yours."

"Cynthia?"

"What were you two doing? Sharing a joint? I could see you through that round window over the sink, and I was getting jealous. Furious, actually, wondering why my fiancé would be getting so cozy with *her* while engaged to *me*. I grabbed a beer and guzzled it down. Found another one and another one. Hoped you'd come looking for me and take me home, but the next thing I knew there was this guy talking to me, an old friend—well, not really a friend but a friend of my parents—and he was trying to kiss me, and he was nudging me toward the bedroom, and I could hardly even comprehend what was going on, and I felt as though I was making you pay for your escapades on the swing and… Darling, please, I'm so sorry. I never meant for it to happen. I wasn't thinking clearly, and now our baby's being punished for it."

"*Our* baby? How do you know it's not his?"

"No, Marsh." She peered up through hair wet with tears. "It's ours."

Marsh's heart felt sucked dry from his chest. He mouthed, "How do you know?"

"I…I know. He didn't…well, we didn't—"

"This is so much bull! You can't know."

Her body was tense, holding back her sobs. He still had one arm around her waist, but the other had slipped to the sofa. Deadened. Like a severed appendage. He stared at it in shock, his vision moving down his bulging veins and curled forearm hair to the sofa's fabric pattern. Orange and brown stripes and frazzled beige knots swam into focus, then every thread, every popcorn seed and potato chip crumb, every pen cap and copper penny. He was holding his breath.

Be prepared. His father's motto. Somehow he managed to ask, "Who was it?"

Her crying came to a stop.

"Who? Do I know him?"

"Darling, I don't think it—"

"Tell me!" He gripped her shoulders and forced her to face him.

"That hurts. You have to promise you won't go after him. You can't tell anyone."

"Now you're protecting him."

"No. I simply can't go through this, darling. Please," she said. "Promise me."

"Fine, I promise. There, is that what you want to hear? Now tell me who it is!" The very thought ate at him, and although he feared the answer, he thought it would be better to know than to wonder and suspect.

She said, "John."

"John? My running buddy, John Garvey?"

"No. Goodness, no. He'd never take advantage of me like that."

"John who?"

"Braddock."

Marsh tried to keep his voice from shaking. "The cop."

"He was off-duty, said he didn't mean for it to turn into anything, that he really needed to talk to me, to keep an eye on things—"

"On my fiancée?"

"He'd also had a few drinks. Wasn't quite himself."

"And now you're defending him? Defending the father of your—"

"He's not the father!" Kara stood to face the couch; tears rolled from the corner of her eyes. She looked very small and fragile with her arms limp at her sides and the left collar of her blouse folded underneath.

"I'm not raising someone else's kid," Marsh informed her.

"Marsh, please. How can you be so cold?"

"You can go see the doctor, right? I'm sure he'll support any decision you make. Especially in light of the baby's blood problems."

"That is not an option I'll consider. This is my baby...our baby."

"Hmm. Wish I could believe that."

Kara, grabbing her purse and stomping out the door, left Marsh's ears ringing with a list of epithets that he had never heard her use before.

During the following week, Marsh held the magnifying glass to her guilt in hopes of diverting the focus from himself; instead, the glass became a mirror, reflecting back his own litany of improprieties. Rather than face his faults, he dug his inner well a bit deeper and tossed down the shaft her sins and his own.

So long—*kersplassh*—farewell.

They loved each other, didn't they? They'd move on. And after a small ceremony in the shadow of Addison Ridge, they stepped into the future determined to make this marriage work. Following his parents' example after losing their firstborn son, Marsh Addison buried himself in the work of the vineyard and squeezed solace from the grapes of success. Hour upon hour. His father's legacy.

Until recent years this remedy had served its purpose.

"Marshall, I'm so sorry. You didn't need to share all that. I'll keep it to myself. You know I will. Attorney-client confidentiality. Not to pour salt on old wounds, but do you think she could be...that she's with someone else? We can't ignore that possibility. It's happened before, as you've just shared. Have there been suspicious signs?"

Marsh pushed himself from the dresser. "No, Casey. Definitely not."

"How can you be certain?"

"Neither one of us has done anything like that since college. It was different then, I guess. Plus, she was drinking socially quite a bit, part of what got her in trouble. Until recently she'd hardly even touch our own wine. That's how much she distrusts alcohol."

"Until recently?"

"Hey, it's all behind us. I've let it go."

"Have you?" Casey let her purse slip to the floor. "I'm sure you know that I find you attractive. You're a handsome man, confident, and you know what you want."

"The only way to be."

"And I like it. Quite a turnon. There're a lot of men out there who'll barely look me in the eye. Friends tell me it's my attitude, that I should back off a little, let the men take the lead. Well, that'd be fine—if they'd take it. *No más*, señor. I'm tired of that game. Most men act like they've never before seen a woman with legs."

"Standard equipment, from what I hear."

"Standard?" Casey slid one thigh over the other. "Or above average?"

Marsh let his eyes slide up her satiny calves. His throat turned dry, but he told himself he was within bounds. *You can look. You just can't touch.* Wasn't that the going code of morality? Married but not dead yet. Conscious of his limited apparel, he let his towel slip into his hand and drape over the front of his boxers.

"What're you trying to say, Casey?"

"Do I need to spell it out?"

He said, "I've got things on my mind, all the stuff that's gone on today. Can't be staying up too late, not if I'm going to be mentally sharp."

"That gives us a good hour or two."

He glanced at his Bulgari on the nightstand.

"Marshall, I'm a working woman. If you think I have time for the emotional roller coaster of a relationship, you're wrong. Two ex-husbands are baggage enough, capice? But I know the male routine, and I can live by those rules. No guilt, no commitment, no expectations. Fair enough?"

"What's in it for me?"

"Wouldn't you like to know." Casey stretched out on the bed, arched her back. Her mascara accentuated her luminous green eyes. Outside the suite, wind and rain were punishing the building in frequent gusts.

He gripped the towel. "Let me think this through. I'm taking my shower first."

"Don't forget to splash on some of your cologne."

"Hugo?"

"Smells so good. I'll be putty in your hands." As Casey rolled onto her stomach and propped elbows, her black heels fell to the carpet.

~

There was no emotion left. Numbness. Nothing more.

Kara drifted in and out of sleep, a rag doll tied to a chair. On occasion, stinging nettles would run down her legs and across her feet as blood circulated again. She'd stamp her feet with the inch or so provided by the rope strapped around her thighs and shins. Scuttling sounds moved in the blackness, and she knew that she would be terrified under normal circumstances. These were anything but.

Numb. Impervious. Damp and dirty and hollow.

She tried to ignore the cold. What if she froze to death down here? How long till someone found her? Entombed in her own beach house. In her husband's wine cellar.

Marsh!

He might very well be blamed, she realized. The evidence would not look good.

Wherever he is, Lord, give him wisdom, give him strength. Don't hold my mistakes against me. For my husband's sake, answer my prayers.

~

Marsh locked the bathroom door behind him. Turned on the fan, the shower.

What was he thinking? A fling with his defense attorney? This would only complicate matters, providing a possible motive to go along with the existing questions. She was a good-looking woman, no doubt about it. She knew how he ticked, respected his work ethic. Sure, she'd hinted at things before, feeding a thought or two in his mind.

No more hints though. This was an in-your-face offer.

In the shower, he watched the steam billow. His face hovered in the hot cloud, removed from his body, cradled by the mist as though in a crystal ball. He ran a finger over a childhood scar on his chest where phantom pains still poked at him on occasion. His eyes stared, dead and unfeeling. He closed them, let water and shampoo run down his face as he ducked beneath the showerhead. What were emotions anyway?

Chemicals, plain and simple. Mixing, reacting. No harm in that.

Yet something restrained him from responding to the woman who was waiting.

Done rinsing, he found the soap on the ledge and fumbled with the hotel wrapper. He was scrubbing his arms when he saw—no, he *felt* the mist swirl in a black-and-white checkered vortex that began to suck him in.

He gasped as a specter in a low-cut dress joined him. Casey?

Confident face, green eyes, sly smile.

What the heck? I thought I locked that door.

"Hold on," he said. "Be right out."

"You want me to wait? Oh, but I want you now."

"Don't push me, okay? I don't like this. This isn't a good idea."

Despite his protest, the face pressed through the mist, and its skin peeled away to reveal a cage of bone with gleaming emerald eyes. Hair, once a stylish brown, turned pale and dry as cut grass. Fingers, skeletal probes, linked around him and pulled him into an unearthly embrace.

"Come on," said the specter. "It'll be even better than you imagined."

"No. I can't do this."

"Really now, Marshall"—the voice was scotch over ice, golden and potent and cold—"why resist the irresistible?"

Marsh met the hollow stare and, despite the malevolence, despite the skin-stripped skull, felt his temperature rise. The pearl necklace glowed. A slave to the prospect of pleasure, his body responded against his will.

"Don't fight what you know you deserve," the voice teased.

The promises of tanned curves and smooth skin danced in silhouette behind luminescent eyes. Raw arousal reared its head; the water played on his back, churning the steam and pressing him deeper into the hellish embrace.

This creature was a representation of his own lurking lust. The battle of the flesh. Black-and-white swirls, writhing shapes… Illusion.

Stumbling from the shower, Marsh almost brought down the vinyl curtain. As he landed on the faux marble floor in a crouch, the fan overhead sucked tendrils of vapor from his skin, sapped composure from his thoughts.

Splash! Splash!

In the corner he saw Kara. She was huddled, tears falling from her cheeks and striking the marble with echoing force.

Splash! Splash!

"Kara? You're alive." Another illusion. He wouldn't be fooled, not again.

"I tried to warn you, Marsh."

"For heaven's sake, not now, okay? Where have you been?"

"Marssshall." The specter's voice was a sedative, a siren song. "Why'd you let *her* in?"

Splash! Splash!

"Who in? Who're you talking about?" Maybe Kara wasn't an illusion.

"Her! Kara!" The specter jabbed an accusatory finger toward the corner, then stepped between husband and wife, long bones in nylons straddling Marsh, fingers beckoning. Avoiding the gem-cut eyes, Marsh set his jaw and took the offered hand so that the creature smiled with pleasure.

"Not so fast!" Marsh growled, grasping the necklace and wrenching it into a noose around the ghastly neck.

The creature froze. Hacked. Choked.

"Not this time." Marsh spoke through gritted teeth. "Score one for me."

The eyes burst into emerald flame, and the voice burned like alcohol in his face. "You'll never win. You logical ones—ha!—you're the easiest to fool. How can you defeat something that you don't even believe exists?"

"Like this!"

With a yank on the noose of pearls, he tried to bring the creature down. His shoulders and chest strained until sweat broke through his pores, yet to no avail. The eyes taunted him; the hands pried him loose with supernatural strength.

"No!"

Kara was astride the bony back, tears streaking her cheeks. Her hands

clawed at the dry hair, came away with clumps of dead grass. The specter collapsed to its knees and fell back onto Kara so that, in Marsh's grasp, the
twisted necklace ground into bone. He heard a snap. It wasn't, however, the
sound of victory; it was the sound of jewelry splitting apart at the clasp. Pearls
slithered down the broken strand, rolled off bony shoulders, and dissolved
into drops of sizzling acid.

Landing one by one on Kara's chest.

"Aarhh! My...heart," she groaned. She was pinned beneath the cadaver-
ous being. "Marsh, why did you... *Aarhh!*"

He stretched out his hand to intercept the burning pearls and caught two
in his palm. On his own skin, they had a numbing effect. His hand became
a nerveless slab, an ice sculpture attached to an arm. The pearls ran in beads
off the specter's shoulders, and from the milky white curvature of each one,
coy faces winked in Marsh's direction. Faces from a pool of cyberimagery,
harmless visual stimuli.

Hey, it wasn't cheating to browse around on the computer. He was a man.
Only natural.

But why the faces? Why now?

As the single remaining pearl landed on Kara's heaving ribs, the specter
cackled. Then, in an instant, the being crumbled into a powdery silt, lingering midair before rotating up into the suction of the fan blades. The blades
screeched, the motor seized, and the bathroom lights sparked in a meteoric
shower of orange that faded into black.

"Kara?"

On hands and knees, Marsh searched the floor. Where was she? She was
gone. He was alone in the darkness with the hiss of the shower, the screech of
the fan, and the sounds of his wife's pain still ringing in his ears.

God, forgive me. What've I done?

29

Hate Letters

The light went off. Josee's eyes analyzed the darkness. The lamp was still at her back, the digital clock read a quarter to eleven, and the music had played itself out, leaving her with the sounds of fading thunder and the swoosh of cloth behind her.

"Who is that?" She whiplashed in the bed to face the intruder. "What're you doing? Why'd you turn that off?"

"Shhh, it's all right. Just me, babe."

"Scooter, that's not even funny. What're you doing sneaking in here?" She reached for the switch, but a hand clamped over hers.

"Don't do it," he said. "It's their fault. I don't want you to see me."

Josee wrested her hand from his and turned on the lamp despite his warning. Scooter's face floated near hers, a visage of fear and conflicting emotion. "You scared the heck outta me," she told him. She stood and wrapped the bedspread over her shoulders. Waiting by the door, with her back to the wall, she said, "Go back to bed, okay?"

"I'm afraid of what they'll make me do."

"They? What do they want you to do? Scoot, who're you talking about?"

He lowered his eyes, took a step toward the hallway. His shoulders were quivering with immense struggle; his breath, cold and dank, lifted the tiny hairs on her arm. "They want to control me. Not just me. They also want—"

With a movement too quick to counter, Scooter pinned her arm to the wall and tugged at the lamp cord. The blackness left her momentarily blinded. Josee shoved back against him, but he evaded her, and without warning his mouth was pressed against hers, grinding, teeth colliding, freezing cold, before she wrenched her face from his and thrust a knee up between his legs.

Scooter collapsed on the floor with a grunt.

Josee dove across the bed and turned on the other lamp. She crouched there on the floor, breathless, and watched him pick himself off the carpet.

"Scooter!" she gasped. "You're supposed to be my friend. I'm supposed to be able to trust you!" Tears swelled at the corners of her eyes and burned trails down into the collar of her shirt. "What's got into you? You try to deny what happened yesterday morning, but I saw it. You were poisoned by...by something evil. You've never done this to me before. Never! Scoot, I can't handle this. I'm not gonna put up with it. Are you hearing me? Say something!"

"Josee, it's not me."

"What is it then?"

"I'm trying to hold them off. I really am." The shame in his eyes was real, yet as he lifted his countenance into pink illumination, the bite marks on his cheek bulged, and cords rippled beneath the skin, knotting his face, tugging at his lips. He avoided her eyes, then locked on to them with brown irises ablaze. "No, that was not nice of me. I didn't want to. But they're...telling me things to do."

"Well, don't freakin' do them!"

He whispered, "You know, you were right about what you said. I did see what happened yesterday. Right as that snake reached my ring, it turned on me." He twisted the moonstone on his finger, and a pallid light swirled in the stone. "I don't know what to do, Josee, don't know how to deal with it. I mean, how did you stop it?"

"I called for help. That's what I did."

"Nobody can help."

"It was a prayer of faith." *A withered seed... Please, Jesus...save us.*

"To God? Jesus?" His words turned colder, a glacial wind sweeping over the bed. "Where are they now, huh? Tell me that. I don't see anyone. And you know why? Because God's not here, that's why. Don't tell me you're falling back into that."

"But that's what faith is, believing in something you can't see."

Scooter gripped his face in his hands as the poison coiled beneath his cheeks. He began to whimper. "Sorry, babe, I don't wanna do it. They're telling me things. Bad things. They want your help. They want the key."

"The key?" Josee recalled Chief Braddock's enigmatic remarks in the elevator.

Scooter said, "Maybe together, we can... No, I can't do this."

"Scooter, please go back to bed."

"You hate me. I'm sorry."

"I don't hate you, but don't ever do something like that again. I mean it."

A knock at the door caused them to turn. John stepped in and said, "Everything okay in here? I was lying in bed when a cold sweat broke over me. Got a feeling I should check on you. Scooter, it might be wise to return to your room now."

Scooter shrunk away, his hands trying to hold together the contortions of his face, the ring on his finger guiding him in a death march down the hall.

Josee's lips were cold. Her heart, too.

Breathing deeply against a suffocating sense of danger, she went into the bathroom and locked the door. Double-checked it. Climbed into the shower. She reflected on those first weeks after she had opened her heart to the concept of a personal God. She was nine, maybe ten. Experiencing a peace she couldn't explain and an assurance that she was no longer alone. Put up for adoption, yes, but never truly abandoned.

Prince of peace. Mighty God. Father to the fatherless.

At sixteen, all that changed.

One evening after a game night in the church gym, the youth minister had offered her a ride home. It was late, he said. Dangerous out there. Josee, apprehensive about walking the dark streets of Renton, succumbed.

The streets would have been safer.

What she saw in the man's eyes that night was frightening. Evil. Like spilled ink, it shaded his face and, by the time he was done, scrawled an indelible hate letter on her heart. In the corner of an abandoned lot, she witnessed the spiritual dark side of a man who claimed to be in the light. Begging her silence, he apologized with tears, explained how lonely the job was, how attractive he found her.

Which only deepened her hatred.

Josee never returned to that church. And she never told a soul.

Only you know, Lord. Where were you, huh? And what about Scooter tonight?

As she had those years ago, she stood under the shower's stream and cranked up the heat until it was almost unbearable. Back then, she had taken two, three, sometimes four showers a day. Scalding away the dirt. Burning the filth from her skin.

Josee heaved a sigh. The water ran down her face in huge drops as she remembered the day she'd heard the news that the youth pastor had been caught. She hadn't been the first victim, or the last. The church was torn over it, and two of the council members resigned, saying that when they had seen disturbing signs and called out a warning, no one had responded. Had God been trying to work through those two members?

Maybe he *had* been there all along.

Yet the senior pastor had sloughed off the council members' concerns.

Okay, so people had free will. God wasn't going to force them to listen and act; he hadn't programmed people like robots to carry out their master's every whim. Still, if the heavenly plan was to work through earthly servants, it was no wonder things got so messed up. Could she pin all of that on God?

Josee felt the myrtlewood cross wet against her chest. She clutched it and closed her eyes. The spraying water drilled against her eyelids. She thought: *To hold on is to believe; to believe is to wrestle with my doubts and questions; to wrestle is to risk injury from a God who seems large and strong yet distant.*

But hadn't he also risked injury—even death—to draw near?

Jesus, was it hard for you down here? Not on the grandiose scale, but in the day-to-day things. I'm so tired of it all. Only twenty-two. Does it get any easier?

⁓

Timberwolf Lane led Stahlherz through the storm's aftermath back toward the highway. He stepped over fallen branches, trudged through piled sand. By the time he reached the Sand Dollar Diner, his leg bones had turned into cinnamon toothpicks—hot and ready to snap.

He saw no sign of Darius or the Aerostar van.

Stahlherz remained calm. He had instructed his driver to check back every half-hour. A quarter to eleven now. A fifteen-minute wait.

He went into the diner to keep watch from the window but found himself in a haze. Two burly men in red-and-black flannel shirts smoked at the bar, tapping ashes into their water glasses while glowering at the sitcom on the television above the food-prep station. At a corner table a teenage couple held hands and giggled.

"Just one, or you got more comin', sweetheart?"

"One." Stahlherz held up a finger for the waitress. "Nonsmoking, please."

"It's all nonsmokin'," she told him. "Don't mind Donny and Red."

"The smoke irritates me, ma'am. Would you mind—"

"They'd mind, and our regulars get special privileges. If that's a problem for you, you'll have to take it up with the management."

"Where is the manager?"

"Home. Sleepin'." She teased her bangs, went cross-eyed for a second as she assessed the results, then handed him a plastic menu. "Find yourself a spot to get comfy, and I'll be with you in a minute, sweetie."

Stahlherz sipped coffee for the next ten minutes. Still no sign of Darius.

The news, however, provided satisfactory distraction. He warmed to the face of young Beau Connors on the television. The news anchor reported that a respected and well-liked Corvallis woman had vanished, her car had been discovered in a ravine, and this young man had turned himself in only hours ago, claiming to be her abductor. The police were investigating the claim, as well as his threats against the citizens of Oregon. A live feed took viewers to a condemned shack in Philomath where detectives had discovered a van linked to Beau Connors. A bomb squad had ruled out any attached explosive devices, but a Detective Randolph had found in the glove box an envelope laced with white powder. In light of similar scares after 9/11, investigators were sending the envelope to a lab to determine whether anthrax was involved. As for Mrs. Kara Addison, she had not yet been found. The anchor instructed viewers with any information to call the number on the screen.

Stahlherz leaned back in satisfied appraisal. "Deflection"—that's what chess players called it. The anthrax was a ruse, nothing more. A means of deflecting the authorities' attention. And it was working.

The public was just as easily fooled. Stahlherz eavesdropped on the men at the bar.

"Get a load o' that, Red. Anthrax. That's some downright nasty stuff."

"Whadda they expect?" Red took an extended drag, let smoke curl through his nostrils and ruddy beard. "I seen it on *20/20, Dateline*—one o' them shows. Can buy the stuff through the mail, you believe that? Universities, whatnot, they study it—guess it's got somethin' to do with some animal disease—and they'll send ya samples like it's shampoo to rub through your hair." He chortled and dropped his cigarette butt in his glass.

"World's a sick place anymore. Line up the head cases, and I'd mow 'em down."

"Free o' charge," Red agreed, "with my Peterbilt."

"We got families to feed, bills to pay. Save the taxpayers some moola."

Stahlherz ingested the exchange with a growing sense of justice. See, these men had no clue. They were uneducated, backwoods screwups blind to the fact that they added to the system's sickness. Talk, talk, talk. Was that all they could do? Let them gag on their self-righteous blabber. Tomorrow the talk would be over.

Time for action.

Throughout the Willamette Valley and along the Oregon coast, ICV cells now waited with the twelve canisters he had disbursed. Each canister was a binary weapon composed of two chambers. Boomslang hemotoxin filled the first. Tomorrow night, with Josee Walker's help and the assistance of other recruits on standby, Stahlherz would supply the other ingredient. Crafted by Nazi biochemist Doktor Ubelhaar, the nerve gas accelerant would fill the secondary chambers of each canister.

Serpentine malice and human endeavor—a deadly concoction.

Fill your cup… Drink up!

On its own, the hemotoxin was hazardous, but the accelerant multiplied the potency a hundredfold. The result: a highly concentrated biochemical weapon capable of poisoning tens of thousands. Perhaps more.

Huddled in the armchair, Josee pulled the bedspread tighter.

How could she trust Scooter? The grind of his mouth, the stale breath. He had violated a boundary long established between them. He'd not only tried to force himself on her, he'd also written himself into those inky memories she wanted to forget.

Forgive and forget.

She couldn't forget. How could she ever? But then, maybe forgiveness was simply the first step on a road leading away from the darkness. Could she learn from the past and still walk into the future? Was forgetting nothing more than releasing her rights to seek punishment for the wrongdoers?

What they did was so wrong! Lord, how can you sit by?

"Vengeance is mine. I will repay those who deserve it."

She knew that was God's line somewhere in the Bible. One day he would deliver justice. A judge, weighing the evidence. And all were guilty—every last one. Black ink. Whether scrawled or printed painstakingly, the ink was still a stain on white paper. Only the sacrifice of one could erase the hate letters of the many.

Jesus, I don't want to hate. Not anymore. But I can only take so much.

With sleep elusive, Josee advanced the CD player to the fourth track and absorbed the syncopated bass and delicate cymbals of U2's "Walk On." The lyrics drew her feelings and thoughts into a soothing embrace. She began to drift off, the words holding her by the hand as they led her down a path of dreams.

30

The Game Book

"Might want to see the news, Marshall. Come on out."

Marsh unlocked the door and stumbled from the bathroom's darkness with a towel around his waist. Before him, Casey Wilcox was lean and radiant, her clothes dry, her hair styled. On the television, a commercial was playing.

"You slip on the floor, mon cher? Sounded as though you fell, and then I heard mumbling but couldn't tell what you were saying. You took forever in there." Casey scooped up her heels and purse. "Go ahead, I'm a grown woman. You were avoiding me, is that to be my assumption? A change of heart?"

"Something like that." He edged her through the hotel suite door. "Time for you to go. Let's just pretend this never happened."

"Nothing did happen."

"Exactly. Good night."

Casey braced a foot against the door. "Marshall, there is some good news to share. While you were in the shower, I checked my office messages. The sergeant called to say that Corvallis PD's pulling the crime team from your estate. As of tomorrow morning, you have the all clear to go home."

"Home?"

"I thought you'd be glad. You'll have back the manor and your Tahoe."

"Kara's not there."

Casey set a finger on his shoulder. "Then, Mr. Addison, I suggest you do your best to get her back. I wish you—and your wife—all the best. Genuinely. Guess I misread you earlier. My error. I see now that you do love her. It's sweet actually."

"Bye, Casey." Marsh chained and deadbolted the door.

On the news the wreckage of Kara's BMW Z3 was filling the screen. Marsh clicked the volume button. The anchorwoman gave a chronological rehash of events surrounding the disappearance of Kara Addison, wife of

Corvallis vintner and owner of Addison Ridge Vineyards. The anchor mentioned the initial questioning of Marshall Addison, then Sergeant Turney appeared with news of a young man's confession to the woman's abduction. The police force, he said, was investigating and looking for anyone with pertinent information. "When we return," the anchor promised, "we'll bring you the story of a related terrorist threat and how it could affect you, and we'll take a closer look at the local political race as things heat up for next week's election…"

The sacrifice had been made. Beau Connors. A measly pawn.

Marsh felt the burden of suspicion lift from his shoulders, yet Steele Knight's maneuvering served notice that he was in this game to the death.

As he faced the barren room, Marsh saw his night bag opened at the foot of the bed. Casey must've been searching for his cologne. In defiance of her advances, the leather corner of a Bible protruded from his folded clothes.

A Bible? Strange. He didn't own a personal copy.

His fingers touched the cover and tightened as a current issued forth from the weathered book. *Kara Addison.* In silver filigree, her name commanded attention. Had Turney scooped this into the duffel bag while at the estate? A simple mistake?

As opposed to the bathroom's apparition, the nearness of Kara's Bible lent Marsh a sense of calm. Wherever Kara was, he realized she was not alone.

He thumbed the pages. The book fell open.

Hoping for a glimpse into her world, he began to read.

⸺

Thubba-hisssh, thubba-hisssh…

Trapped in the dark hole beneath her husband's trophy room, Kara woke to the grating sound. In her mind, she could see the prickly arm of a ponderosa pine bumping and dragging against an outer wall above.

Thubba-hisssh, thubba-hisssh…

Years ago, in the dark stairwell of Good Samaritan Hospital, she had heard a similar sound as she worked the steps, hoping to hurry the delivery of her daughter. Was it an old wives' tale, or would this work? One step, then another. Marsh, her fiancé, was holding one hand while she gripped the guardrail with the other. Her belly was swollen and heavy, her legs bowed. This was her first child. Had a baby ever dropped straight out? It seemed imminently possible. Her lower back was a cord of knotted muscle that squeezed down with each step.

Footsteps…*thubba.* The brush of a jacket…*hisssh.*

Thubba-hisssh…

This time they both heard it. Kara turned her head in time to see a white-jacketed figure arrive on the landing above. She couldn't see the face; from this angle, she saw only a silver blue object with a gaping black mouth. Behind the figure, she saw the door open. The gaping mouth roared.

Ka-boommm!

The crack of thunder echoed through the stairwell, deafening. She felt a tug at her hip. A bullet? She was falling, clutching at Marsh for support, crumpling into a heavy ball. He braced his legs and gripped her elbow with one arm, her waist with the other. *The baby!* He let her down gently. She winced, felt hot sticky fluid pumping from the hip wound. Above, the landing had cleared, and the door had closed them off. Marsh was speaking soothing words. She was getting blood on his clothes.

"I'm sorry," she said. Then her voice failed her. *Sorry.*

Like salt on a wound, Detective Braddock was the first on the scene. The tension between Marsh and the detective was palpable.

Sorry, sorry.

After preliminary treatment of the bullet wound, an emergency Cesarean ushered a daughter into the world. Little Josee. Six pounds, eleven ounces. *Perfect,* Kara thought. In her arms, the tiny form sparked to life, awash in the color bursts of the Independence Day fireworks outside. A pink cap warmed the infant's head.

Marsh stepped in. "You beat the fireworks," he said. "Just like you wanted."

Kara's hair was plastered to her cheeks. "Here. Say hi to her."

"No use getting attached, gonna have to let her go. We already agreed—"

"I know, I know." Tears pooled on Kara's eyelids. "Just let her hear your voice before you say good-bye for good. You can do that much at least."

Marsh said, "Hi there, little one. Uh, how are you?"

Together they stared transfixed by the infant's ribbon-thin lips and pudgy nose, by a band of turquoise that twinkled through moist, squinty eyelids.

"My baby girl," Kara whispered as she adjusted the receiving blanket.

Marsh watched. "Taking it better than I thought you would, Kara."

Without looking up, she said, "I don't want her to feel my pain. I want her to know joy." Then, focused on little Josee, she cooed, "You'll always be my baby. Please remember my voice. This is your mama talking to you. You'll always be my precious girl." Despite herself, she let the tears fall as her lips convulsed in quiet whimpers.

Then the commotion at the door shattered the night.

Kara was rushed to safety. Josee was rushed from their lives.

Now, tied to a chair, Kara Addison held on to the hope of that pink knitted cap in her pocket. Out there, somewhere, Josee Walker was looking for her mother. Perhaps a twist of fate would join Josee and Marsh in their efforts to locate her.

Not that everyone made choices within God's will. Many disobeyed.

But didn't he cause "everything to work together for the good of those who love God"? Hadn't she underlined that verse? At the moment it seemed an empty consolation, considering that her Bible was at home on her nightstand, far, far away.

Marsh contemplated the pages. His heart was drumming. He had never imagined this book could have any relevance to his life and was amazed by its detailed description of his struggle through the past two days.

"We are not fighting against people made of flesh and blood," it read.

Tell me about it! What was that thing in the shower?

"...but against...mighty powers of darkness who rule this world."

Do skeletons in the bathroom count? This actually makes sense!

"Use every piece of God's armor to resist the enemy in the time of evil."

Deep within him, the simplicity of the words resonated with authority. Marsh closed the Bible and placed it on the pillow next to him. The silver filigree shimmered, and the musky scent of the leather rose as incense. Like the tomes of Homer and Sophocles, the book had its place as a literary master-piece, as an ancient document, and yet on a deeper level it exuded a dignity and—he could think of no other word for it—a *presence*. A part of history. A life of its own.

He opened the book again to the preceding passage.

He was a man savoring each course of a meal.

"You husbands must love your wives with the same love Christ showed the church. He gave up his life for her."

I've kept Kara at arm's length. Am I willing to love deeply? Would I die for her?

" 'A man leaves his father and mother and is joined to his wife, and the two are united into one.' This is a great mystery."

Got that right! And in light of my dad's journal, it's a bigger mystery than ever.

Interesting side note: Kara hadn't underlined the verses that dealt with his spousal mishandlings; she'd underlined the one directed to wives. In typical fashion, she had taken the burden of guilt upon herself. Had he, by his actions, pounded her down one notch at a time until she was less than a woman in her own mind?

A new determination took hold. The reading had cleared his head.

With his thumb, he tapped at Sergeant Turney's card on the nightstand. He needed Steele Knight's true identity. Without it, what hope did he have of catching his opponent off guard?

Marsh pulled on his loafers and found a pay phone in front of the hotel where he could avoid having his calls traced. He was disappointed to get an answering machine at the sergeant's number, but he refused to turn back. He could not do it all alone.

"Sergeant," he said into the machine, "I spoke with you in Barkley's today. I am taking an extreme risk in contacting you. Please keep this between us. I do not believe Beau Connors is acting alone, and I suspect you'll agree. Earlier I received a suspicious call on my cell, but my service provider will not release the info on the blocked number. Maybe, with a subpoena, you could gain access to the user's identity. Just a thought, but Officer Lansky told me this morning that a mobile caller phoned in about my wife's car in the ravine. Compare the two numbers. You might find a match."

After providing the relevant details of his phone account, Marsh dialed Henri Esprit.

"Did I catch you in bed?"

"No, no. Seems I never sleep. What can I do for you?"

"How's your nephew doing on the computer? Has he come up with anything?"

"Steele Knight is registered in the gaming zone. That much he's confirmed. The Webmaster refuses, however, to release any personal info without a court order. With a valid e-mail address—and, as you're well aware, those are a dime a dozen—technically, just about any wise guy can register in the zone."

"So that's it?"

"Not at all. Nick's wondering if you intend to play Steele Knight in the morning. I told him of your online habit, and he thinks such a match could provide a chance to trace the modem connection and pinpoint a phone number."

Marsh scanned the walkway. "We meet at 7:00 AM in the zone. I don't know if Steele Knight'll show up tomorrow, but it's worth a try."

"From there, Nick theorizes, he can track down his mailing address. Unless, of course, he's operating from a public site, such as a library or phone booth."

"That seems unlikely. We've been playing nearly every day for years."

"The other possibility is a mobile phone. That could also put us off the scent."

"True," Marsh conceded, "but as long as he shows up online, it's worth a try. I'll pull a surprise from the game book and give him a fight he won't forget."

Where was Darius?

After grimacing through a fifth refill, Stahlherz weighed the option of returning to the Addison beach house to take charge of the Professor's parked Studebaker. He disliked the idea of abandoning a network member, but he knew he must act. He slapped down his payment on the Formica tabletop and brushed past his waitress, who looked ready for a break. Droopy mouth, dark-ringed eyes, weary stare.

We'll be doing her a service tomorrow by putting her out of her misery.

With a tail of sand, a van swung into the diner parking lot. Before Darius had time to shut off the engine, Stahlherz was out the door and climbing into the vehicle.

"Say, Steele-man—"

"Where have you been?"

"Look, I met this chick pumpin' gas. She start hittin' on me hard. Asked if I wants to meet up after her shift. She got some bud from a friend. Uncut stuff, da bomb—"

"Give me the keys."

"Whaddya want? Here, ain't I?"

"The keys!"

With one hand, Karl Stahlherz grasped at the ignition, and with the other he latched on to the driver's neck and dug clawlike fingers through cotton fabric. He felt acetous rage drain through his talons, sour and raw, then reveled in the man's slumping posture. Stahlherz's eyes formed unblinking orbs that scanned the van's perimeter. A tidal breeze swirled sand over the vehicle's hood. A light patter of rain splayed over the glass and ran in rivulets through the residue.

No sign of witnesses.

In a sudden movement, Darius jerked upright and thrust open his door. He ripped himself free from Stahlherz's grasp, and putty legs carried him to the sidewalk where he collapsed. Straining to look over his shoulder, his face was full of confusion.

A man in a cook's apron peered out the diner's window.

Kre-aaawk!

Stahlherz staggered from the van. Palpable anger had turned his bone marrow to ice. He fell to his knees beside the driver and said, "Get up! You have a job to do." When the man showed no response, Stahlherz set his hands on the mane of brown hair and tried to summon obedience. "Audentes fortuna juvat. Rise, you fool! Onto your feet!"

"You know this guy? He a friend of yours?"

Stahlherz looked up into the face of the diner cook. "He… Yes. I need to get him into the van. He's going into insulin shock. Case of diabetes, see."

The cook helped shoulder Darius through the van's side panel and onto the bench seat. "You got it handled from here?" he asked, lifting his voice over the pounding of surf and wind.

Nodding, Stahlherz thanked the man and climbed behind the wheel.

A few miles out of Yachats he pulled to the side of the highway. As he waited for a pair of cars to pass, he scribbled notes on a piece of paper and then stuffed it into the wallet in Darius's back pocket. He'd already planted the anthrax sample as a deflection, causing the authorities to spin their wheels while he and ICV proceeded with their schemes. Why not spin a few more?

Deflection, ha! With a human twist.

Grunting, he dragged the unconscious man from the van and into the middle of the pitted coastal road. The pavement dipped here. Headlights jumped. Oncoming vehicles would have little chance of spotting the prostrate figure.

Another pawn sacrifice. Road kill.

Back in the van, Stahlherz concentrated on the dash, gripped the wheel, and eased down on the gas. It'd been a long time. He had to do this right, a peerless driver, a model citizen. No reason to risk their schemes over a piddling traffic infraction. He might have some difficulty explaining. *You see, Officer, I have no true identity. I'm a man without a father. On paper I don't exist.*

The imagined response wrinkled his thin lips.

Now more than ever he wanted his birthright. And he wanted Marsh— that usurper!—to be stripped of all he held dear. His wife, his daughter, even life itself.

Kre-acck!

Pain, in the form of a massive black wing, slapped across the backs of Stahlherz's eyeballs, tearing at the optic nerves as if to disconnect his sense of sight. He reeled back with a spasm, held that position, then doubled over, rocked by a set of gaffs that stabbed from his ear canals.

Kaw-kaw-kawntrolll! Screechh!

Stahlherz slammed on the brake pedal and felt the van fishtail. He brought the vehicle to a stop on the highway's shoulder. With a firm hand, he latched on to one of the hooks and began to wrestle the orange talon from the pounding orifice in his head. Then a wild nip sent a jolt through the base of his left thumb, and he let go. Back into his thoughts the blackbird floated, a thunderhead of acid rain.

PART FIVE

I go on a path appointed.
But those who follow me do so of free will....
I shall take the Paths of the Dead,
alone, if need be.

The Return of the King by J. R. R. Tolkien

Though your hearts were once full of darkness,
now you are full of light.... Take no part
in the worthless deeds of evil...expose them.

Ephesians 5:8,11

31

In the Balance

Friday, October 31. Halloween. The city was on the edge of its seat.

Along the block, amid the wisps of dawn's breath, Josee could see black-and-orange flags and bumper stickers parading OSU's colors for tomorrow's gridiron battle. Rabid fans would converge upon Reser Stadium to cheer their team and berate their opponents. In fitting parallel, seasonal decorations of witches and skeletons and bats promised an eventful evening for the neighborhood kids.

From a mailbox across the street, a glow-in-the-dark skull stared at Josee.

She stepped back from the Van der Bruegges' front window and thought of the canister she'd found in the thicket on Tuesday. Since then, her world had come undone. Her mother was missing. Her father was dismissive. Scooter was…not himself.

Wonder if Sarge's heard anything new. My sparring partner, he'd better call.

Before breakfast, Josee did receive a call. From no one she expected.

———

The darkness held him in a barren womb.

Sergeant Vince Turney knew this was a dream, fears and memories stalking the borders of his mind, but that made it no less real. He was running between alley walls, searching for a suspect. He slowed as he neared a garbage container where tentacles of sewage spread from the rusted bottom. Footsteps. Coming close.

He drew his police weapon and skirted the container.

From behind, something brushed his face, and he turned.

Glistening in the moonlight, a blade swept by, and he dodged back. A hulking, toothless man sniggered as he pointed to the side where a newborn slept in a car seat at the base of the alley wall. Knife in hand, the man sprinted toward the baby, and the sergeant aimed his gun. Pulled the trigger. Felt the recoil. The .38 projectile spun through the air with all the speed of a spit watermelon seed.

As the man stretched for the infant, Turney fired another round.

This time the barrel of the gun gagged on the bullet and sagged like a limp reed. Useless. Impotent. Again he had failed at his task. A baby gone…

No, I can't let her down. Not again.

"Josee!"

Turney bolted up in bed. He was breathless, drenched in sweat. He checked the time. Yesterday had taken its toll, but he saw no point in trying to go back to sleep. He pulled on a robe and padded into the kitchen, where he poured himself a bowl of Peanut Butter Crunch. He fetched the nonfat milk from the fridge and unscrewed the cap. Waved off a fly.

But the fly refused to be ignored. The creature circled in random patterns.

Turney peeled back his bathrobe and saw discharge leaking through bandages. Tingles ran from his shoulder down to his fingertips. The fly droned closer to his ear.

"Would you quit that?" he snapped. "Buzz off."

The pest lighted on the gauze; tiny feet tiptoed through the sticky green stain.

"Shoo!" Turney flicked his finger, but the fly took evasive action. Landed again.

What was this thing doing? Laying eggs? Turney knew wounds were ideal cesspools for breeding. Could maggots feed off him? Hatch from his skin? Now that he thought about it, flies had been pestering him pretty much since the reemergence of his scars. What was the deal?

Beelzebub…Lord of the flies!

Like a blow to the midsection, this biblical description of Satan and his activity stole the sergeant's breath away. Yessir, more going on here than met the eyes. Not that he thought this housefly was the devil incarnate, nothing so crazy as that, but the fly symbolized the evil that had been Turney's bane.

These scars… Were they God's ways of warning him to remain humble, alert?

Betcha that's it. Just like the verse says, "When I am weak, then I am strong."

Spreading through his bandages, the pus threatened to erode his resolve. Then he felt a prayer rise from his chest—a lifeboat of faith carried on a tenacious current. The words came as neither shout nor whisper; they came as silent command.

Get outta here, you filthy, unclean thing.

The fly, in the act of rubbing its feet together, froze.

Turney thought of Josee and her Wednesday morning confrontation. Hadn't her prayer halted her foe in its tracks?

"In the name of Jesus," he said, "I'm tellin' you, get lost!"

He aimed, then snapped his stubby finger. The fly shot into the side of the cereal box and fell dazed to the table. Turney finished it off with a crumpled napkin, which he flushed down the toilet. A surge of excitement brushed over his scalp. Surprised, he smiled. He thought he'd buried that feeling years ago, thought he'd buried it for good.

The phone jangled from his stack of phone books by the Gevalia coffee maker.

"Howdy," he answered. The stove's clock read twenty after six.

"Vince, hope it's not too early. John Van der Bruegge." They exchanged banter, then John said, "I'll make this quick. You're a busy man, and I've a class to teach, but I want your help. Actually, I *need* your help."

"Josee? Is she okay?"

"Hanging in there. A likable young lady, but I can see that she has a lot going on behind those eyes of hers."

"Uh-huh."

"Beautiful eyes, too, or haven't you noticed?"

"Uh-huh."

John laughed. "Vince, how long do you intend to hold the opposite sex at arm's length? I've known you long enough to understand your caution, but it's been three years, and your grieving won't bring Milly back. She would've told you to walk on, to keep living life. Am I wrong?"

"I'm hangin' in there."

"You've substituted food for love."

"Whoa, John, that's goin' too far—"

"It's the truth, isn't it? Your fear of getting hurt is jeopardizing your health." Sympathy tamed John's voice. "We all have our weaknesses, Vince. I'm not trying to point fingers, just trying to be a friend. Which brings me to the purpose of my call. Situation is this: Krissy and I've discussed it, and we're convinced that Scooter and Josee are wrestling with some weighty issues, some strong spiritual forces. Last night I caught Scooter in her room, and Josee looked petrified—no other word to describe it. We need to join together. Need to fight on their behalf. At the risk of sounding sensational, I believe their lives could be in the balance."

Turney ran a hand down his tummy and swallowed his indignation. John's reprimands were dead-on. He said, "What'd you have in mind?"

"You remember Jesus' words to his disciples? He told them that some evil spirits would only be conquered by prayer and fasting. I'm sure that's what we're dealing with here, and I think it might be time to make a stand."

"A stand?"

"You and Kris and I, committed to seeing this thing through."

"Hear what you're sayin', but I'm on duty in an hour. Bit difficult to hit my knees while pounding the streets. Not that I won't help, but—"

"I just need you to fast."

"Fast? As in, don't eat?"

"Think of it as a health regimen. Fasting flushes toxins from your system, and in the unseen realm it has similar effects. What about it? Are you with me on this?"

Turney leaned his forehead against the refrigerator door. No food? This was like asking a bear to hibernate in the heat of summer. His arm throbbed as he weighed John's request. He knew the fight of which John spoke. Knew the opponent.

Beelzebub.

"Say, how about I skip lunch? I could—"

"One day—that's all I'm asking. Think you can handle that, Vince? I've seen evil take over when people refuse to make a stand. This is for Scooter's and Josee's sake. Let's hear it. Are we in agreement?"

Turney pressed his head into the crook of his arm and forced out his reply. "Sure, John, I'll give it my best shot."

Slowly he emptied his cereal back into the box.

To Josee, seated in the living room shadows, John looked tall and dapper in his herringbone jacket. He was at the front door, balancing a syllabus and two books atop his horizontal briefcase, when she said, "Out of here already? Not eating this morning?"

"Josee. Didn't see you there in the dark."

"Your wife's making Dutch babies. Says they're delicious."

"They are. Right now, though, Krissy and I have other things on our plates." John winked as Kris stepped into the arched doorway, then pulled her into an embrace. "Should be gone most of the day, but we want you to feel free here in our home, Josee. Fresh towels, coffee, anything. If you want to call and let your adoptive parents know where you are, the phone's all yours."

"It's long distance. Renton, Washington."

"No problem. A couple loads of dishes, and you'll be all paid up."

"John, honestly." Kris pushed her shoulder into him. "He's kidding, Josee."

"Hardy-har-har." Josee wore a grin to dilute her sarcasm. "Anyway, I don't know that I should call them. Moved out years ago. I had to find some space, probably the same as your daughter."

"Annalise," John and Kris said together.

"Not that they were to blame, not at all. Just had to figure out life on my own."

"As a mother," Kris said, "I can tell you that it'd mean a lot to them if you called. I understand the need for independence, but part of growing up is learning to operate under someone else's rules. That's true in college, on the job, in society—"

"Heard this speech before."

"It's not a popular one," Kris admitted. "I'm of the opinion, though, that people can't move fully into maturity until they come to terms with the influence of their parents. Not that parents don't make mistakes, Josee, but the longer you try to escape their influence, the farther you run from the very things that make you who you are. Until you deal with it, the good *and* the bad, you won't be comfortable in your own skin."

"Explains what's wrong with me then, doesn't it? How can I deal with it when I don't even know my real parents? Why do you think I came down here, huh? And now that Kara's missing—kidnapped, abducted, whatever—guess I'm just sorry out of luck."

"Oh, sweetheart—"

"I'll figure it out on my own. Don't worry about me."

"Listen, we're here to help in whatever way we can." John raised an eyebrow, paused to consider a noise from the hallway. "And no matter what happens, you *can* find comfort in your own skin. Yes, parents are the soil, but you're still the plant fighting the elements in order to bloom. Be who God's made you to be."

"Defective merchandise—that's what I am."

"You're so much more than that. Look"—Kris stepped forward and set one hand on Josee's shoulder and brushed the other over her cheek—"in less than two days, we've grown attached to you. Imagine how your adoptive parents feel. Surely, they'd love to hear your voice."

"Hmm."

"Remember, only a couple of loads of dishes." John flipped the phone from its wall mount and extended it like a cure for her melancholy. Then he brought the speaker to his own ear and listened. "Thought I heard someone just hang up. Is Scooter awake?"

"That bum? I doubt it." After last night's encounter, Josee didn't look forward to facing him. Would he act like nothing had happened? Would she? Only time could restore things to normal.

John flicked his eyes at Kris. "I would've sworn… Well, why don't you two ladies sit and relax, and I'll go rouse that sleepyhead."

Before he'd taken a step, the phone rang, and John answered it.

"For me?" Josee asked, when he handed it over. "Hi, who is this?"

"Josee? Oh, my, but I'm glad to have contacted you. My name's Rosamund Yeager. Rosie. I'm the Addisons' household manager, the one you reached on Wednesday. Please, for your mother's safety, allow me to explain. She had to postpone your earlier meetings—difficulties on the domestic front, I'm afraid. My apologies for any consternation this has caused on your part. It's a delicate matter."

"What're you telling me?"

"Marital struggles," Rosie said. "Kara regrets that you've been caught in the crossfire. She doesn't want you to think less of her husband, but she simply could not go on in the stifling environment at the manor. She devised her own escape before things spiraled farther downward. You do understand, I hope."

Josee's heart was in her throat. "But I thought that—"

"Ignore the crackpot claims," Rosie broke in. "She has not been abducted. Inevitable, really, that some deranged soul should try to take responsibility. No, Kara is well, don't you worry. She hasn't stopped speaking of you. She still wishes to meet with you and with you alone—she's quite firm on that—this afternoon, if possible."

"At the park?"

"Yes. Shall we say, oh..."

"One o'clock. Avery Park." Josee felt hope rush back in as rejection rolled from her shoulders. Her mom wanted to meet with her. Yes, Kara was healthy. Alive. Relief squeezed a short laugh from her lungs, and she brushed her sleeve over her cheeks. "Okay, yeah, I can do that."

"Splendid," Rosie said. "She was so worried that you'd turn her away."

"What, are you kidding? This is why I came."

"She does have two requests, please understand. For sentimental reasons, she'd love to see your birth certificate if you could bring it along."

"Sure. What else?"

"Strange as it may sound, she asks that you keep this discussion from Marsh."

The stipulation struck Josee as odd, but she knew little about her parents. Perhaps they'd been struggling more than Kara had let on. She had said Marsh could be distant and unfeeling. Warned that he was not a creature of emotion. Why, though, had she chosen this week to make such a drastic effort to escape?

Figure it out later. This is my chance to see Kara. I can't screw it up.

"I won't say a word," Josee confirmed.

"Settled then. We'll see each other this afternoon."

"We? Wait, I thought it was just me and Kara. And, Rosie, how'd you find me here? No one's supposed to know where I'm staying."

"I'm a woman of many resources. My age demands it."

"Well, I guess I—"

"Kris!" John's voice reverberated up the hallway. "Kris and Josee, I need to see you both. Come and take a look at this, in Scooter's room."

Scooter? Oh, no!

Josee barked a farewell into the phone and lurched from the couch.

"Stahli. What have you done? Why do you persist with your impetuous ways?"

"Professor?" Stahlherz untangled the phone cord and tossed aside his covers. He cleared phlegm from his throat. "What're you talking about? I'm still in bed."

"The morning news, haven't you seen it?"

"I just told you that I'm in bed. Arrived home late last night."

"Your driver, Son. Found dead. Don't you see the attention this'll draw to us?"

"I left him along the road," Stahlherz confessed. "Left misleading information in his wallet as well, so as to deflect attention from our plans. No need to worry."

"I hope you've not miscalculated, the way you've been known—"

"Trust me, Professor."

"What foundation do I have for this trust? You've allowed hatred for your brother in arms to remove all reason from that head of yours. You've always despised Marsh for that which he has. Understandably so. But after your clumsy efforts, even my attempts have been doomed. Sometimes I wonder that I even call you my son."

"Mother!"

Stahlherz felt bile rise like vinegar in his throat, like gall on his lips. How could she reject him? She had rescued him from Chance Addison's abandonment. In his mind, words stolen from the Savior's cross took on blasphemous form. *My mother, my father, why have you forsaken me? Am I so wretched? So worthless?*

"Channel that anger," Rosie directed him. "Harness your dark thoughts, and use them to your advantage. Do not, however, become arrogant in your use of these forces. They'll fight you, even destroy you."

"And by giving them control, you believe *you* are safe?"

"Yes. For 'when I am weak, then I am strong.'"

Stahlherz snapped his neck one way and the other, then hung up on her. Opening his blinds, he ushered in a wave of gray light. What a loathsome view. These bi-level homes and gleaming automobiles served as nothing more than suburban props, masking abuse and betrayal, lies and addictions. Humanity made him sick.

On his cell, he placed an exploratory call to an ICV cohort.

"He's leaving the hotel this very moment, Mr. Steele."

"Keep him in sight. If he notices you, let it rattle him a bit."

"What if he tries to shake us?"

"Crash-Chess-Dummy? I know the way this man thinks: very linear in his reasoning, preferring the direct and tactical approach. Even if he does manage to elude you, we have alternative tracking methods. Keep me posted."

Next Stahlherz phoned and maneuvered through American Express's automated menu. After verifying Marsh Addison's data for a female account manager, he requested a breakdown of the card's activity. "From 4:00 PM yesterday to the present. I've misplaced my wallet with all my receipts in it," he explained. "I'm looking to sort my transactions, so as to avoid any oversights when it comes to paying my balance."

"Was the card in your wallet, Mr. Addison? I can put a hold on it, if you wish."

"Won't be necessary," he said. "I'm sure I'll find it. The recent activity—that's really all I need."

"Let us know if you decide otherwise."

The lady detailed the card's usage, beginning with a payment to Barkley's Restaurant and ending with room charges at the Ramada Inn less than an hour ago. From the charges, Stahlherz deduced that Marsh had been to the golf course, conducted business, visited his mother in Depoe Bay, and spent most of the evening indoors.

Don't take me lightly, Crash-Chess-Dummy. In chess, only one king wins.

Josee sprinted down the hall and arrived at John Van der Bruegge's side. Scooter's bedroll was gone. As was he. Josee took in the emptiness of the bedroom and the open window above the bed. On the floor, piled upon the open pages of a role-playing game manual, eggshells lay like torn scraps of parchment.

Leathery snake eggs. Freshly hatched.

32

Deflected

Marsh Addison's suspicions took shape in the rearview mirror. He had checked out of the hotel early, and as the Bonneville carried him north of town, he spotted a nondescript Chevy Cavalier in the thinning traffic behind him. Was this the same car he'd noticed yesterday? He detoured. Meandered. Backtracked.

The Cavalier followed at a distance.

Okay, Marsh figured, they knew he had been at the Ramada, and they probably knew he lived up Ridge Road. Public info, available in any phone book. Let them follow. He hadn't created a credit trail for nothing.

He turned, and his pursuer pulled into the Dari-Mart at the base of the hill.

Nice try. Soon as I'm outta sight, you'll be back on my tail.

Marsh steered around debris that last night's storm had scattered over the road. He slowed by mile-marker four and considered stopping but decided he did not want to relive yesterday's anomalies. He was short on time as it was. Twenty-two minutes. Would Steele Knight be online for their regular chess match?

Henri Esprit and a university kid were waiting at the front pillars of the house.

"No cops, huh?" said Marsh.

"They've all gone home," Esprit said. "Place is yours again, and your Tahoe's in the garage. Meet Nick, my nephew."

Nick's anemic goatee could not hide the former acne battleground of his face. Stretched over his girth, a white sweatshirt boasted anachronous diagrams and proclaimed the annual da Vinci Days. More reassuring, Nick toted a sleek notebook computer under his arm.

"Hope I can be of service to you, Mr. Addison."

"Me, too."

"Friends and I went online last night, zeroed in on the Web site you provided, but couldn't find a trace of anyone using a local Internet protocol under the name Steele. Might be an alias. We did verify the Steele Knight name in the gaming zone though. Ran a program to log every time he entered the zone so that, by process of elimination, we could home in on his address, maybe pinpoint his modem."

"And?"

"He never logged on. Program's still running back in my dorm, so if he shows up this morning, we'll have a head start." Nick pulled down his sweatshirt to cover a tuft of bellybutton hair. "Plus, I'm gonna check with this other dude who's got connections with the Dead Cow Society—"

"The what?"

"A hacker thing. What'd really help is if we can get Steele Knight to give us his e-mail address. That'd be sweet, save us time in a big way. Not that I mind the challenge, but you're in a hurry, am I right?"

"Could say that."

"Let's do this."

Marsh led them up the flared steps into the vacant manor. He noted items that the crime team had moved, hints of footsteps in thick carpet, straggling yellow tape. A sense of violation formed a pit in his stomach. Despite the confession of Beau Connors, last night's newscast had intimated the police's initial suspicion of Marsh's involvement in his wife's disappearance. He felt dirtied by this whole affair.

From the parlor, *The Lady in Dread* spied on them.

Marsh thought of the art gallery's thank-you message and the smaller note from his opponent. His desire to bless his wife had backfired, instigating further questions and suspicion from the officers on hand. Lansky had even asked if he was turning this empty space into a shrine. Somewhere out there Steele Knight was mocking him.

Rage coursed through Marsh. Fear for Kara's life fueled his emotion.

"This is one *pathetic* joke!"

Swearing, he marched across the parquet and tore the painting from the wall. He smashed the frame into the floor. Brought it down with hammerlike force. Golden wood shards spat like sparks from an anvil. The canvas tore. Down! *Craackk!* Down!

His mother's cautions blinked in his head: *It will find that rage in you and use it against you… "Your anger can never make things right in God's sight."*

Marsh flung the misshapen frame into the corner. He was bleeding.

He removed a sliver from his forearm and said, "Let's go nail this lunatic!"

—

As they entered the study, his computer was launching itself onto the Internet.

"Give me a few minutes here," Nick said, plopping into the desk chair. Marsh noticed that the black leather was scrubbed, devoid of yesterday's evidence of blood. "We'll enter the gaming zone," Nick explained, "in a sec. I'm gonna hook in and run some software, try to track down this guy's IP. Once you're in the cell playing the game with him, I'll try to finger his service provider." The kid set up camp on the desk, running cables into Marsh's computer tower beside the desk.

Esprit beamed at Nick, then at Marsh. "Brains must run in the family."

"Esprit," Marsh said, "I need some of that wisdom of yours."

"I thought I'd never hear you confess such a thing."

"Miracles never cease. Listen…"

While Nick made connections, Marsh drew his winemaker to the tinted window overlooking the vineyards and condensed the account of Kara's abduction, the note from Steele Knight, the demand for his father's journal, the threats regarding Josee.

Esprit remained stoic throughout, but sinews popped along his jaw.

Marsh said, "On the business end of things, Esprit, I'd like you to get ahold of the crew foreman and get everyone back up here ASAP. No more sloughing off. We have to catch back up in the vineyards. As for Rosie, she's at our beach house, so when she's done with her work there, tell her to come on back."

"Consider it done."

"Now, on the personal end, I have some ideas."

Marsh expounded, then Esprit departed to his tasks.

"Ping…ping…*pinggg*."

Nick's imitation of sonar was inept, but his look of satisfaction brought Marsh back to the computer. He was in the gaming zone and had located Steele Knight. Nick jabbed a finger at the monitor. "Cell 522. Game time.

Remember, try to snag his e-mail address, if he'll let you. You ready to go in? Let's finger this rapscallion."

"Ready. So I should just play the game, make moves like normal?"

"You got it. Take your time, the longer the better. We'll see what we shall see."

Marsh directed his Crash-Chess-Dummy persona through the cell door. At the table, a hooded, brown-robed creature tapped his gauntlet on the wood. Marsh typed: "Surprised you actually came."

"Came, saw, and conquered," his foe replied. "Aren't you the one who's skipped out on me the past few days?" Without further ado, a king pawn advanced, and Marsh shoved his queen's bishop pawn ahead two squares. Steele Knight keyed, "The Sicilian Defense revisited."

"That's right. Do you dare risk another Wing Gambit?"

"I enjoy the challenge." Steele Knight offered his queen's knight pawn.

"A patzer move. When will you learn?"

"Ah, but did I not capture your queen two days ago? You're destined to lose… Time to pay your dues. Today, CCD, I'll have my way with your bishop."

Josee? Not if I can help it. Soon Esprit'll bring her here to me.

Marsh captured the pawn, and his foe offered another, which Marsh took as well. "What if I send you the journal?" he asked. "Isn't that what you want? I've stored my father's info in a PDF file, which I could send to you right now. Let's get this over with."

"You'd risk turning over the journal before getting your wife back? I think not, CCD. I'm not so ignorant as to trust you with my e-mail address. My dear brother, what's to stop you from releasing a virus or hiding some 'back orifice' program in an attempt to compromise my hard drive? Alas, your efforts are in vain."

"Can't blame me for trying."

"Nine hours till our meeting of war. You'll be there, won't you?"

"I want my queen back. Of course I'll be there."

Nick was waving his hand in a circle. "Keep playing. I'm getting close."

The foe typed: "And you'll bring the journal? Remember, no journal, no wifey."

"You'll get what you want."

Marsh deliberated, made his next move. He tried to concentrate on the game while Nick tapped away on his notebook keys. He felt his excitement begin to rise as Nick's incomprehensible mutterings intensified. Were they getting close to nailing this slime bag?

Ker-thumpp!

The table jumped across the cell's flagstone floor as Steele Knight rose and pointed a finger. "I know what you're up to, CCD. You take me for a fool?"

Marsh feigned innocence. "Giving up so soon? Ready to resign?"

"I believe that was my question to you yesterday. Resign? I'd rather die first. No, my gatekeeper software indicates that you're trying to finger my location. So long."

A message leaped onto the screen indicating the connection had been severed.

"Did you get him?" Marsh queried.

"Dude saw it coming," was Nick's feeble response. "He deflected me."

⁓

Turney stared at the kitchen cupboard. From behind that door, the box of Peanut Butter Crunch was calling his name.

John's words came back: *I just need you to fast.... One day—that's all I'm asking.*

The phone rescued him from his ravenous thoughts. Henri Esprit was on the line. Turney had met the winemaker at a charitable function the year before and found him to be an agreeable sort. An older man, witty and wise. Now he had two simple requests.

Turney assented, then set down the receiver, only to have it ring again.

"Grand Central."

"Sarge, Chief Braddock here. We're under the gun. No excuses, mandatory meeting in thirty down here at the station. Just got off the horn with the county boys out on the coast. Last night they found a man on Highway 101 carrying details in his pocket pertaining to an anarchist demonstration. Looks like ICV's involved. Judging by the scribbles on the note, it appears that they've targeted city halls throughout the state. The plan, if the county boys're deciphering it correctly, is for something to happen tonight. Says 'Boom!' across the bottom of the page."

"Sounds a bit over the top, don't ya think?"

"We're not taking anything lightly, not after Beau's video segment."

"A bomb, is that what you're thinkin'?"

"One possibility. Of course, with the anthrax threat, I can't rule out anything."

"What about the man at the coast? Has he coughed up any useful tidbits?"

"Zip," said Chief Braddock. "Guy was barely breathing when they arrived on the scene. He was hit by a motorist who's all torn up over it. Swears he didn't see the guy lying there in the middle of the road till it was too late. Dark out, wet and all. Fifteen minutes later he was pronounced dead at the scene. Gruesome sight from what the sheriff tells me, and they see some nasty ones out on those curvy roads."

Turney's thoughts turned to Kara Addison's Z3 on the curves of Ridge Road.

"Comin' right now, Chief."

A quarter after seven, in the station's briefing room, Turney bypassed the table of pastries and coffee and grabbed a bottle of water instead. Being good, yessir. He found a seat behind three rows of yawning officers. Chief Braddock replayed the Connors tape and explained that the kid had been shown the video feed in his cell yet still refused to divulge Mrs. Addison's location. Beau had seen no transcripts of his speech in today's newspaper and vowed the cops would pay if they were tricking him.

"We can't ignore this kid's vitriol," Braddock stated as he turned off the monitor next to the podium. "'Allhallows Eve' is what he says. That's today…Halloween. We now have two separate sources indicating that a violent demonstration will take place. Officer Flynn? You tuned in to what I'm saying? You think this is child's play?" Braddock studied the roomful of people. "This is no joke. Even if it is, which I doubt, we cannot afford to shrug it off. In the past, ICV has shown anarchic malice, and this country's war on terrorism doesn't allow us to ignore credible threats. You want me to light a fire under your tired butts? Take a look at this."

Canary yellow papers circulated through the room. Turney held one to his nose so that the fresh ink warded off the pervasive aroma of donut glaze.

"This," Braddock elucidated, "is an excerpt from an early '90s congressional report. According to the Office of Technology Assessment, a small plane dispersing about 220 pounds of anthrax spores could be more lethal than a hydrogen bomb. On a clear night, in an area such as Washington, D.C., it could kill upward of three million people. Is young Mr. Connors bluffing? Could be. But if this hits the fan, I'll be the first one dragged through the blades, and I'll take all of you with me. We clear?"

The mood had turned somber. "Yes sir."

On a rolling chalkboard, Braddock diagrammed the tasks before them. He would meet with the mayor and the Benton County sheriff to coordinate local emergency services and request discretionary funds. The Investigations Unit would partner with the FBI Regional Terrorism Task Force. Oregon's Chemical Stockpile Emergency Preparedness Program would be brought in to guide their efforts, while the Centers for Disease Control and Prevention would be requisitioned for early-warning field kits. The American Red Cross would be alerted, pharmaceutical people, too. "Get ahold of anthrax and nerve gas antidotes," the chief ordered. "Those disposable types, the auto-injectors. Jamison, you make the calls, and don't take no for an answer." He also demanded that Beau Connors's past be combed "like a lice-ridden scalp" for any terrorist, anarchic, or militia-group connections. Meanwhile, they would shake down the streets for rumors of weapons caches or chemical labs or anti-American sentiment.

"Get moving. You all know your assignments. If not, you weren't listening."

Turney pushed his way to his office and hunkered down to the tasks at hand.

Phone calls. Paperwork. Printouts and press releases.

To break the drudgery, he rummaged through yesterday's uniform, now wrinkled and draped over his dented file cabinet. From the shirt pocket, he collected and tagged the items in evidence bags, inserted them into a padded envelope with an official CODIS request form, then dropped it in the mail pouch.

By noon it would be headed to the FBI's Combined DNA Index System.

—

"Not giving up. Not yet. More than one way to ensnare a fish in the Net."

Despite this assurance, Nick's hubris had diminished visibly with the disappearance of Steele Knight. He muttered and tinkered, tapped at the folding keyboard in his lap, then checked the monitor on Marsh Addison's desk.

"I'm no computer genius. I'll leave it to you," Marsh said.

He stepped to the study window and watched migratory workers arrive in the company van. They milled about and joked alongside the warehouse, then snapped to attention when the foreman marched from the tasting room and shouted orders in Spanish. The carpool of household staff—two women and a man—pulled up. They entered the manor through a side door, their voices floating up from the kitchen downstairs.

Rhythm and routine. Addison Ridge Vineyards was back in gear.

But where was Josee? Would Esprit be as efficient at finding her?

Josee Walker. Biological daughter or not, she was the one with access to the safe-deposit box at the Bank of the Dunes. She was an integral part of Steele Knight's plan, and without her, the journal and bank key would prove useless. Marsh had directed Esprit to get her whereabouts from Sergeant Turney, then bring her to the estate.

Marsh saw a pale lemon sun squeeze over the ridge. A new day.

Questions tumbled through his head. His heart. He was adroit at handling business uncertainties but less comfortable with these emotional concerns.

Was Josee in danger? Where was Kara? What had she meant by the Black Butte Ranch clue? Who was Steele Knight? How did he factor into the schemes of Trudi Ubelhaar? Who was tailing him? Were they still out there, ready to hound his every move? The journal had mentioned a protector, one commissioned by Chance Addison to watch over the Addison household. Who and where was this protector?

Not that Marsh intended to sit around waiting for protection.

Come on, Esprit, bring Josee safely to me. I have a plan of escape.

33

The Sorceress

They located Scooter in the backyard at the base of a walnut tree. The rabid look in his eyes caused last night's terror to rise in Josee's throat. She slipped behind John as he advanced over the spongy grass. In a corner of the yard, birds that had been chirping now settled into vigilant stances along a marble birdbath.

"Back off," Scooter said. "Came out here to get away. Gotta keep movin'."

"Where're you headed?" John's face grew solemn.

"Anywhere but here." He pointed to Josee. "You have to get away from me."

She bent to his level and said, "It's okay, Scoot. I don't hold anything against you."

"Stay away."

"I forgive you. For last night. At least let John help you."

"I'm poison." Scooter's eyes brimmed with self-loathing. He rocked with his bedroll in his arms. "You're my closest friend, and look what I did. It's because they're trying to make you…"

"Make me what?"

"Trying to reach you"—his rocking accelerated—"through me. Wherever I go, they follow. They want you." He mumbled to himself, pressed his hands to his eyes.

John Van der Bruegge stood tall at Josee's side. "Scooter, I'm here to help. I know what you're dealing with. We saw the hatched eggs."

"What's in it for you?"

"You think you're able to handle this on your own?"

"Maybe. Dang it, I don't know! What do you care anyway? I don't know you from Adam. Okay, so we shot some pool, ate some food together. That doesn't mean you know squat about me. Yeah." He nodded and stood to his feet. "I can handle it."

Josee felt water drip from the walnut branches into her hair. She tried to keep her composure as a twitch flexed through Scooter's cheeks. She said, "Don't brush us off, Scoot. You said they were trying to get you and you couldn't hold them off. What are they? Snakes, like the one we saw the other day?"

"Stop looking at me, babe. They're after you! Aah, I hate this, *hate* this! Till last night I was maintaining. What happened? Everything got worse when we came to this place. Why?" He was pacing. "I thought they'd leave me alone. That's what they told me. But they're eatin' at me. I can feel it."

Kris emerged from the back of the house and joined them beneath the tree. "I made some calls, and word's passing around," she told John. "We're not alone."

Josee said, "Let John and Kris help you. They're good people."

"They've only made it worse. Somethin' about this place."

John took his wife's hand. Along the marble bath, the birds quieted and kept watch over the proceedings. John said, "The reason you feel that way, Scooter, is because Kris and I try to let our home be a place of refuge, of grace. Not that we're perfect, not at all. Don't believe us? Ask our kids. But where mistakes abound, grace also abounds. Nothing unclean is welcome here. It must either run and hide or show itself. That's why you want to run. You think you're trapped and there's no way out."

"Sheesh, what's wrong with all of you? I'm fine. Look, I cut off the scraggly long hair and beard. What more do ya want?"

"Scooter, that's not the point. God looks at your heart."

"Try tellin' that to some of the creeps Josee and I've run into."

Kris said, "What've they told you? You think God's put off by Josee's eyebrow ring? By the way you wear your hair or the clothes you put on? Fairly superficial, if you ask me. No, God's much bigger than that, and if he's not, we're all wasting our time, aren't we?" She elbowed John, threw Josee a mischievous grin. "Why, maybe I should get that tattoo I've always wanted."

The grin washed over Josee with cool acceptance. No fronting here.

"Let them help," she implored Scooter. "Come on, hon."

He tucked his chin into his chest and continued pacing. "I'm not about to jump through any hoops, you hear me? 'Do this' and 'do that.' Nah, we've heard all that before. Thanks, but no thanks." The cinch cords on his bedroll seemed to unravel as he moved. "Maybe I'm not good enough, but hey, at least I don't pretend I got it all together. What about you, Josee? You gonna conform? Let's get away from here." The cords spiraled down, brushing against Scooter's legs, curling along his sleeves.

"Scooter," John admonished, "please give me that bedroll."

"Back off, man! This is my stuff."

"You won't be free until you let go."

Scooter rocked again. His voice took on a deeper tone. "I'm free, free to roam. Who are you to hold me down?" He halted to remove a cord that had slithered between the buttons of his shirt. "Why won't this thing let go?"

"Because somewhere along the line it's found a foothold."

"A foothold? Yeah, man, whatever."

"Something little. That's all it takes. A spot of unresolved bitterness. This enemy you're fighting is a thief, and he'll take whatever you give him."

Scooter ignored the rejoinder and tugged at the bedroll's cover flap.

Ker-popppp!

Josee and the Van der Bruegges started at the sound. The clasp sprung open, and Josee watched threads of snakes unwind over the lip and drop to the grass. Baby vipers spilled over the legs of Scooter's khakis; together, the threads wove themselves into a single dark entity that coiled back up his body and poised over his shoulders. It was a sorceress, a haughty queen on a chessboard.

Was this for real, Josee wondered, or some comic-book apparition?

"S'okay." Scooter dropped his belongings. "Back off, I'm okay."

"Scooter, it's a lie," said Kris.

"This thing that you're fighting," John said, "is a deception, nothing more."

The fabric of intertwined serpents formed an undulating cloak behind the sorceress. Once more Josee's eyes seemed open to an unseen realm so that she doubted her own clarity of mind. Was she going wacko here? Yet, clearly the Van der Bruegges were aware of an additional presence as well. They might not be able to see it, but they seemed to know it was there.

Scoot said, "Uh-uh, everything's cool. Just back off."

The morning's tedium was about to drive Turney bonkers. Facing bomb threats and terrorist acts, he was irritated to no end by the details of the job. What he needed was a little pick-me-up, a sugar rush. He thumbed through the case files on his desk, lifted the morning paper, but found nothing to satisfy his urge.

The top drawer? Nope. How about the middle one?

Yup, there it was.

Even as thick fingers closed around the tin of almond roca, his vow to John Van der Bruegge reasserted itself: *Fast? As in, don't eat?... I'll give it my best shot.* Why'd he ever agree to such an idea? Sure, he saw its value, but what difference could he possibly make? This was why he shied away from New Year's resolutions; they practically begged to be broken.

He opened the tin, caught a whiff of rich—

Nope! Gotta honor my agreement. For John and Kris, for Scooter...for Josee.

Time for a change of scenery, otherwise he'd cave to the candied temptation.

Turney wandered through the station's hubbub to the mail slots near the water cooler. He sucked down a double helping of water—better than nothing—aimed the cup into the wastebasket, then scanned his three most recent messages.

The first referred to an employee at a drive-through espresso booth in the nearby town of Philomath. Apparently, the young lady had seen this morning's news report about a man hit and killed by a car on coastal Highway 101. She recognized the picture. She knew the man. She'd served him white mochas every now and then. He always drove up in a family-type van, a tan one, and always had an older guy with him in the passenger seat.

Turney noted at the bottom of the paper that the lady had been put in contact with police counselors. She must be pretty shaken up.

The second message, from Chief Braddock, demanded his appearance at Good Samaritan Regional Medical Center. Twelve o'clock in the hospital administrator's office. Don't miss it; drop everything.

Hoo boy, what now?

The third, per Marsh Addison's earlier inquiry, provided the cell number of the motorist that had called in Thursday morning's accident on Ridge Road. Under the cloud of a potential police investigation, the phone company had released the name and billing address attached to that number. The address was of no immediate help—a local post office box—and it appeared that the phone belonged to a business account. The name, in a slanted scrawl, looked misspelled.

House of Ubelhaar…Sponsor of the Arts.

Armed with a bottle of water, Turney paid a short visit to the Corvallis postmaster and discovered that a "Karl Stahlherz" had signed the original post office box agreement. The account had remained in good standing for over five years. The average count of delivered mail was nothing out of the ordinary; never had a package been called into question; the box was emptied on a regular basis. In all, an unremarkable account.

House of Ubelhaar? Karl Stahlherz?

Both names were new to Turney. Sounded Dutch or German.

———

Scales formed a scepter that the sorceress swished down Scooter's arm. Her fluid shape nestled behind him, writhing in an offer of unearthly comfort.

Don't even go there, lady! Josee stepped forward. *He doesn't belong to you.*

The hazy face angled her way.

Josee turned to stone. She recognized those eyes, the same flaming pinpricks she'd seen two mornings ago in the woods. She recalled Scooter's reaction to the attack… *Submissive and accepting of his fate? Or reveling in the experience?*

"Scooter, you're not alone in this," John said. "We have friends praying for you, and we're right here. Let us help."

As though in response, the birds along the marble bath took wing. In staccato bursts, they swept down at the serpents, short beaks pecking at and shredding the dark fabric. The sorceress cried out, swatting at them with her scepter. They swooped in a second time; again she batted them away.

"See there, you can resist this thing," John called.

"This? Oh, she's nothing." Prompted by the scepter, Scooter's fingers brushed back through the ropes of vaporous hair, and the sorceress drew closer. "She's a companion, one of the characters from a role-playing game I'm into. You don't wanna get on this lady's bad side, tell you that much right now.

She's got one razor-sharp mind and a...a wicked..." His voice weakened as she nuzzled at his neck.

"Can you see her?" John inquired. "You're in a spiritual skirmish. Do you recognize that? We can't see what you're fighting, not physically, but we can feel its presence. This is a pagan entity, one you should never have flirted with."

As Josee had suspected, only she could see the creature's physical form.

"Push her away," Josee demanded.

"Babe, I can't...can't do it."

"You can."

"She's too strong. Too many...necropoints."

"Necropoints?" Kris waited for an explanation.

"Death points," said Josee. The birds continued to hover, striking in bursts.

"But, Scooter, you've given her those points," John stated.

"She took 'em."

"Yes, but only after you gave her control."

"It's a game, that's all," Scooter countered. "I'll be fine, you hear me?"

A game? Fat chance. Josee thought back to a few weeks ago in their trailer by the lake. She had curled up in a beanbag with a bag of sea-salt chips while Scooter and his buddies played one such game. Some, in the spirit of the night, had dressed as warlocks and wizards, but nothing quite like this sorceress. Josee thought of the times Scoot had gone into Seattle, claiming to meet his friends for a game or two. What had he really been up to?

"You can resist. You must resist," John was saying to Scooter.

"Nah. She...won't let...go. Not like she's tryin' to hurt anyone. It's all good. It's cool." Scooter's tone had gone flat. While the sorceress's right hand took erratic swings at the birds, her left ran black fingernails down his arm. The fingers turned to handcuffs about his wrists.

"Stand firm," John said. "You need to make your choice."

"I...can't. How... Help me, man. What can I do? Help."

John Van der Bruegge stepped in, waving his hands over Scooter's arms. With this motion, he seemed to knock the encircling fingers loose. He looked into Scooter's eyes. "See, you gave me the opening to step in. You made a brief decision to seek help. You *can* resist, so long as you retain your ability to make choices. No one takes your free will from you, but you *can* hand it over, and once you do so, it's no longer free, is it? In fact, it can cost you everything."

Scooter softened. "I'm trapped. They're using me to get to Josee." He looked down. "They followed me to the hospital…the snake, the snakes. They came with me." His words were slurred, but he forced them out. "An…ambush. I didn't mean to, Josee. I'm sorry…too strong."

"Told you I forgive you, hon. Like John says, you can resist. Come on!"

"I…no, I can't."

"You can! You've gotta take a stand. Why do you do this? Why do you back down? Listen to me, Scooter, you have to fight!"

"Too late, babe. She's…she's gonna eat us alive."

His words pressed the Replay button in Josee's memory. *Scooter…a prey numbed, yet alive, heart still beating to provide fresh sustenance on demand.* Josee had sensed impending danger in the thicket. Here it was again, insatiable, grasping for more. Although she wanted to hug Scooter, to comfort him, she also wanted to flee. She pressed down her fear. "Scooter, you have to make a stand to get rid of this thing, this…enemy."

"Enemy, huh?"

"The enemy of our souls," Kris joined in.

The scepter hooked Scooter's mouth and a paroxysm of laughter shook him. "Oooh, sounds spooky."

"Scoot, it's nothing to kid about," Josee said. "You think you'll survive by letting this thing hang around, but it'll take you down. You have to stand up to it."

Though sagging on weak legs, Scooter raised an eyebrow. A flicker of hope?

Briefly the apparition loosened her grip as she ducked from a new onslaught of darting birds. Beaks tore fiber from her fabric, tatters hung lifelessly from the cloak, and Josee began to believe that this thing could be defeated. Perhaps the Van der Bruegges' circle of friends was beginning to prevail; perhaps their prayers were taking effect. With feathery attack, the birds were providing shelter from the sorceress.

Shelter, Josee recognized, in the shadow of the Almighty's wings.

"God is on your side, Scooter," Kris said. "Call on him boldly. Jesus is freedom, but you must take hold of him."

"Hold o' what? What can he do?" Behind Scooter, his captor spewed doubts into his ear. Her cloak clung at his legs, seemed to sap his strength. His face clouded as he said, "Jesus doesn't give a rat's tail about me. It's…no use…too late! You know the saying, 'Live fast, die young, and leave a good-lookin' corpse'? Well, maybe that's all I am, huh? Nothin' but a walking corpse."

"You're not dead," Josee insisted. "Keep fighting!"

"After what I did last night…I can't risk it, babe. Get away from me. I can't let them hurt you." He gathered his bedroll in his arms. "I'm no good. Unclean. I've gotta get away—from you, from them. Just leave me alone!" He shoved his way past John and Kris and stalked along the house to the front walkway. "And don't come after me."

Josee ignored the Van der Bruegges' appeals and followed, jogging to keep pace. "What now, Scoot? You're going to take off like usual?"

"Told you not to come after me!"

"It won't solve the problem. If you leave, I'm afraid that—"

"Afraid? See, you *are* afraid of me! Don't blame ya, not one friggin' bit. Heyya, what if I *am* a corpse? You don't deserve that, and you never have." He broke into a wild-eyed sprint, trailing tatters and threads. Against the sky, the birds flitted but made only one or two attempts to further weaken the viper-spun fabric.

Josee found herself falling behind. Her lungs and eyes burned.

Scoot, you're a stinkin' idiot! Why do you always refuse to fight?

She doubled over to regain her breath and felt a knot of sorrow tighten in her throat. He was going to get himself killed, she just knew it, and there was little she could do to stop it. She let him go. Around the corner, out of sight. She trudged back up the block, past store-bought gnarled witches and huge black plastic spiders.

Ahead, she saw that a car had pulled up at the Van der Bruegge home. An older man conversed with John and Kris on the walkway, then turned as she drew near.

"Josee. I'm Henri Esprit."

She wiped a drop of sweat from her chin, then lifted her fingers to her eyebrow ring.

"He's okay," John clarified. "He's been cleared by Sergeant Turney. He's here to take you to your father."

"As in Marsh? Marsh Addison? Yesterday the man told me to get lost."

"He's feeling a bit lost himself," Esprit said. "He'd very much like to see you."

"Oh, goody. Glad to know he can finally pencil me in."

———

The gaming zone confrontation was over. Back to the scuffle of human pawns and motivations. In the basement studio, Stahlherz tapped at his keyboard, checked the appropriate addresses in his database, then pressed Send. Unseen, the messages sliced through cyberspace. A call to arms.

He lifted a glass and squeezed a tube over the water's surface.

One drop…*drippp!*

The blue food coloring swirled, indigo tendrils coiling into the crystal depths.

One drop…polluting, permeating, poisoning the entire glass.

The plan was devastating in its simplicity. Tonight, once Josee had utilized the safe-deposit key, ICV would distribute the long-hidden venom vials to members posted along deserted logging roads in the coastal mountain range. By midnight they would pass on the toxic payloads to fellow units throughout Oregon's westerly half. Specially trained, these units would fill the historic silver canisters with the accelerant to form a deadly biochemical agent. A few liters, nothing more. Drops. Dissolving into invisible evil. For the past year, recruits had reconnoitered reservoirs and water storage facilities, narrowing the targets to a dozen.

Twelve targets. Tens of thousands of potential victims.

"Come. Let the thirsty ones come," Stahlherz said, parodying that which was sacred. In one extended gulp, he drained the glass of tinted water. He wondered, would tonight's victims have time to alert their loved ones before all their bodily functions went haywire?

34

Telltale Signs

"An escape plan," Josee said. "That's why you brought me up here?"

"Basically." Marsh stood beside her beneath the portico as they watched Henri Esprit and his nephew drive down the hill between grape trellises still beaded with last night's rain. "Short notice, I know. Thanks for coming."

"That's not what you said yesterday."

"Yesterday I was dealing with the fact that my wife is gone."

Josee's eyes locked on to him. Piercing. Discerning. "Maybe you're to blame."

"True, I've made mistakes, but it's time to deal with the problems at hand. The clock's ticking as we speak."

"First, tell me what's wrong between you and Kara."

"First, tell me what you know about a key to a safe-deposit box," Marsh said.

"A key? Wait, that's the same thing Chief Braddock asked."

"Chief John Braddock? Once again sticking his nose where it doesn't belong."

A smile tugged at the corner of Josee's lips. "Least we agree on something."

Marsh met her eyes and felt his heart thump against his ribs. Josee reminded him of Kara. Different coloring, sure, but similar features. She was younger, rougher. Her shirt was untucked, black, with tiger's-eye buttons; her jeans loose, brown, with a peace symbol patch on one knee. And she was beautiful. He could see that now. Why hadn't he noticed yesterday? What had he missed out on all these years?

"Josee," he said, "I'm sorry for my abruptness at Barkley's. I was worried about you, and I thought I could protect you from getting involved. I was wrong. You, me, Kara—we're all part of this. We're being watched, even now. By tonight, one way or another, this issue'll be resolved."

"You know where Kara is?"

"No, but I think I know who's responsible. Not that Beau Connors kid either."

Josee shot him a quizzical stare. Looked as though she wanted to say something but couldn't let it out. She hefted the knapsack she'd brought along.

"So," Marsh said, "are you ready to get muddy?"

"Excuse me?"

—

Donning a daypack that he had stuffed with clothes, tennis shoes, and his nine-millimeter semiautomatic, Marsh led Josee down the grand staircase. She said little. He could see her assessing the manor, weighing the life that might have been hers. Her hands kneaded the loose ends of her shirt; her teeth pulled at her bottom lip.

"Ever been in a wine cellar, Josee?"

She snorted. "Me, an uptown socialite? Talk about a whole different world. When I was growing up, my version of a wine cellar was chugging Boone's Farm with my friends in their garage."

"I shudder at the thought."

"Can we spell *pretentious?*" she chided.

"But Boone's Farm? Around here that's heresy."

He led her through French doors onto the back deck, past the hot tub, down cedar steps. Set into the earth at the base of the house, the cellar door was padlocked. Marsh let them in and hit a switch on the wall. One bulb sparked and died, but others revealed wooden racks and discarded oak barrels. He said, "My father's humble beginnings. Chance stored his vintage here, half a century ago."

"He's the one Kara told me about? The one who died after the war? How'd it happen? He wasn't that old, was he?"

"Be easier if you read it for yourself, Josee. I have something for you to see. In here." Marsh patted the daypack. "First, let's give ourselves some space to breathe."

They wound through a series of tunnels, then up stone steps into a boiler room.

"We're in the warehouse now, nearly two hundred feet from the manor. Around the corner, docking doors face the woods out back. We can escape unnoticed."

In the equipment room, he mounted a Honda quad and fired it up. Josee joined him, but he had to direct her arms around his waist and her feet onto the proper pegs. The sputtering engine shook the vehicle. It'd been some time since he'd taken a spin on one of these. In times past, he'd ridden the estate's perimeter, spot-checking for ripeness and signs of blight. Nowadays, financial ventures consumed his schedule.

"Eh, *jefe*." No doubt drawn by the engine, the foreman found them, waved, dipped his head. "You go get dirty? You have good time, sí. Sí, señor, we still work hard for you. *Mucho trabajo*."

"Thanks, Alex. Even the boss has gotta have a little fun every now and then."

Alex gave a knowing nod. *"Hasta luego."*

Marsh cranked the throttle and released the clutch. Josee's grip tightened as the quad rocketed down the ramp. He waggled the handlebars so that the tires spun and spat bits of quartz and wet dirt. She cried out. In no time they had bypassed the old pump house and zipped between fir trees that spilled down from the ridge. Old paths carried them over fallen timber and moldering leaves. Despite a wrong turn and a detour around a flooded gulch, Marsh knew they were still on schedule.

As he navigated the quad, a renewed vigor took hold. The roar of the engine precluded conversation, but Josee's nearness communicated ideas he had shoved away for twenty-two years. She was a woman. Surely she'd gone through first grade, had her first kiss, found talents and interests, faced heartache and pain.

I've seen it all there in her eyes. And she's seen it in mine.

His mind sharpened. The task, he reminded himself, was to get Kara back. Wife and mother, she was at the heart of all that had gone on. Marsh replayed the events of the past two days. Specifically he mused on Kara's answer to his question regarding this weekend: Black Butte Ranch. Marsh envisioned a map of Oregon. Had she given him a directional clue? Black Butte was located near the town of Sisters, right? Or maybe that was it. Maybe she was trying to share that she was near her sister's place. That seemed unlikely, considering her sister lived in Colorado.

Stabs in the dark. That's all he had.

By the time they reached their destination—a gravel road on the border of the McDonald-Dunn Research Forest—their clothes were mud caked. With a turn of the key, the forest fell silent again. The engine ticked. From his pack, Marsh loaned Josee a set of Kara's brushed corduroy pants and an aquamarine pullover. Then, behind a thick tree trunk, he changed into pleated Dockers, deck shoes, and a maroon, collared shirt and a light jacket.

"Sorry, Josee, I know I'm not much on fashion, but it should keep you warm." He shook open a plastic trash bag. "Dirties can go in here. So tell me, what'd you think?"

"Of your driving? You're insane." Josee grinned. "Best ride I've ever been on."

"Why, thank you."

"Would've been even better if I had been driving."

"Have your license handy? Here's your chance."

They turned to see Esprit pull roadside in a white economy rental car. At Marsh's direction, he handed the key to Josee. "Long time no see," Esprit quipped.

"A Metro?" She wrinkled her face at the prospect. "A real speed machine."

Marsh gave a hearty laugh. Then, pointing to the quad, he said to Esprit, "She's all yours. Have fun riding back. When you get there, put on one of my ball caps and one of my coats, then take the Tahoe for a spin. In fact, I want you to drive over to Black Butte and check out our condo. Make sure that nothing's been disturbed and that Kara's not there." He saw Josee twitch but went on. "Call me once you've arrived."

With one long breath, Esprit straddled the filthy quad. "That's a four or five hour round trip, Marshall. You wish for me to go *today?*"

"Paid time off. Grab a bite to eat while you're there. Here, use my AmEx card."

"If you insist."

Following Josee, Marsh folded himself into their four-cylinder escape vehicle. He relished the idea of his pursuer still twiddling his thumbs back on

Ridge Road. Would he fall for the trick and follow Henri Esprit? Maybe, maybe not. But Marsh and Josee would be long gone by the time he recognized the hoax.

—

At the Tattered Feather Art Gallery on SW Second, Marsh cupped his hands and peered through the storefront. He had hoped to question the curator about yesterday's delivery. Who had paid for the painting? Who was the artist? A list of inquiries.

"Closed," said Josee. "See the sign on the door."

"On a Friday? Midmorning? Seems unusual."

Perplexed, Marsh circled to the back of the store. The sight of the jimmied back door ripped the air from his throat. Confirming his suspicions of foul play, he saw scuff marks and a trail of dime-sized drops in the gravel.

"You see anything? Hold it. That looks like dried blood."

"Stay back, Josee." Marsh strode from the scene. "That's just what I need right now, cops asking questions again. We'll make an anonymous tip from a phone booth."

In the Metro, Josee turned sullen. As though her trust in him was waning.

—

"Have you any idea what the name Corvallis means?"

"Sir?" Sergeant Turney stepped into the office, closed the door.

At floor-to-ceiling windows, the Good Samaritan hospital administrator stood silhouetted. The vista was spectacular. Remnants of storm clouds dragged patchwork shapes over the city, and between the coastal mountains to the west and the foothills to the east, the farmlands were a quilt of greens, browns, and reds, stitched together with threads of glistening rivers.

Turney shifted his weight, wondered what sorta trouble he'd gotten himself into this time. He knew Dr. Duvernoy on limited terms.

"Corvallis. Come now, Sarge, you're a public servant. You should know the answer." Duvernoy turned so that the sunlight showcased the fatigue behind his spectacles. "The name's self-explanatory actually."

"Doesn't it mean 'heart of the valley'? Think I saw that in some brochure."

"Well done." Dr. Duvernoy rounded his broad oak desk, gesturing for Turney to take a seat. He made a show of polishing his spectacles with a chamois. "Fun and games aside, these are weighty matters before us. Yes, Sarge, our city sits squarely at the heart of the Willamette Valley. From here, veins of industry and commerce flow statewide, even worldwide. Hewlett-Packard, a case in point. And now we find ourselves harboring an invisible enemy, one that may pump out death."

Feeling unkempt, Turney tugged at a strained shirt button. He hadn't slept well. With little idea where this conversation was headed, he decided to linger around the edges of the ring so as not to take any unexpected blows.

The blow came anyway.

"I know about your childhood snakebite," Duvernoy said.

"My fall onto the guard's broken mug. Isn't that what you mean?"

"A snakebite. I owe you an apology. See, years ago an army intelligence officer approached me in secret to warn that a chemical weapon had been lost in this very valley—'temporarily misplaced,' in military parlance—during transport to a restricted site. A Nazi weapon, I was told, brought over after the war in the race between the Russians and Americans to exploit Hitler's scientific advances. In fact, the success of our space program owes a debt to such technology. Anyway, the officer instructed me to keep an eye out for particular symptoms among our patients and to report telltale signs."

"Who was this officer? Did you check up on him?"

"Naturally. Although the Umatilla Army Depot refused to tell me much, they confirmed that she was stationed there."

"She?"

"The intelligence officer, yes. Later, Sarge—in July of '81—I did as requested and reported to her your episode here in these hallways. She was intrigued by your symptoms, ordered me to suppress the facts surrounding your case."

"What facts? What don't I know?"

"Certain…details were tampered with—for the sake of national security, I was led to believe. The officer explained how the Nazis thought they had crafted the perfect biochemical weapon during the war. With a chemical accelerant incorporated into a snake venom—a specific hemotoxin that thins the blood and chokes off oxygen to the cells—they assured Hitler that an antidote would be nearly impossible to create. Indeed, experiments with varying subjects proved the weapon highly effective."

"Effective?" said Turney. "Do I wanna hear this?"

"Aside from a handful who were measured for long-term effects, the majority of the subjects perished. Jews mostly. Whether distributed in aerosol form or percutaneously, small concentrations killed in minutes. Even highly diluted doses induced slow and horrific deaths with most subjects suffering hallucinations of grotesque serpentine images, presumably instigated by the venom." Dr. Duvernoy inspected his eyewear. "They thought they'd been physically bitten."

"By a snake."

"Naturally."

"The same as what happened to me." Turney's mind swung from the factual overload to the sudden connection: *It was a snake. And a big one! Like a stare down before a fight.*

Duvernoy slipped a sheet of onionskin across the desk. "Have a look, Sarge. That's a portion of the report from your medical file. The stats and figures may be indecipherable, but you'll notice there near the bottom—"

"Boomslang," Turney read the word.

"An African tree snake, deadly as can be. Large and green, it feeds primarily on chameleons, secreting its venom through sharp rear fangs. In the US the boomslang is nonindigenous, impossible to find outside of zoological exhibits or private and illegal collections, but the Nazis first stumbled across it, literally, during their campaign in Africa. Resourceful types that they were, they collected the species and found use for it in their laboratories."

"So I didn't make it up. That's what you're telling me?"

"Your hallucinations were certainly warranted. And, though I can't say I have all the answers, yes, traces of boomslang venom were found in your blood. Not that we knew it at the time. Only after analysis—complete blood count, coagulation profile, blood typing and urinalysis—only then could we pinpoint it definitively."

"Twenty-two years, Doctor? Why wait so long to cough up the truth?"

"We never found the canister you described. That left us with doubts."

"Two decades?" Sergeant Turney drilled his eyes into Duvernoy. "Over two decades! All this time I've lived with ridicule and guilt. Thought I'd failed somehow."

"We only dug into this again recently, when you brought Scooter in." Duvernoy turned to the windows. "I called Chief Braddock yesterday when Scooter's blood tests turned up results similar to yours. Nothing verified by outside sources, of course, but the symptoms are remarkably alike. The chief wanted me to tell you that he feels bad about it."

"But Chief Braddock couldn't tell me this himself, could he? Not his style."

"He felt that my qualifications would lead to a clearer explanation."

Turney's stomach knotted. All along Braddock had known. *Figures!*

"Back in '81," Dr. Duvernoy prattled on, "I was in my early forties, fairly new to this position, and your case planted itself firmly in my mind. Yesterday, as I compared files, the parallels became readily evident."

Turney rolled back his sleeve. "Take a look at that! My scars're oozing again. You've left me in the dark, while I just keep on sufferin'. Why didn't you treat the wounds properly in the first place?"

"Did our best, I can vouch for that."

"And what about Scooter? Is he gonna be fightin' this for years to come?"

"We have no adequate antivenin, no specific means of treatment." Duvernoy tapped on the glass, then looked back. "I'm mystified, actually, by Scooter's sudden turn for the better. How he managed to walk out of here on his own two feet, I do not know. Cannot be attributed to our efforts, if truth be told."

"Food poisoning—that's what I was told it was."

"Per my instructions, yes, Dr. Dunning provided that diagnosis. No reason to stir the public's fears. Additionally, I needed time to call the intelligence officer and let her know that we had another case."

"And what'd she have to say?"

"Actually," the administrator said, "I didn't speak with her personally. All along we've communicated through a liaison. Over the years the number's changed a few times, but the liaison has remained the same—a man close to my age, by the sound of it. Always been polite, passing on my messages promptly. This time, however, I suspected something was wrong."

Turney pushed himself up with palms on his thighs. His belly growled.

Duvernoy said, "When Scooter walked out of here on his own accord, I thought I might have jumped the gun, perhaps raised a false alarm. I redialed the liaison to let him know, but after failing to reach him, I called the Umatilla depot, hoping to directly contact the intelligence officer. When I asked for her, I was put through to a high-ranking official who told me she had retired a few years back. That aroused my suspicions."

"What's her name?" Turney asked. "You tried tracing this woman?"

"Trudi, that's what she had me call her. At the depot, she was listed under her full name, Gertrude Ubelhaar. When I checked yesterday, I found that the liaison's number is registered to a company called—"

"House of Ubelhaar," Turney blurted out, recalling his visit to the post-master.

Duvernoy's eyes lifted over his spectacles. "Yes, but how did you know that?"

Marsh waved to the truck-stop waitress for a refill on their coffees. As Josee tore open a creamer, he located two items from his daypack. Stained by the ride through the woods, the pack elicited a curious stare from a young girl seated with her father in the next booth. She wore a Pocahontas costume, with her hair braided beneath an Indian headband. Marsh rued the fact that he could never retrieve the years lost between him and Josee. The object now was to preserve the years ahead.

"This belongs to you," he said, slipping the filed bank key across the table.

Josee sipped her coffee. Added one more creamer. "What's it for?"

"A safe-deposit box. In this envelope is a copy of my father's journal, which details all that's led up to this point. You won't like everything in there—I didn't—but it's your grandfather's story. Chance Addison's legacy. I owe it to you to provide access to the truth."

"Is this the key Braddock referred to?"

"Probably so, though I'm not sure how he knew about it." Marsh leaned forward. "Josee, keep it somewhere safe where it won't be found. I'm gonna make a few phone calls outside. Need to get ahold of my boys down at the golf course. Don't give me that look. It's not as frivolous as it sounds."

Josee lifted her hands. "Hey, did I say a word?"

"Go ahead and read the journal," Marsh said. "It'll explain a lot."

35

Among the Bones

Avery Park. Almost one o'clock.

Josee stepped from the car and slung her knapsack over her shoulder. Using the contents of the journal as an excuse for time alone, time to think, she had solicited Marsh's help in delivering her to this park. She regretted withholding information from him, but Rosie had made it clear that Kara wanted a confidential meeting. Yeah, Josee had noted strange actions on Marsh's part, yet the journal convinced her to trust him. Whatever the conflict between husband and wife, that was their own private affair.

"Marsh, thanks. For, you know, letting me see the journal, for bringing me here. I'll be safe, so don't worry about me. No one's followed us, not that I've spotted anyway."

"You're right," he said. "Feeling edgy, that's all. Sure you don't want company?"

"Nothing personal, just need to settle my nerves. That journal gives me a lot to think about, you know." *And that's no joke. Now I know why I was damaged equipment from the start.*

"I'll come back for you, Josee. How about that? Say, one hour?"

"Relax, okay. It's not that far to the Van der Bruegges. I can walk it."

"Watch yourself. That's all I ask."

"Yes, Daddy, I promise to be good." Though she said it in a mocking little girl's voice, she noticed that Marsh stiffened. Despite his candor regarding the past, he seemed resistant to this new mantle of fatherhood. She wasn't going to force him.

"I can take care of myself," she amended. "See ya later."

Josee headed into Avery Park, crunching leaves and puffballs underfoot. According to the car's dash clock, she knew it was five minutes to one. A couple of minutes to spare. Why had that Beau kid claimed responsibility for

Kara's kidnapping? Maybe he was obsessed—that'd been Sarge's theory last night—living out some fantasy in his mind.

Ten minutes passed. A pair of bikes followed a path through the trees, and a woman jogged by with a St. Bernard on a leash.

Josee climbed onto a Georgia Pacific train engine. On display, the black machinery spoke of past achievements. She propped herself on the coal box and scanned the park. If nobody showed, she didn't want to look stupid; she'd play this cool. She shifted her knapsack onto her lap. Inside, photos and poems, drawings and thoughts awaited Kara's viewing.

And the birth certificate.

Josee didn't know what she would say to her birth mother, but she counted on these items to open windows into each other's worlds. She turned the pages of her notebook and, in passionate purple pencil, put down her thoughts:

> Am I close? Are you real?
> Have you lied? Have I been blind?
> My thoughts are a ball of sticky tape
>   rolling through the grass,
>   collecting stray items, coins, leaves,
>   and shreds of a baby photo…
> Am I close? Have you lied?
> My thoughts are a ball of sticky tape

She slapped the cover shut and made her way down a grassy incline to a scattering of sculptures that looked like fossils of a prehistoric beast. She wound her way between them, peeked up to see if anyone had appeared.

Nope. What'd she expect? This quest had been cursed from the start.

Maybe Kara had chickened out after Rosie's call.

Josee wished that Sarge was here. He would understand her frustration. In three days he had shown himself capable of sparring with her, deflecting her punches and throwing a few of his own when necessary. Most men pandered to her. In their eyes, lust and flattery joined hands.

Not so with Sgt. Vince Turney.

Forget the extra padding. The way he looks at me with those chocolate eyes… I start to melt.

A Studebaker slowed at the curb. An elderly woman poked her head through the window, saying something, gesturing. Josee glanced around. She was alone among the bones of the sculpted beast.

"Josee?"

The breeze lifted her name. Could this be Rosamund Yeager?

"Josee? It's you, isn't it? I beg your forgiveness for being late."

A flare of irritation. "I've been waiting. Where's Kara? Is she coming?"

"She's anxious to see you. I'm Rosie, the one you spoke with on the phone. I've been instructed to take you to her." Seated in the driver's seat of the vintage car, the old woman wore the face of a black-and-white movie star, glamorous in a dated way, sterile and serene. There was no one else in the car.

"Why isn't she here?" Josee said.

"Of late, she's had more than her share of attention. She feared she might be identified by the police or by whoever's out to harm her. Her husband perhaps. Kara told me to show you this." Rosie's age-marked hand held an envelope with a Washington State postmark and Josee's handwriting. "She said this would secure your trust."

"Kara gave you this? It's one of my letters to her."

"Are you ready to meet with her?"

"Yes," Josee said. "Of course I'm ready."

"Climb in then. A bit of a drive but nothing too horrendous."

As Josee rounded the automobile, she heard strident yells. She was tossing her knapsack into the passenger seat when a white Metro swerved into view with head beams flashing.

"Let's not delay," Rosie urged.

The Metro slid to a halt, and Marsh popped out.

"Climb in, please," Rosie said. "Let's go."

"Josee," Marsh called, pacing to her side, "don't take it personally, but I had to come back to be sure you were okay. Call it a feeling. Not that I believe in that sort of thing, but in my mind I saw this picture of you… Anyway, are

you okay?" His eyes roved the park. He leaned to look into the car's cab, allowing his hand to rest on Josee's forearm.

She stiffened. Afraid that if she moved, he might let go.

"Rosie?" he said. "What're *you* doing here? I didn't know you drove a
Studebaker. Where've you been hiding such a car?"

"At my relatives', sir. For recreational use."

"No fault in that. Did Esprit get ahold of you?"

Rosie continued. "He left a message at the beach house. Said we had an
all clear to return to the manor. Should've gone there straightaway, but I
thought a stroll through the park might be pleasant before diving back into
the hustle and bustle. Does an old woman good."

"Strange that we should end up here together," Marsh noted. "What with
Josee being here and—"

"Jooosseee!"

The scream caused all three to turn.

"Josee, get outta here!"

She felt Marsh's fingers tighten on her arm. She craned to look over the
car and saw Scooter running full tilt through the trees and over the bike path.
Behind him, a cloaked rider revved his motorcycle and closed the distance.

～

"Marsh is heading toward Black Butte Ranch. That's my guess."

"Alone?" Stahlherz collected cash from a regular art customer, then hurried the woman from his basement studio. He pressed the phone to his ear as
he locked the garage door. "But wasn't Josee with him at the manor? Is she not
accompanying him?"

The voice was tinny on the phone. "I don't think so, Mr. Steele. Haven't
seen her, but she could be ducked down in the back. About an hour and a half
ago, he pulled his vehicle from the garage, a forest green Tahoe, and sped by
before I could get a good fix, you know what I'm sayin'? Guess where I am
right now? Shadowing him from a distance, humming along Highway 20. He
made one stop in Cascadia, let the attendant pump the gas."

"Did he have a journal with him, something along those lines?"

"He had some sort of book with him last night. He took it when he left the Ramada. I didn't see anything with him now, but the Tahoe was parked in the garage. Who knows what he loaded in there?"

"Black Butte Ranch—that's where you think he's going."

"Just a guess, Mr. Steele."

"Keep me posted. He needs to be heading back this way by early afternoon."

Stahlherz punched the End button and stood over his onyx chessboard. The center was a conflagration of threats, combinations, and tempo-gaining exchanges. His head blurred. So many strategies. Which ones were correct? Marsh was known to use the occasional gambit, but what was he up to now? Searching for Kara? Confirming plans for their weekend getaway?

Scree-akkk-akkk!

The beast was rising yet again, refusing to grant a moment's peace. Stahlherz wearied of combating this creature. The beak pecked at him, tearing at his sanity, shredding it bit by bit...*s-a-n-i-t-y!* He could feel reason taking flight.

Dark thoughts, the Professor had told him. *Use them to your advantage.*

Resistance was in vain, he knew. Perhaps the wiser option was to release himself. He stretched his thoughts across the powerful, soaring wings and became one with the flight of the rook. Wind flushed over him. Charged him in its superheated draft. The acid of his vengeance crackled and sizzled beneath his skin. Razor talons, his newest weapons, carved at the edges of his mind.

Unblinking, he viewed the framed photo above his desk. The man in Wranglers. Young Chance Addison, indolent and smug. In a swing of his talons, Stahlherz catapulted the photo into the air where it made contact with the suspended birdcage. Feathers and birdseed scattered. Glass broke upon metal bars in a shower of angry tears. The photo floated toward the carpet, curling and browning at the edges as though put to a flame. It disintegrated into ash.

Why had he fought so long? Resistance had only brought pain.

"Facilis descensus Averno... The descent to hell is easy," he mused aloud.

Only one secret remained, the whereabouts of the venom vials. He would find it in Chance Addison's journal tonight. Before the appearance of the

Halloween moon, Karl Stahlherz intended to acquire the poison, using Josee as the key.

—

"Scoot?"

"Josee, get away! Go!" Frantic, Scooter waved his hands at her while careening down the incline. The motorcycle was gaining. Shredded by the wind, the rider's clothes whipped violent shadows over the lawn.

"You know him?" Marsh questioned.

Josee nodded, starting to move forward.

"No," Marsh said. "Listen, he's trying to warn you off."

"But he's in trouble!"

After this morning, she wondered what had prompted Scooter to come here, but she had no time to consider it. The motorcycle engine was screaming, the tires spitting clumps of grass in aimless trajectories. In a blur of motion, the rider drove onward, clearly bent on destruction.

Marsh directed Josee into the Studebaker and handed her the knapsack. "Hurry! This is what I was afraid of. Rosie, can you get Josee outta here? Take her away from here. Or…yeah, take her back to the beach house. You two should be safe there."

"Certainly, sir. Whatever I can do to help."

"Move it! I'll deal with these guys. I'll call you later. Go!" He closed the door and slammed a hand against the side panel as though to hasten their departure.

Josee turned in the seat to catch sight of him. She wanted to see her mother, yes, but behind her was a man who'd affirmed a familial bond between them. His touch was still tingling along her arm. And what about Scooter? After all that had happened, here he was. How did he know she'd be here? Fighting his own inner demons, had he come to warn her of danger?

Hurry, Scoot. Don't let them get to you. Run!

The Studebaker was gaining speed. "We mustn't wait," said Rosie.

Through the rear window, Josee watched Marsh Addison assume a combative stance at the curb, ready to face Scooter and the approaching marauder.

Marsh's shoulders were broad, his jaw set, his stance courageous and challenging.

But his imposing figure could do little to help Scooter.

"Babe…" Scooter's yell was fading. "No*oo!*"

Rosie glanced into the mirror and met Josee's eyes. "Might be best not to watch. This whole matter is ugly, Josee. I simply don't understand."

But Josee could not pull away. She marked Scooter's dash through the display of prehistoric bones, his lateral jigs and his hurdling of an obstacle. The bike roared down the knoll, vaulted a gap in the sculptures, swerved in the soft turf, then continued in pursuit. Scooter skidded across the sidewalk and landed curbside in a sprawl.

"Get up!" Josee's fingers gripped the seat. She could see his gaping scream, but the sound was muted. He was looking in her direction. His mouth formed her name.

Too late.

Hunched over the handlebars, the driver propelled his machine into Scooter's fallen figure so that the front tire folded Scooter's legs into unnatural shapes. Leaping, the motorcycle came down upon him, then, with tires finding purchase on his crumpled form, spun sideways to evade Marsh Addison's angry arms. An iridescent tail of green grass and dirt clods whipped the air, spattering the parked Metro and Marsh's clothing. In a plume of smoke, the machine caromed onto the pavement and sped off in the opposite direction of the Studebaker.

"Go back!" Josee told the elderly woman at the wheel.

"We mustn't," Rosie insisted. "You heard Marsh. I need to take you away."

"Scooter's hurt!"

"Marsh'll look after him. Truly, I can't risk any harm coming to you. What then would I tell your mother?" Rosie put the car in gear and followed signs toward Philomath and Highway 34. "She so desperately wants to see you."

"Where is she?"

"At the Addisons' beach cottage, of course."

"Does Marsh know that?"

In the airflow from the vents, Rosie's honey-tinted curls shifted. "No, of course not. And Kara prefers that it remain so for the time being. They've had their troubles, as I told you on the phone. This is to be a private meeting."

Josee's waning attachment to Scooter gave way to her overwhelming desire to see Kara. This was what she'd come for, wasn't it?"

—

Josee's desire to see her birth mother overrode her fundamental distrust. The Studebaker was comfortable enough, and she pretended to nap with her head against her knapsack for much of the journey.

Only eight miles to go, according to the last sign.

The images from Avery Park gnawed at Josee's heart. Although she tried to switch her attention to the vast swells shimmering in the October sun, the picture of Scooter tumbling beneath those screaming tires remained. She felt a craving for a cigarette; instead she slipped a red gel capsule from her vial into her mouth.

As the town of Yachats came into view, Josee saw a sea lion bobbing in the ocean. Trees swayed before the bellows of surf and sky, and she lifted her head to sniff the salty air. Her eyebrow ring turned cold against her skin, but she kept her face windward and latched on to Marsh's rekindled interest in her. She would tell Kara of it. Previously he had tried to talk his wife out of making the connection with their long-lost daughter, but maybe his new resolve would melt the ice between them.

Between Kara and Marsh. Between Kara and Josee. One big happy family?

Stranger things had happened; Josee knew that for a fact.

"We're nearly there, dear," Rosie cooed. "Left at the sign and half a block."

The car crunched over gravel past a sign for Timberwolf Lane. Josee ran a hand through her hair, tugged at a few strands with her fingers, then ran the other hand through. What would Kara think? Would the life-size view repulse her?

"This is it, the Addisons' beach house." Rosie followed the half-circle drive and parked behind another car. "You'll feel right at home, I'm certain."

"Kara's here?"

"She is."

"Are you gonna be hanging around? I mean, no offense but—"

Rosie's look turned cold, then she tilted her chin in a play for sympathy. "You prefer that I go? I made this drive for your sake, Josee. I had hoped that you'd find a soft spot in your heart for this lonely old woman. Never had a child of my own."

"Thanks for the ride. Nothing against you. Just want some time alone with Kara."

"Certainly, I can understand that." Rosie patted Josee's leg. "Forgive my silly notions. Time alone? With Kara? I'll be certain you have that opportunity."

Josee trailed the older woman onto the porch. Her pulse pounded. One part of her wanted to throw open the door and find her mother's arms, while another part said to click off the emotions and take things as they came. No more disappointment.

Rosie knocked twice on the sliding glass door, paused, knocked three times.

"Who knows?" Josee said. "Maybe she went out for a walk."

"I sincerely doubt that."

The curtains shifted behind the glass, and a hand brushed into view. The lock disengaged, the door slid open, and a guy about Josee's age stepped before them.

"Good afternoon, Wade," Rosie said. "Are you going to allow us in?"

He held back the curtain and ushered them into a room with vaulted ceilings, open rafters, and a stone fireplace. Would she have played here growing up? Josee wondered. Would these have been her stomping grounds? The dim surroundings surrendered no sign of Kara, but there were others in the house; their shapes took on distinguishing features as her eyes adjusted. What were they doing here?

"Meet Josee," Rosie told Wade.

He gave a slight nod. "Josee."

"She's here to see her mother," Rosie said. "Would you be so kind as to show her down the hall?"

"Now?" Wade was hesitant.

"Maybe now's not a good time," said Josee. "Doesn't seem like she's exactly hurrying out to see me. Maybe this wasn't such a great idea."

"Nonsense, dear," Rosie said. "Don't be silly. Wade, show her the way."

The young man indicated for Josee to go ahead of him. Some reception, Josee thought, trying to suppress her doubts. As she started down the hall, Rosie issued a final instruction from the living room: "Wade, make sure that they won't be disturbed. Josee and Kara aren't going anywhere right away, but they'd like the chance to talk, to have some uninterrupted time together. Make sure they get it."

"As you say, Professor."

Professor?

Josee turned even as additional weight creaked and sagged the floorboards behind her. A cloth pressed over her face, jabbed her eye, and caused it to water. Then the hallway spun away, revealing a whirlpool of strobe lights that faded into black.

36

Timberwolf

Turney almost hit the gurney as he prowled down the Good Samaritan corridor. He swung his wide frame aside, trying to skirt along the wall. Flanked by a team of medical personnel, a heavily bandaged figure was prone beneath bloodstained sheets.

"Excuse me," Turney mumbled. "Sorry."

"Sarge?"

Turney heard the voice but ignored it. He was still agitated by the meeting in the administrator's office. This roller coaster of a day had hit some real highs and lows, and he was feeling queasy. Not to mention he was starved.

"No! Go back. Hey, Sarge!"

"Sergeant?" A hand on his shoulder. "Sorry to bother you, but this kid here seems to know you. Spare a sec? Gotta make it quick."

Turney discovered Scooter hidden beneath bandages that capped a lopsided head; the bandages were caved in on one side, slightly discolored. Scooter's voice was weak, his one uncovered eye a mere slit. A nurse held an IV bag beside his arm.

"Where're they taking me, Sarge? Couldn't get away. I tried," he said in a strangled voice. A spasmodic chuckle brought blood to the front of his mouth where it pooled behind his lips. "It got me, no doubt about it. Nailed me good."

"What're you talking about?"

A wet cough. "Josee okay?"

"Josee." Turney looked up and down the hall, saw no sign of her. A paramedic gave an impatient shrug to indicate he knew nothing. "Yeah, she's okay. You know, kid, you should've never left here without the doc's permission."

"I'll be fine, big guy."

"Rest easy." Turney set a hand over Scooter's. "You hang in there, okay? Your voice's full of mush, and you're not even thinking straight. Believe me, I know the feeling." Turney rolled back his uniform sleeve to reveal gauze that was crusty and discolored along the edges. "Looky there. See what I mean?"

"You got tagged too."

"Don't give in to it," Turney insisted. "If you give it an inch, it'll take a mile."

Another chuckle. "Too late now." Blood spilled over the young man's lips, and his one visible eye began blinking rapidly.

A doctor rushed up. "Sorry, Officer. This patient's going into OR *now*."

"Understood. Stay tough, Scooter." But there was no response.

Turney watched the team regain steam and burst through double doors at the end of the hall. He wondered if he'd see the kid again. Whatever this fasting from food was supposed to accomplish, it didn't seem to be working. John Van der Bruegge had described it as a form of joining together in battle. Was it worth the effort?

Please, God. Looks for the life of me as though Scooter's losing the war.

A shell-shocked soldier keeping watch, Marsh paced the hospital waiting area.

He felt little connection with Scooter, but at the Avery Park curbside, responsibility for the kid had fallen upon his shoulders. Josee's friend had been lying dazed in a pool of blood and contorted limbs. With a quick call, Marsh had beckoned an ambulance; the eleven-minute wait had allowed him time to assess Scooter's wounds.

One detail, in particular, caught his attention.

Where he expected to find deep tire tracks and rubber burns, he found instead a pattern that resembled overlapping scales. Tattooed across Scooter's chest and legs, the pattern was one to match the belly of a serpent.

Marsh wanted to write it off as another apparition—that would be so much easier to deal with—but he knew he was beyond filing away the facts for future consideration. No, the truth was, he'd been viewing things through some otherworldly filter. A spiritual lens. Try as he might, crazy as it seemed, he couldn't purge this line of thinking.

Okay, then. The facts, as he'd experienced them firsthand.

One: He'd seen his own necktie corded around Kara's throat. *Two:* He'd found her bound and gagged in his desk chair. *Three:* He'd talked to her at the stream before a glass figurine took her place. *Four:* He'd spotted Josee on the sidewalk, only to find a chess bishop on the pavement. *Five:* He'd wrestled with some apparition in the shower and watched his wife's image suffer while his own dirty secrets burned into her skin.

And now this? Scooter's physically wounded, that's a fact, but he seems wounded at a deeper level, at a...soul level.

Marsh snatched a sports magazine from the waiting-room table. He was losing touch with reality; he must be. A soul level? Where did these thoughts come from? He flipped the pages, almost tearing them. Not seeing a thing.

Now seeing everything.

Kara's prayer: *Please, God, open his eyes.*

His own prayer: *God, forgive me. What've I done?*

The magazine plummeted to the carpet, and he lowered himself into an armchair where he sat with fingers wrapped through his wavy hair and deep breaths flaring his nostrils. He, Marsh Addison... *One:* He had choked his wife by not letting go of her sins. *Two:* He had bound her, gagged her with his self-promoting and self-fulfilling career. *Three:* He had stayed by her side, yes, but he'd lost sight of who she truly was. *Four:* He had tossed aside their daughter in the process, in this very hospital. *Five:* He'd deceived himself into believing his own indiscretions had no bearing on his family.

A king on a chessboard. The central figure. The weakest piece.

He had played his part to perfection.

Marsh heard a door open and saw a doctor approach with a solemn gait. The waiting area was suffocating. Marsh retrieved the magazine from the floor, then shook the doctor's outstretched hand.

In words that both sanitized and underlined the horror, the doctor relayed the news of the surgical team's success in saving Scooter's vital organs and stanching his internal bleeding. "He has, however, sustained massive head trauma. At 2:27, we believe he slipped into a coma on the operating table."

How, Marsh asked himself, would he break the news to Josee?

Marsh was convinced he had shaken his pursuers. He and Josee had escaped.

With that in mind, when he spotted Sergeant Turney in the corridor, he invited him to a short powwow in the hospital cafeteria. They found a court-yard table surrounded by plants and pale October sunlight. They were alone. The hefty sergeant filled a chair, wringing his hands around the neck of his water container, then wiping the condensation on his police trousers.

"Not hungry?" Marsh said. "I could've grabbed you something."

Turney's jowls shook beneath his deep-set eyes. "Food'll come later. Still got battles to fight."

"If you say so." Marsh dipped a spoon into hearty vegetable soup.

"Had a rough few days, haven't you, Marsh? Between Kara, Josee, and Scooter, you've been put through the wringer."

Dip, *slurp*. Dip, *slurp*.

"You haven't been real helpful from the police's point o' view. Lawyered up, acting suspicious, but I can see that your mind's racing. So this Connors kid says he has your wife. Whaddya think about that? Has someone threat-ened you? A ransom maybe? You have an image of wealth that could be temptin' to some."

"The vineyard's doing well." *Slurp*. "A lotta hard work. Not as lucrative as you might expect, but, yeah, I'm sure there are those who think we live in the lap of luxury."

"More to life than money."

Marsh looked up, wiped his mouth with a napkin. "I'll admit, I've had reasons for avoiding certain people in your department. Personal business. Goes way back."

"Somethin' between you and Chief Braddock?"

"What makes you say that?"

"The truth? Heard rumors about the chief's ways in the early years, when he was a detective—rumors about one party in particular. Not gonna beat around the bush. I've got issues with the chief myself. Still, I'm committed to my job."

Marsh buttered a roll and took a bite.

Turney averted his gaze. "Marsh, tell me this. Do you know where Kara is?"

"Wish I did. Did you track down that phone number for me?"

"Assigned to the House of Ubelhaar. Some art supply and review company."

Marsh dropped his spoon. "U-b-e-l-h-a-a-r?" He spelled it out.

"Bingo. Name Gertrude Ubelhaar mean something to you?"

Mean something? For crying out loud! Gertrude... Trudi!

Marsh's mind raced through his father's journal, aligning the facts. The US Army had provided Trudi personal living quarters in Benton County, Washington, across the Columbia River from the Umatilla Army Depot, where she had worked as a consultant. A crafty woman, she had found a way to survive all these years.

But is she still alive? She'd be in her seventies by now. Still seeking revenge?

"Mean something to me?" Marsh said. "Yeah, Sarge, you might say that."

"Then let me be of assistance. Why don't ya tell me what you know."

Marsh surveyed Sergeant Turney's face. In the business world, Marsh had honed his ability to detect subterfuge. What about this cop though? Turney seemed aboveboard. Josee, too, seemed to trust this guy. Maybe it was time for a little help. *Facts are power—even the power to care, if needed.* Isn't that what he'd told Kara's image in his study? With the facts between them, perhaps he and Turney could piece this puzzle together. Worth a try.

"You ready for this?" Marsh pushed aside his soup bowl, crossed his arms on the table. His watch told him it was a quarter to three, less than two hours before the rendezvous at the Camp Adair marker. "Sarge, this is between you and me..."

Marsh highlighted the history of Chance's betrayals and Trudi's abuse, of the imported biochemical weapons and the gift Trudi bestowed upon her former lover—a gift of spite, *Gift 12*. "In German, the word means poison. And now," Marsh said, "it's as though the poison of old wounds has resurfaced."

"Boy, tell me about it." Turney tugged at the sleeve of his shirt.

"When I read my father's journal," Marsh went on, "I assumed Trudi was dead. But what if she's still here, masterminding my family's demise, like the final moves of a chess game?"

"A jilted old woman, you think? With a hatred for men."

"Look at what the guys in her life did to her—the SS officers, her father, my father. She's gotta be one determined old crone. Where is she though? Did you find an address for this House of Ubelhaar? A name to contact, anything to help us?"

"Sure did. Dug around and found out they're billed monthly for the phone through a local PO box. Dug deeper and got a look at the name on the box's original lease. Funny thing is, although the name's not in the phone book, the account's been gettin' paid on time for over five years. In cash, mind you. Good thing I could read the signature on the receipts."

"Whose was it?"

"A Mr. Stahlherz. Mister Karl Stahlherz."

Steele Knight? Karl Stahlherz? Are we talking about one and the same man?

Marsh observed the police sergeant as he took a swig of his water, gave the container a disappointed look, and pushed his elbows against the chair's arms.

"To add to the mystery," Turney said, "this same phone number came up in a conversation in the administrator's office."

"Here? You mean the hospital administrator?"

Turney nodded. "Guess he's been commissioned to call that number anytime someone shows up at Good Samaritan with snakebite symptoms. Little more complicated than that, actually, but you get the idea."

Snakebite? Marsh considered that pattern over Scooter's legs and chest.

"I'd say you're onto something, Marsh. This phone call you got yesterday. Was it a threat? What can you tell me about it?"

"Guess I've told you this much…" Marsh divulged the details of the meeting with Steele Knight, including his own steps to counter any trap. He baited Turney's attention, watched him angle his head and push his eyebrows together. He asked for unofficial, off-duty, out-of-uniform help.

"And I'll have Henri Esprit call you with the final details," he finished.

"Marsh, I hope you know what you're doin'. Can't say I approve on the official end, but I understand your desperation. Where's Josee in all this?"

"She's safely tucked away. Far from the action. Our household overseer, Rosamund Yeager, drove Josee over to our place in Yachats."

"Josee's not exactly a pushover. One tough little cookie."

"You noticed that too."

Turney grinned. "Think Ms. Yeager can handle her?"

"Sure. Rosie's still got energy. She can hold her own, doesn't let any of our staff push her around. That's part of what I appreciate about her. Give her a task, and she'll see it through to the end. Do or die—that's her motto. Don't worry. She'll keep an eye out for Josee. One thing Rosie's always wanted was a child of her own."

"What about you? You glad to have your daughter back?"

Words stuck in Marsh's throat. Although he was tempted to challenge the paternal bond, the words sounded cheap and hollow in his own head. Sure, Kara had made her mistakes, but what had he done in return? He had used them against her to shirk the burden of child rearing. He had answered his father's mandate by pouring his energies into the vineyard at the expense of all else.

"It'd be nice to have proof that she's my flesh and blood," he responded. "But, yeah, all doubts aside, I am glad."

Turney flashed a wink. "And so am I."

Sgt. Vince Turney escaped the cafeteria with his tummy grumbling overtime. He'd watched Marsh eat. Smelled the rich soup. How did people do it, thinking on an empty stomach? How about John Van der Bruegge? Odds were good that he'd fudged somewhere along the line today. Anyway, what would one little nibble hurt?

John's appeal: *Some evil spirits would only be conquered by prayer and fasting.*

Well, it'd have to be God's power, all right. Turney could scarcely function.

He pulled alongside the Willamette River and, from the warmth of his patrol car, watched the waters eddy northward. Time, like the current, was continuing to move, and he had things to consider before the clock ticked to zero.

Beau Connors? After hearing charges of abduction and attempted assault, a judge had set bail at twenty-five thousand dollars, which Beau's father refused to post.

House of Ubelhaar? Turney had been unable to find a phone-book listing, nothing in the state of Oregon. Calls to local art galleries profited little. They had brochures but not much else, other than the phone number already established. He had assigned a detective to keep watch over the PO box at the downtown post office. As of yet, the box had not been emptied for the day.

Henri Esprit? Per Marsh's request, the winemaker had contacted Turney earlier and enlisted his help for a four-thirty meeting near Camp Adair. Did Turney think he would play the hero in this? Now that he knew the details in full, he questioned his wisdom in agreeing to join Esprit at Fred Meyer's supermarket at a quarter to four.

John Van der Bruegge? Though relieved to hear that Josee was safely away, John was worried about Scooter. John promised to visit the kid at the hospital, sit by his side, pray for recovery. He confessed that he, too, was struggling with hunger but felt it was important to see this through. Over the phone, he asked, "And how're you doing, Vince? Staying strong? Remember, we're in a battle. Keep your eyes and ears open, and for the sake of all things holy, keep your mouth closed!"

If it was meant to be funny, Sergeant Turney forgot to laugh.

⌒

Set on silent mode, Marsh's cell phone vibrated against his chest as he browsed through a used bookstore downtown. The blocked number doubled his pulse rate.

"Karl Stahlherz," he announced.

"Well done, Marsh. You've tracked down my full name. Busy at work, I see."

"Are we still on for our meeting? I want my wife back."

"Do you have your father's journal?"

"I do. And you'll have Kara there? Let's get this over with, clean and simple."

"You uphold your end of the bargain, and I'll uphold mine. See you shortly."

An hour and forty minutes, Marsh reassured himself. He could make this work.

Before returning to the rental car, he made a book purchase. Pricey but worth it. The book was wrapped and left behind the counter. He was coasting beyond the city limits when the phone vibrated again, a different pattern from the first. He had missed an earlier message. The display read "Timberwolf Two," the phone's ID at their time-share condo at Black Butte Ranch. The condo was situated in a cul-de-sac called Timberwolf Circle. In light of his father's military history, the name's significance had instigated Marsh's purchase of that specific property. A sentimental link. A sign.

The voice mail was from Henri Esprit.

"Doubt anyone's been to the condo in a while." Esprit's tone was apologetic. "I found the place empty and in immaculate shape. Checked at the resort office, and they confirmed that the last visitor left weeks ago. Things quiet down this time of year, they say. As for this afternoon's plans, I'll proceed as discussed. Got a call from a Sergeant Turney, a trustworthy sort. The decision to include him seems a wise move on your part. Sorry nothing panned out here, Marshall. Waste of a trip? Your call."

Not at all, Marsh thought. Just part of his plan.

He took a second look at the alphanumeric display: Timberwolf Two.

There it was, spelled out right before his eyes! For heaven's sake, how could he have missed it? This was Kara's clue to her location. Timberwolf Two was at Black Butte Ranch on Timberwolf Circle. Timberwolf One was the phone's ID in Yachats, the beach house on Timberwolf Lane. Indeed, she had tried to communicate with him through her answer to the weekend getaway question. Unable to tell him directly, she'd conveyed her location with a near-identical designation.

Timberwolf One…Timberwolf Lane.

You're in Yachats, aren't you, Kara? Should've known you'd give me a clue!

The jubilant pounding of his heart crashed to a halt. Rosie. Hadn't she spent the night in Yachats?

A dark realization clamped around his ribcage. He laid the facts from his father's journal over the grid of his own experiences and charted the corresponding reference points. On his hands he counted out the years, while Rosie's soft accent purred in his ears.

Good grief! Rosie? Could it be you?

But, of course, he'd made the observations to the sergeant less than an hour ago: *She can hold her own.... Give her a task, and she'll see it through to the end. Do or die... One thing Rosie's always wanted is a child of her own.*

Trudi Ubelhaar was alive, he felt convinced. She'd been there beneath their noses all this time. Toying with them. Playing this game Chance had instigated so many years ago. With Josee's arrival on the scene, Trudi was ready for end-game maneuvers. Rosie...Trudi. The same lady.

And he'd sent Josee off with her! Practically packed her into the car himself!

Marsh made quick calls. His chess game needed some new tactics.

———

Sergeant Turney pulled into his driveway as the phone rang.

"Sarge," said Henri Esprit, "I may be a few minutes late, but I still intend to meet you in front of Fred Meyer's. Be patient if I'm not as prompt as I'd like to be. I have something to pick up."

"I'll be there. Gonna change outta my uniform, then head out."

"I have other news. My nephew Nick—he's a computer whiz, a student at OSU—he's been monitoring Marsh's opponent online. Don't expect me to decipher the lingo, but I guess this man's logged on and off a couple of times in the past twenty-four hours so that Nick, by process of elimination, has managed to identify his modem. With an unspecified computer program—that for now I will assume is legal—Nick's gained access to the man's hard drive and copied his e-mail address base. He believes the information could prove indispensable to your department's investigation of local terrorist threats."

"I have no official comment. Off the record? Sounds like he hit the ol' jackpot."

"More significantly, he says he should be able to identify the user's physical address, as well as others from the database. Particularly those within Oregon."

Karl Stahlherz? Is this our guy? I'll bet the addresses read like an ICV roll call.

"Here, Esprit, let me give you a number that Nick can call to hook up with some guys on the state level who specialize in trackin' Internet-related crimes. Being as we're under the gun, they'll be able to speak his language and jump right on it, get the ball rolling." Turney dictated the appropriate info.

"Thanks, Sarge. I can only hope Nick follows through on this. He's a loner, not much of one for working with the powers that be. He might resist on principle."

"People's lives are at stake."

"I'll urge him firmly, but gently, to get over it."

"That's the spirit."

Turney signed off and climbed the carport steps that led into the kitchen. He closed the door, loosened his belt, and slipped off his shoes. What was he missing? Some crucial element had eluded him.

At the fridge door, his stomach rumbled like a concrete mixer. He set fingers on the handle, felt its cool comfort.

That's when the second call came to his aid.

"Sarge," said the detective, "we have a visual at the House of Ubelhaar PO box. Short, college-age Caucasian male with a bleached crewcut, wearing loose-fitting corduroys and an off-white, button-down shirt. He emptied the box. Now he's hanging around at the corner. Waiting, it seems. He was dropped off by a tan Ford Aerostar."

"Could be the van," Turney said, releasing the fridge handle. "The one the espresso-booth girl mentioned. Don't let him outta your sight, you got that?"

"Yes, sir, but he's... Hold it, a vehicle just pulled up. An old Studebaker, Sarge, you believe that? I didn't know there were any still around. Okay, looks like the kid's handing stuff through the window. Unable to view the driver from this angle. Should we tail them?"

"You betcha. You go after the Studebaker. Have your partner follow the kid. I'll be dropping below radar for a while, but you can keep me posted on my voice mail."

"Consider it done, sir."

"And, Detective? Call for backup if you sense any trouble. With the threat of an attack tonight, I don't need ya takin' any chances."

He turned from the humming mechanical preserver of all things cold and delicious and headed to the bedroom where he changed clothes, cleaned and re-dressed his seeping scars, then slipped on his shoulder holster.

Maybe there *was* something to this fasting exercise.

Thunder Turney was feeling lighter on his feet. Ready to fight.

Ten minutes after three.

Stahlherz wrapped himself in a long black coat, swelling his chest and stretching his arms into the loose sleeves. He repositioned the curved dagger in his pocket, then dropped the phone and stolen glass queen into another.

Years ago he had signed the PO box contract in his own name, protecting his mother's identity, since his own could not be linked elsewhere. Apparently, Marshall had put together the facts, calling him by name in their phone conversation.

I knew you to be a worthy opponent. Alas, your plans'll shatter like glass.

Stahlherz wrapped himself in the coat's folds and stared into the mirror across the room. His was the form of a shiftless black rook. He drew on his chess parlance and selected the term "doubled rooks," two castles working in unison.

Yes, he and the rook had become one.

37

Necessary Evils

"Josee?"

Her name. Being called. From another planet.

"Josee?"

With a massive effort she pried her eyes open. Saw nothing. When she closed them again, remnants of bright colors whisked around and connected to the dull throbbing in the middle of her skull. She kept her eyes open this time, detecting a movement in the nothingness. An indefinable shape.

"Hello there." A woman's voice. Familiar. Like a piece of music heard long ago.

"That you?"

The response was gentle. "It's me, Josee. Your mother."

"Kara." Her tongue formed the word with difficulty. "I can't see you."

"No windows down here. We're in a storage cellar."

Josee reoriented herself. The beach house. Town of Yachats, on the Oregon coast. "Can't we turn on the lights?" Even as the question left her lips, she realized she couldn't move. She was propped in a wooden chair, hands cinched behind her back, knees taped together, feet tied between two posts.

The posts shifted. Legs. Her mother's legs?

"We're bound together." Kara's voice was hoarse. "Facing each other."

"It's you?"

"It's me."

Josee blinked in the blackness. She tried to ignore the cellar's smells. She doubted that she could've restricted her own bodily functions in this creepy tomblike space. "Kara, you're not hurt, are you? Are you okay?"

"I am now." Kara's voice trembled.

"It's hard to believe it's really you. Is it true you got shot in the hip years ago?"

"Unfortunately, yes. Happened the night you were born. The doctors had

DARK TO MORTAL EYES   349

to do an emergency C-section. Can you feel that? That's me wiggling. I've been trying to keep moving in every possible way to stay alert and to keep from cramping."

"So it is you, Kara. Your voice sounds smoother on the phone."

"Throat's parched. Haven't had anyone to talk to, and they've kept me gagged. I've been tied up here since Wednesday, fairly miserable. Two days, and I've… It's been so lonely. And I'd hoped to bring you to this house myself."

"We're together now. How's that for irony?"

"Here we are." Kara sounded small, engulfed by the cellar's darkness. "Some guy I don't even recognize—tries to act calm, but he frightens me—he came down last night. Says that he's not interested in money, that he's using me as bait to trap my husband. How is Marsh? Have you seen him?"

"He's looking for you. Yeah, I saw him. And guess what?"

"Oh, darling, don't tell me. Was he rude to you? I warned you that he—"

"We started off rocky, all right. He came off as a real jerk. But something's changed, I guess, like he's opening to the idea. He showed me his father's journal."

"Chance's journal? I wasn't aware it still existed."

Across from Josee, Kara's shape seemed to hunch forward. From above, Josee thought she heard far-off footsteps and the whine of an engine. She squelched the pain in her head and the fear, then shared what she had read in the truck stop. Kara listened with minor interruptions.

As Josee finished, Kara said, "On my end, I have something to share."

"There's more? My brain's already toast."

"I'm quite serious on this matter, Josee. Not that I want to tell you, not really, but it'll explain some of Marsh's reservations in accepting you as his daughter. He's a good man. I'm partly to blame for the walls he's erected."

"No, that's what women always say. Don't take his junk and call it your own."

"Some of it is my own." Without further preamble, Kara jumped into an abbreviated version of a long-ago indiscretion at a campus party, spelling out the facts as though rehearsing them to herself in the black cellar. Her voice took on the steadiness of one trying hard to maintain control. "It's an evening

I'll always regret, an incident I should never have let happen. Marsh's never believed me, though, never let me explain that it went no further than some kisses and…caresses."

"So Marsh is my father? As in, the real deal?"

"Beyond a shadow of a doubt. Please, Josee, I've lived with this over my head long enough, even blamed myself for letting you go. As though it's been my fault entirely. At times I still wrestle with those regrets."

"But the journal. Don't you see? I'm like some freakin' curse in this family. No wonder Marsh and his mother were afraid of keeping me around, afraid that it would lead to others getting hurt. This whole thing's so twisted."

"I should've insisted on keeping you. I could've taken care of you."

"Hey, we're here together now, aren't we?"

Kara's legs moved against Josee's in the darkness. "That's right."

"And I've gotta say it, Mom. You're looking real good."

"You, too."

"Talk about a *captivating* conversation."

Paralyzed by their bonds, they chuckled. Then Kara said, "I'll take whatever I can get, a chance to be with my daughter. That's been the hardest part of being down here. Being hungry and dirty and scared—that's been bad enough. But knowing you would think I'd run out on our reunion—that was torture. I thought about you all day, cried and prayed. Asked God to open your eyes to all that's gone on, past and present."

"Open my eyes? If you only knew."

"Darling, I'm so sorry it's happened like this."

Josee felt her throat tighten. She soaked in her mother's voice.

Kara said, "I was sure that when I didn't show up, you'd never contact me again."

"I called," said Josee, "and your housekeeper told me it was postponed. Next thing I knew you were gone, and nobody knew where you were. Then they found your car down in a ravine, and some kid on the news said he'd kidnapped you, even had your earrings to prove it."

"I recognized him. He did work at the vineyard."

"Yep. Well, for a while they even suspected Marsh. Cops searched your place and everything."

"Does he know that I'm alive?"

"He thinks you are. There're things he's still not telling me. And now he thinks I'm safely tucked away from the action. In fact, he put me into the car himself."

"What do you mean?"

"Well, there's that kid on the news, but the woman who drove me over here, she must be as deep in it as any. She lied to me, stinkin' lured me into that park. Says she works for you and Marsh. Rosamund Yeager, does that sound right?"

"Rosie? She's here?"

—

In jeans and a camouflage hunting jacket, Sergeant Turney stationed himself outside of Fred Meyer's supermarket. The vending machines glowed behind him. He stamped his feet and rubbed his hands against the nip of the early-evening air. Twenty minutes to four. Esprit would be here soon, driving Marsh Addison's forest green Tahoe.

Minutes passed. The parking lot boasted a bevy of SUVs. Still no Esprit.

"Would you like to buy something, mister?"

"Come again?"

It seemed a cruel temptation that a table near the market doors flaunted Halloween candies and chocolate bars, a fund-raiser for some local scout troop. Backed by a dad in a lawn chair, the preteen boy was trying his hand at sales. His missing tooth and spatter of freckles only aided the attempt.

"Sorry, kid. No cash on me."

Turney surveyed the parking lot once more. *What am I even doing out here? Should've reported this to the chief. Gonna get myself in trouble all over again. Who knows what sorta mess we'll be walkin' into?*

Ten to four. The proximity of the vending machines was washing away his resolve. He was alone—in camouflage even—and he couldn't remember the reason he was withholding food from himself. Self-imposed starvation—what was the sense in that?

To the side, the freckled kid was plying another customer, and Turney thought he saw an exchange of money and chocolate. He tried to find something else with which to occupy his mind. A flier with curled corners and errant doodles caught his eye from its location near a bank of pay phones. He read, in shadowed letters, an invitation to artists, poets, writers, and dreamers: *Frustrated with life? Discover the gift of art. Join our family at the House of Ubelhaar. A place to set yourself free. For more information, call 541-555-GIFT.*

Ubelhaar? Gertrude…Trudi…Rosie. Was this how she had recruited for ICV?

GIFT? Or, as Marsh had translated for him from German, "poison."

Turney's mind swam with the repercussions of this fresh insight. He understood more than ever what had drawn the ICV recruits into the web of anarchy and rebellion. By appealing to their dreams and abilities, Trudi Ubelhaar had molded their thinking. She had perverted God-given talents, twisting them into instruments for destruction and vented rage. How many youth had been screened and brought into the fold? Where did they plan to attack, and how?

Whoa, now—it's enough to give me a headache. Can hardly think straight.

Sustenance, that's what he needed. Whatever this silly fasting idea was supposed to accomplish, surely it'd been done by now. How could this self-torture be a source of strength? Oh, he remembered the words, all right— *"When I am weak, then I am strong"*—but what did they mean anyway? He felt weak; that much was true. Sick to his stomach, on edge, and irritable. So now, he argued, it must be time to get strong.

Which meant food.

Nope!

He thrust his hands into his jacket pockets, knowing that as long as they remained in place, they couldn't get him into trouble. Without his hands, he couldn't feed his face. Well, theoretically he could, but—

Fingers touched something wedged in the corner of a pocket. A ball of lint, he thought, plucking it out. But the texture was all wrong. It was a five-dollar bill that looked as though it'd seen the belly of a washing machine on more than one occasion.

Five dollars? He turned his back on the fund-raising table. No, too obvious.

But let's face it. It's gotta be more than coincidence. A gift in my time of need.

Before he could change his mind, he spun around and sauntered to the table. "What're you sellin' there, kiddo? What's it going to?"

The kid smiled and went through his spiel, while Turney examined the choices. "Here, this'll do. How much?" He handed over the five and got three bills and quarters to go along with the thick orange-wrapped chocolate moon. He returned to his waiting place. Peeled back the foil one fold at a time to show he was in control.

The first bite was incredible! Food had never tasted so good.

He had his teeth into the second when the Tahoe pulled up. A poised older gentleman spoke from the cab window. "Sergeant Turney?"

"Uh-huh." He swallowed a chunk whole. "Howdy, Mr. Esprit."

"Glad to be of service. I assume you're ready to do this?"

Ready? With the evidence of guilty pleasure in his mouth and in his hands, Turney felt anything but. He clambered in beneath the vehicle's hatch, finding his hiding spot as planned, and wedged himself into the musty space. He sensed a prickly heat beneath his arm bandages. As city lights gave way to the countryside, as evening shadows took over, he adjusted his holstered .38 and wondered what lay ahead.

"Nearing the site," Esprit called from the front. "Stay low."

"Urhh-kay." Garbled words.

"I'll spring the hatch as I'm backing into a spot. That way you'll be able to exit the vehicle unnoticed when you deem it propitious."

The sergeant buried his mouth in the crook of his elbow. He'd failed again. He'd let himself down, and the Van der Bruegges, Josee, and Scooter. Who was he tryin' to fool? He'd even let God down. He was a lard belly, scarred and apathetic, a loser of a cop—and everyone knew it.

Feeling miserable, Turney took another nibble of the chocolate moon.

———

Light poured down the concrete steps. Josee squinted. She saw legs descending, then looked back to her mother. As her pupils adjusted, she found Kara's face no more than a yard in front of her. Though pale and bruised, Kara's skin was still soft over fine features. Her lips were thin, cracked, blood-encrusted. Her hair was the color of Josee's golden-wheat sketching pencil, touching her shoulders in thin waves, cupping delicate ears. But it was Kara's neck that transfixed Josee; the contours spoke of a grace and beauty nearly impossible to put on paper.

"It's you," Josee said with a shy smile.

"Josee." Kara, too, ignored their approaching abductor. "You're so pretty."

"Wasn't sure what you'd think. What you see is what you get."

"You're a grown woman. Don't change a thing. No matter what happens," Kara added in a whisper, "you'll always be my baby. I said those words to you long ago, and I meant them. Don't you ever forget it, Josee. I love you."

Josee's chest clenched. "I won't forget."

The cellar was awash now in the light from upstairs. Before them stood an elderly woman whose smile did even less than her facial powder to soften her features.

Josee glared up at her. *Wipe that smile off your face.*

"Rosie?" Kara said. "I didn't think it was true. What's this all about?"

"Have you two enjoyed your little tête-à-tête?" Rosie inquired. "I hope the talk was worthwhile. A happy reunion, I trust? Regrettably, the afternoon's upcoming events demand that we gag the two of you. Time to depart."

Kara stared at her as though she were a stranger. "How'd you get involved in this? Does Marshall know what you're up to? Is someone coercing you?"

"Coercing me? No, frankly, it's the other way around. I'm the one manipulating the terms of engagement. It's been my show from the beginning. Nothing against you, Kara. You're an honorable woman. Gullible but honorable. You've played your role without flaw. As for Marsh, tonight's his farewell performance. And Josee"—she chortled in obvious relish—"Josee is the key to it all. Sorry, ladies, time to split up."

"You're not taking me from my mom!"

"But, Josee, I have no choice. You both have your roles to fill."

"My role is as a mother." Kara's dry voice cracked. "Please don't take Josee from me. Not now."

"A mother… Why, motherhood's something I've never truly experienced."

"Who'd want you?" Josee snapped.

The old woman's eyes caught the light from above and took on a spectral glow that sent a shiver through Josee's body and caused Kara to stiffen.

"You deceived us," Kara said in hushed shock. "Marsh and I trusted you."

"When you left, you gave me an opportunity I couldn't resist."

"You had me ambushed! I nearly crashed into the ravine."

"You did, according to the reports. Your car's quite a mess. I had my cohort send it over the edge. Then we called it in the next morning. Marsh was so worried." Rosie primped her hair with spotted fingers. "Necessary evils, my dear. Greater issues at stake. You're a means to an end, a way of getting Josee and Marsh to toe the line."

"You have no right to involve my daughter in this. Think about it, Rosie—"

"*Ich heisse Gertrude Ubelhaar,*" the woman corrected in German. "Gertrude Ubelhaar…but you can call me Trudi for short."

"This is wrong!"

"How can it be wrong," Rosie jeered, "when it feels so gloriously right? Sorry, ladies, the time has come. You had your little reunion, yet your voices have grown wearisome to me. The gags, I fear, are not negotiable."

As Rosamund bent to tie a cloth about Kara's mouth, Josee worked her tongue, sucked in her cheeks, then spit on the old woman's blouse. It hurt, yes it did, when a slap of punishment came whipping back across her face, but she still felt a sense of victory born from the fact that she had been with Kara and that the two of them, mother and daughter, were in this together.

Separate. Apart.

Either way, they were joined by much more than this old hag's filthy ropes.

The second blow, from the other direction, sent her sinking into the waters of a frigid sea where light and warmth had no home and only the cry of a mother's love kept her scrambling back to the surface for air.

—

Stahlherz would drive himself tonight. The rendezvous was nearing.

He placed a call to the beach house and had one of the ICV lackeys put the Professor on the line. He said, "You're coming soon, I hope, bringing Kara along." Stahlherz rolled the glass figurine in his pocket. He'd grown so attached to her.

"She's being loaded into the car as we speak, Stahli. The Studebaker's trunk has more than enough room. Are you certain Marshall will honor our arrangement?"

"He says he has the journal."

"That's vital. Without the key or bank info, Josee does us little good."

"No need to worry. I've been tracking Marsh's movements by credit card, as we discussed. A final check confirms that he made a midday visit to Black Butte—where he had lunch—and, most recently, a refueling stop at a station east of Corvallis. Nothing unusual. He did attempt to locate me on the Internet this morning, but I deflected his probe back to his own modem. He knows better than to try such tricks. No, there's nothing to indicate that he's taken flight or gone to the police. I made it clear to him that any such maneuvers would endanger his wife."

"Odd. Why, may I ask, would he visit Black Butte?"

"Well, I know he's taking Kara there this weekend. He wanted proof that she was alive and, as a test, had me ask her where they were going for a romantic getaway. Kara's answer seemed to placate him."

"A romantic getaway?" Trudi's voice had chilled.

"Did they tell you differently? Was this part of their plans? You sound dubious."

"Oh, it's nothing, Son. Nothing at all. Why, they're under no obligation to share their schedules with me."

"Do you get the sense Marsh has more feelings for Kara than we estimated?"

Trudi gave no response.

"Is there something I should know, Professor? What is it?"

"All's well. No, you proceed with your plans. I'm sending my Studebaker—with the queen on board, of course. Along the way, the driver'll pick up the items you requested from the PO box so you can proceed to your rendezvous at Camp Adair."

"I'll be waiting," he replied.

Part Six

So we come to it...the great battle....
There is no longer need for hiding.
We will ride the straight way...
and wait for none that tarry.

The Return of the King by J. R. R. Tolkien

Resist the enemy in the time of evil....
In every battle you will need faith as your shield....
Pray at all times.... Stay alert.

Ephesians 6:13,16,18

38

Ready to Strike

Marsh knew that he'd been duped by the enemy queen. Time to change plans.

Far out to sea the sky glowed with the warmth of a dying ember while Marsh parked the Metro at a Yachats convenience store. It seemed silly to sneak up on his own beach property, but he was counting on the element of surprise.

Here, on the edge of the Pacific, on the edge of the chessboard, the battle for his family was about to take place. Back in Corvallis, at the board's center, Sergeant Turney and Henri Esprit would play out their strategies, yet the focus of the battle had shifted. Shifted back, Marsh realized, to where it had all begun.

Would he find his wife and daughter, the queen and bishop, here?

Would his credit trail keep Trudi off balance? Or would she be waiting for him?

As he loaded a clip into his Glock nine-millimeter, Marsh decided to make the call he'd been avoiding. He could no longer do without the help of law enforcement; he had drafted the sergeant, and now it was time to go after the chief. With the rash bravado of a nineteenth-century chess player, Marsh jabbed at the numeric pad.

After a series of holds, Chief Braddock's gruff voice broke through. "Hello?"

"Braddock, this is Marsh Addison." He checked the safety on his weapon, then shoved it into his belt beneath his light jacket.

"What can I do for you? If it has to do with Kara, I'm listening."

"As if you have any say in what happens with my wife."

"We're both concerned for her safety. It's my job, Marsh. You've been under a lot of stress, I'll give you that much, but at least your name's been cleared."

"What about yours? I should make you pay for what you did years ago!"

"Everyone pays a price. Do you think I haven't?"

"Listen. I don't know, I don't care. Right now, we have a serious problem."

With wind gathering at his back, Marsh walked along the highway and found a break between outdated motels. He couldn't let personal vendettas get in the way, not at this point. He plugged through the sand, feeling dune grass poke at his legs as he explained to Braddock what he needed. He informed him of a biochemical weapon hidden on the coast in a safe-deposit box. This could be part of a larger scheme.

"You've got my attention, Marsh. You ever heard of ICV?"

"The local anarchists? Sure."

"Well, if you've seen the news, you know about the anthrax alert. Threats've been made, and I have teams working overtime on it. Camp Detrick, a longtime center of chemical warfare research, one of their classes had a motto: 'We seek something which cannot be seen, smelt, or felt, discovered by means which we do not have.' That might give you an idea of the challenge we face."

"Can't you simply tell the bank what's going on and seize the deposit box?"

"No, I can't just walk in and demand free access. Despite any snide remarks you might have, my badge is not a license to do as I will. I've learned that much."

"Bank closes at six, Braddock. If I want to free my wife and daughter, I have no choice but to turn over the key and box number to people intent on using those vials. I'll delay them as long as I can, but I refuse to lose Kara and Josee. Of course, I don't want others hurt. All I'm asking is that you'll intervene. You can do that much for me."

"I don't know that there's time to secure a warrant. Without the key, I'd have to drill that box. Not the wisest choice, in light of the alleged contents. We have nothing to counter the hemotoxins."

"You're making this more difficult than it is. Honestly, if—" Marsh stopped walking. Through gnarled branches and over a dune crest, he could see the vaulted roof of his beach house. "Braddock, I didn't say anything about hemotoxins. Where'd you come up with that word?"

Braddock's silence served notice of forthcoming secrets. When he did speak, there was defeat in his voice. "Got some things I should share with you, Marsh. I know about the box. I know about Josee—"

"Know what? How could you—"

"And I know about Trudi Ubelhaar, leader of ICV. For over a year, I've had a paid informant among the ranks of In Cauda Venenum. He's been trying to identify her, but he was killed last evening, left as road kill just north of Yachats."

This revelation pumped cold sweat onto Marsh's brow. Had he driven past the spot on his way here? Hadn't he noticed spillage on the opposite side of the highway?

Marsh said, "You knew that Trudi was masquerading as my employee?"

"Trudi? She worked for you?"

"Used the name Rosamund Yeager. She's managed our housekeeping staff for over three years. You might've warned us. Now Kara's gone, thanks to you."

Braddock's voice brimmed with indignation. "I didn't know of this. I never knew. She's had us all fooled. Should've guessed she'd be right under our noses, but things're always obvious in retrospect. Barely four years ago Trudi completed her job at the Umatilla Army Depot and received a government pension. Here she is again."

"Wish I'd been brought into the loop. This is—"

Braddock jumped in. "Are you going to give me the number of this deposit box?"

Marsh considered the campus party so many years ago, reflected on Kara's teary couch-side confessions. This man's actions had been a stain on their marriage. Then, in contrast, scenes from the Good Samaritan stairwell clouded Marsh's mind. Braddock rushing up the steps, offering aid.

He leaned into the bole of a tree. "Why should I trust you?"

"Strange question, Marsh, considering you're the one who called me."

"But who gave you the right to push your nose into my family's business?"

Braddock's laugh was deep and cheerless. "Do you want my help or not?"

"You owe an apology at least. Or a—"

"Next subject, Marsh. Right now, we need to stop the contents of this deposit box from being distributed, am I right? I'll do my best. Now, tell me its location."

From the trees, Marsh studied his house. Emotion surged in his chest, and he knew that his mother had been right when she had said that love was a powerful weapon.

I'd do anything right now—anything!—to ensure Kara's and Josee's safety.

"You still there?" the chief asked. "Don't have a lotta time."

He said, "The box is in Florence. Number 89, Bank of the Dunes."

"Thank you, Marsh. Hard as it might be to swallow, I am on your side."

"Yeah? Sure hope calling you wasn't a mistake—"

The chief had already disconnected.

Lights off. Zero movement. No vehicles in the driveway.

From here, the beach house looked deserted, but Marsh kept wide of the motion-activated lights near the back entry and angled through the scrub brush. He gripped his gun, buttoned his jacket. He skirted the house and ducked beneath a bedroom window. Poking up at the windowsill, he saw no movement inside. Two more windows. Same results.

Had he misinterpreted the clues? Were they even here?

Rosie…Trudi. She was at the heart of this, and she had transported Josee here from the park. Kara had used a wordplay to guide him to this same site.

He was too late; that must be it.

At his trophy-room window, between sailboat curtains, he glimpsed his liquor bar and the mirrored shelf of decanters. By the sink, a single shot glass sat empty. He never left those out. And if Rosie were innocent, she would've straightened it in her cleaning routine.

Someone's been here. That's a fact!

Feeling cavalier, Marsh followed his nine-millimeter around the house, into the activated circle of light on the front porch. The door was unlocked. He clicked off the safety on the Glock and stepped inside. The dining room was still, the kitchen clean. By the hall light, he scanned the living room, bedrooms, bathroom, on down to the final door.

The trophy room.

Aware of the evidence on the bar, he pressed his back against the linen cupboard, turned the trophy-room doorknob, and kicked open the door.

He found no resistance. No intruders. Only an odor wafting from within. With sweat beading under his arms, Marsh stepped in and turned on the light. Beside the bar and the wayward shot glass, he noticed the bearskin rug had a wrinkle along one edge. He unrolled the rug. Lifted the door to the cellar.

They were gone. His gamble had backfired.

In the light, he counted two empty chairs—that explained the vacant spots at the ends of the dining table upstairs—and a paint bucket in the corner. Perhaps that was the smell he'd detected. But there was nobody down here. Sure, he'd set the trap for Stahlherz; sure, he'd deduced Kara's location. On the other hand, he'd sent Josee to her fate with Trudi and wasted valuable time trying to help Scooter at the park and hospital. Not that he should've abandoned the kid, but he'd fallen behind, lost a tempo.

"So what now?" he called into the emptiness of the cellar. "What now!"

I'm no king. I'm nothing but a pawn in this game…

It was helpful to couch this fiasco in the metaphor of a chess game; it served as an emotional buffer. *Pawn promotion,* Marsh told himself. Hadn't the old master Philidor said that pawns were the soul of chess? He had to find Trudi. He would go as a pawn, marching to the board's back row to give himself up.

Self-sacrifice. A pawn for a knight, or a bishop…or a queen.

He ducked beneath a strand of cobwebs and circled the damp space one more time. Facing the first chair, he tried not to think of the anguish Kara had been through. What had they done to her? He saw stains and sliced strips of cloth.

Then he saw the note.

———

Four thirty. The Camp Adair historical monument. A private rendezvous.

"Shame, shame," Stahlherz whispered. "The end of the game."

He parked beside the forest green Tahoe in the gravel lot. Though the dying sun revealed little evidence of others nearby, he was certain his ICV network was dispersed within fifty yards. No doubt they could see him even now and were relieved by his arrival. As instructed, they would be prepared to detain any unwanted intruders.

With a renewed sense of purpose, he emerged from the van. He had seen a picture or two, but this would be the first face-to-face encounter. How he'd longed for this day.

Marsh Addison. Crash-Chess-Dummy. His lifelong foe.

"You're here, Stahlherz. I was beginning to wonder." The voice carried over the grass from beside a marble marker bearing the timberwolf symbol of World War II's 104th Infantry. The speaker wore slacks and a sports jacket over a cable-knit sweater. Beneath the brim of a homburg, his face was shaded.

"Marsh? Marshall Addison?"

"Here as requested. Where's Kara?"

Steele Knight was cautious. "Tell me, what opening did you play this morning?"

"The Sicilian Defense," came the reply. "But you disconnected."

Stahlherz grinned, for even as he detected an unfamiliar tone, he spotted the object in his opponent's hand. Thick and clothbound. The long-sought journal? He moved down the gravel path to join Marsh. Once the journal was in hand, he would phone the Professor and tell her to drive from her waiting spot only moments away at Adair Village. The exchange would be made, and then—with or without his mother's approval—he would carve his pound of flesh from this man who'd usurped all that was rightfully his.

Marsh, you wish to meet your father? Well, you can join him—in hell!

In the breeze, an American flag fluttered, its fasteners clanging against the metal pole. Stahlherz's coat, too, flapped about him as his strode over the path. He palmed his dagger, kept its hilt pushed from view in his black sleeve.

Doubled rooks. Taking wing. Harnessing the darkness.

He scanned the park's perimeter, where shadows moved. On one side a fence bordered them; on the other, Camp Adair Road. Ahead, a crumbling concrete structure spoke of a former military presence, while at his back a wildlife sanctuary teemed with cooing pheasants and quail.

Or were those imitated bird calls?

"Marsh." Stahlherz arrived at the marker. "Let me see the journal. If it's the real article, if it's not been tampered with, I'll call to have Kara brought forth without delay."

"Where is she?" The brim of the man's homburg lifted.

Skre-accck!

"Who are you? Where's Marsh!" Stahlherz tapped his fingers so that the dagger slipped into his hand. A curved talon. Ready to strike.

⌐

With strips of gas-scented cloth over her eyes and mouth, Josee kicked at the heavy duct tape around her ankles. The trunk held her captive. Cold and cramped, she listened to the hum of the road beneath her. Through her gag, her intermittent cries went unnoticed.

Where were they taking her? Where was Kara? Even as she had declined into unconsciousness, she'd found comfort in her mother's nearness. Now that was gone.

Fighting panic, she worked her ankles and wrists against her restraints. She found a metal ridge, a part of the trunk's structure, against which to rub the tape, but then the car lurched to the side, thwarting her efforts and tossing her back into the wall. She tucked her head to avoid serious damage and braced herself against the motion.

Lord, help me here. Protect Kara. Don't let it end like this.

Scarcely able to breathe, Josee felt a peace beyond her own understanding wash over her. The helplessness of the situation negated any schemes of escape, and in the trunk's inky space, she surrendered herself to the events of the past few days. She thought of the viper in the woods; of Sergeant Turney's fang marks and his warm Hershey's kiss eyes; of Scooter's fleeing the slithering sorceress and later coming to the park to try to warn her away from Trudi. How had he known to find her there? She thought also of the nurse—the angel?—in Room 223. She remembered the Van der Bruegges' kindness; the flexing muscles in Marsh's back and his pine-and-cloves scent as she held on to him during their ride through the mud and trees; the light shining down the stairwell onto Kara's face, and the lilting tenderness of her mother's words: *No matter what happens…you'll always be my baby.*

She could die knowing her mother's warmth and her father's strength.

But I'm not ready! Did Scoot survive? We can't just let this hag carry out her plans, whatever they are. Where's Sarge?

—

Sergeant Turney wiggled his toes. Okay, he still had some movement.

He maneuvered so he could see over the Tahoe's seats into the park where Stahlherz and Esprit were talking. He'd heard the van arrive and watched Stahlherz head across the grass. Good time to make his exit through the released hatch. He swiped his sleeve over his mouth to remove the last remnants of chocolate and failure, then eased his bulk under the door. His right leg stretched down to the gravel. Left leg.

Thunk. Click.

The hatch bumped him in the head as he completed his exit, then landed on its catch with a metallic sound. As he tried to regain his balance, rocks shifted beneath him.

Focused on the moment, Turney ignored the brief head pain and the gathering moisture around his scars. He was ringside, prepared to jump into the fray

All 238 pounds of me. You still in my corner, God? Or have I ruined everything?

—

"Who are you?" Stahlherz could feel himself shaking. "Where is Marsh?"

"I'm Henri Esprit, the winemaker at Addison Ridge." Although the man looked to be in his late sixties, his wide shoulders and strong face bore a passing resemblance to his employer. "Marsh is far from here, I can assure you. He sent me to deliver this."

"Impossible. He was here, here in town not long ago. I checked."

"Oh, you mean this?" Esprit waved a card.

Stahlherz snatched it. American Express, Marshall R. Addison. He had been monitoring this credit card's activity, and to think that it'd been in the hands of this impostor before him. Disbelief hammered against his temples. Bile filled his throat. The dagger was a talon in his grip, poised to inflict damage. The creature had control.

Esprit said, "I've been enjoying the privileges of that account, Mr. Stahlherz—"

"*Herr Stahlherz!* It's German, you idiot. *Ich heisse Karl Stahlherz.*"

"I'm quite fluent in many languages, Herr Stahlherz. From the beginning, Marsh suspected that you would monitor his moves. A diversionary tactic, that's all this was. From your reaction, I gather that little card did the trick."

"But he *has* to be here. Marsh has disregarded our agreement. With a single call, I could have Kara killed. I would take pleasure in ripping away all he holds dear!"

Esprit lifted an object wrapped in oilcloth. "Here, isn't this what you're after?"

"Unwrap it. Show it to me." Stahlherz tightened his grip on the blade.

39

Beyond Hope

Marsh plowed through the trees and dune grass, back toward his car at the convenience store. He huffed into his phone. "I found the note. I called this number. Now what?"

"Tell me, sir, would you enjoy a stroll along the beach at Devil's Elbow?"

"Devil's Elbow?" He shuddered. Trudi's voice sounded so familiar, yet so foreign. "I can be there shortly. Will you have Kara with you?"

"Will you have the journal? Do you have the key and the information I need?"

"You know that I do. It's how I put the pieces together. You're Trudi Ubelhaar."

"Marsh, did I ever tell you how much your voice sounds like your father's?" She sighed into the phone. "Chance loved me, you know. Simply wasn't strong enough to turn against his dear wife. Men are weak, mere pawns in the hand of a determined woman. So, in answer to your question, yes, come along, provide that which I need, and I'll allow you and your precious bride to reunite along the shores of the Pacific."

The edge of the board. The eight row. Almost there.

Forgoing emotion, Marsh found strength in the chess metaphor.

"What about Josee?" he said. "Is she with you too?"

"Thanks to you."

He ignored the gibe. "You never intended to show up for my meeting with Stahlherz, did you? What did you plan to do with my wife?"

"Oh, I was going to send her, true to the agreement Stahlherz brokered with you, while I waited here, covering our bases dependent on the bank's location. Stahli's become a liability though. Dead weight. To obtain victory, I've had to change plans."

"It's not over yet." Marsh emerged from between buildings, saw his car up the road.

"You?" She scoffed. "You're no threat. I've anticipated your every move. I knew you'd skip the rendezvous and head for the beach house. Your little trick alerted me. May have fooled Stahli, but I know of your plans to fly to Paris this weekend, so naturally I wondered why you and Kara would collaborate in a lie about getting away together. An attempt to gather information, was that it? I see it worked."

"Once a chess player, always a chess player."

"Who'd you send in your stead? Esprit? He's similar in build."

"Why reveal my tactics if you won't reveal yours?"

"Aha. Clever, Marsh. You've inherited some of your father's intellect."

"And you've been a positive addition at the manor—efficient, resourceful." Marsh softened his tone. "Rosie…Trudi, I know of your history, the mistreatment you suffered. I can't even imagine. There's no excuse. Your anger's understandable, but you can still turn back. You're not locked into this course of action."

"Let's not wax sentimental at this point, please. Are you en route?"

He reached the Metro, opened the door. "Yes, Trudi, I'm coming."

"No dallying, you understand, or your wife will go on a stroll from which I fear she'll never return. Really, Marsh, is that what you desire? Devil's Elbow. For old times' sake, be there below the lighthouse. Call me once you're in position."

—

"No more tricks," Stahlherz said. "Show the journal to me."

"First," Esprit said, "bring Kara out. Her welfare is our primary concern."

Stahlherz silently ridiculed this man's naiveté. With the ICV recruits surrounding the park, Stahlherz knew he could take ownership of the journal at will. However, in a show of sportsmanship, he placed the call. "Move the queen forward three spaces," he said, using the code words. "We're ready to exchange the pieces."

Within ninety seconds the Professor's Studebaker rounded the corner and pulled into the gravel lot. Two figures stepped from the car, cautious. There was no sign of the Professor. Had he misunderstood her? Wasn't she to be present?

Stahlherz led the way to the vehicle and barked at his acolytes, "Let's get moving."

"The items you requested, Mr. Steele." The driver handed over a packet.

Steele Knight tore at the padded envelope, leafed through the documents, let the scent of ink and paper arouse his desire for recognition. As requested, the Professor had provided his proof of identity. She had watched over him, shaped him, forged him with undying attentiveness. He paraded a booklet and a sheet of paper for all to see. "This," he proclaimed to his ring of listeners, "is my ticket to notoriety—my name, my identity, all the corroborating evidence to state unequivocally that I am who I claim to be. I am Herr Karl Stahlherz. Soon the world will know of me."

"Kara Addison?" Esprit said. "Show her to me. I want to know she's safe."

"Open this up." Stahlherz knocked on the trunk. "Let's see how she is faring."

The ICV driver inserted the key and opened the trunk for inspection.

"No*ooo!*"

———

The sounds Sergeant Turney had generated were covered by the approach of a vintage automobile. He removed the gun from his shoulder holster and edged along the Tahoe. Based upon his earlier phone conversation, he assumed his detective wouldn't be far behind the Studebaker. Even now the man could be watching.

With gun in hand, Turney made a visual check of his surroundings—the parking area, the tall grass and brush, the aviary. In the hospital cafeteria, Marsh had told him how he'd enlisted the help of his Trysting Tree golfing buddies, many of whom, he confided, also made a habit of practicing at the shooting range on Saturdays. They knew how to watch after their own. Armed and concealed, they had positioned themselves to take on any ICV subversives who showed up here at the scene.

In the trickery of the fading sunlight, Turney welcomed their presence. Keeping low, he inched forward to lock in his angle of attack.

Karl Stahlherz was staring into the Studebaker's trunk. "No*ooo!*"

The burst of vehemence sent the ICV recruits back to their seats in the car. They looked nervous. Ready to run.

—

Empty? The trunk is empty!

Stahlherz felt his nostrils flare. He harnessed his fury and punched in the Professor's number on the cell phone. "Where are you? Where is the queen? She's not in the trunk."

"My son, do you have the journal?"

Stahlherz was dazed. He rocked on his feet. This wasn't what they'd outlined.

"Demand that Esprit show it to you, Stahli."

"I... How do you know Esprit's here? You *are* close, aren't you?" Now his suspicions seemed juvenile; he should never have questioned her.

His mother emitted a high laugh. "Marshall fooled you, didn't he? After years of playing him over the board, you still allow him to subvert your authority. Stahli, when I first began nurturing your bitterness in childhood, I never realized how deeply it would root. You've let it corrode you, let it distort the truth before you. By attempting to control it, you've turned it into something perfidious."

Steele Knight, short of breath, swallowed against the beak in his throat.

"Marsh is headed to Europe this weekend for an international wine festival," the Professor elucidated. "He's had it planned for quite some time. I might've suspected he'd use it to his advantage. He manipulated you to help determine Kara's location. Even at this minute, he's coming my way."

"Where are you?"

"With Kara. With Josee. When you called earlier and I realized Marsh's scam, I decided it'd be best to keep them nearby."

"You deceived me, Mother?"

"Only as a part of the overall design. Did you get the documents I sent?"

Stahlherz looked at the identification papers in his hand, stuffed them into the pocket of his jacket. "So this is it? I'm no more than a pawn in your schemes?"

"*Our* schemes, Son. The goal must be kept in sight. Now, with your identity officially established, you can shoulder the legal repercussions for ICV's actions. Time to be a man, to take the blame. After tonight's deadly results, after thousands have partaken of the tainted waters, I'll simply disappear, a free woman at last."

"You're leaving? Abandoning me? I thought tonight was your new beginning."

"Oh, but I'm getting old. Time to enjoy the fruits of my labor."

"And I'm left to face the consequences. This was never part of our agreement."

"Stahli, Stahli, never underestimate the power of a pawn." And she hung up.

She disconnected! She's manipulated me to play the fool!

He called back. No answer. The subterfuge seemed clear. He'd been told all along that he was a master of the game, but he was nothing but a plaything. He'd been given identity so as to make his mark, only to uncover this deception, which tore all other concerns away. In a flash, his years of work and solitude had become scraps of meat in the claws of the rook. He'd been sliced and fed to the Professor's monstrous designs. She'd used him from the start.

The Professor…Trudi Ubelhaar…Mother.

In Cauda Venenum: "Beware of what you cannot see."

A zephyr of anger billowed his black jacket about him and lifted his arms—his wings—in a gesture of aggression. He whipped his dagger to Esprit's throat. "Very slowly," he commanded, "let me see the journal."

The man unwrapped the book with painstaking care, as though to honor and protect the contents. The oilcloth folds fell open over his hands, and he turned the tan, faded volume for Steele Knight's approval. "Marsh thought you might find this handy, even wrote an inscription. See here…"

Stahlherz watched Esprit open the cover for his viewing.

Steele Knight,

I hope this book brings you all the success and knowledge you seek.
Without it, I fear your game is beyond hope.
Better luck next time…

Crash-Chess-Dummy

A flicker of hope quelled Stahlherz's anxiety. Perhaps this was authentic. By some means, he might yet race his mother to the venom vials and stand victorious.

With his free hand, he turned to a dog-eared page. What would Chance Addison's handwriting look like? This man who had risked his life to save a fellow soldier, then, on the other hand, discarded one so helpless. Left him to die. What would Chance have to say for himself? Would there be apologies, regrets? For Stahlherz, this journal carried personal significance far beyond its value to ICV.

But the words were not handwritten. Fresh black ink underlined faded type.

By threatening to promote to a queen, an isolated passed pawn can dominate an otherwise clinical ending. If the opponent ignores the march of a passed pawn, he sets his own head upon the executioner's block.

"What's this?"

"A warning," Esprit stated. "To you from Marsh."

"This is a chess book!"

"Appears to be," Esprit agreed, motionless at the dagger's tip. "*Modern Chess Tactics,* sixth edition, 1939. Purchased today at a used-book store downtown. Is it true? Have you ignored Marsh's march into the light?"

Stahlherz lifted his gaze, dropped his weapon to his side. In his chest, the warning burned. Where *was* Marsh Addison, the passed pawn? Victory was fading, and Stahlherz saw all else as meaningless. Pointless. Emptiness deeper than he'd ever known.

Closing the book, Esprit took a step back. "The game nears its conclusion, and you find that you've been taken advantage of all along. You can still choose the right path."

"The right path? Ha! And you think I've taken the wrong way?"

"There is a path before each person that seems right, but it ends in death."

Acid churned to the surface, a maelstrom of wrath. His bones ached. Although this winemaker's words carried hints of reprieve, Stahlherz saw no room for turning back. He'd come too far. Worked too hard. Invested his soul and identity in a lie.

Why? Oh my...but to die!

—

The setting sun chopped tree shadows into strips of deep mauve, stacking them across Marsh Addison's path. He'd parked the rental car at the top of the road leading into Devil's Elbow State Park. Now, on foot, he reconnoitered the stretch of sand that was embraced by knobby-fingered cliffs. The wind tasted of brine and seaweed. From here, at the tree line, he viewed a woman's silhouette.

Kara? Without a doubt.

A lump formed in his throat. He could see the soft curve of her back, the roll of her shoulders, the manner in which she rested her weight on one leg, favoring it over her scarred hip. She took a few steps, sat down on a section of driftwood.

This was his queen. Where, though, were his enemies? And Trudi Ubelhaar?

Marsh controlled the urge to call out to Kara, to run to her. He stood studious and calm, surveying the environs for any hidden threat. The mauve shadows made investigation of the woods difficult. Across the waves, the sun was a sliver of gold.

He hit the Redial button.

—

From this angle at Stahlherz's back, Turney could see that the man had dropped his dagger to his side, but his stance remained aggressive. Beyond him, Esprit's eyes had the calm of a dove. For an older gentleman, he handled himself well. Around the park's perimeter, Marsh's accomplices would have to cover while Turney made a dash past the recruits in the Studebaker and intervened on Esprit's behalf.

An inhuman scream ripped over the gravel lot.

Esprit stumbled back as Stahlherz's dagger made an arcing swoop. The winemaker collided into the marble marker before collapsing in a bed of flowers.

"*Skerr-reeechh!*" Stahlherz had gone berserk.

Should've moved quicker, Turney chastised himself. *Curse this lard belly!*

"Aah!" Pistoning his legs, he left the Tahoe's side. As the black-coated foe lifted his dagger a second time, Turney became a battering ram that slammed him against the monument in a rush of pebbles, sweat, and gross tonnage.

—

Rough hands half dragged, half lifted Josee from the trunk. She found herself propped on cramped and tingling legs and winced as the constraints were torn from her ankles. Her arms remained taped. Still gagged, she stumbled forward, feet slipping on sand-dusted asphalt. In her left sock, she could feel the bank key against her heel. She angled her head back and saw two cars. Beyond them, stepping through the sand, a pair of figures held Kara between them.

Kara…Mom.

A brief look passed between daughter and mother, then they were torn apart.

"Press onward," Trudi said. With a walking stick, she prodded Josee along a path between trees and brush. Up ahead, bathed in the sun's last rays, the Queen Anne–style lightkeeper's house shone on a cliff. In the darker section of sky, the moon was already present. "Soon enough, Josee, Marsh will arrive. I hope you'll forgive our searching through your knapsack, but I'm pleased to see that you brought along your birth certificate. Isn't it nice to know you're part of a family?"

Josee marched on, sucking breaths through the gag. One step at a time.

Trudi touched her arm. "Have they told you of your portion in the inheritance?"

Inheritance? Josee's eyes flickered in the old woman's direction.

"Yes, dear, your grandfather left you the contents of his safe-deposit box.

Of course, that's nothing new to you—if you've seen the journal—but it's no wonder that Kara and Marsh abandoned you at birth. They haven't mentioned the fortune to you, I surmise. Of course, why would they?"

The accusations fought for a hold in Josee's mind. Was this true?

Trudi caressed her honey-tinted hair. Her face was a mask of powdered wrinkles. "Is it any wonder that Kara's allowed you back into her life? You're the key. That's all you are to her. To be used and tossed away. Quite simply, she sees you as the means of expropriating her fortune."

The cloth was cutting into Josee's lips. Duct tape held her hands.

Trudi was toting a wicker picnic basket. She described the family meal they would share together—soup and bread and vintage wine. She pulled an item from within. "Do you recognize this?" She was holding a metal canister.

Josee's eyes widened. She choked against the cloth in her mouth.

━━

Stahlherz was stunned. Esprit had shielded himself with the thick chess book so that the dagger plunged deep into the heart of the pages. Nevertheless, the force had rocked him back into the marble, where he stumbled into a backdrop of flowers.

Infuriated, Steele Knight arched his arm for another blow.

Behind him, gravel crunched, and a pile driver rammed him into the monument. The dagger struck the bronze description plate. The blade snapped. Caromed back into his own shoulder. Sprayed blood.

A talon… *You filthy beast, you've turned on me!*

Stahlherz landed facedown, shook off heavy hands from his back, and twisted to confront his attacker. Dressed in a camouflage jacket, the man was bulky. He was balanced on one knee. Aiming a gun. Across the grass Stahlherz saw a grappling trio of men and realized his recruits were also under siege, unable to come to his aid. An unmarked car skidded into the lot, and a detective hopped out with his weapon trained on the front seat of the Studebaker.

In the aviary, the squawking of birds reflected the afternoon's burst of activity.

Warm blood. Spilling around the dagger's tip in Stahlherz's shoulder.

"Give yourself up," said the man facing him. "I'm Sergeant Turney, Corvallis Police Department. We'll getcha some help. Looks like you cut yourself deep."

Surrender? No, it's all or nothing!

Stahlherz gripped the blade. With blood spurting from the wound and his hand, he plucked it out and raised it in defense. The pain was nothing; the game was everything. A "spite check," they called it in chess. His chance to spread the agony.

"Set that down." The sergeant's gun was unmoving. "Put 'em up nice and slow."

Stahlherz wagged the blade at an oozing spot on the sergeant's jacket. "What happened there? One of my recruits get to you? Or did the beast catch you, too?"

"The beast?"

"Ha! See, I'm not the only susceptible one."

"These scars? They're my way of knowin' when trouble's around. A reminder."

"Double the trouble." Stahlherz chuckled.

"I've been sittin' on the sidelines long enough," Turney said.

The sidelines... *The horseman was sliding from the side toward the center. From the muck into the fray... Out of shape as he might be, he seemed determined to do his part.* "You're the one," said Stahlherz, shifting to a perched position. "You!"

"Stay still!"

"But you're the knight, the one on my board. The kid who got in the way years back. This is the cruelest of all jokes. You!"

With his laughter as a cover for his coiling body, Stahlherz planted both feet beneath him. He launched forward, jabbing the bloodied dagger tip at the center of the sergeant's arm wounds. The hefty man swiveled away so that the blade caught but a sliver of skin as it tore through his sleeve.

The gun in Turney's hand roared. Amid the acrid scent of detonation, a bullet grazed Stahlherz's ribs. He growled in torment but used his momentum to spin around and lock one arm around Sergeant Turney's wide belly, the other around his throat. He pressed the wet and jagged blade to the man's corpulent neck.

"Drop the gun, or this knife becomes forever one with your vocal cords."

Turney's sidearm clattered onto the path.

"Now let's get to our feet. Easy now."

Stahlherz dragged the big man to an upright position. He saw the detective in the parking lot with weapon drawn. In the flower bed, Esprit had rolled into a kneeling position, a priest pleading mercy over his parish.

"That's it, Sarge. Stay in front of me."

"You're just askin' for trouble," Turney told him. "Best to surrender now."

"On the contrary. You're going to make certain I leave this place alive. I don't know who these other guys are, but I have one move yet to make. If it's the last thing I do, I'll find Marsh and Trudi—to remind them of all they have taken from me."

"You're wounded. You need medical attention."

"Oh no, I'm far beyond that now. Don't you understand? No more turning back. Walk slowly." He let the broken and bloodied talon hover at Turney's throat. "Tell your friends to let us by, or you'll be tasting metal, even through your double chin."

40

Blades and Birds

Trudi cradled the canister just as Scoot had done in the thicket. She lofted it so that the moon gleamed in its dull surface, a twinkle in the eyes of the skull and crossbones. One finger played over the metal surface, and as though summoned by the warmth, a thin vapor began to twine from the canister's seam. Trudi moved behind Josee and tugged at the gag. "Josee, you have an assignment to fulfill. I'll remove this nuisance if you are willing to behave yourself as a young lady. No spitting, agreed?"

Josee nodded her head. Whatever it took to breathe freely.

The gag came off, and Trudi said, "Now, my dear, we come to the point of this entire exercise. You've been an important part in a little game stretching back to the end of the Second World War. Your grandfather and I were quite the item, but he saw fit to disentangle himself from me in favor of his homegrown bride. Surely you can empathize. You, too, have been abandoned by one close to you."

"What're you talking about?"

Trudi set down the basket. "Why, Scooter, of course."

Josee wished her hands were free. She'd gladly deliver a blow to this old witch. "Is he here? Is he okay?"

"Don't you know? Your friend's still in the hospital after that nasty collision with the motorcycle, driven by one of my recruits, I'm proud to say. Scooter slipped into a coma, according to the last report."

Josee wanted to challenge the statement, but Trudi's hands had moved to her neck, encircling her throat, twisting the myrtlewood necklace the nurse had given her. Josee drove her head back against the woman's collarbone.

Get off me! Stay away!

"You think you can resist me?" Trudi hissed. "Like Scooter has tried to do? He betrayed you. How do you think he knew you would be at the park today? Minutes before you and I talked on the phone this morning, Scooter called to reveal your location at the Van der Bruegges'. For three days he's been my pliable servant. Kept tabs on you."

"Your words mean squat to me."

Trudi gloated. "He's been one of mine longer than you think."

"But he tried to warn me. I heard him there at Avery Park."

Trudi jeered. "A final act to appease his guilt. No, he's been dabbling in ICV for over a year, starting with a small cell at the University of Washington. He allowed the venom to take hold in the thicket, gave full access to the serpents in his hospital room. No wonder he recovered so quickly. Even that nurse couldn't make the choice for him. Give this baby an inch"—she tapped the canister—"and it'll take a mile. Scooter was a virtual breeding ground for these babies. You've been a bit more difficult, I daresay."

"I've had a little help."

"Help?"

"I'm not alone." Josee thought of her childhood seed of faith—withered and small but growing. "You're wasting your time."

"I'm not one to quit so easily. You've still a role to play, a bishop cutting across the board to empty a safe-deposit box. You may have avoided Scooter's chums, may have dodged the efforts of my coiled friends, but you will not— you *will* not!—leave me empty handed. Not if you have any desire to see your mother and father again. Though I must point out, there's still some question as to your parentage."

"Kara already explained to me what happened—"

"Did she now?"

"So I don't need you to try messing with my head, you got that?"

"You're ready to cooperate then?"

"What're you gonna do to Marsh and Kara?"

"Nothing. Yet. Their fates rest entirely upon you."

Trudi's cell phone chimed. She answered in a husky voice. "Hello, Marsh. Do you see your bride? As you may've noticed, yes, she's a bit weakened by hunger and inactivity, in need of a bath, but healthy nonetheless. For the time being. Are you ready to make the exchange?"

The big man coughed. "It's okay, boys. Back off. Just let us on through."

"Sarge, we can—"

"Just let us pass through."

"And," Stahlherz instructed, "tell them to remove the keys from their car and from the Studebaker, then throw them out into that tall grass over the fence." He knew they could be tailed with a call from the detective's radio, but all he needed was to buy a few minutes. *By then, this bird will've flown the coop.*

Turney parroted the order to the detective. The blade's pressure encouraged compliance, despite the detective's look of disgust. Keys disappeared into thick grass.

"God, I've let them down," the sergeant muttered. "I can't do this on my own."

"Too late for prayers, my friend. Get moving, and don't pretend to be a hero."

"Couldn't be one if I tried." The defeat was evident in Sergeant Turney's voice.

"Yeah, I see her," Marsh said into the phone. From the edge of the trees, he scanned the beach for a clue to Trudi's position. "But where are you?"

"That's inconsequential."

"What do you want me to do?"

"I want you to deliver the journal to me. For years I've looked high and low. Black Butte, the manor, the beach house, Depoe Bay. Where was it, if I may ask?"

"That's inconsequential."

"Touché."

"So where do we go from here? Let's get this over with."

"First, you provide me the journal with the key and the bank information. If you go to your dear wife beforehand, you'll be shot by those hiding in the woods."

"What about Josee?" Marsh stood motionless, eyes searching the trees.

"She has a bank errand to run."

"I want you to release her as well."

"You know I can't do that. Without her, the bank manager will never provide access to the safe-deposit box. It's just about five, Marsh, only an hour left. We don't have time to make a court case of this. What do you propose?"

"Here's the deal. Josee takes the key and goes with one of your cohorts to fetch the contents of the box. It's not far from here, I'll let you know that much. Kara and I'll join you. Once Josee reaches the bank, she calls, I provide the correct box numbers, then we all wait for her to return."

"And risk having Josee slip through my fingers? That's unacceptable."

"Your men will be guarding her. She won't try anything funny. Besides, the whole purpose of her trip has been to connect with Kara. She won't leave her mother behind, not if you hold Kara and me as collateral."

"You'd willingly place yourselves in my care?"

"Until Josee returns, yes. Then, once you've obtained the box's contents, you'll have no further reason to keep us, and we can go our separate ways."

More likely that you'll kill us, but what're my options? We'll take it as it comes.

The line was silent while Trudi considered his proposal. He heard voices in the background. When Trudi spoke again, her voice was full of irritation. "Where's the journal? My men have searched every inch of your car. No sign of it."

"They broke into my rental?"

"We haven't time to dillydally, as you well know."

"The bank info's safe in my head. It's not going anywhere."

"Marsh! This was not the plan. What about the key? Did you swallow it? Must we wait for it to pass through your digestive system?"

"Josee has it. I gave it to her earlier. Go ahead. You can send her now so she doesn't get to the bank after they've locked the doors. It's the best idea. We all maintain some control, and we all hold on to something the others need. What options do you have, Trudi? Without Josee's key and my knowledge, you're up a creek."

"I could've inflicted damage long ago!"

"Yeah, but you want to do it the right way—with your father's poison, the Nazi venom. Isn't this what you've plotted for, been destined for? Why settle for less?"

"Okay," Trudi surrendered. "I'm sending Josee off now. She has her birth certificate. Yes, she says she has the key, and we need you to tell us where to go."

"Bank of the Dunes," he said, "in Florence. Should be there within a half-hour."

"Marsh, if you fail to provide the correct box number, my men will kill Josee. You had better toe the line. Enjoy your brief solitude with Kara. You are being watched, so don't try to escape. Others'll be down shortly to escort you back up to my position."

"Your position. Where?"

"Up here, on the cliffs by the keeper's house. We'll gather for a candlelight family picnic with a special vintage to soothe our palates. From your father's original harvest—Vintner's Reserve, Addison Ridge Vineyards, 1951."

Marsh stepped from the shelter of the trees and saw etched against the darkening sky the elderly woman's distant wave from a jutting promontory. From there, he realized, the canister had gone over the edge years ago. On the crags beyond her, Heceta Head Lighthouse stood as wary sentinel, beams feathering through the sky.

He turned toward his queen's form on the beach. *Chess. Pawn promotion.*

Kara's tears were hot streaks down her face. Her hands and feet were free. Her swollen lip, her bruised cheek, her stained and smelly jeans. She had accepted the fact that she could die there in the cellar, but then she'd seen her daughter. And now here she sat on a strip of driftwood in the salty breath of the Pacific Ocean. Before her, the waves were white-lipped mouths, champing at the sand and the cliffs.

She loved it here. Was it true Marsh'd be joining her? Was this a trap?

She wanted to warn him away. She wanted to hold on to him.

To think that he had been suspected in her disappearance. To think that his father had betrayed them, fashioning them as pieces in a game. What'd been going through Marsh's mind all this time? He had held Chauncey Addison on a pedestal.

A game of Chance? God, help us bring this evil game to an end.

From perilous cliffs, the lighthouse scanned the sea and sky.

⌣

The key was cold in Josee's hand. Seated in a red Buick that had waited near the keeper's house, she weighed her instructions. Pretty basic: If you wish to see your mother and father alive, go to the Bank of the Dunes, sign in at the register, enter the vault to open the safe-deposit box—number to be provided soon—and carefully transfer the entire contents into the carpetbag.

An inheritance. *Could that part be true?*

Josee hated the doubts that now nested in her thoughts. At the very moment she'd begun opening up to her parents, Trudi had contaminated her with accusations. The proof was in the deposit box. Regardless of its contents, she would return to the keeper's house to be with Kara and Marsh. Newfound connections. She couldn't toss those away based on the words of some bitter old Nazi chick.

"Almost there," the driver said. "You're not going to give us any trouble, I hope."

They descended a long hill, crossed a bridge. She shook her head. "Nope."

One of the guys leaned forward from the backseat. "Good answer, cutie."

⌣

Forced at knifepoint to crawl across the center console into the driver's seat, Turney tore the Tahoe through the gravel and speared back toward town. On duty, he gave tickets for this sort of driving, but these circumstances were a bit different. And this fellow riding shotgun... Stahlherz was intense, quiet, his dagger tip poised at Turney's neck, his eyes roving the mirrors and the road for trouble, his shirt globbed with blood.

By his watch, Turney saw it was 4:57. They'd never make it to the coast in time.

"Turn here," the wounded man said.

"Here? I thought you—"

"Here!"

Turney slowed. They were at Elks Drive. He made a right, then followed the fork up to Good Samaritan Regional Medical Center. Even as he rounded the hillside, he spotted the rescue helicopter on the pad and knew what Stahlherz had in mind.

He pressed on the gas. Maybe he could outrun or outdistance this crazy plan.

"Slow it down." Stahlherz dug the blade deeper. "Time to take flight with your badge as our ticket. Over there." He directed them to the helipad, where a pilot circled the white-and-red machine, alternately sipping on a Mountain Dew and making marks on a clipboard.

Turney said, "Without proper clearance, he'll refuse to lift off. Against policy."

"And sleep each night with your death on his conscience?" Stahlherz's snort sprayed blood droplets from his nose onto the dash. "Believe me, he'll do as I say."

~

With his blade hand at the sergeant's throat, Steele Knight leaned into the big man and did little to fake his own infirmities as they crossed the grass to the helipad. The loss of blood was numbing his body. His bones felt brittle and cold. He snarled into Turney's ear, demanding action.

"Hey, there," Turney called out. "You the one flyin' this bird?"

The pilot looked over his clipboard.

"Got an injured man here. Help me get him on board."

"I've received no such instructions. Got no flight plan."

"Pilot"—Turney whipped his badge into view—"this is an emergency."

Training overrode the pilot's initial suspicion, and he strode forward to assist. He could not ignore a police sergeant and a bleeding man. As he reached out an arm, he noted the dagger tip in Stahlherz's hand. "Hey, what's going on? Listen, I'm not—"

"You are. You're taking us on a quick ride."

The man slapped his clipboard against his leg. "No, I'm not! This is my bird, I'm responsible for it, and it's not going anywhere."

"Then you'll live with this police officer's life on your hands." Stahlherz allowed the evening's bitterness—*kreeackk!*—to creep along his arm, to direct the dagger's edge. The curved talon pierced his hostage's skin, producing a red trickle.

Turney gurgled in pain.

"You ready to watch?" Stahlherz asked the pilot. "Or ready to fly?"

The pilot cursed, threw his clipboard down on the floor of the chopper, and climbed into his seat. He pulled on a headset and flicked a switch to ignite the motors. The limp rotors jerked to life, then began a lazy spin that accelerated as the engine's whine grew louder.

Stahlherz swallowed his own blood. Watched his captive do the same.

"Get on board," he told Turney. "Move it!"

The pilot was speaking into his mouthpiece. As Stahlherz boarded, he snagged the set from the man's head and demanded radio silence. He flung the object to the grass below and told the sergeant to close the door. He settled into his seat and, to air his wounds, peeled off his black jacket and shoved it beneath the seat. In the cockpit's cocoon, he imagined the Professor's surprise when he arrived at the coast.

This is one pawn that won't go down so easily. Kaw-haahaa!

From the front, the pilot's invective was relentless, audible over the rotors. He tried to warn Stahlherz of the legal consequences of his actions. He insisted the fuel levels were too low to accommodate an excursion over the coastal mountain range to Heceta Head Lighthouse. He spouted off about his ex-wife and the way she'd robbed him blind in court and how he wasn't going to be taken advantage of again, especially by some old guy with a broken knife and Shredded Wheat for brains.

Stahlherz said simply, "You're no different than me."

"How so?" The pilot glanced over his shoulder.

"We're both driven by anger and bitter disappointment. We're both—"

"Don't feed me a line! Whaddya know? You're no better than the next guy."

"And we're both driven by our respective birds." At that, Stahlherz cackled. Feather tips, bristling through his head, tickled his thoughts and stirred his acrimonious swill of emotion. "If we let them, oh yes, they'll swallow us whole."

"Huh?"

"The descent to hell is easy, my friend. Facilis descensus Averno."

"Bite me, pal!"

Strapped into the seat behind Turney, Stahlherz absorbed the pilot's hatred, pressed it to his heart as part of his acidic poultice. He'd been betrayed by Chance—*abandoned at birth!* By Marsh and Esprit—*card trick, ha!* By the Professor—*an empty trunk!*

At this point, death and darkness sounded inviting.

41

Knee-Deep

Marsh strode the hundred yards to Kara's thin form. With the Glock tucked into his belt beneath his jacket, he surveyed the broad beach and saw no sign of others. Although he distrusted Trudi Ubelhaar, he was certain she would withhold drastic action until Josee had acquired the items from the deposit box.

That gave him time to think. To speak with his wife.

"Kara." He moved closer. "Kara, is that you?"

She was standing now on the driftwood log, facing the waves. She was a queen at the board's edge, waiting to be returned to the game. She turned. "Marshall?"

"Took me awhile, but I figured out your clue," he said. "I went to the beach house, but it was too late. Saw where they'd kept you in the cellar. Are you okay, hon?" He drew alongside her. He put his hands on her arms. "I swear, if they did anything to hurt you…"

She nuzzled against him. A sob erupted from deep in her chest.

"Shhh." He drew Kara down from the driftwood and into his grasp. They stood as one, arms around each other, listening to the pulsing life of the sea. The waves, lured by the rising moon, drew closer until water lapped at their feet.

Marsh said, "We're gonna settle this for good. Tonight."

"They left me here to wait for you. What're they planning to do to us?"

"In a little bit we're supposed to meet up by the keeper's house." He glanced at the cliffs, considered whisking Kara far away from here. But that would leave Josee on her own. There was, of course, the possibility that Chief Braddock had contacted the local authorities, that perhaps there would be officers at the bank to detain any suspicious latecomers. Marsh, however, refused to risk the alternative.

"Kara, how many others did Trudi bring along?"

"Trudi? So it's all true, what Josee said about the journal. Trudi Ubelhaar."

"She had us all fooled. She also has a team of people around her. She's the leader of that anarchist group, ICV. I've seen them in the news a couple of times. So did you count any others?"

"Two, three, maybe more. I don't know. I was taken to a car, tied up in the trunk, and brought here. I've thought a lot about you, darling. I...missed you."

He paused to look at her. He moved her back so he could take her in. The wind flipped golden strands of hair into her eyes. A bruise had turned pale green on her cheek, but her skin was soft and luminescent in the growing moonlight. On her lip, a crust of blood bespoke violence. What had she been through? What agony? And to think of all the emotions he had subjected her to over the years...

With one hand slipped along her neck, he bent to kiss her torn lip.

"I'm sorry, Kara. I've been...I've been trying to find you."

"You found Josee."

"I did."

"She told me about it. Isn't she beautiful, Marsh?" Kara's eyes were moist. "The past few days have been horrible, but seeing her has been worth it all. My baby. I was so afraid that I'd see contempt in her eyes, or judgment, but there was none of that. She looked at me as though...as though I was the most incredible thing she'd ever seen. Called me Mom."

"I left her with Trudi. I didn't know."

"Josee knows it was a mistake. All along I kept holding on to the hope that you'd come. When that creepy older guy—Stahlherz, is that his name?—when he told me that you wanted the answer to where we were going for the weekend, the only thing that made any sense was that you were fishing for information."

"I hoped you would figure it out."

"Darling, I know how you think. Twenty-two years. We've been together too long for me not to have learned a thing or two about your thought processes."

He looked into her caramel eyes. "Kara, I've tried so hard to see what's going on, but in many ways I've been blind. Spent the past two days trying to find you."

"That's all I've ever asked."

"There're things I'd like to change, things in me, things with us. I'm forty-four years old, pretty set in my ways, and I'm not sure I can do it. Or undo it. Don't know if you'll let me."

"I won't stand in your way."

"Intentionally, no. But—"

"You'll just have to convince me, I guess."

As she turned to face him, he thought of their last confrontation near the manor's front pillars. After the horror she'd been through for the last seventy-two hours, it didn't surprise him to find skittish fear in her eyes. There were deeper feelings, too: love that had been lost and found, contentment, and joy.

He reached out and took her hand. "It meant a lot to you, didn't it?"

Kara needed no clarification. "Yes, she's so…so grown up. Josee's a woman." She closed her eyes, turned her palm out to hold off the rush of emotion. "I was so scared for her, for all of us, but you don't know how amazing it was to sit there in the dark and listen to her, to feel her near me."

"What else did they do to you? Other than your lip and the bruise?"

She shook her head.

"Because whatever happened, hon, we'll work it through. I'm right here."

"Mostly," she said, "I'm just hungry and thirsty and in dire need of a bath."

Marsh stared out over the waves that curled, crested, and flattened, then receded in a timeless cycle. He pulled her forward. In an act that seemed so appropriate, yet so ludicrous, he asked Kara to join him in removing their shoes. Then—not without a sideways glance from Kara—he tossed both sets of shoes and socks up onto dry sand and led her toward the next wave. They were ankle-deep in the October surf. She squealed at the freezing waters and gave him a look that said he had surely lost it.

And maybe he had. What did it matter? He knew Trudi was up there on the cliffs, probably following his movements and deriding his intelligence.

File this one under you-only-live-once.

They stepped over the next roller and landed knee-deep. With the stress of the past three days, he let out a yell. It felt good. He opened his mouth wide, found his tongue wet with salty foam. He spit it out. Laughed aloud. Kara joined in.

"Marsh, what's come over you?"

"Good question," he called out.

"This is cold. Insane. You sure you're all right?"

"Isn't it great?"

He had noted her embarrassment regarding her soiled clothes; now he saw her give in to the washing of the sea. Hand in hand, they jumped and shivered and giggled at the absurdity of the moment. How was it, Marsh wondered, that the craziest actions sometimes seemed to make the most sense of all?

The edge of the waves…the last row…a pawn for a queen.

He knew that historically servants had washed their masters' feet. Knew also that Kara's Bible spoke of the washing of feet as an act of humility and love. The image took on new significance as the water swirled about them. He caught Kara with both arms in a splashing spin.

Knee-high water, freezing and foaming. Cleansing. Pure.

"Kara"—his eyes fixed upon hers—"can we forgive each other and start over again? We've been at this too long to quit now. Let me learn how to love you."

Sea spray mingled with the tears in her eyes. The froth of the waves curled at their knees as they faced one another in an embrace. Numb legs aside, this wasn't so bad, Marsh thought. And then he saw fear flash over his wife's face.

He turned back to face the beach and saw a pawn storm.

Swooping down from the woods, a quartet of youth advanced in long-snouted gas masks and head-mounted lamps. Cycloptic creatures of the dusk, each held a sleek metallic container. Where sea and sand met, they formed a half circle.

The ringleader said through his mask, "I need you to follow us."

From his seat, Turney could see the fuel gauge's decline. The dagger was still pressed to his throat, with Stahlherz holding him from behind.

"Told you, but you wouldn't listen." The pilot muttered choice names for his abductor and fingered the gauge, his gesture crude and emphatic. "Already dipping into the reserve tank and we've just cleared the range. Bet you feel stupid."

Sergeant Turney felt the arm tighten around his neck.

"Just get us there in one piece," Stahlherz said.

"Why're you doing this?" Turney asked. "What've you done with Mrs. Addison?"

"You expect me to confess all now that you have a witness? You're about as asinine as they come, Sarge. You think I'm a blubbering fool, is that it?"

"Forget I asked."

Which was all the invitation Stahlherz needed to proceed. "You realize, of course, that Marsh's wife has been the bait all along. In chess, a player can often harass his opponent's queen until the opponent crumbles to the pressure and loses another piece, a different piece. In this case, Josee is the piece we're after. The key to our plans."

"Kara's still alive?"

"Safe and sound. At present."

"You had Beau kidnap her, then drive her car into the ravine to throw us off the scent. Should've seen it right away. But the blood they found at Marsh's place. How'd ya manage that? Was that your doing? Did you send him the painting too?"

"I was the artist. And I had to buy it myself to see the plan set into motion."

"And the blood?"

"Nothing but a sample taken from dear Mrs. Addison. Beau left it by the guardrail for Trudi to pick up. Later, right behind Marsh's back—ha!—she found an opportunity to apply it to the chair. Dropped his belt and robe sash, as well. But she really had him going when she wiped the blood on his face. She told him she was wiping it off. He thought it was his own blood."

"Pretty slick. Gotta hand it to ya." Turney paused, not wanting to push his luck. "Stahlherz, I figured out your identity at the post office with your signature—"

"I'll give you credit for that."

"But I don't get the connection between Trudi and the Addisons. How'd she get into their place?"

"Not so clever after all, Sarge. You're boring me with these superficial insights—as if sitting in a helicopter with a knife to your neck indicates any great ability on your part. Now, if you'd be so kind, shut up!"

Above the mountain range, the pilot reinitiated his diatribe on domestic ills and, as an afterthought, turned on the cockpit heater so that condensation peeled back from the center of the curved windscreen. Turney, as a bonus, regained some movement in his limbs, but sat stock-still for the majority of the flight. Although his knife wound was superficial, his sense of defeat was debilitating.

Should never have bought that chocolate. I broke my promise to fast.

"In your weakness—"

I know, Lord, I know. But now what? What good've I done?

"You can never triumph by your own righteousness. By my grace alone."

The engine spluttered. A small cough. A hiccup.

Turney clamped a hand over his arm where the fang marks from so long ago continued to remind him of his weakness, of his failure. These wounds, he believed, could be windows into others' struggles. He could either focus on their pain and wallow along in self-pity, or he could see their needs and fight for them.

He gritted his teeth against the stinging slice along his neck. Just one more, he decided. Thunder Turney would wait for his opening, for one final blow.

⌐

Marsh debated pulling his gun. His hand inched around his back. He and Kara could escape and rush to the Bank of the Dunes with the box number in his head. Sure, Josee had gone ahead, but if they could catch her before—

"Get rid of your weapon."

Marsh's hand stopped at his spine, fingertips on the grip of the Glock.

"If you refuse, we'll release our containers' contents." The leader's hand clamped around the cap. "You and your wife are woefully ill-prepared for this. Highly concentrated, it'd kill you both in minutes."

"The wind's blowing inland."

"You can take that risk." The man's hand circled the cap.

"First you'd have to get them all open."

"You think you're so accurate with a gun? Think you can take us all down while standing in the ocean, with the waves, the wind, and your wife right beside you?"

"You're bluffing. You don't even have the vials yet."

"This is one of the Professor's newest concoctions."

"And what about you guys? You think some lousy, outdated masks'll protect you? Shouldn't you be wearing Tyvek suits or something?"

In the masks, the four ICV members wore blank, bug-eyed stares. Their leader voiced their unanimity. "We're prepared to die, if need be. Audentes fortuna juvat."

"Audentes fortuna juvat!" a muffled chorus swelled around him.

Marsh felt Kara press closer, clasp tighter. She said, "No matter what happens, darling, I'm glad you came for me."

"So am I."

From the descriptions in his dad's journal, Marsh knew they could not afford to take this risk. He had no desire to breathe in even a minute particle of poison, new or old. In the journal, with scientific exactitude, his father had detailed the formula for a chemical weapon's aerosol effectiveness: $L(Ct)_{50}$, the lethalness to 50% of the population, based on concentration and time. How long could they hold their breath? Could they dive under the waves and swim away? None of the options seemed viable.

"Your weapon," the leader demanded. When Marsh drew the gun into view and ejected the clip, the long-snouted man was not fooled. "I know you still have a chambered round. Toss the whole thing. Do it!"

With posture erect so as not to reveal his trepidation to Kara, he flung the Glock into the pounding tide. His strategies had been stripped away.

Here we are, God. At your mercy. And I'm all outta bright ideas.

Side by side, bound at the wrists by ample lengths of duct tape, and guided by the group's mounted lamps, Marsh and Kara made the ascent to the top of the cliff.

"Well, well, my distinguished guests…"

From the path between the trees, Marsh and Kara arrived to the beckoning arms of Trudi Ubelhaar. The gas-masked sentries positioned themselves about the candlelit picnic table that had been set not far from the keeper's house. Trudi nodded, then gestured for them to join her for dinner alfresco.

Marsh took a seat, noting the metal canister at the head of the table.

Kara broke in. "These are our dishes, Rosie. Trudi. Whoever you claim to be."

"And I'm serving you dinner," the older woman said. "Is it not the routine you've enjoyed for over three years now? Only I'm no longer relegated to silent subservience. Truly, Kara, you should know the feeling of which I speak. I've observed your relationship, seen you abdicate your personality by playing humble wifey. Well, learn from my example, dear heart, for this time I shall speak my mind."

"I want to know that Josee's okay. Will she be coming back?"

"First, she's fetching a gift for us all."

Gift 12. Marsh caught the play on words. *Poison. Vials of venom.*

———

A half block from the bank, in the lee of a sand dune where spikes of grass waved in the wind, the ICV driver parked and tapped a knuckle against the radio clock: 5:39. "Hope your papa has some numbers for us," he said to Josee, "or you'll be a little orphan girl. Of course, I'd be more than willing to watch after you."

"In your dreams."

The driver shirked her rebuttal and dialed his cell phone. With pen in hand and a notepad on his knee, he waited for a reply. "Professor? We're here, no problems… Still open, yeah… Not many cars in the parking lot. Nothing out of order… I'll stick to her like glue, you betcha… You got the numbers for us?"

Josee, for her parents' safety, fought the impulse to dart from the Buick with the box number he scrawled down. Problem was that her parents were stuck with Trudi. For the time being, she would have to cooperate.

The driver was scowling into the phone. "Are you sure that's what you want—" He stopped short. "As you say, Professor." With a set jaw, he stretched an arm over the backseat, gestured, took possession of the snub-nosed revolver.

"What's that for?" Josee inquired. But the driver did not answer.

———

Trudi answered her chiming phone. After a short dialogue, she shot Marsh a look, and he checked his watch: 5:39 PM. "The box number, Marshall? No time to squander, knowing that Josee's life rests upon your reply."

Marsh touched Kara's tightly taped hands beneath the table. "Number 89."

Trudi repeated the digits into the phone, her fingers tracing the skull and crossbones on the canister before her. She issued a last order: "And once Josee's retrieved the contents, remove her from the board... Yes, do it without delay."

From the wooden bench, Marsh tried to stand. "What do you mean, 'remove her'? What about our agreement?" At his side, through the fence, he caught a glimpse of billowing waves below.

"You're not that naive, sir. You should know that every game exacts its toll."

"You said we'd see her!" Kara shouted, wide eyed. "What'd she ever do to you? Leave my daughter out of this! You can't do this! Whatever grievances you have with Marsh and me, let's sort them out, but for goodness' sake, let Josee go. Please, Trudi."

"You've always been the innocent bystander, Kara. My heart goes out to you."

"Then call them back. Tell them to leave Josee alone!"

Marsh grabbed for the phone with taped hands. Maybe if he hit the Redial button, he could undo this unthinkable wrong. What he really wanted to do was wrap his fingers around Trudi's neck, wringing from her any possibility of further damaging his family, but an assault would be counterproductive now that she'd issued the order.

Trudi swiped the phone from the table and stepped back. Her hair whipped about her face in the breeze. Marsh, caught short by his thighs against the table's edge, stumbled and knocked over a candle. Strong hands grasped him from behind, and masked men planted him back on the wooden slab. Others subdued Kara, and after a valiant struggle, she eased into a rocking motion made all the more troublesome by the droning moan that escaped through her lips.

"Kara."

She continued to rock, showing no reaction to Marsh's voice.

God, please—after all that she's gone through... What's going on?

Trudi was on the phone again. "Yes, you must hurry," she said. "The key is in Florence. Have the couriers rendezvous at the designated point north of town. All twelve of them, yes."

42

The Vault

Trudi Ubelhaar circled the table, offering crusts of bread and bowls of borscht on fine china. "Allow me to serve you a last meal together. Time to 'eat up,' as the guards were so fond of saying to me. Go ahead, Marsh. Try a bite."

"No thanks."

"Eat!"

"Our hands are tied. We can't."

"I won't touch it." Kara ceased her moaning. "You've done something to it."

"You're both mistaken. Dip your heads and eat, *eat!* There's nothing wrong with it. I should know. I survived on this for months in your army's internment camp near Frankfurt. The camp's code name? 'Back porch.' A fitting title, considering that they fed us scraps no better than they would feed vermin at the back door." The old woman circled again, pushing heads into bowls, forcing mouths against stale crusts.

Marsh felt the heat of the candle near his forehead. He meant to resist, but as the woman's hands made contact, he found his neck muscles give. His nose dipped into the hot liquid. He came up, shook off the pain, found himself slurping at tasteless gruel. Alongside, Kara sucked up the borscht. He heard a whimper in her throat.

"Now, please," their host said, "have a sip of the wine. Carefully, yes. See, it's not so difficult when you have no alternative."

With his mouth, Marsh tilted back the glass. The wine snatched away his breath as it seared his throat, but a second, slower sip was lush and flavorful. Over their heads, the lighthouse continued to stab long beams across the waters.

"Isn't that delightful?"

Marsh nodded in reluctant appreciation. Kara, however, wore an expression of self-loathing as a rivulet spilled from her mouth down her neck. She looked away. Ran her tongue over her split lip.

"Vintner's Reserve, 1951." Trudi ran the cork beneath her nose. "Your father's gift to me." Her fingers twined through her hair. "I do take some credit for its success."

"You deceived him, Trudi. The pesticide poisoned his system."

"The way you speak my name reminds me of him. Chance—my one and only love."

"You did him in," Marsh ridiculed. "What sorta sick love is that?"

"Your father was the only man that made me feel desire. I'd given myself to others but always for my own motives. He was different." Trudi remained wrapped in recollections. "And then," she continued, "he confessed that he was married. He told me that it was a terrible mistake, that our relationship could not continue. Yes, he found me passage to America, but he said that it was over, nothing more. This was unacceptable. I made arrangements—made them in ways a woman learns when she is otherwise powerless—and, with a good doctor's help, met Chance one more time, a final opportunity for him to change his mind."

"And when he didn't, you gave him a parting gift. This canister."

"The only one that contained the accelerant." Trudi laid a hand on the metal, a devotee drawing blessing from a profane idol. "With this small gift, he was able to plant and harvest a bountiful crop, free of phylloxera or other pests. And thus we have our wonderful vintage." She twirled a strand of hair, then waved the finger, unfurling vaporous streamers that spiraled down as her fingertip landed on the silver canister. "Of course, my father mixed his bio-chemical weapon for a different sort of pest."

"For Jews." Disapproval was heavy in Marsh's voice.

Kara took a second deep swig from her wineglass.

"*Juden, ja.*" Trudi traced the canister's black-stenciled symbol. "The problem was that an antidote was never perfected. It's the reason Hitler never implemented Gift 12. He'd been victim to a gas attack in World War I and, as a result, quailed at the thought of unleashing similar weapons without an available antidote. Hitler was a short man...the little corporal. That was the highest rank he ever attained in the German army. Haven't you ever wondered how my dachshund came by his name?"

"Li'l Corporal."

"In honor of der Führer."

The wind gusted stronger, extinguishing a candle, and their captor once more embraced her canister. The metal reflected the moon's rays. Trudi's face hovered in the milky glow. Her eyes were set back in darkness.

From afar, Marsh thought he detected the sound of a helicopter. Kara turned.

"Of course, there are forces that could've revived Hitler's war," Trudi said with conviction. "I myself made an appeal to him, to reveal the powers available. No, no, he wasn't to be disturbed by Doktor Ubelhaar's delusional daughter. It was at that time Hitler signed papers sending me into the program. I obeyed. Blindly."

⌇

"Stay calm." The recruit stared hard at Josee as they neared the entrance to Bank of the Dunes. His scowl was a tug of war between feral attraction and gender aversion. "Just don't forget, I got my eye on your every move."

"Couldn't have guessed." Josee lowered her voice. "Eighty-nine?"

"That's it. Don't botch this, hear me?"

"Stay calm." She patted his arm and, with a toss of her head, strode into the pristine chambers of the Bank of the Dunes with Trudi's carpetbag in hand. She mustered her courage and advanced to an open window where a teller appeared to be organizing papers before closing time. Halloween decorations hung from the counter. Customers and early trick-or-treaters had already depleted the bowl of candy.

The clock behind the woman read 5:47.

"Next." The woman looked up, uninterested.

"Hi." Josee glanced around. Her escort was the bank's only other customer. In a corner to the left, at a desk in front of wing chairs, another woman typed at her computer while hugging a phone to her ear. Behind them, posted near the door, an elderly security guard flashed the relaxed smile of one who has lived life to the fullest and feels no need to hurry it along. With lips together, she smiled back.

"Are you ready, ma'am?"

"Yeah." Josee spread out her birth certificate and box key. "I'm here to get into my safe-deposit box. It's my first time. My grandfather willed its contents to me."

"Well, what a kind gesture. Uh, why is the number filed from the key?"

"Greedy relatives. Coming outta the woodwork."

The teller gave a knowing look.

"The number's 89," Josee clarified.

The woman tapped at her keyboard, scanned the monitor through fashionably oversize glasses. "Yes, I see it here. Granddaughter of...Chauncey Dean Addison?"

"That's me."

"And your full name?"

Josee wrinkled her nose. "Josee Melinda Walker."

"A nice name"—the teller perused the birth certificate—"nothing to be ashamed of, sweetheart. Need to see your photo ID."

Josee provided her Washington State driver's license.

The teller compared the picture to the real thing, seemed satisfied. "Been a long time since anyone opened that box. I'll need to have you sign in at the register."

Josee added her signature with an unexpected sense of pride.

Josee M. Walker. A member of the Addison family. *I belong.*

Then, as she followed the guard into the vault area, the suspicions planted by Trudi sprouted again. An inheritance—is that all her parents sought? Were they merely using her? Would the contents of the box shatter her newly discovered sense of place?

———

"Hitler's breeding program?" Marsh specified.

"*Ja.*" Trudi ran a hand along the canister and up through her hair. "I resigned myself to the task, to carry children in my womb, raising them for the good of my country and for *mein Führer.* The children were to be my contribution to the rise of the Third Reich. I felt, at least, that I'd been given a part in the unfolding drama."

"But you were barren. There's no excuse for the things they did to you. None."

The helicopter's whine indicated it was not far off.

Trudi's eyes twitched with uncertainty. "Ha, what do you know?"

"I know it's possible to put this to rest," Marsh said. "You can move on past the turmoil you've put up with. You hear what I'm saying, Trudi? You've done so much for Kara and me at the manor. You've proven yourself to be a reliable worker, and I'm sure a judge would consider your case with leniency. You know me, Trudi. You know how I like to deal in facts, in tangible proof. Well, these past few days have been an eyeopener. I'm willing to accept that maybe I can't fit all my ideas into a box. What about you? Are you ready to break free?"

Trudi looked away. Around her, the recruits stood motionless, gas masks hiding their faces. An icy gust swatted at the cliff, and Marsh noticed that Kara was shivering in her damp jeans. He, too, was cold.

In a frail voice, Kara said, "Trudi, God is merciful. He knows what you suffered."

"Too late for that!"

With her sleeve, Kara brushed the wine from her chin. "He sees your heart—"

"Precisely. Therein lies the problem."

"I've got my own burdens, Trudi. Things I regret, things I'm still dealing with. But he sees past all that. That's the hope that keeps us going."

"Enough! You'll say anything to try to save your daughter." Trudi turned from their pleas to the unfathomable recollections of an SS barracks. Her pale lips spit words with Teutonic precision. "In the eyes of my leaders, I was *unfruchtbar,* infertile, of no purpose to the Fatherland. I became no better than the *Untermenschen.* And who was going to stop the men of the SS from violating a mere subhuman? My own father would not come to my defense. *Es macht nichts.* The past is the past. Must it linger with us always?"

"No," said Marsh.

"Ye*ssss!* It mu*ssst!*" Her eyes glowed, and her face grew livid, a map of twisted memories. Her hair bristled. "That's the whole point. I could not bear

children. Despite my faithfulness, I became worthless. I gave and they took—
till there was nothing left."

"But this happened long ago—"

"In whose mind, Marsh? Yours? You self-centered fool, you weren't even
born yet. I've been patiently holding on for this opportunity to be *fruchtbar*,
to be fruitful. And in so doing I'll let others eat of their own dark fruit. I am
hastis humani generis."

"The enemy of mankind?" Kara translated. "Only one deserves that name."

Trudi's face hardened. "Beware, the House of Ubelhaar shall no longer
crouch in the corners."

"The House of Ubelhaar?"

"A sponsor of the arts, Kara. Private art lessons have been our means of
weeding through young, malleable recruits. With simple fliers in grocery
stores, we've harvested people with a common vision throughout the Northwest, training them to drive away the oppressors who attempt to shape us for
their own self-serving devices. I've instructed some within the very walls of
your own manor—"

"At Addison Ridge?"

"All in the name of the arts."

"Your weekly lessons—"

"Yes. In cauda venenum: Beware of what you cannot see. Indeed, we shall
demand payment for the wrongs society inflicts."

Cresting the northerly crags as though responding to the old woman's
threats, a helicopter beat the air with powerful rotors. The sound grew louder.
As the metal bird approached, the engine hiccuped, and the entire thing dipped.
The pilot was coaxing every last bit of elevation from his machine, climbing,
climbing from the chasm over the sea. Beside him, a large man was seated.

Sergeant Turney? Could it be?

Marsh's thoughts raced. What had transpired at the monument?

⁓

Behind the door of reinforced steel bars, the vault was still and cold.
Tomblike. The guard's shoes clicked on the marble floor as he directed Josee

and her escort toward the appropriate box. He inserted the master bank key into the left slot, let her turn hers in the right. The reinforced door opened as though this were a daily occurrence.

Over Josee's shoulder, the ICV escort was intent upon her actions.

"I'll be just outside," said the guard. "Lemme know when you're finished."

"Actually, sir?" She set her chin at a demure tilt as the guard turned back around. "I'd like to view the contents alone. Do you mind if…" She blinked twice.

"Yes?" he said.

Through her sweatshirt, the ICV man was pinching her back.

She put this to use, allowing a tear to well in her eye. Every word she spoke was true. "Well, not trying to hurt anyone's feelings, nothing like that. It's just that…this is private. My grandfather's gone"—she saw the guard's eyes soften—"and this is all that he left to me. I'm…I just need a moment, if it doesn't sound too silly."

"Of course not, dear. We're closing up just now, but don't let that hurry you. I can let you out, no problem." The guard took the ICV recruit by the arm. "Come along, young man. Certainly we can understand a lady's request for privacy."

Her escort shot her a look as the guard led him back into the lobby.

Alone in the cryptlike chill, Josee carried the safe-deposit box from the locker to a viewing table. She set the carpetbag alongside, noticed overhead cameras recording the moment. She lifted the top and peered into the rectangular space.

Josee left one item in the deposit box, shoved another into the front of her jeans. She clipped shut the carpetbag and slid the box back into its slot. Closed the door, heard it click. She was turning for the security guard's assistance when a fierce tug on her wrist caught her unawares.

"Follow me, you little wench!" The ICV escort dragged her along the floor. He was wielding his revolver. "Think you're real clever, huh? Well, take a look at gramps over there. You proud of yourself now?"

In a sitting position against the wall by the entry, the older man had his head on his chest. His palm was turned outward at his side, his hat upturned on the floor.

Josee shoved at her captor, tore from his grip. "You didn't have to hurt him!"

"What's done is done. Come on."

Josee saw the teller peek around the counter, undoubtedly with her finger on a silent alarm. It was a minute past six. Closing time. The accounts manager was hiding, invisible save her high heels protruding from the side of the desk.

Her escort grabbed the keys from the fallen man and unlocked the door. She trailed him outside to the waiting Buick. The other recruits breathed sighs of relief.

"Get it all?" The escort plucked the carpetbag from her hands, looked inside.

"Should be twelve vials. In that padded tray."

The car carried them to a side road on the north end of Florence, ferried them through puddles to the edge of a lake. There, under cover of dusk, a dozen vehicles of all makes and colors crouched in waiting. With little fanfare, the Buick's driver visited each one, distributing the vials and instructions. She saw one of the contacts stretch from a window, unscrew a thermoslike container, and slip the vial in before capping it.

The entire maneuver took less than five minutes.

One by one, the vehicles went out the way they'd come in, dispatched to their clandestine tasks. Josee thought of escaping into the lakeside trees, but the two men in the back relieved her of that idea. The driver returned and yanked open her door.

"You did it, cutie. All there, no tricks."

He called Trudi to let her know they were heading back and the vials had been sent forth. "No, Professor," he said before hanging up. "Haven't done that part yet."

Josee thought she saw movement in the trees.

"Okay, Josee." The driver's snub-nosed revolver appeared in his hand and directed her to exit the car. "Appreciate the help, but it's time for your treat."

—

"Looks like someone's down there," the pilot said.

On the headland, a lightkeeper's house stood protected high above the surf, hosting a group of stick figures around a table on the lawn. To her credit, it appeared that the Professor had kept to her plan and led the troops to this spot. The point of origin. Here, in 1945, the canister had escaped, then come back to her on the beach below. Soon, a loop extending over five decades would come to its conclusion.

"Set her down there, and your job'll be done." Stahlherz pointed to the skirt of grass within the white fence. His ribs and arm were aflame. The bullet that had grazed his chest had drawn blood that now affixed his shirt to the wound. The dagger had left its talon beneath his skin.

"Good thing," the pilot said. "We're running on fumes as it is."

In confirmation, the engine coughed and issued an obvious burp.

"I'd better set this bird down, and quickly!"

43

Momentum

Turney's heart thumped along with the beating of the rotors overhead. Below, the sea was angry. Steep rocks shot upward, grasping for the failing machine.

"What do we do?" he blurted. The thought of an ejection seat rambled through his head. Wouldn't that be a pretty picture?

The pilot was intense. "Hold on and shut up!" Cursing in an unbroken stream, he skimmed beneath the beams of the lighthouse, fought an upsurge of air from the tide below, and rounded the crags toward the keeper's house.

Sputt-sputt-whirr-whirr-whirr...sput!

With the rotors' remaining motion, the pilot coaxed a last spurt from his machine and cleared the cliffs, twisted the tail around and over the fence, dropped, bounced once along the grass, then planted the skids. Turney saw him, in the same motion, thumb a switch marked Fuel Interrupt to ward off an explosion from residual gas.

The contraption's momentum was too much. In his effort to vault the fence, the pilot had squeezed the final drops of fuel into the engine, and the resulting thrust was not to be denied. As the skids caught and the engine died, the weight of the machine continued forward, dipping the nose. Turney felt his seat lift. Felt his head strike the windshield as the helicopter smashed its bubble-eyed cockpit into the grass.

The man's breath was cold against Josee's ear. The gun was in his hand. He pressed her on into the thickening branches and plants. The ground was wet, sucking at their feet as the darkness collapsed in around them.

"Just leave me out here," she bargained. "Go do what you have to do. I don't even know your names or anything. I mean, what's it gonna hurt to deal me a break?"

"Deeper."

"These bushes, they're all tangled. Can't walk. It's dark."

"Fine. Right here then." The revolver nosed into her.

The night broke open with a charge of bright lights and cops and bullhorns.

"Freeze right there! Hands up!"

Adrenaline fired through Josee's limbs like lit gasoline. She dove to the ground. Skinned her nose in the dirt. Foliage crashed around her. Yells and gunshots. The ICV guy. His arm was shredded. He was writhing in the bushes beside her. Then she was up again. Running. Tripping. She fell, then arms reached for her. A voice cut through the chaos. Familiar. Cheerless. Deep.

"Josee, get up now. You're okay. Up, onto your feet."

"Chief Braddock?"

"Your favorite person."

—

With the ground rising to meet them, Stahlherz withdrew the broken dagger and pressed back into his seat, gripping his straps. The windshield buckled and disintegrated in an eruption of grass and dirt and glass shards. Even as strips of skin opened on his forearms, he perceived a cold and precise pain along his forehead. The impact of a rotor spinning into the hard earth sent a shudder through the hull.

In death, the engine protested. *Screechhh!*

Stahlherz felt the rotor's torque as it tried to complete its circuit. The helicopter lurched down and twisted on the collapsed passenger-side skid. Then, in an earsplitting moment, the rotor snapped. In his peripheral vision, he watched it spin through the air, glance off a railing, and drop into the chasm between the cliffs.

Ka-snappp! Whirrp-whirrp-whirrp…Spulasssh…

Epinephrine heightened all his senses. The pain was distributed evenly now—through his ribs, his face and arms, his skull. He unbuckled himself, shook the debris from his hair. The sergeant was slumped in his seat, unconscious. Beside him, the pilot was lifeless, thrown forward into the mishmash of dials and gauges, his thigh impaled by the helicopter's steering mechanism.

What had Stahlherz told the man earlier? *We're both driven by our respective birds. If we let them, oh yes, they'll swallow us whole.*

He shook his head at the irony of it all.

～

Chief Braddock commandeered the red Buick over a bridge as they climbed the road out of Florence. Fiddling with her eyebrow ring, Josee offered him a short glance. "Okay, I'll say it. Thanks."

"Thank your father. He called to warn me. I rushed over here to join with the local officers in keeping an eye on the Bank of the Dunes. From there, we followed you to the meeting point and crashed the party. Were the vials in the vault?"

She nodded. "Did Marsh tell you about them?"

"I knew they existed. I just wasn't sure where."

"You're too late. You've gotta stop them. Those cars, they're already—"

"Already what, girl? Don't get yourself all worked up. You're in capable hands. With the help of the local authorities, detectives are even now tailing those vehicles. Once they reach their destinations with those vials, we aim to round up the troops. Get as many as possible in one big sweep. Shut ICV down for good."

Braddock shifted, watched the mirror. "Was there anything else in the box?"

"Hey, it's not your deposit box. Why should you care?"

"Not trying to fight you, Josee. The other day we got off on the wrong foot, but I am here to help you."

"And how do you plan on doing that?"

"By getting you safely back to Heceta Head. Isn't that what you want? Isn't that where you said Marsh and Kara are? Where Trudi Ubelhaar is?" Above Braddock's rawhide cheeks his eyes narrowed. "Thing is, I want the same thing you do, Josee. I want fathers and children together, safe and warm in their beds at night, free from worry about what tomorrow may hold. I want this brought to an end."

Josee held up an envelope. "There *was* something else. Addressed to you."

Braddock snatched it from her hand. He pulled to the side of the road and smiled as he read the note inside. A note of thanks, Josee knew; she'd gone over it at the vault but didn't understand the reasons behind it.

He found the photograph next. Yellowed. Curled.

"Father," he said, filling the one word with admiration, questions, and anger.

He removed a set of wedding rings last. His Adam's apple jumped.

"Chief, I'm lost. Why'd my grandfather put these in his deposit box?"

"He knew my parents," Braddock said as he slipped the diamond-studded rings into his shirt pocket and pulled back onto the highway. "My mother died of influenza during the war while the men were off fighting. They returned to a world of changing parameters. These rings belonged to my parents. Unbelievable. I didn't even know they were still around."

"Worth a fortune, by the looks of them."

Braddock nodded, almost as if the thought hadn't occurred to him.

Josee watched the road whir by. Reflected in the sea, the moon was a lemon orb on blue-black fabric. In the distance, visible from bends in the coastal highway, Heceta Head Lighthouse was a stalwart guardian, offering light to all who would come.

"Almost there. Hope you've got a plan of action, Chief."

Although his laughter boomed through the Buick, dark intentions filled his eyes.

———

With his legs, the ICV recruit gripped the reinforced case on the passenger-side floorboards of the Toyota pickup. Inside, Styrofoam mounts cradled the canister that Mr. Steele had provided. Once the accelerant was introduced, the poison would be unstoppable.

This was it. Finally. A year of prep and recon, and now the grand finale.

In his mind, Travis rehearsed the plan. They'd turn at Mapleton and head east on Highway 126. Within an hour, they'd skirt Eugene on Green Hill Road, cut into the north end along Barger Drive and head for River Avenue. They'd nose into the parking lot of a bingo hall—just two guys hoping for a lucky streak…hilarious!—then cross over to the property of a city water treatment facility. Since 9/11 was now a memory, security measures had softened. Penetrating the property, that would be the fun part. By morning, the reports would start coming in.

Convulsions. Loss of control. Bodily functions gone berserk.

Victims by the hundreds, by the thousands.

The driver angled his rearview mirror. He said, "We're being followed, Travis. That car's been behind us since we left Florence."

"This is the fastest way to Eugene. Could be coincidence."

"Maybe I should try going the long way, through Triangle Lake."

"No," Travis said. "That'd put us at the target too late."

"What if it's the cops?"

"They can't pull us over unless they have something to go on. Take it easy."

The driver shifted into a lower gear, his eyes darting between his mirrors as he followed a bridge over the Siuslaw River. Ahead, the road was dark and wet, hemmed in by towering conifers. "That's the problem. Got a warrant out on me. See, I skipped a court date last week."

Travis exhaled. "You idiot!"

"There's a corner up here and this narrow driveway. I've got an idea." Braking the vehicle with two quick downshifts, the driver switched off his headlights and aimed toward the gap in a fence across the road.

—

The helicopter was a smoldering heap. Glass and metal glistened in the grass. Kara, along with the others, waited for movement in the wreckage. Apparently, though, no one had survived.

Will any of us survive this night?

Kara felt numb. The way she had in the cellar. Trudi had ordered her daughter's death, and here Kara sat with soup and wine and bread crusts down the front of her shirt. The vintage wine bottle stood in the center of the table, flanked by candles. The canister in Trudi's hands bounced moonbeams across the tableau.

"They should be here by now," Trudi said. "Not that far from Florence."
But Josee won't be returning. My daughter. Gone.

Kara dipped her head to sip again at her wineglass. Her pants were sticky with salt and wet from the dash through the waves with Marsh. That'd been a surprise. He seemed different. Maybe one good thing would come from this mess—if they survived.

Trudi scooped her beloved canister to her nose and sniffed. With a mischievous grin, she puffed her aged chest and arms as though possessed by unearthly might. To her four adherents, she said, "Tonight's deadly distribution shall be our pièce de résistance. With the vials released, ICV shall make its mark for eternity."

They answered in spirited unity: "Audentes fortuna juvat!"

A red Buick was easing into the parking area on the far side of the keeper's house, and Trudi eyed it with elation. "At last."

With her attention diverted, Marsh was sawing the tape on his wrists against the wooden table leg. Kara tried not to check his progress, afraid she might telegraph his movements to the others. She waited for the Buick to park.

Before it could stop, a figure emerged from the disabled helicopter.

———

Old Man Ridder made a point to let out his wife's cocker spaniel every night before the reruns of *Seinfeld*. He loved the show. Reminded him of his East Coast relatives. Abrupt. Self-absorbed. A million miles an hour.

"Go on, girl. Do your thing."

The spaniel was getting up in age. She waddled through the screen door.

Standing on the porch, Ridder heard the chattering burp of a semitruck's air brakes. Up there along the tree line, Highway 126 was the site of many a fender bender. Fool trucks. The road was rain soaked and dark. The blast of a horn confirmed Ridder's fears, even as a Toyota pickup slashed across the pavement, nothing more than a rodent caught in the rectangular sweep of the truck's headlights.

But the Toyota's lights were dimmed. Now if that wasn't the dangedest thing.

Old Man Ridder forgot about the spaniel, about the rerun, and shook his head. "They just never learn, the fools. Never learn."

With the blare of a horn, the hurtling tanker swerved to avoid the smaller vehicle. It skidded and began to jackknife. To escape, the Toyota kicked mud and hopped over the grate, but a front tire dropped into the drainage ditch, and the driver's eyes shone white as the front grill slammed into the escarpment. A star crack appeared where his forehead hit the windshield. For a moment, he and his passenger were stark silhouettes in the glare of the overturning semi's lights. Then the entire night became an outline of trees and metal against the orange-blue explosion that erupted from the toppled tanker as it careened into the paralyzed pickup in the ditch.

A fist of heat punched Old Man Ridder back through his screen door. He felt slivers and metallic threads snag at his overalls. His head bounced against the carpet.

He groaned. Gritted his teeth. Extracted himself from the heap of wood.

The smell of burnt hair pierced his nostrils, the enormous blast still rang in his ears, but there at the top of the drive the wreckage was a sight to behold. From the cauldron of fire, from the heart of the flattened pickup, green flames rose like departing spirits. In matching color, wisps of smoke snaked down toward the house and passed over the still form on the front grass.

He never did like that dog.

Old Man Ridder took a deep breath, steeled himself to make an emergency call and to face the reaction of his wife. Within seconds, however, he was aware of nothing other than the pain sparking through his extremities and the convulsions rippling through his muscles.

⌒

Allhallows Eve. The night for trick-or-treaters had arrived. Emerging from the torn cockpit of the helicopter was a man Marsh assumed must be his online foe. The man stumbled forward dazed, a jagged blade in his hand. As though part of a macabre costume, lacerations and blood marked his arms and face.

This was no trick; the man needed medical attention.

"Stahli," Trudi whispered. "You're a fool."

"He needs help." Marsh worked his wrists against the duct tape, using the distraction to his advantage. *If I can just...*

Two bug-eyed recruits took steps to assist the crash victim, but a command from Trudi stopped them short. "Let him be. He should never have come." She cocked her head, amused by his advance on ungainly legs.

The man swayed. Halted. "At last we meet, Marsh. I'm Karl Stahlherz."

"Steele Knight, your chess skills are weakening. You fell for my gambit."

"Game's still in progress." Stahlherz coughed, spit blood. "I had to meet my brother before handing to him a final defeat."

"How'd you get dragged into this? I understand Trudi's motive here, but why'd you choose me and my family to torment? I don't get it."

"Aren't you listening? I just told you, Marsh. You are my brother."

"I don't have a brother."

"Virginia can verify it for you. She gave birth to me years before your arrival."

"My brother was stillborn."

"Stillborn? No, that's where you're wrong. Is that what they've told you, the lie you've believed while frolicking in the role of favored son? No, no, see I deserved all that which you claim as your own. It should've been mine. I was the firstborn."

Marsh felt like yelling at this impostor. Was there any truth in his words?

"I don't see a resemblance. I don't believe it."

"Think as you will. You've usurped all that should've been mine, assumed the role that belonged to me. Chance did not want a child. With an army orderly's help, he deceived even his own wife and left me for dead. But Trudi stepped in. Rescued me."

"And she's the one who's fed you these lies? She's full of it, Stahlherz."

"Ha-ha! Yes, I've come to see that." He glared at the old woman.

"It's all been a lie," Marsh said. "Let's put the whole thing to rest. Call it a draw."

"Nooo! All or nothing. I'd rather die than let you claim even partial victory."

"Stahli." Trudi shook her head with pity.

Marsh was shell-shocked. No wonder this had become personal. Could his opponent's claims be true? He was sure that Virginia knew nothing of this, but perhaps Chance had taken the truth to his grave. Perhaps they would never know for certain.

From the direction of the Buick, a lone figure was walking their way. She was a cutout shape against the lights behind her, but Marsh couldn't mistake the silhouette.

"Josee!" He and Kara and Trudi called out her name in unison.

⌒

As arranged, Josee took her time. She moved along the keeper's house, giving Chief Braddock an opportunity to slip from the Buick and circle around by the demolished helicopter. Her step quickened though when she caught Kara's eye at the table. Disregarding the others, she pressed in beside her mother on the bench seat. Felt her nearness. Overhead, beams of light from the tower sliced the darkness.

"Josee. We thought they were going to kill you."

"Guess you thought wrong, I'm here in one piece."

Trudi was agitated. "You're a survivor, Josee. That's to be admired. Have the vials been distributed and sent out? The driver told me they had been."

"Yep."

"Then why," Trudi asked, "are you here? He was to remove you from the game."

"Guess his aim was off."

The old woman closed her eyes with exaggerated languor. Holding the silver canister over her head, she seemed to squeeze from it a vile green vapor that encircled her head and washed down over her body. Her recruits watched with masked stares, and judging by their backward steps, Josee decided they must share her sense of foreboding. The profuse vapor formed tight curls about Trudi's scalp. Thus empowered, she strode around behind Josee.

"What happened? Tell me! Something happened, I'm quite certain of it."

"I got the stuff from the bank like you said. Then the guys split it up and went their separate ways."

Trudi leaned in, and Josee felt a tug at her eyebrow ring. "I told them to kill you. You could have been my granddaughter, but no, you shirked that connection."

"Think you've got the wrong chick." Josee jerked her head from the invasive touch. "I'm done helping you with your psycho little plan!"

Trudi cupped her hands over Josee's tufted hair. Josee tried to move forward, to shake off the old cow, but a burst of heat seemed to ooze down her cheeks and jaw. She was staring out at the rolling breakers, paralyzed by fear. A set of white fingers lowered before her eyes. Curved fangs. They latched on to her eyebrow ring.

"Leave my daughter alone," Kara protested.

"You've disrupted the game, Josee. Your fabrications are self-evident. I can smell that you're not telling me everything. My orders—disobeyed!" Trudi tugged at Josee's ring, fangs hooked into pewter, stretching her skin to the breaking point.

"Arhhh!"

Josee's scream was involuntary as the fangs created a tear. The searing heat was intense. The eyebrow ring was still there, held by the remaining tissue.

"Hands off!" Marsh rose from the bench.

"Stay *back!*"

Marsh ignored Trudi's warning.

"*Baaccck!*" Trudi clutched fingers to Josee's ears.

Marsh stopped. Josee could feel droplets down her cheek.

"In your seat!" The fangs clutched tighter at Josee's head. "Do it now!"

From behind them, a snarl broke through the darkness. "Gertrude Ubelhaar!"

———

With bits of glass dug into his skin, with scars throbbing and left elbow hanging useless, Turney's reserves were dwindling. He was shaking, and his head was spinning. He lifted himself upright and fought to regain awareness.

"Sarge." Chief Braddock was crouched at the pilot's side door. "You're alive."

"What're you doin' here?"

"Shhh. Been trying to wake you up. Didn't know if I'd be able to, thought you might be a goner. Long story, but I heard about the hijacked helicopter over the radio. Should've known you'd have your backside planted in it." Braddock eased through the mangled cockpit. Together they faced the table at the edge of the cliff. Turney noted the Addisons, Josee, Trudi, and four recruits. Good thing the chief had his firearm.

And Braddock looked ready to use it. Finger on the trigger. Pacing forward.

"Out of the way, Sarge."

Wait, what's he doing? He's got a target in mind!

With an explosion of words, the chief stepped out toward the group. "Gertrude Ubelhaar!" His finger flirted with the trigger of his gun. "You murderer, destroyer!"

"Who are you?" she said unperturbed.

"After my mother was gone, my dad was all I had left. And you killed him! I'm the son of Major Johnson Braddock Sr., the colleague you murdered."

"An accident. I'm quite certain that's what the reports indicate."

Braddock leveled the barrel at her, ignoring Turney's arrival at his side. "You were there with him at the depot. You released the chemicals in that lab. You knew he was suspicious of your movements about Umatilla, and you removed the threat."

Trudi's head was alive with frayed and wild hair. Turney marveled at the sheer mass of it. With a twitch, she whipped a rope of hair at her uniformed aggressor.

Braddock's eyes widened. He yelled, then drilled a round through Trudi's calf. It exited in a bloom of blood.

Trudi looked down. "*Shhh*ouldn't have done that."

A revelation hit Turney: His superior, his chief, had every intention in the world of maiming and killing this woman before them. The evidence was in his stance, the position of his gun, the look in his eyes. Turney moved from the wreckage toward the others. "Don't do this, Chief."

First degree murder, with witnesses to spare? He'll lose his career and more.

"Stay out of it, Turney. What do you know about standing up to this thing?"

Turney begged him to reconsider, but the chief had lost all restraint. "She killed my father, and she's aiming to kill others! I'm doing us all a favor." He scanned the audience. "Don't you know, Marsh? I was the one Chance commissioned to protect your family. I've been here all along, watching out for you. Staying close."

"A little too close," Marsh shot back. "Why you? It doesn't make sense."

"Your father, Marsh, saved my dad's life in the trenches during the war, and he felt I owed him a favor. As a young detective, I agreed to help. I admit that in my desire to warn Kara about your contaminated offspring, I got myself in trouble—and I'm sorry. Okay, is that clear? I'm sorry. My intentions were to guard you from this insanity."

Turney saw Trudi advancing on her good leg. "Trudi, don't make him fire again!"

She was tugging at her hair, her voice purring with ridicule. "Mr. Braddock, if you're going to throw but one punch, I suggest you not even step into the ring."

One punch…

"Come on, *shhh*oot me again! Let your hatred have its way. *Come onnn!*"

Without a word, Braddock swung his firearm up and—

Kerrackkk!

Turney's staggering uppercut was a masterpiece of leverage and motion that he could feel spring from his legs, gain momentum in his hips, and collect power from his arms. His meaty fist cracked into Chief Braddock's jaw from below, lifting him on his feet and driving him back a yard through the air. The gun misfired into the night.

Satisfied, Thunder Turney rubbed at his sore knuckles.

Sorry, Chief. Just thinking of your career.

44

Hair-Raising

At the picnic table, painted in weak candlelight, the Addison family sat stunned by the eruption of violence around them. Braddock was out. Stahlherz was weak but enraged. Trudi was gathering strength, flanked by her cohorts in bug-eyed masks.

Turney shook the fog from his head. He met Josee's eyes. Nodded.

Gotta help her, but I need backup. Can't do this all alone.

He was sure that the county's patchwork of airport radars had monitored the helicopter's hijacked flight. A good chance that even now officers were on their way. Not that he could sit around and wait, no sir.

Disoriented, the sergeant moved toward the group.

So here I am, ready to serve and protect. What next, Lord?

The response was not what he expected. In a sudden spin, Karl Stahlherz circled behind him and, once again, laid the broken blade along his neck.

—

Josee felt blood drip down her jaw and spill onto the china. She leaned ahead, set her chin on the rim of a wineglass. Felt the fangs' needle tips touch her earlobes. She sat still. Beside her, Kara's face was wet with tears; beneath the table, her mother's legs moved against hers.

And there, on the grass, stood Sarge. A mess, just like her. But still standing.

"Josee, you've survived," said Trudi, "longer than expected. With your genetic disorder, your debilitating symptoms… Tell me, dear one, how have you managed all these years? Tell us, what's kept you so healthy, so vibrant?"

The ruptured skin of Josee's eyebrow was throbbing. She felt far from healthy and vibrant. Her cross necklace slid against her chest. *Show me a way outta here. Please. What am I, a stinkin' pincushion?*

"Tell us, Josee!" Trudi bellowed. "What's your secret?"

"Gel capsules."

"Capsules?"

"One each day."

"No, there's no remedy so mundane as that. Come now, tell us the truth. This poison that has invaded your genes, altered your blood, has no cure. A long slow death—that's what you can look forward to, my dear. Don't be fooled into—"

"You're a freakin' liar!" Josee cringed against the reaction she was sure would come. "I've heard enough of this. You tried to turn me against my parents. Every step of the way you've deceived us."

"Leave us alone, please," Kara added. "Josee's place is with me. With us."

Across the grass, Turney found Josee's eyes and gave a nod. Her throat tightened. She wished she could respond to these gestures, but the clasped fingers at her ears were shoving her face down. It was her turn to share in the soup and bread dinner. The swill was cold now, but the liquid burned as it touched her torn eyebrow.

She was coming up for air when she saw Sergeant Turney take a step in their direction. Lightning quick, Stahlherz wrapped behind him and pushed gleaming steel to the officer's neck.

Groaning, Sergeant Turney shuffled across the grass, hostage to this madman.

"Keep those fat legs moving," Stahlherz said.

"What good am I to you?"

"I'd like you to meet my mother." At the table, Trudi watched with amusement.

"Gertrude...Trudi? She's related to you?"

"She rescued and nurtured me. I also find out that she's manipulated me."

"Then let's bring her to justice. You can have a life of your own."

"Too late for that." The man poked at him. "I want her to see you, to witness this pesky knight who's bumbled about, unwittingly protracting our goals past and present. I want her to see how easily her shrewd schemes do crumble."

Certifiably loony tunes! I'm not doin' a thing this guy says.

"Keep moving, Sarge."

The plan hit him like a load of bricks. In apparent compliance, Turney took three rapid steps that startled and dragged Karl Stahlherz along. He whispered, "When I am weak"—step four, step five—"then I am strong!" Thunder Turney let his muscles collapse and dropped to the grass like a prizefighter down for the count.

⸺

The weight of the police sergeant was overwhelming. Like a stone, Turney dropped through Steele Knight's arms and, despite the upward dagger slice along his heavy jowls, fell in a heap on the lawn.

"Then I am strong!" His words echoed over the cape.

Before Stahlherz could react, the mountainous cop rolled backward upon his own wounded arm and pinned Stahlherz's feet, snapping him at the kneecaps. Stahlherz cried out, felt his legs turn to jelly, then did a marionette's untethered fall over the obstacle beneath him. As he thrust his arms out for support, he saw his broken blade, saw the sinews of his own hand where the edge had dug deep, saw the dagger's tip turned upward as it landed with his fist on the path and waited for his unblinking eye.

Shloo-kerr-pawshhh!

The rook could now see through only one eye. His other was draining over his cheek. He tried to rise again upon feathered black wings, found little reaction. Far off, as if in a dream, he heard his mother's voice.

"Stahli..."

Her deceptive nature rang through that one simple word. Even his name was a deception. So she had provided him proof of identity, but who was Karl Stahlherz really? Would he ever know his lineage with certainty? No, too late now. By his own line of reasoning, he had lost. *It's over! I won't keep living in defeat!*

With the talons that had clawed through his ears, that had wrapped through his skull and scraped at his sanity, Steele Knight managed to crawl to the fence. He leaned an arm on the wood and crawled over. Removing the dagger from his ruined eye, he stumbled down the incline and wondered if this was the path taken by Trudi's canister so long ago. His bitterness had nowhere to turn. All over now. He drew one deep track across his own throat and let his body carry him down.

Through the brush. Over the cliff's gnarled brow.

Tumbling. Falling…in an easy descent.

Facilis descensus Averno! It was the last phrase ever to pass through his mind.

—

With hands on the fence, Trudi peered out at the cliff as though to convince herself of her henchman's outcome. She shook her head. "You see, Marsh, Stahli always liked a rousing game of chess, the opportunity to strategize. He could've gone about all this far more simply, but he insisted we play it his way. I tried to warn him, but he wouldn't listen. That male ego of his… He could not bear to lose."

"You let him walk into my trap at the monument." Marsh was appalled by her obdurate tone. "You set him up to taste defeat. You poisoned his thinking, Trudi!"

"He deserved punishment for his failure to take heed."

"And now," Kara said with disgust, "he's punished himself. Are you happy?"

"Don't you have any reaction whatsoever?" Marsh pitched in.

"Not at this time, no. I raised him with vengeance as a goal, feeding him stories of abandonment and cruelty. This action he's committed is consistent with his thought processes. He could not live to face defeat from an Addison. Stahlherz was the son your parents allegedly lost at delivery. You were their second, Marsh."

"You know nothing about my father. What proof do you have?"

Trudi laughed. "Sins of the fathers passed to the third and fourth generations. A biblical concept, am I correct? Familial transgressions."

"Under the old law, that's true," said Kara.

"Old law, ha. I've read the words myself. Sins must be paid for!"

Marsh was attentive. This was the curse he'd been striving under the past few days, even years. Sins of the fathers. Was there a way to break the cycle?

Chance's indiscretions… Braddock's intrusion… My own mistakes…

"Yes," Kara conceded. "But the curse has lost its power. Jesus' sacrifice on the cross broke the power of separation and death, reuniting us with his Father." Kara was gaining confidence; her voice was less shaky. "Once God adopts us into his family, we're no longer enslaved to the rules of the old household. We're given a clean slate."

"Sounds too good to be true, particularly from the lips of an adulterer."

Kara wavered. Wrestling with her own shame.

Trudi was relentless. "And as we can all see, you've been imbibing again of late."

"I'm not perfect. Yes, I know that."

Marsh came to his wife's defense. "Trudi, your accusations are immaterial. As Kara said, the curse has no power. She's been forgiven. She's part of God's family."

"All very charming. Light applause." Trudi chortled, then her tone changed as she spewed words that would seal her decision. "How dare you sit and offer smug forgiveness? You are filth! You slap the face of the afflicted! I don't think that you've seen the real power of the curse. A serpent's poison can be deadly, yes, but a family's sin… It's an accelerant that increases the potency. Now that you've been forced to swallow your father's betrayal, don't try to convince me that you're immune to its effects. You think you can combat this venom? No, I don't believe you're ready for it."

"You're the one who's not ready." Sergeant Turney had clambered to his feet.

—

My sparring partner!

Josee's pain turned into determination. The old woman's finger fangs still clung to her head, but Turney was advancing. With Trudi intent on this newest opposition, Josee drew her feet up beneath her. If she could just get the right leverage…

Trudi droned, "Come and join us, Sergeant. All I wanted was a simple meal by the sea. Let's all sup together, shall we?" She swerved from Josee to the head of the table where she placed a hand on the metal canister. "We shall once and for all drink and be satiated. All a matter of surrender." She spread both arms in a gesture of abandon, summoning coiled vapors from the canister before her.

Although Trudi Ubelhaar was now positioned two yards from Josee's seat, the fangs still hovered over Josee's ears. With all that had happened in the past few days, Josee was more incensed than surprised by the apparition emerging at the head of the table. She watched Trudi's honey hair change color in the night. The cords of hair congealed into writhing shapes of green—snapping around her neck, slithering about her eyes and ears. On the woman's scalp, the mass of serpents moved with tongues alive and scales flexing in the moonlight.

Most of the snakes were small, but others were fat and outstretched.

Two extended back around Josee's neck to her ears. Others zeroed in on Marsh and Kara. One large viper drifted in Sarge's direction.

"Driiink!" Trudi reached for her quartet of gas-masked cohorts.

Josee knew they couldn't see the snakes, but the venom in the air was palpable.

The ICV recruits flinched and drew together. They were unprepared for Trudi's reaction as she lashed out in consternation, hooking vipers into arms, spreading appendages in involuntary surrender. The recruits fell, frozen, to the ground.

She hissed blasphemies. "You, too, shall taste this cup. Drink in my memory."

The cone of the ancient canister twirled open with ease, and Trudi tipped it like an urn, dispensing poison over each wineglass. Miasmic orbs hovered there, chained to the confines of the glass rims.

"Josee…"

The whisper followed a nudge beneath the table, and Josee's eyes shifted down. She saw that Kara had worked taped wrists beneath her thighs and feet.

Her fingers were tugging at her hip pocket, working a swatch of pink into view.

"This is yours—"

"Halt dein Mund!" Trudi's gaze whipped along the table. "Keep quiet!"

Still whispering: "Your birth cap, Josee, from the hospital. I've saved it."

"That's enough!" Trudi roared. "I did not ask you to speak."

Josee palmed the tiny hat, felt its warm knit texture on her skin. She tucked it into her pants, lifted her face to meet Kara's soft expression—soft, yes, but hardening with a protective mother's resolve. At Kara's neck, a set of fangs yawned. The creature's breath turned to steam in the cold air.

"Mom!"

Josee was about to dive at the thing when her mother made a move.

In a sweeping motion, Kara ducked forward and cleared the table of fine stemware. Wineglasses, deep red liquid, and wisps of poison littered the air in a kaleidoscope of color. The glasses struck Trudi's abdomen, splattering wine in crimson stains. Taking her cue, Josee shifted her weight to her feet and sprang to the tabletop. She toppled bowls and soup and smashed the candle-holders. Pain clawed through her ears as fangs ripped back, and her vision reeled. The breeze stung her eyes. Stars spun.

"Marsh," Kara cried. A snake had encircled her ankle and now coiled upward.

Josee dodged a pair of serpents that struck at her head. She kicked once at the vintage wine bottle in the center of the table, aiming it toward Trudi. A viper struck her arm. She kicked again. Her feet connected this time and catapulted the Addison Ridge bottle. The object cut through her attached viper's translucent form, bounced from the table's ledge, then broke its neck in a shower of glass that sprayed toward Trudi's Medusalike head. The shards wedged between the fangs of myriad snakes.

The snakes followed their larger kin toward Marsh and Kara.

Josee slipped in the pools of spilled wine and fell backward onto the table. She found herself prostrate over silverware and plates. Her head was pounding, a rock wall crumbling piece by piece, giving way to the lingering poison.

"Jesus!" Another beast was hovering over her, rear fangs extended amid a shower of spittle and hot venom. Her cry was a statement of faith. "Help us!"

The ocean was spewing frosty breath over the crags and cliffs, and the moon was a pale eye watching the proceedings. Turney knew that he should be weakening from the poison Trudi had released. To his surprise, he felt invigorated.

But hadn't he failed in his fasting exercise? Yes, and in so doing, he'd been reminded of his true source of strength. Although his scars were moist beneath his shirt, he realized they might indicate his growing immunity to the poison. Twin shots. Inoculations. Building resistance to ward off the disease. He'd held his ground, even removed a length of Trudi's hair as it snaked along his chest. Around her scalp, her tresses had formed a dance of green fire. He didn't understand it exactly, but her power had seemed to emanate from the metal canister.

That thing's gotta go. No more messin' around!

Turney took a breath and vaulted toward the silvery object in her hands.

Vaporous poison had stripped away Marsh's clarity. He was sullen. He worked his hands free from the duct tape and sat wringing his fingers. Fading, drifting. Through drooping eyelids, he watched his wife and daughter take action, yet remained paralyzed on the bench. This entire scenario was impossible. Ropes of creatures swirling about Trudi's face? Orbs of poison in the air?

No. Madness setting in. Losing touch.

He could always crawl to the cliff's edge and let go…like Karl Stahlherz. *Do it!*

Then spotlights came on. In his mind. The words from Kara's Bible: "We are not fighting against people…but against…mighty powers of darkness.… Use every piece of God's armor to resist the enemy."

God, give me strength to stand—to stand firm!

Marsh pulled himself to his feet, drilled his eyes into Trudi, and spotted vipers directed at Josee and Kara. Josee was down on the table; Kara was standing. The creatures stabbed toward them. Banging the table's edge with his knee, Marsh clawed over the wood to thrust himself between attackers and prey. His arms flung forward.

Sets of scimitar fangs carved through both hands. Nailed him in place.

Impaled above the table, he groaned, then fell onto the planks as fangs retracted. Beads of blood and venom pushed through the holes in his skin. His nerves began to riot. Quivering in the poison's grip, he realized that this was a picture of Christ on the cross. Marsh could only follow the example: "Love your wives with the same love Christ showed the church. He gave up his life for her."

But I'm only a man…a mortal.

Each nerve was screaming now. Each cell a torch. A million torches…running their flames beneath his skin. An unholy fire, consuming him.

Then the fire shut down. His nervous system threw the switch.

No more signals. No more pain. Nothing.

—

Ignoring Trudi's stale cinnamon breath, Sergeant Turney moved in. He set aside his fear and doubts and determined that he could show no more pity for this wretched old woman who'd made choices to impose her will on the world around her.

He wrested the canister from her grip and jerked his head away from the hair that beat in the wind and slapped at him.

With an outpouring of strength, he launched the metal object out over the fence, toward the precipice, toward the mist and the waves that crashed far below.

—

Josee's voice was useless on her swollen tongue. Flashes…venom…needles and bright lights… All the horrors of childhood came back: the transfusions, abuse, neglect, the search for her birth parents. Now her future was fading before her eyes. Kara was crouched alongside the table, coughing. Marsh was sprawled over the bench with mouth gaping, eyes unblinking. Spasms arced through his limbs. Tiny drops formed in his tear ducts. Thinning blood.

The elements of survival…

Groggily, Josee plucked at the braided cord around her neck, emptied the red gel capsules from the vial into her hand. Three of them. She was so weak. She set one on her tongue and watched the others drop through her fingers.

———

Convulsions…in gathering waves. Locked jaws. Wetness at Marsh's tear ducts. Drops of blood hit the grass before his eyes. Whose blood was it? His own? Kara's?

No. Gel tablets…Josee's saving grace…doctor's orders.

With his last vestige of awareness, he forced one into Kara's mouth, the other between his own clenched teeth. The medication tasted metallic. Pungent on his tongue.

———

Midair, the canister reflected moonbeams in somersaulting patches. Trudi's scream, in Josee's ears, turned into the hiss of multitudinous serpents. The old Nazi's hair slithered out into the wind, snakes reaching over the fence in an attempt to snatch back the coveted object. They formed a net that draped beneath the canister, caught it, and bounced it once and again before a huge viper snagged it between pale-lined jaws.

"Ah, you *sssee,*" said Trudi. "I give for no one! I thrive in the night. I drink it in like a tonic. The darkness is on my breath, in my *sss*weat, in the very *sss*pit of my mouth." Her lips closed over her withdrawing tongue.

"The darkness," Kara whispered, "cannot extinguish it."

"What?" Trudi looked down at her in bewilderment. "Extinguish what?"

"'God is light.' Guess you'll never understand."

"Game's over," Marsh said.

Despite his ragged tone, Josee recognized it as a declaration of faith. The moment the words left his mouth, a spoke of Heceta Head's light caught the viper more than fifty feet off the ground and swung it in a circle. As the incandescent beam panned back along the wooded hillside, it dragged its prey and lifted Trudi on her aging tiptoes. Her hair and the flailing serpents stretched and circled over the sea, then inland, bumping through the trees, over the ground. The serpents spread out in an effort to escape—until alternating spears of light skewered each of them in turn.

For a millisecond that Josee thought she might have only imagined, the golden spokes retracted, leaving the snakes suspended. Then, in a blaze of heavenly rage, the light shot out again, flinging canister and creatures far out into the brooding sea.

As far as the horizon.

As far as the east from the west.

Trudi Ubelhaar, broken and bruised, tried to rise to her feet. On the third attempt, she collapsed on the grass. Most bizarre of all, above her wrinkled brow and blank, reptilian eyes, she was totally bald. Not a strand of hair remained on her head.

Through hazy eyes, Marsh looked from the table and saw Trudi's cyclical journey in the skewer of light. The wind gusted. The spinning beams of the lighthouse seemed to accelerate, slicing the gloom as with a cognitive purpose. About Trudi's head, each serpent strand stretched taut to impossible lengths. The old woman's pale lips opened in a scream as the wind yanked away her sheaf of hair.

She tumbled to the earth. Tried three times to stand. Fell unconscious.

On the tail of the breeze, the lighthouse probed the night and discovered a slowly falling object.

Trudi's wig…

Captive to the upthrusts of air, the wig tossed and peeled apart, then fell seaward, eventually dipping from view beneath the ocean's vast blanket of mercy.

Hidden Things

Addison Ridge Vineyards, Thanksgiving Day

"I'm so pleased that you could join us."

"But, of course," Virginia said. "This is a time for families to come together."

Kara nodded at her mother-in-law over a platter of sliced turkey. Her community dinner was only an hour away. Her orange fliers had drawn over two hundred responses from individuals and underprivileged families that would be bused from downtown Corvallis to the Addison Ridge warehouse. Directed by John and Kris Van der Bruegge, teams of servers made preparations: filling punchbowls and coffee carafes, placing decorative centerpieces, heaping silver tureens with holiday standards.

Virginia sighed. "Goodness, I don't know that my heart could've handled what you went through a few weeks ago. Glad to have that behind us."

"Trudi put you through quite a lot as well. We have much to be thankful for."

———

"I knew it'd rain," Marsh grumbled. "Typical Oregon weather."

"A little rain? Bright side is, those without shelter were even more thankful to be here," Kara said. "Glad to see Virginia made it. Been a while since your mother turned out for a social event. She's cornered Esprit on the back deck for his version of the confrontation at the memorial marker. They're swapping stories from the good ol' days. They seem to be getting along fabulously, better than ever."

Good ol' days?

Marsh frowned. Sure, in the past month his future had brightened—he'd been cleared of suspicion, he'd found his missing wife and long-lost daughter, he'd nurtured a budding faith—but his view of the past was dimmer than ever. The pillars he'd built his life upon had crumbled. His own father had deployed him and others as pieces in a real-life game. Even Josee's adoption had been instigated by Chance's indiscretions.

Kara's prayer had opened Marsh's eyes. He knew that as a fact. Thankfully, the apparitions had ceased, but he understood his misdeeds as never before. So many hurtful words over the years, careless actions.

And there would be more. He wasn't perfect.

He recalled the words of reconciliation he and Kara had exchanged on the beach, and the words of spiritual adoption, of the breaking of cycles. Where, though, was the joy in the process? Hadn't he extended and received forgiveness?

A thought struck him: *I haven't forgiven myself.*

The rain was clattering along the portico, pooling in puddles. Cleansing.

"Hon?" Marsh took Kara's hand. "I know we have a lot of straightening up to do, but why don't we leave it for a few minutes? I have something else in mind."

She shot him a glance. "Nowadays I don't know what to expect from you."

"How about getting all wet?"

She looked out at the downpour. Smiled. "Oh no, Marshall, not again."

                        ~

Addison house rules: no smoking inside. Josee stepped through the front doors, hoping to light up. Dinner had been great, but the mob of people, overwhelming. She was still outfitted in her long gingham dress. A wreath of fresh flowers circled her hair. On a leather necklace she wore her myrtlewood cross.

"Marsh? Kara? What're you doing?"

Josee hadn't seen any visions of late, but this was strange enough. The couple was dancing in the white-pebbled drive, drenched with rain and laughing like a pair of fools. And she was supposed to belong to this gene pool? She grinned. She tossed the unlit cigarette to the ground and dug it in with the toe of her sandal.

"Afraid to get wet?" Marsh gibed. "Can't handle the cold?"

"This?" Josee gestured at the dimpled puddles and the clouds that crawled over the hills. "This is nothing compared to some of the stuff I've been in. Been in even worse with Scooter." She fell silent. Removed her wreath and poked at it.

"Still no word?" Kara said.

"Nope."

"Hasn't come out of it yet, huh? Have you gone to see him?"

Josee held up a finger. "One time." Since that visit, she'd made a point of avoiding Good Samaritan. Once had been enough, sitting beside Scooter's comatose form, receiving zero response—as if he'd died and left a breathing corpse. She shook her head and reset the wreath. "Not ready to deal with it just yet. I mean, maybe after I've sifted through all that's happened. A lot to process, you know?"

Scooter had violated her trust; he'd refused to make a stand and had allowed his own demons to turn him against her; he'd stinkin' ratted her out to Trudi.

Of course, he'd also thrown himself in harm's way to warn her at Avery Park.

I will visit again, Scoot. Give me time.

Her eyes brightened as a police car came up the driveway.

"What do you know," Marsh said. "Looks like Sarge has decided to show up."

⁓

Sergeant Turney parked the cruiser beside the company van and jogged through the rain, splashing water. Though his pain had lessened, bandages and scabs still covered his arms and face, testimony to the wounds he'd endured in the helicopter crash.

"I come bearing gifts," he said.

"How generous," Kara said. "But isn't it a bit early for Christmas?"

Josee met him on the steps. "How's it going, Band-Aid Man?"

Turney smiled. "The inquiry cleared me. That's a good thing. Ruled Stahlherz's death as a suicide. Sorry, Marsh. They haven't found a body, which means there's little chance of ever gettin' your answer on his connection to you—if there ever was one. Could've been one big lie. The station received your father's journal, the original you dropped in the mail, and with the account matching the events we've been through, my guess is that Ms. Ubelhaar'll be spending the rest of her days behind bars. We can all breathe easier. She'll be out of our hair."

"Sarge, you have a sick sense of humor," Marsh said. "What about Beau Connors?"

"Seems he was nothing but a—"

"Pawn sacrifice."

"Yup, stole the words right outta my mouth. The kid'll be facing psychiatric evaluation, if the judge has his way. So far, we've found three separate safe houses for the ICV network and have broken things up, but we'll still be keeping an eye out, just in case. With the e-mail database that Esprit's whiz kid snagged on the Internet, the members the detective rounded up near Camp Adair, and the cars that got tailed on Halloween, we've listed more than ninety people involved. We have star witnesses ready to go on the stand if this ever goes to trial—the espresso-booth worker and Suzette Bishop, art curator. Suzette, as you know, suffered a blow to the head, but she's okay."

"Quite a little network of terror."

"You're tellin' me, Marsh." Turney raised a finger to make a point. "Wanna know something scary? The thermos things those kids threatened you with on the beach had actual poison gas in them. Somethin' close to tear gas but authentic juice all the same. As for the canisters with the truly dangerous stuff, all but one of 'em have been recovered and transported over to Umatilla. They'll be slated for the incinerator—if the authorities ever get that thing up and going."

"What about the missing canister?" Josee's concern was obvious.

"Went up in flames. We've confirmed that now. The ICV boys had a little run-in with a tanker on Highway 126. Sad thing is, at least thirteen people died within a mile of the site. Lotsa animals, too. Pets and livestock.

A couple of wisps of the stuff must've gotten into the air, but we haven't had any casualties since the week after the collision. The poison's dissipated, thank heavens."

Marsh nodded. "Life goes on. We're all falling back into our routines."

"I've been thinking. What with all the sleaze bags runnin' around, I'm not so sure I wanna keep workin' a beat. Might switch to consulting for criminal investigations."

"Would that be any safer?" Josee asked.

"Least I could call my own shots. Anything for a chance to go a few more rounds." Turney turned to Marsh and produced a sparkling glass chess piece. "Here, this is yours. It's from the evidence they've released. Found it near the spot Stahlherz went over the cliff. Little dinged up but otherwise ready to go. Your queen, I believe."

"I'll take good care of her."

"You do that. Oh. One last thing." Turney handed a plain white envelope to Josee. "Ran the tests, a little side job, just to settle things once and for all. Between the saliva from Marsh's lunch fork and a piece of your hair, Josee, it didn't take the labs long to determine a paternal match. Don't worry. Go on, you can take a look."

Josee scanned the results, folded the paper with care, and reinserted it.

"Sarge called me earlier," Marsh told her. "Said it was official. You're my daughter." He reached for her.

Turney watched for Josee's reaction. With arms at her side, she leaned into Marsh's embrace. Inch by inch she melted until at last her thin arms lifted around her father in return.

Monday morning. Back to the grind for her parents, Sarge, Henri Esprit, and the operations at the vineyard. Which meant Josee had some time alone.

Soon after that night on the cliffs, she had made a trip back to Washington, where she refilled her dwindled prescription, where she made an impromptu visit to her adoptive parents. She had needed that. So had they. For the past three weeks back in Corvallis, she'd been sharing an apartment and working part-time with Suzette at the newly renovated art gallery on SW Second. The gallery was closed on Mondays.

Time for a solo excursion.

Borrowing Marsh's Tahoe, Josee headed for the coast. She pressed a hand to her collarbone where, under her turtleneck, she bore a small tattoo. She smiled, recalling Turney's uneasiness. Out of uniform, on their second lunch alone together, he had put an arm around her shoulder. "Somethin' I been meaning to ask you, Josee. You're gonna think it's stupid."

"Probably."

"Well, it's what you said that first day we talked. You remember? In the hospital cafeteria?"

"Oh no, don't hold that against me."

"You asked if I'd like to see your newest tattoo."

"And?"

"I would."

Grinning, she'd shown him the butterfly on her collarbone. Silly man. Thirty-one years old, and he turned brighter than a beet. Sarge was quite a guy. He'd had stinkin' three years since Milly's passing; it was time to move on and live a little. That boy needed a girl in his life.

And maybe, just maybe, that girl will be me.

In Florence, she lurched to a stop at the Bank of the Dunes, hopped out, and twirled the key chain on her finger. One of the keys went to safe-deposit box 89.

The vault felt less cold this time, and her fingers had no difficulty with the lid on the box—her box, her inheritance, her sole connection to the grandfather she had never known. What was she going to do with the one item she'd left wrapped inside? She had no clear direction. She'd mentioned it to no one. And no one had asked.

If, as Trudi had accused, her parents were primarily interested in an inheritance, why had they not even fished for information? It was as though they knew nothing about it. Yep, she was sure this was her secret and hers alone.

One more look so I know I'm not going wacko.

Her eyes weren't deceiving her. She drew the object from a felt bag, marveling at its exquisite shape. She had read about such treasures. Doubtlessly

ransacked by the Nazis from an imperial museum or palace, the four-inch
Fabergé egg was encased in translucent turquoise enamel. Gold cabriole legs
lifted the object on a garnet-encrusted stem, where a stamp with the initials
H. W. spoke of hidden things. Even in the vault's bland electric light, a band
of rose diamonds glittered with sophisticated elegance.

Freakin' thing has to be worth a fortune!

Dated March 1960, a fragile paper rested in the bottom of the bag. She'd
read it hurriedly on her first visit, but this time she felt no pressure. She
savored each word:

Precious grandchild,

This egg is a symbol of new life and of grand designs that await. With
it comes all the love I'll never be present to share. Don't do as I've
done, allowing petty pursuits to escalate into monstrous evils. Rather,
give of yourself to kith and kin. Exemplify the riches of an uncluttered
life. Forgive me for this game I've involved you in, and remember…to
the winner go the spoils! Indeed, I hope you prevail.

Love, Grandpa Addison

Josee tucked the treasure back into the bag, locked the box, and left the
vault.

In the past few weeks, her eyes had seen many things, both beautiful and
fierce. It would take time to digest it all. She would have decisions to make
and, eventually, secrets to unveil. For now, she'd take each day as it came, one
step at a time.

Okay, Lord, I'm gonna need some help here. I'm ready to listen.

The answer was simple… *Walk on.*

Acknowledgments

Dudley Delffs and Don Pape (editor and publisher)
for grace and support, for taking a chance on this book and making it so
much better, for coming up with a title after my brain had turned to mush.

Jan Dennis (literary agent)
for finding me in a haystack and further sharpening me...
You made it happen.

The team at WaterBrook Press (those behind the scenes)
for the cool cover art, marketing, and lots of hard work... You're incredible.

Carolyn Rose (wife)
for sacrifices at every turn and for deepest kisses on the roughest days...
You're music to my ears.

Cassie Rose and Jackie Renee (daughters)
for laughter and hugs, for sharing a room
so that Dad could have a place to write.

Linda Wilson (mother)
for loving, teaching, nurturing, and for removing this kid's correction
ribbon so that he would actually finish something.

Mark Wilson (father)
for unending belief, love, loans, and a computer to complete the task...
Of course, you deserve a ton of credit too, DeeDee.

*Shaun and Jade Wilson (brother and wife), Heidi and Matt Messner
(sister and husband), Mike and Debbie Monaghan (parents-in-law)*
for enduring ears, munchies, baby-sitting, computer advice,
and tons of love.

*Sharyn McCrumb, Jefferson Scott, Ted Dekker,
Robert Whitlow, and David Ryan Long (award-winning novelists)*
for well-placed kicks, encouragement, and editorial comments...
Jeff, the Sobe's on me.

*Jacquie Manning, Patricia Miller, Sean Savacool, Matthew Guise,
Barbara Guise, Linda Frizzell, Marissa Dowell, Sandra Houmes,
Lyle Edwards, Jim and Nancy Jordan, Sherry Shippentower (advance readers)*

for comments, chuckles, and the encouragement to continue…
Jacquie, Patty, and Sean, your books are next.
Espresso Yourself customers (you know who you are)
for the business, moral support, and caffeine-enhanced friendships.
*The Moodys' Home Group, the Youngs' Kinship Group, Vaughn and Laurie
Forbes, Luci Stolle (spiritual partners, seen and unseen)*
for prayers and belief that this book would sit on shelves
around the country…
Vaughn and Laurie, thanks for helping me over that final hump.
Mike and Carol Korgan CEC (Heceta Head Lighthouse Bed & Breakfast)
for fantastic food, lodging, and a late-night tour of the lighthouse.
Nashville Public Library Staff (Hermitage and Donelson Branches)
for great fiction, research facilities, and an office away from home.
Corp. Larry Larson (Junction City Police Department)
for patience, advice, and no share of the blame.
Gary Horner (Benton-Lane Winery)
for great Pinot Noir and help with the details.
*U2, Evanescence, Linkin Park, Switchfoot, King's X,
Audioslave, Collective Soul, and P.O.D. (modern rock bands)*
for shaking the walls while posing questions and/or answers
in meaningful ways.
Vinny's Pizza (Nashville's most incredible pizzeria)
for keeping this starving artist's family alive
with large doses of the good stuff…
Lantz and H. J., keep Music City rockin'.
Readers everywhere (that means you)
for sharing a few hours with the characters in this novel…
May you, too, walk on with renewed vision!
I welcome your feedback at my Web site or e-mail address:
wilsonwriter.com
wilsonwriter@hotmail.com